Preying in Two Harbors

Books in the Two Harbors mystery series:

Convergence at Two Harbors (2012)
Seven Graves, Two Harbors (2013)
A River through Two Harbors (2014)
Preying in Two Harbors (2015)

Preying in Two Harbors

Dennis Herschbach

NORTH STAR PRESS OF ST. CLOUD, INC.
Saint Cloud, Minnesota

Copyright © 2015 Dennis Herschbach

Cover photos © Diane Hilden

ISBN 978-0-87839-792-1

All rights reserved.

This is a work of fiction. Names, characters, places, and incidents are the products of the author's imagination or are used fictitiously. Any resemblance to actual events or persons, living or dead, is entirely coincidental.

First Edition: May 2015

Printed in the United States of America

Published by
North Star Press of St. Cloud, Inc.
P.O. Box 451
St. Cloud, Minnesota 56302

www.northstarpress.com

Dedication

Preying in Two Harbors is dedicated to my children, Letty, Jennifer, and Karl. I'm proud of you for who you are, for what you have accomplished, for the grandchildren you have given me, and for the support you have been to me.

A very special thank you to my wife, Vicky Schaefer, for all the time she spent proofreading this manuscript and supporting my efforts during its writing.

Preface

Extremism, whether right or left, whether secular or religious, can be, and many times is, dangerous. Ideologies become so firmly entrenched in an individual's or a group's thinking, irrational decisions become the norm and those involved become blinded by fear, by distrust, by hate.

Preying in Two Harbors is totally fiction. True, many of the places are real, and even some of the characters were inspired by people the author may have known. Most of the characters are composites of persons, drawing from an incident in one life, another incident in another's. Yet, the theme is one that is real. In Minnesota, a self-proclaimed minister was charged with fifty-nine counts of sexual assault involving underage followers. He escaped being taken into custody and is currently wanted by authorities. According to an article in the *Minneapolis Star Tribune*, August 14, 2014, he was spotted in Washington. Incredibly, he was seen with a young woman, who he escorted to a waiting car.

In another article, the *Star Tribune* described a person with alleged ties to a white supremacist group who was apprehended while in possession of grenades, bullet-resistant vests, a fully automatic Uzi, a Sig Sauer AR-15 rifle, three fully loaded, thirty-round AR magazines, and a fully loaded sixty-round magazine.

An FBI posting begins, "Last March, nine members of an extremist militia group were charged in Michigan with seditious conspiracy and attempted use of weapons of mass destruction in connection with an alleged plot to attack law enforcement and spark an uprising against the government." The article went on to say that many militia groups subscribe to the idea they are protecting the U.S. Constitution.

"The celebrating began before the coroner could collect the bodies of two Las Vegas police officers who were ambushed and executed while eating at a pizzeria." An entry on a Facebook page said to celebrate because there were two less police in the world. The entry received 6,300 "likes" before it was taken down.

The Two Harbors mystery series is fiction, but any reader can do their own research and discover that the topics written about are very real societal problems, and the author has attempted to draw to the public's awareness that these problems do exist.

Chapter One

It was the last week of April, the first real spring day in Two Harbors, and on the corner of Waterfront Drive and First Avenue, Reverend Isaiah (at least, that's what he called himself) waved his floppy, tattered Bible, thundering to anyone who would listen.

"Wake up, America. Repent or experience God's wrath. Repent before it's too late to be saved."

His piercing blue eyes were sunk deeply into his face. They, along with a sharp, hooked nose, gave him the appearance of a hawk hunting prey. Reverend Isaiah thrust a bony finger toward The Pub, a local watering hole across the street from where he held sway, and continued his harangue.

"There, my brothers, is a den of iniquity, a place where the sinful prepare their places in hell!" He swept his wizened hand in the direction of the bar and grill. A burly man in biker garb tried to pass on the sidewalk, but the reverend stepped in front of him. "Are you saved, brother? Because if you're not, time is running out, and you're going to be judged by God Almighty."

The man tried to step around the gaunt figure blocking his path, but the old man would not get out of his way. Finally, the befuddled biker said something and pushed his way past, crossed the street and looked back at the corner where the reverend was standing. He opened the door to The Pub, but before he could enter he heard one last salvo.

"You just opened a gate to hell, my friend. I'll be praying for you," the preacher bellowed.

Across the street two middle-school-aged boys were jostling each other as they walked. One had his arm thrown over the shoulders of the other. They turned and stared as Reverend Isaiah railed at them.

"Abomination! That's what it is, abomination! Get your arm off his body. God commands men to stay away from men, demands that women stay away from women. This is how it begins, unnatural affection for each other. Do not fall into the trap set by those who would say that God is love. God is an angry God, a jealous God who demands our obedience. He is a God who punishes us for our own good. The Almighty God has told me this town, your town, is an abomination to God, and like Sodom and Gomorrah, he is about to destroy you unless you repent of your sinful ways."

The two boys looked across the street at Reverend Isaiah in disbelief. One shook his head and said something to his friend, and they laughed. But they stepped apart as though a barrier now existed between them and walked on down the street. They weren't laughing or jostling each other. That moment of innocence had been extinguished by the reverend's unwarranted judgment. He continued his tirade until a cold breeze picked up off Lake Superior, killing the spring day.

Reverend Isaiah stomped away from what he considered his corner, murmuring under his breath as he skulked down the street. He climbed behind the wheel of a battered, ten-year-old Ford Escort and pulled away from the curb, not bothering to look over his shoulder to see if traffic was coming. An alert driver slammed on his brakes, averting what otherwise would have been a collision.

*****

CLIMBING GRADUALLY, HIGHWAY 2 ran straight north out of Two Harbors. About three miles from town, the grade rapidly increased until cars, and especially trucks, labored to clear the crest. Near the top of what locals called Five Mile Hill, the highway intersected on the right with Gun Club Road. A little way down that road, on the left, sat what had been a country school in the 1920s.

After students began to be bused into town for classes, the school was closed. The building became a township hall, then a community center, then stood abandoned until a biker group bought it for their clubhouse. They hand-painted a sign with the Harley-Davidson symbol on it and the words DEATH RIDERS in large black letters.

"That crazy old coot, Reverend Isaiah, was in town again today," a man with "THE HAMMER" tattooed in blue and red letters on each forearm said as he leaned back in his chair. He and a half-dozen other bikers were sitting on the porch, soaking up the April sun. He got up and plucked a beer from a cooler, popped the top, and returned to his chair. On the wall was nailed a notice, NO FAGS ALLOWED. Without waiting for anyone to respond to his announcement, he continued.

"He stopped me on the street and asked if I was saved. I said, 'Hell no, and I don't want to be. I want to go down in a blaze of flames, just like a comet burning itself out.' The old goat kept at me until I pushed him out of the way." Hammer stopped to laugh at his own private joke.

A couple of the others laughed, and the one called Blackie gave him a verbal jab. "Better be careful, that old man'll put you on your back!" She took a toke on the weed she was smoking. Hammer mumbled something under his breath. He was six-foot-six and weighed in at two hundred eighty pounds. The scarecrow reverend would hardly have stood a chance in a physical altercation.

"Tell you what, another two weeks and we'll be riding our bikes anywhere we want. I'd like to take a road trip far away from here. What say, anybody up for that?" Most of the group was too wasted to respond.

One of them looked at the blue sky and responded, "Sure, Hammer, sure. We'll ride with you. Why don't you go inside and make the plans? We'll follow you." He rolled in a ball and laughed and laughed as though he had made the greatest joke of all time. Then he instantly sobered and stood up. "You dumb shit. We ain't goin' no place. You're as nuts as that preacher."

Hammer charged from his chair and hit Scy, short for Scythe, in his midsection with a full shoulder tackle. Together they tumbled off the porch into the cold mud and wrestled until they were covered in the red-clay goop. The two men were of equal size and neither could gain the upper hand. Finally, each lay on his back, exhausted.

"Come on, you dumb shit, let's get another beer," Scy capitulated, and they slogged their way back onto the porch. Hammer went inside, but before sitting down, Scy grabbed another beer, then took a puff of what Blackie was smoking. Five minutes later, Hammer returned to the porch. He had washed the mud off and changed into cleaner clothes, and he wore a baseball cap, backwards so it wouldn't fly off. Above its brim was his name, HAMMER, and underneath the Harley symbol.

"I'm going into town to see if there's any action. It's getting too cold to sit out here. Any of you numb-nuts wanna come?" No one answered. "Don't forget to lock up when you leave," were his final words. He fired up his Harley and roared away in a spray of mud and noise.

*****

DEIDRE JOHNSON STOOD at the kitchen sink, doing dishes. Her husband, Ben VanGotten, had driven their twin daughters to soccer practice in town, and she had stayed home to clean up after supper. It was a beautiful Saturday evening in the country, the end of the first nice day of spring, but as she looked out the window, she experienced a feeling of unrest that had gradually crept into her life the past few months.

She and Ben were married when his daughters were five. Now they were ten, almost eleven. Awhile ago, reality hit her. She was thirty-seven years old, had never had a child, was a stay-at-home mom, and was becoming a regular Suzie Homemaker. The girls didn't need her the way they had when they were little, and she sensed their growing independence would only leave her more isolated. Not that life was bad.

After they married, Ben had stumbled onto a real gem, forty acres of rural land fronting the west branch of the Knife River. It had a wonderful building site, and they constructed a home that fit the property perfectly. She had a garden, solitude when she wanted it, and a wonderful family. Still, she couldn't shake the unrest that gnawed at her when she was alone.

Deidre had been involved in law enforcement since her graduation from college, first as a deputy, then sheriff, and after she was forced out of that job, as a special appointee of the state's Bureau of Criminal Apprehension. She had worked tough cases, dangerous cases, and thought she was ready to give up all that excitement and settle down. Now she wasn't quite sure what she wanted.

Her introspection was interrupted by the sound of a car pulling into the yard and of two doors slamming in unison. Megan and Maren, her adopted daughters, stomped into the house. "How'd the game go, girls?" Deidre asked, not really needing an answer.

"We lost," Maren pouted.

"Bad," Megan added. Both made a beeline for their rooms without pausing. Ben stood in the doorway.

"Those two. I don't know what we're going to do with them. They're so competitive they embarrass me. Megan wouldn't shake hands with the opposing team members, and Maren told each of them as they passed, 'Next time, sucker.' I told them we were considering not letting them play in their next game. Can you talk to coach tomorrow?"

"Oh sure, make me the bad cop." She smiled and wrapped her arms around her husband's midsection. "Let me talk to the girls in a few minutes. If I can't make any progress, I'll see her tomorrow and figure out an appropriate punishment. Okay?"

"Okay," he said, and led his wife outside so he could cool off. As they walked on the path that followed the riverbank, he stopped and put his arm around Deidre's shoulders. "What would we ever have done if you hadn't come into our lives? I think that every day and give thanks for what I have." He kissed her on the cheek. Deidre said nothing but leaned closer to him. They were silent for many minutes as they watched the clear water spill over boulders buried in the streambed. Suddenly, a steelhead, a lake-run rainbow trout, broke the surface and leaped from one of the riffles. As it disappeared in its own splash, Deidre and Ben gasped in surprise. They laughed and returned to the house. That night Deidre and the girls had a long talk about sportsmanship and enjoying the game.

After watching the ten o'clock news with Ben, she decided it was time to have a serious talk with him. She didn't quite know how to begin. She turned off the TV and cleared her throat.

"Can we talk for a minute or two?" She looked at Ben from across the room. He was sitting in his recliner, and reacting to Deidre's words, he brought it upright.

"If this is about the girls and their coach, I'll be glad to handle it. I didn't mean to push it off on you." He looked worried, afraid he had expected too much.

Deidre laughed at his discomfort. "Don't be foolish. We're in this together, and I want to hold up my end of the deal. No, it's not that at all. Really, what I want to talk about is how our family is changing. The girls don't need me as much anymore. I'm alone all day while you're at work and they're at school. I think I'm beginning to become too much of a recluse. What would you think of my trying to find a job? I know you support us well, but I think I need to get out more, you know, be with people. What do you think of the idea?"

Ben took a minute before answering. "You don't need to ask my permission. I want you to be happy, to live your own life. I've no doubt you'll never put anything ahead of me or the girls, so I say go for it, if that's what you want. Any idea what you'd like to do? Just don't tell me you have your heart set on working at the plant in Silver Bay." He was referring to the taconite processing facility that was dirty, noisy, and dangerous.

Again, Deidre laughed. "No, nothing dirty, noisy, or dangerous. I was thinking of trying to get on at the school as a teacher aide, or maybe getting a job at The Pub as a waitress. Thanks for your vote of confidence. Maybe I'll begin looking around on Monday to see what's out there."

Hand in hand, they climbed the stairs to their bedroom. Ben gave her a loving pat on her fanny as they entered the room.

Chapter Two

"Nine-one-one," the dispatcher intoned. "What is the problem?"

"Send an ambulance as soon as you can! We need an ambulance!"

"Please slow down and speak calmly. Now, where are you located?"

The 911 operator heard the man on the other end of the line take a deep breath. "I'm near the soccer field off Paul Antonich Drive. There's a man lying by the side of the road, and he's unconscious. It looks as if he's been hit by a car, or something."

"Is he breathing?"

"I think so, but he's in a bad way. Can you hurry?"

The operator asked him to stay with the injured man. "An ambulance should arrive in minutes." She continued to talk, keeping him on the line.

"I hear it coming." The caller sounded relieved. "I can see its flashing lights." He ended the call.

*****

Officer Dan Zemple of the Two Harbors Police Department made a note of the time. 9:46 P.M. He had started his Saturday shift at eight and was looking forward to getting off at eight Sunday morning. That meant he would have four days before having to start another stint of four twelves in a row. He liked the arrangement. It meant he could spend several days fishing the many rivers that flowed into Lake Superior. Right now, he had something else on his mind. A Ford F-150 pickup was parked near the breakwater of the harbor. Its motor was running but all its lights were turned off. He shined his flashlight through its side window.

A large, bearded man lay slumped over the steering wheel, and he didn't move when Officer Zemple rapped on the door. He opened it slowly, not wanting the person to fall out, and immediately picked up on the smell of alcohol. Dan reached across the man's lap and turned off the ignition, and then, with a great deal of effort, rocked him back in the seat. An empty vodka bottle rattled to the floor. Still, the man didn't rouse. Dan needed backup for this one and called for an ambulance. It arrived in minutes, and soon they had the intoxicated driver on his way to the hospital.

Officer Zemple was in the process of filling out his report at the hospital while he waited for the results of a blood alcohol test being run on the man. A nurse handed him a copy of the printout, and he wasn't surprised at the .270 reading. As he suspected, the rough-looking character was terribly inebriated and would be placed in detox. He watched as an orderly untied and removed a pair of heavy boots from the man's feet and then wheeled him away to his assigned room.

Dan was in possession of the man's wallet, and he searched through it for an ID, finding the driver's license. He copied the information onto the arrest form: James Peter O'Brian, height six-foot-six, weight 280 pounds, brown hair, blue eyes. Dan was glad he hadn't had to wrestle the man down. As he was finishing his paperwork and preparing to leave, the relative quiet was interrupted by a burst of activity. He sensed something serious was happening.

*****

THE MEDICAL STAFF in the ER were waiting for the ambulance to arrive. Before it came to a complete stop, Joannie, the nurse, and an orderly were at its back door, pushing a gurney. With an efficiency honed by practice, the unconscious patient was transferred from the ambulance and wheeled through the sliding doors into the confines of the hospital. Joannie automatically looked at the clock above the nurses station and saw it was 10:35 P.M. She was the head ER nurse working the Saturday night shift, and would have to record the time in the patient's chart.

Three people rushed by Officer Zemple, pushing a gurney with a seriously injured person lying on it. As they rushed by, he heard the nurse giving orders to the other attendants. "Cut his shirt and pants off," she told the orderly in measured words. They disappeared behind the curtain of one of the ER rooms.

"Jill, take his blood pressure. Mark, hook up the EKG electrodes," Joannie said when the gurney was in room five. She pried the patient's eyelids open so she could test his pupils. "Dilated and unresponsive to light," she announced as the ER doctor pushed aside the curtain.

Joannie stepped back from the bed and surveyed the bloody scene. The comatose young man was a mess. Not a square inch of his face was unmarked. Both eyes were swollen shut, his nose was bent off to one side, and his lips were cut and bleeding. His left ear hung by a thread of tissue, and teeth showed through a gash on his left cheek. She could hardly bear to look at him.

"I think his trachea has suffered severe trauma, and I'm going to do a tracheotomy. I'm pretty sure we'll have to hook him up to a respirator." The doctor's calm tone seemed out of place considering the obvious emergency. "Call an X-ray tech. I want a full set of pictures, and a CT scan. Start a Ringer's Solution drip as soon as you have that IV in." Joannie was in the process of inserting the needle in a vein in his arm.

The doctor abruptly left when his pager beeped, and Joannie continued to administer care. He returned before she finished, looked at the monitors, and decided the patient had to be moved to X-ray. They wheeled him and all of the equipment attached to him to the elevator and took the two-floor trip downstairs, where they were met by the tech who was putting on her work smock.

It took the three of them—the tech, the doctor, and Joannie—to get the pictures he wanted. Then they moved him to an adjoining room where the CT scanner was located. Another technician took over, and the scan was started. From her vantage point behind a glass window that was treated to block radiation, Joannie watched the monitor screen as section after section of the man's body was displayed.

She heard a thump each time his body moved a few inches so another image could be taken and watched as it progressively scanned toward his head. Though she was not a trained radiologist, the compound fracture of his right tibia, or shin bone, was easy to spot. As the scan moved upward, more gross damage became visible. His right hip was dislocated, and a piece of his ischium, the lower part of his pelvis, was broken off.

Joannie couldn't interpret damage to the soft tissue—that would take a trained eye—but when the patient's ribs were scanned, she instantly recognized that three of them on his left side were not only broken but caved into his chest cavity. *No doubt they damaged his lung,* she thought. She almost turned away, but the machine had reached his head, and she stood mesmerized.

What had been facial bones looked like a bowl of cornflakes. His nasal bones were mashed to one side of his face, and his zygomatic processes, cheek bones, were pushed so deeply into his eye sockets that she couldn't make them out. His maxilla was caved into his mouth cavity, its attached teeth flattened against the roof of his mouth. She could see at least five fractures of his lower jaw, and above his ear, his temporal bone appeared to have been struck by a heavy object, maybe even a kick from a heavy boot. She could easily discern the point of the blow, because fine cracks radiated outward from its epicenter. Joannie shook her head.

"He's in big trouble, isn't he?" The ER doc didn't answer but nodded. Together, Joannie, the orderly, and the radiological tech maneuvered the patient's bed back to his room in ER.

"We've got to try to make an ID on him and contact his next of kin," the doctor said. "Call the trauma center in Duluth and have them send a Life Flight copter to pick him up. He's too fragile to survive the trip by ambulance. The way it is, it'll take more time than we may have for them to get here."

Chapter Three

Just as the medical staff in ER rushed past him with the critical patient, Officer Zemple's pager went off, and he took the call.

"Dan, we need you over here right away. We have a probable crime scene just off Paul Antonich Drive, near the soccer field. You'll see our lights when you get here." The officer ran to his squad car, started it, and turned on his flashing lights. In four minutes he was at the soccer field and was met by the other officer on duty.

"What's up, Bill?" he asked as soon as they were close enough to talk.

"Not sure yet. The ambulance just left with a young man who's in pretty bad shape. I don't know what happened to him. We might have a hit and run, or we might have a beating. I don't know what else it could be. He sure as heck didn't do it to himself, that I know."

The area had already been cordoned off with crime scene tape, and the two officers began to assess the situation. "We'd better get the chief out here. Another set of eyes will be good, and I think this is going to end up being a serious case. We'll let him give the orders. That's why he gets the big bucks."

Bill made the call, which was answered by the groggy police chief. He grumbled something into the phone but was at the scene in fifteen minutes. Two Harbors is a small town, barely three thousand residents, and it didn't take long to get from one end of the community to the other.

"What you got here?" he asked. Bill was tired of answering the same question, but he went through the same explanation he had given Dan.

The chief, Sig Swanson, surveyed the scene. "Let's get some spotlights set up. I don't want to wait until morning to do a search of the area." He punched a number into his phone and ordered the person on the other end to bring a generator and some lights so they could get started with their investigation.

Dan shined his flashlight on the ground inside the taped perimeter. "Looks like something on the ground over there." He pointed at an object in the grass. "I'm pretty sure it's a baseball cap."

Sig shined his light where Dan was pointing. "Yeah, it is, but let's wait to retrieve it until we have better lighting so we don't trample evidence we can't see." They shined their flashlights around while they waited for the spotlights to arrive and be set up.

Within fifteen minutes the lights came on, illuminating the grassy area enough that the investigators could move in for a closer look. Sig pulled on a pair of rubber gloves, carefully made his way to where the baseball cap lay on the sod, and picked it up. He mumbled to himself as he examined it, "Whoever wore this had one big head." The adjustment strap was on the last notch. Then he turned it over and took note of the Harley symbol. In bold letters above the visor was embroidered the word HAMMER. Sig dropped the hat in an evidence bag, signed and dated it, and wrote the time, 11:05 P.M.

"Sig, take a look at this," Bill called to his superior. "This will answer some questions."

Sig kept the evidence bag in his hand and walked over to where Dan and Bill were standing. When he got closer, he saw they were looking through a wallet.

"We've got an ID on someone." Dan held the wallet in one hand and his flashlight in the other. "It's a Minnesota driver's license for a Justin Peters, seventeen years old, five-foot-nine, one hundred fifty-five pounds. He lives only a few blocks from here, on Sixteenth Avenue."

Sig looked over Dan's shoulder. "I'll tell you what. We definitely have evidence of two people being here. The cap I picked up sure as heck wouldn't fit this person. Take care of this evidence. I'm going to the hospital to find out what I can about the guy the EMTs picked up here.

"Don't be sloppy. We're going to have to vouch for our methods in court. You can bet on that." Sig left as his officers finished sweeping the area for clues. He would return in the daylight with fresh eyes to check one more time before the tape came down.

At the hospital he stopped at the nurses station. "A person was brought in a couple of hours ago. I need to talk to somebody about the patient." The nurse looked up.

"Which one? Two came in at about the same time. One is in the drunk tank and the other is just coming back from the CT lab. He's in room five, but he'll be transferred to Duluth as soon as Life Flight gets here." Sig told her he wasn't interested in some drunk.

"Did the victim have an ID on him when he was brought in?" Sig wanted to know. He strongly suspected he knew the answer, and the nurse shook her head. Sig checked his notes. "We think he is Justin Peters. He lives on Sixteenth. Can I use your phone book to check on a number? Maybe we can get somebody over here to tell us who he is."

There were four Peterses listed, but only one on Sixteenth Avenue. Sig dialed the number.

"Hello," an anxious woman answered.

"Is this the Peters' residence?" Sig began, but before he could continue, the woman blurted out, "Is he okay? Justin, I mean. He was supposed to be home two hours ago, and I haven't been able to get him to answer his cell phone. Where is he?"

For a minute Sig was speechless, then he asked, "Are you Justin's mother?"

"Yes, yes. Can you tell me where he is?"

"Try to calm yourself, Mrs. Peters. Justin has had an accident, and he's in the hospital emergency room. From the address on his license

I see you live only a few blocks away. Will you come immediately?" Then Sig caught himself. "Please, Mrs. Peters, don't speed or drive recklessly. You can't do your son any good if you're in an accident. Are you okay to drive, or do you want me to send someone for you?"

Sig could hear her crying on the other end of the call. "I'll be all right. It'll take me only five minutes to get there." He heard the call disconnect, and he hoped she wasn't going to get in trouble in her haste to be with her son. Sig went outside to wait. Two minutes later, as he looked down the highway, he saw a set of headlights approach the road from the direction of Justin's address. The car made a rolling stop and sped into the intersection. Luckily, no other traffic was on the road. Its driver didn't signal but made a left turn into the ER parking lot, and a middle-aged woman sprang from the car.

"Where is he. Where is Justin?" she demanded without breaking her stride. She rushed into the hospital with Sig close behind. He caught up with her and slowed her at the nurse's desk.

"This is Mrs. Peters," he announced. "She would like to see her son in room five." Sig didn't wait for permission. He escorted the distraught woman to the victim's bedside.

"Oh, Justin, my poor child. What have they done to you?" she moaned as she touched his hair. There was no response. She turned to Sig. "Who did this," she sobbed and then went back to stroking the boy's hair.

"I'm sorry, Mrs. Peters, but I need you to confirm that this is Justin. Can you make a positive identification?"

Mrs. Peters looked at the boy again. "Yes, this is my son, Justin. It's him."

Sig led her away from the bed as the doctor and nurse pulled back the curtain. The doctor demanded, "Who are you, and what are you doing back here? Who gave you permission?"

Mrs. Peters was too upset to answer, but Sig spoke up. "The person on the bed is Justin Peters," he said, not answering the doctor's question. "This is his mother, and I wanted her to be able to see her son as quickly as we could. I'm sorry we didn't follow proper protocol." He wasn't, but he knew this wasn't the time to ruffle feathers. "Is it okay if she stays by his side?"

The doctor was hardly listening as he viewed the monitors. The steady beeping of the equipment matched the peaks and valleys of the line display. Suddenly, the line became irregular, with periods of rapid peaks followed by a flat line. The peaks appeared more and more random and decreased in amplitude. Sig put his arm around Mrs. Peters' shoulders as they heard the doctor bark orders and saw the nurse disappear to get help. In an instant, four people were huddled over the boy, working feverishly to restore a normal heartbeat. The monitor's signal became a monotone buzz, and the doctor stepped back from the bed.

"Time of death, eleven forty-eight." He hung his head and left Justin's bedside as he stripped off his gloves, turned to Mrs. Peters, and placed his hand on her shoulder as Sig gently removed his own arm. "I'm so very sorry. We tried everything to save your son, but sometimes the damage is just too great. I'm sorry."

Joannie stepped forward and put her hand on Mrs. Peters' arm. "Is there anyone you want me to call for you? A member of the clergy, a relative, perhaps a friend?" Mrs. Peters shook her head.

"I knew someday this could happen," the bereaved mother said, her voice monotone.

Sig gently asked, ""Why do you say that, Mrs. Peters?" She shook her head again as though not really believing her boy had died.

"My son was gay, and over the years he suffered so much abuse. He was mocked in school, pushed about outside of the building, humiliated every time he turned around, it seemed. I just knew someday the harassment would escalate to something more violent." She buried her face in her hands

Joannie asked if she wanted to be alone with her son's body, and Mrs. Peters mumbled that she would like that.

Chapter
Four

WHEN HIS PHONE RANG the next morning, Officer Zemple had a bad feeling that his long weekend off was about to become overtime. "Dan, this is Sig. I'm afraid I'm going to need your help out here this morning. Meet me in my office as soon as you can. I want the two of us to go to the crime scene and look around in the daylight. We could have missed something last night."

Dan mumbled into the phone that he'd be right there and cursed out loud when the chief cut off the call. Fifteen minutes later he was sitting in Sig's office, sipping a cup of coffee. He needed the caffeine.

"I hope we can find something else," the chief groused. "All we have right now is a cap, and that won't be much help. What did you think of the word above its visor? Mean anything to you?"

Dan looked surprised. "I didn't see the cap. You bagged it and took it as evidence."

Sig shook his head. "Could have sworn I showed it to you. Must have been Bill. Anyway, it had the word HAMMER stitched on it."

"Holy shit!" Sig looked up, shocked at Dan's words. "I brought a guy into the ER last night. Picked him up down by the breakwater. He had HAMMER tattooed on each arm. Great big guy. I thought I was lucky he was passed out. Now I know why."

Sig had his hat on and was already to the door. Dan caught up with him. "Ride with me. We've got to get to him before he gets away."

"We don't have to rush," Dan reminded him. "He's in the drunk tank for forty-eight hours. We've got time."

Sig didn't say a word to Dan as he sped to Seventh Avenue, rolled through a red light as he turned right, and was at the hospital before Dan could get his seatbelt adjusted. Together they rushed to the reception desk.

"We need to find the man I brought in last night," Dan explained before Sig could take over. "His name's James O'Brian."

The receptionist ran her fingers down a list of names. "Mr. O'Brian is in lockdown right now. You'll have to stop at the nurse's station on the second floor and have one of them let you in."

Both men hurried up the stairs. The elevator was notoriously slow.

"We need to talk to the guy who was admitted to detox last night," Dan said as they reached the nurse's station. "Can you let us into his room?"

The nurse, a recent hire, looked up at them, slight panic in her eyes. "I don't know. Let me check with my supervisor." She turned to a woman standing nearby. "Jane, would you come here a second? These officers have a request."

Jane looked up from the chart she was holding and smiled. "Sig, what can we do for you?"

Sig explained the situation to her, leaving out the information about Justin Peters. She retreated to behind the counter and came back with a key. "He's pretty sedated right now, lorazepam, but he might be able to talk to you. Make sure you lock his door when you leave … and don't forget to drop off the key," she scolded and nervously laughed at the same time.

It was obvious that Dan and Sig were on a mission as they marched down the hall. Sig unlocked the door to the room and gave a short knock. Not waiting for an invitation, he pushed the door open.

James "Hammer" O'Brian was reclining on his bed, but his eyes were open. Groggily, he tried to sit up. "Huh? What do you want?" he slurred.

Dan could see that the man's eyes were glazed, and he was having a difficult time focusing on their faces. "Are you James O'Brian?" Sig questioned.

James had thrown his legs over the side of the bed and sat with his head in his hands, his elbows resting on his knees. He spoke without looking up.

"Yeah, that's me. Nobody calls me that unless I'm in trouble, though."

"What do they usually call you?" Sig wanted to know.

"Hammer."

"Do you remember me from last night?" Dan broke into the conversation.

Hammer looked at him through bleary eyes and shook his head. "Should I?"

"I brought you to the ER. Do you remember anything?" Hammer shook his head again.

Sig picked up the questioning. "Did you wear a baseball cap yesterday?" Hammer tried to remember.

"Yeah, yeah. I think I did. Do you have it?"

"Maybe." Sig wasn't going to provide information. "Could you identify it if you saw it?"

Again the drugged man had to think hard. "It's black, and has a Harley symbol on it. And my name. It's got my name, Hammer, on it."

Sig dropped the subject. "Got pretty wasted yesterday, didn't you?"

Hammer sort of snickered but then held his head as though it hurt pretty bad. "Guess so. I don't remember much. I was out at our clubhouse."

Sig interrupted. "The one up by the Gun Club Road?"

"Yeah, that's the one. Had a few beers was all. Then I came into town."

"Alone?" Sig asked.

"Yeah, alone. I stopped at The Pub and had a couple more beers. Then went over to the Legion. I think I had a couple shots of vodka there."

"Where'd you get the bottle?" Dan asked.

"Bottle, bottle? Oh yeah, I think I stopped at the liquor store and bought a bottle."

"Of what?" Dan pressured.

"Vodka. I only drink vodka. Oh, and beer." Hammer ran his fingers through his hair and continued to hold his head.

"Looks like a pretty nasty cut you have on your hand," Sig said as he glanced down at Hammer. "How'd you get that?"

Hammer looked at his bandaged hand and touched the spot where blood had oozed through the dressing. He shook his head.

"What's the last thing you remember?" Dan asked.

Hammer thought for a good thirty seconds. "I think I ended up down at the breakwater. Then I don't know what happened. I suppose you're going to get me for a DWI, and I'll lose my license."

"Something like that," Sig said. "We're going to leave you while we take care of some paperwork. If you think of anything else that happened last night, let us know."

The officers left Hammer's room and locked the door. At the desk, when they returned the key, Sig asked Jane, "Do you have his personal effects stored someplace?"

Jane left for a minute and came back with a plastic bin. "Just the clothes on his back and his wallet," she said.

"Dan, run down to my car and get some evidence bags. They're in the trunk." He turned to Jane. "Is there a conference room we can use for a few minutes?"

"To the end of the hall, on your right. It's labeled "Family Conference Room." You're welcome to use it."

Dan hurried down the stairs, and Sig carried the bin of clothes to where they would be examining what had become evidence. In minutes, Dan returned with a kit and several evidence bags. They each put on rubber gloves and began digging through the bin.

Hammer's shirt was a mess, and it looked as if he had rolled in muddy grass. They looked it over closely but found nothing. It went into one bag. The jeans he was wearing when Dan had called the ambulance were in the same condition. They pretty much skipped his underwear, which was repulsively dirty. Dan picked up Hammer's left boot and held it to the light.

"Sig, look at this." He positioned the boot so Sig could get a good look.

"Looks like dried blood on the toe. Geeze, that must be a size thirteen, with a steel toe." He dug in the evidence kit and came up with a sterile swab and a bottle of distilled water. After soaking the swab, he ran it over the stain on the boot and was rewarded with the swab tip turning red. He put it in a sterile envelope and marked it time, date, place, and the origin of the sample.

"The lab should be able to get a good read from this," he said. "If not, there's plenty left on the boot. How about the other one?"

Dan bagged the boot and picked up the other. Neither man could spot anything that resembled a blood smear. After an hour, all of Hammer's belongings were bagged as evidence.

"I'll take this down to the car and lock it up," Sig said. "Meet me at Hammer's room. I think it's time to visit him again."

Dan picked up the key at the nurse's station and waited outside the detox door until Sig returned. They unlocked the door, rapped once, and entered the room. This time Hammer was sitting on the edge of his bed, but his eyes said his brain was still in a fog.

"What?" he said as he looked up at the officers.

"James Peter O'Brian," Dan said, "you are under arrest for the murder of Justin Peters. You have the right to remain silent. Anything you say . . ." Dan finished reading Hammer his rights.

The words had an effect on Hammer, and he stood up. "Wait . . . wait. What are you talking about? I never killed nobody." Then he scowled. "I want to call a lawyer, right now."

Sig shrugged. "I'll have a nurse get you a phone. In the meantime, Dan is going to guard your door. You'll be under guard for the remainder of your stay here, and then you'll be transferred to the jail. That should be day after tomorrow. Do you have anything to say?"

Hammer was in a daze and shook his head.

Chapter Five

SUNDAY WAS ANOTHER beautiful spring day, and Ben drove his family into town to attend church. Deidre didn't buy into all of the ritual of the Lutheran faith, but she had to admit that attending church each Sunday provided a comfortable rhythm for her life.

During the sermon, she allowed her mind to wander as she usually did, and by the time the pastor finished his message, she had worked through part of her dilemma. She was convinced she needed more than being a stay-at-home mom. She needed a purpose. As the congregation finished singing the hymn of the day, Deidre stood in silence. She was sure her voice would draw unwanted attention, being she always sang a little off-key.

The service ended, and Deidre joined the other members of the congregation as they filed past the pastor, and she heard comments like, "Wonderful message," and "I just loved the last hymn we sang. It was so meaningful." When it was her turn, Deidre shook his hand and murmured, "Have a nice day." She regretted that she couldn't think of anything more spiritual to say.

When they arrived home, Deidre instructed the girls to change into play clothes so they wouldn't soil what they wore. She jabbed at Ben, "You too. Don't you dare go into the garden with your dress pants on."

"Who, me?" Ben clowned, knowing she had a valid reason for saying what she did. She poked him in the ribs again.

"Yes, you." By that time they were in the house, and Deidre busied herself fixing lunch. Soon everyone was fed, had scattered to do what they wanted, and Deidre was left to think over her options. In a small town like Two Harbors, they were few.

"Come on, Deidre," Ben called through the open door. "Let's take a walk up the road before the sun sets and it cools off. It's too nice a day to sit inside." He came to where Deidre was sitting looking out the window, took her hand, and helped her out of the chair.

Hand-in-hand they strolled down the dirt road, not really walking for fitness, but for the joy of being outside together. Their talk was random, skipping from topic to topic, and soon they were a mile from home.

"I wonder what goes on back there?" Deidre asked as they passed a gated driveway, knowing Ben had no answer. "Ever since they put in that road, I've wondered if there's some building going on back in the woods. They can't be logging, or we would see haul trucks going past our place."

Deidre was referring to a large tract of land that abutted their forty acres on the back and on one side. In the 1950s it had been owned by a paper company, but for one reason or another the board of directors had decided to divest themselves of the thousands of acres they owned in Lake County. One of the tracts, over seven hundred acres, was the parcel she wondered about. The company sold off its holdings for under two dollars an acre, and some was bought by individuals. Most was grabbed by investors.

Two years ago, heavy equipment moved in, and a road was pushed into the property next to them, "no trespassing" signs went up, and a heavy steel gate barred anyone from entering. Since then, they had witnessed little traffic going in or out.

"It's a puzzle, isn't it?" Ben mused. "I seldom hear any noise, and when I do, it's from way back in. Sometimes, I think I hear gun shots, but the retorts are so close together, only a machine gun could hammer that fast. Then I wonder if it's a jackhammer. You don't suppose they're drilling into bedrock for some reason? Not long ago, I thought I heard an explosion. Well, as long as they stay on their side of the line, we don't have anything to complain about. You know the saying, 'Good fences make good neighbors.' I suppose that's true, even if there isn't a literal fence."

Still hand-in-hand, they walked home, had supper, and enjoyed the evening together after the twins went to bed.

*****

SIG PAID ANOTHER VISIT to the hospital Monday morning. Dan had returned to his post at Hammer's hospital door and joined Sig inside the patient's room. Sig called ahead to tell Hammer he was coming, and when he and Dan entered the room, they were greeted by T.J. Compton.

"Mornin', Sig. How's it goin'?" the attorney asked in his down-home way. T.J. had a way of playing an uneducated person.

"Good, T.J. And how are you, Counselor?" Both men knew the pleasantries were nothing but fronts. They had no animosity toward each other, but they knew they were on opposite sides of the fence.

"We'd like to ask your client some questions this morning."

T.J. took out a notepad and sat down on the one chair in the room, forcing Dan and Sig to remain standing. "We can't stop you from asking, but we may not be able to answer."

"All right. Hammer—"

"Excuse me, Sig. I don't want to have to butt in already, but my client's name is James, Jimmy is okay, and from now on I'd like him addressed in that manner."

Sig half smiled and nodded. "Jim." He didn't want to give in entirely. "Jim, were you anywhere near the soccer field by Paul Antonich Drive last Friday?"

Jimmy shook his head. "I don't remember."

"Do you remember where you were at all last Friday?"

"Like I told you yesterday, I came in from our clubhouse around evening, ditched my bike, and drove my pickup downtown."

Sig made some notes on his pad. Jimmy hadn't told them that yesterday. "Then what?"

"I drove to The Pub and had a couple of beers." While Jimmy answered, T. J. watched the officers' reaction to his words. Sig nodded as though what Jimmy said was in agreement with what was known.

"I walked down the street to the Legion Club and had a few more beers. After that, I remember buying a bottle of vodka at the Municipal Liquor Store."

Sig interrupted. "What brand did you buy?"

"Svedka. That's all I ever drink. It's good stuff, you know."

Sig nodded his head as if in agreement. "Was that the empty found in your truck when Officer Zemple took you in?"

Jimmy shrugged. "I suppose. Don't think anybody would have thrown an empty in my pickup while I was passed out."

"Did you ever get out of your pickup between the time you left the liquor store and when Officer Zemple found you?"

Jimmy thought for several seconds, and Sig gave him time to dredge up any details of that night.

Finally, Jimmy answered Sig's question. "I sort of remember having to take a leak and getting out of the truck to go."

"Do you remember where that was?"

"Not really. I think I walked through some short grass. Oh, and I tripped over something. I remember rolling ass over teakettle. That must have been when my cap came off. After that, I don't remember anything. Oh." Sig straightened up in anticipation of something more concrete. "I remember having a tough time getting up the ditch bank to my truck. I must have made it, because he," he nodded toward Dan, "found me down by the breakwater. That's all I know."

"Just a couple more questions," Sig said. "Jim, do you know a Justin Peters?"

T.J. abruptly stood up. "I'm sorry, Sig. I'm going to advise Jimmy not to answer anymore of your questions. He was brought in here on Saturday night, and yesterday you informed him he was under arrest. Jimmy's told me you read him his rights, and we aren't going to contest that." T.J. began to push a few papers into his briefcase. "My client will be transported to the county jail tomorrow. When do you intend to arraign him?"

Sig expected that question. "Tuesday. I'll have it scheduled this afternoon, and you can check the court docket for the time."

"Thanks, Sig." T.J. extended his hand. "By the way, you are not free to question my client about any aspect of this case without my being present. Just thought I'd remind you. See you tomorrow, Jimmy. Dan." T.J. nodded to the officers and left the room.

"We'll be back to pick you up tomorrow," Sig said to Jimmy. "Dan, I want you stay at your post until you're relieved at five."

Chapter Six

On Monday morning, Deidre sent her family off, Ben to work, Megan and Maren to school. She was standing at the sink, mindlessly humming a tune while she did dishes and looked out the window. A deer, a pregnant doe, crossed the yard, and she smiled to herself at the thought of a fawn cavorting around in two or three weeks. She was jolted from the idyllic moment by her cell phone ringing. *I wonder which one of them forgot something?* she thought. She looked at the caller ID and was surprised to see it wasn't one of her three.

"Hello, Deidre speaking."

"Deidre, this is T.J. Compton. Do you have a minute to talk?"

Deidre was rather speechless for a moment but was able to respond. "Sure, what's on your mind?"

T.J. was a familiar figure in town. He was a Two Harbors boy made good, graduated from the local college, UMD, and then from the U of M School of Law. He came back home to set up practice and had a small law office on the main street of downtown. Everyone knew him or of him.

T.J. began his pitch, and Deidre could picture him sitting behind his desk. He didn't look like an attorney. He was prematurely bald and sported a "cookie-duster" moustache, and with his stocky build and spectacles, he didn't make an imposing figure. But looks could be deceiving, and Deidre remembered seeing him in action. She had thought to herself if she ever was in need of a defense attorney, it would be him.

"Deidre, I have a proposition for you." He laughed over the phone. "Now don't go running to Ben with this news. It isn't that kind of proposition. I'd like to hire you to work for my law firm."

Deidre answered without thinking. "T.J., I don't know anything about working in a law office. I type with two fingers, know nothing about filing systems, and am a complete idiot when it comes to computers."

The attorney cut her off. "I'm not asking you to do those things. Tell you what, I'm in court for the rest of the day. Are you willing to come into my office at eight tomorrow morning? I'm always more persuasive face to face than over the phone." Deidre could hear him chuckle. "Will you hear me out?"

"I suppose I can at least do that, but don't get your hopes too high. I have no clerical skills whatsoever."

T.J. didn't argue. "See you at eight sharp tomorrow morning. Have a good day."

Deidre mulled over his words all day, and that evening, she told Ben what he had said.

"T.J.'s a good guy. Just a day ago you were telling me you needed something meaningful to do. Be careful what you wish for. You just might get it." He smiled and took her hand. "See what he's offering. It might be too good to turn down. I'm behind you whatever you decide to do."

*****

DEIDRE WENT THROUGH the usual early morning ritual: fixed breakfast, made bag lunches, and ushered her family off to their destinations. Then she headed to T.J.'s office. He was working at his desk when she cracked the door, wondering if she should just barge in or knock first. The lawyer saw her and rushed to invite her in.

"Deidre, great to see you! What have you been up to, working the land or becoming a hunter-gatherer? I haven't seen you in town for ages." She could tell by the smile on his face he was glad to see her.

"Oh, I've been around. I guess our paths just haven't crossed." T.J offered her a chair and pulled up another near her.

"I don't have too much time. I have to be at the courthouse for an arraignment at nine. Here's my offer." He wasted no time getting to business. "My practice has grown this past year, and I'm having difficulty keeping up with some of the things I have to get done. I think I've gotten the reputation of being a decent criminal defense attorney, because many of my cases lately have been of that nature. I'm to the point where I have to hire a private investigator to do some of my investigative work for me, and you're the person I'd like to hire."

The thought had never crossed Deidre's mind, but she quickly recovered. "But I'm not licensed, and I have no experience."

"No experience?" T.J. echoed. "No experience? What do you call the years you were a deputy, or the years you were sheriff, or the time you spent on the seven graves case with the BCA? You've got more than enough experience. Add up the hours and you far exceed the state requirements."

"But I don't even know the registration process," Deidre argued while she tried to wrap her mind around the idea.

Again T.J. torpedoed her objection. "I've got the forms run off." He handed her a folder. "The filing fee is eight hundred dollars. I'll pick up the tab on that. I even have a friend in the registration office who has told me he'll speed up the process. Said he can run it through in two days. After that, there are some continuing ed requirements to keep your license, but that's about it. What do you say? I think you'd make a great PI."

Deidre was silent for several seconds. "T.J., I need time to think this over. I have to talk to Ben and run the idea past my girls. When do you need my answer?"

"Well, I was hoping by nine o'clock, but I guess that wouldn't be fair to you. How about coming with me to the nine o'clock preliminary hearing? Watch from the gallery to see what your first investigation would be about. You can give me your answer tomorrow morning. Okay?"

Together, they walked to the courthouse. Deidre took a deep breath, and the freshness of spring was in the air. Spring is a special time in Two Harbors, and it was impossible to not experience a sense of elation over the demise of winter.

Deidre was sitting in the gallery when a deputy of the court marched in with Jimmy, who took a seat next to T.J. behind the defense table. The bailiff announced, "All rise. The Minnesota Court of the Sixth District is now in session." The Honorable Jeremy P. Quinn took his seat on the bench, and instructed everyone to sit.

Jimmy's appearance wasn't exactly what Deidre had expected. He was large, she expected that, but his beard was neatly trimmed and his hair well groomed. He wore long sleeves that covered his tattoos.

The court administrator announced the case, "The State of Minnesota verses James Peter O'Brian."

Judge Quinn looked over the top of his reading glasses. "Mr. O'Brian, are you represented by an attorney today?" Jimmy looked totally ill at ease.

"Yes, I am," he said in a weak voice.

"You are accused of second degree murder in the case of Justin Peters. How do you plead?"

"Not guilty, Your Honor." Jimmy hung his head in disbelief of his situation.

The judge continued. "You do know that by law in Minnesota, because this has been deemed a hate crime, any sentence against you will be of a higher degree?"

Jimmy's head came up and his eyes widened. "I didn't know that," he responded in a sharper voice.

"Well, I'm telling you now," the judge instructed. "I find evidence sufficient to not require a grand jury being seated. The trial date will be set by the court administrator. Until then, you will be held in the Lake County Jail."

"Your Honor," T.J. said as he rose to his feet. "About the matter of bail, my client is not a risk—"

Before he could finish his sentence, the judge snapped, "Bail will be set at one-point-five million. Bailiff, you will escort the prisoner back to his cell. Next case." T.J. had no opportunity to argue.

*****

THAT NIGHT, WHEN DEIDRE and Ben were finally alone, Ben asked, "So, what did T.J. want to talk about?"

"I think we need a glass of wine before we get into that." Deidre went to the kitchen and came back with two goblets of chardonnay filled a little more full than usual. She handed one to Ben and sat down.

"He wants me to become a licensed PI and work for him." Before she could continue Ben cut in.

"A PI. That would be a perfect fit for you." He caught himself. "If that's what you want."

Deidre laughed. "So much for wanting to ask for your input. But really, what do you think of the idea? It might interfere with some of our fun, get in the way of family time, you know, things like that."

Ben thought for a moment. "You can't sacrifice your training and what you do so well just to sit around waiting for us. It's not your job to make us happy or to create our fun. That's our responsibility. Seriously, I say if you'd like the challenge, go for it. I'll back you a hundred percent."

Deidre went over to the sofa where he was sitting, plunked down next to him, and pulled his arm around her. "Thank you." She laid her head on his chest.

Chapter
Seven

Deidre called T.J. at eight the next morning, wondering if he would be in his office that early. He asked if she could come in right away to fill out the PI application and to give her impression about the case she observed in court the day before. She was at his office at eight thirty.

"You've made my day," T.J. exclaimed as he came around from behind his desk. He shook her hand, then directed her to a chair and took one facing her.

"What did you think of Jimmy?"

Deidre pondered the question for a moment. "I felt sorry for him. He looked totally confused. How did he hook up with you?"

"Oh, Jimmy and I go way back. He lived on the same street I did, down on South Avenue. He was kicked around quite a bit by his drunken dad. We played together when we were kids, were friends in grade school. We kind of kept in touch in high school, but our paths took different routes. He hardly graduated, got a job as a welder. I went to school and got my law degree. We only say hello, been that way for at least ten years.

"He was pretty shook up when he called me last Sunday. After I met with him, I walked away believing he's innocent. I doubt if he'll ever be able to pay me, but I can't get the good times we had as kids out of my mind."

T.J. convinced her with his sincerity. "What do you want me to do now?" Deidre asked. "Do I have to wait for my license to come through before I can do anything?"

Her new employer said he wouldn't ask her to do anything requiring a license until it came. He did ask, though, "Do you have a conceal to carry permit?" The question stopped Deidre.

"No, do you think I'll need one?"

T.J. nodded. "I wouldn't let you work for me unless you did." The thought made her uncomfortable. "I have court this morning. The first thing I want you to do is to meet with Mrs. Peters. I'd like to know more about her son, Justin. Think you're up to it?"

Deidre didn't like the idea of visiting a grieving mother so close to the time of her son's death, but she realized they had limited time before a trial would be held. T.J. would try to stall for more time, but it was conceivable they would be in a courtroom in less than two months.

*****

DEIDRE STEPPED UP to the door and rang the bell. She heard movement in the house, and the door was slowly opened to her. Behind the screen door stood a haggard woman, and Deidre recognized the look. Her eyes were red-rimmed, and her hair was flyaway. She wore a disheveled robe. "Yes?" she asked softly.

"Mrs. Peters, my name is Deidre Johnson. I'm so sorry to have to bother you at a time like this, but I have a few questions I'd like to ask, if you can find it in yourself to talk to me."

The lady looked at her for a second. "Aren't you the woman who was sheriff? I suppose if your questions will help convict that man who did this to Justin, I'd better cooperate." She held the screen door open. "Come in."

Deidre was offered a chair at the kitchen table, and she took out a small notebook as she sat down.

"Thank you for being kind enough to see me. I'll be as precise as possible so I don't interrupt any more than I have to. Is there anything you can tell me about your son that might help?"

Mrs. Peters wiped her eyes and shrugged. "He was a good boy, kind, gentle, intelligent. As a child he was a real loner who loved to read. Justin spent a lot of time with me. We both loved gardening."

"Did he have many friends?" Deidre could tell she hit a nerve.

"No. Like I said, he was a loner. Besides that, many of the other kids bullied him, because he didn't stand up for himself. The older he became, the more isolated he was. In high school he did meet some boys he hung around with, but they were more or less outcasts like himself."

"Did he have a girlfriend?" Deidre asked, thinking it was a safe question.

There was a long silence. "Justin was gay. Oh, how I prayed that he would survive in this crazy world, that no one would want to harm him because of the way he was. So much for prayers, and don't tell me God had a plan that I don't understand. That's pure garbage." Deidre could see Mrs. Peters was becoming riled.

"Was he still being bullied in high school?"

Mrs. Peters didn't have to think before she answered. "Bullied? Continually. Finally, things became so toxic I had to go to the superintendent and threaten a lawsuit. He set up a meeting between the students who were bullying, me, and their parents. The bullying stopped, but the shunning was almost worse. Even some of the teachers went out of their way to ignore Justin. I thought if he could last until he graduated, he could escape this place and have a new start somewhere. Then he'd be safe. That's why I didn't want him out at night. He was at his best friend's house just a few blocks away and was supposed to be home by nine thirty. He never made it."

"Can you tell me who the bullies were?"

"Over there, a folder. It has all the information about our meeting with the superintendent in it. Help yourself." She wept into a towel while Deidre copied down several names and closed her notebook.

"Mrs. Peters, I am so sorry this happened," Deidre said as she finished. "I'm sure whoever did it will be caught and punished. I'm sorry."

The distraught mother looked up. "Get caught? You have him in jail, that biker. Who else could it be?"

Deidre didn't answer the question but stood to leave. "Thank you, Mrs. Peters."

"No. Thank you. It's comforting to know that you officers are on the job." Deidre felt a pang of guilt, but she didn't correct Mrs. Peters.

She stopped at the courthouse to find T.J. Deidre wanted advice about where to turn next but was told he had left for his office. She caught up with him there, where the attorney was busy at his desk.

"Discover anything?" he wanted to know.

"It's strange being on the other side of the fence. Mrs. Peters didn't ask who I was working for, but I know she surmised I was law enforcement. I didn't tell her I wasn't. Hope that's all right."

T.J. raised his hands to signal he didn't want to hear.

"Sometimes, the less I know, the better," he said, and Deidre expected him to plug his ears and sing "la-la-la-la."

"Did you know Justin was gay?"

T.J.'s brows furrowed. "I surmised that, especially after the judge gave his spiel about the stricter sentencing guidelines. Did she tell you that?"

Deidre nodded. "She told me how he was bullied when he was in school. Should I check out that angle?"

"Do that, and also, I want you to check out the biker hangout. Find out what you can about the members. Better jot these down," he advised Deidre, and she reached for a notepad on T.J.'s desk, slightly embarrassed that she had not been prepared. "I want you to interview Jimmy's employer. He's a welder for Two Harbors Steel Fabricators. Before you do that, I'd like you to run up to the soccer field and go over the crime scene with a finetooth comb. I doubt there's any evidence left, but you never know, they might have left something behind."

Deidre looked up. "I don't think I can get all of that done today. My girls get home from practice at six, and I'd like to be there for them."

T.J. laughed. "Don't burn yourself out on the first day. Try to get through the list by the end of the week. Take it as it comes, but take care of your family first. Sometime we might get in a real bind, but until then, don't kill yourself. Work at it like any other job."

Deidre took him at his word. "Oh," he added. "You don't have to check in all the time—unless you come across something that's too hot to wait."

Chapter Eight

On the way to the soccer field, Deidre mulled over what her boss had said. She knew herself and how driven she could become. She would have to learn to leave her work outside when she got home.

She parked partway down the ditch where Justin's body had been found. The scene was easy to discern by the matted-down grass. First, she slowly walked the area, her head down, scanning for any sign of something significant that had been missed. Then she expanded her search beyond the perimeter. By the time she finished, she had found nothing. Deidre decided she would literally crawl over the site.

As she slowly moved on her hands and knees, she roughed her hand over the beaten-down grass, standing it up, even bending it over in the opposite direction. She had nearly covered the immediate area when a swipe of her hand exposed something shiny. It was a piece of metal that had been stepped on and pushed into the dirt by someone's heel. She could see the imprint left behind.

Deidre was in a quandary about how to proceed. She had hastily put together a few things she thought she might need, but they were of little help at this moment. She stuck her ballpoint pen in the ground near the find so she would be able to relocate the spot, planting it deep enough so it couldn't be seen from the road. Fifteen minutes later she was back from the hardware store with a bag of plaster of Paris, a small plastic bucket, and a jug of water. Now her dilemma was if she should first remove the metal object or make a cast of the heel imprint. She decided on the former, but then it dawned on her she should call her boss.

A myriad of thoughts rushed through her mind. How could she preserve the integrity of the site and still collect the evidence? She knew a good prosecutor would claim she had planted it, even if that wasn't the case. While she waited for T.J. to arrive, she decided to scrutinize the ground around her find more closely. On her hands and knees again, she gently moved the grass from side to side. Again, she caught a glint of something partially buried in the wet soil. Parting the grass, she was sure she was looking at the jagged edge of a broken bottle. Not only that, but there appeared to be dried blood on the glass.

"Deidre, what have you got?" T.J. wheezed as he made his way down the sloping bank. "Here, let me see." The attorney bent down so he could take a closer look. Deidre didn't think he'd kneel on the ground and soil his expensive suit, but he surprised her. After a close look, T.J. stood up, wet patches on the knees of his trousers. "Photograph the site, get pictures of me touching the pen. I want pictures from every angle so the spot can be identified. Then you can remove whatever is in that heel print."

Deidre snapped a number of pictures to document the object. Setting aside her camera, Deidre teased the metal object with a set of forceps she thought might be handy when she put together her makeshift inspection kit. To her surprise, as she gently lifted it from its place, an empty shell casing emerged. Without touching it, she dropped it in an evidence bag and labeled it. Taking a cursory inspection, she noted the inscriptions on the shell: USCCO, and the number ten. Setting the bag off to the side, Deidre took more pictures of the heel impression, sans the shell.

It took a few seconds to mix the plaster, which she poured into the depression. When it set, she gently lifted it from the ground. *Whoever made this had a very large foot,* she thought. *Wonder if it will match Jimmy's boot?*

"Let's get going," T.J. urged. "I have court in an hour, and I'm going to have to change before then." He started to walk away.

"Wait!" Deidre blurted out. "There's one more thing over there in the grass." She pointed to the spot where the glass shard was buried. "I found what looks like the broken edge of a glass pop bottle over there. I'm almost certain it has blood on it." T.J. wheeled around and rushed back to her side.

"Where?" he asked excitedly. Deidre pointed to the spot where she had stuck a small twig in the ground. "Make sure you don't touch it with your bare hands. We'll have it tested for blood, and if it is, then we'll run a DNA test on it." Deidre excused his telling her how to do her job. He was excited.

With the pair of forceps, Deidre lifted the glass from the ground. It was the bottom of a soda bottle that may have been broken by a mower when the grass had been cut. The jagged edge was wicked, and she took care as she dropped it into a collection bag. She labeled the bag, noted the date and time of exchange, and turned it and the bag containing the shell casing to T.J. "Take good care of these," she instructed.

Deidre collected all of her paraphernalia and stored it in the trunk of her car. She checked the clock. Still plenty of time to visit the biker's clubhouse. On the way up Five Mile Hill she mulled over the difference between being a PI for an attorney and being an officer. Her job now was to find any wiggle room for T.J.'s client, anything he could use to place a fragment of doubt in one juror's mind. Before, as law enforcement, her job had been to erase any fragment of doubt. Before she could reconcile the difference, she arrived at her destination.

As she walked up to the front of the building, the first thing she noticed was the black-and-white sign, NO FAGS ALLOWED. Strike one against Jimmy. She poked around back, but all she found was a garbage bag of empty beer cans. *They don't look like recyclers, but who knows?* she thought.

A rusted-out, twenty-passenger school bus sat beside the building, its district logo obliterated by a swipe of black paint. So far she had found nothing significant but the sign. Deidre decided to go up on the porch and look through the front window. She had just cupped her hands around her eyes and bent forward to peer in when the door burst open.

"Who the hell are you, and what do you want?" Deidre was so surprised she stumbled backward, caught herself by the porch railing, and stared at her accuser. A muscular woman with black-dyed hair, a cigarette hanging from her mouth, and a broom in her hand glared at Deidre.

"I'm so sorry," she blurted out. "I didn't think anyone was here."

"Well, yeah. I figured that much out for myself. You didn't answer my question. Who are you and what do you want?"

"I'm investigating a case involving one of your members. That's why I was poking around. I'm sorry."

"Do you have a search warrant? Because if you don't, get your ass out of here."

Deidre knew she was in the wrong. "No I don't. In fact, I can't get one." The woman stepped closer.

"Whaddya mean you can't get one?"

"I'm not an officer. I work for T.J. Compton, the attorney representing James O'Brian." Before she could say another word, the woman butted in.

"Hammer. That dumb shit got himself in a real jam this time. What's his chances of getting out of this one?"

Deidre sensed a little thaw in the woman's brusque manner, but she couldn't be sure. "I don't know, all I'm doing is gathering evidence for T.J. If Jimmy gets off, that will be up to him." She thought she'd take a chance. "Look, can we talk for a few minutes?"

"You sure you ain't the law?" The woman squinted at Deidre. "I'm Blackie." She thrust out her hand, and Deidre noticed her grime-packed fingernails. "Come on in." Blackie held the door open and Deidre entered the clubhouse. Blackie signaled for Deidre to have a chair and sat across from her at the table.

"He didn't do it," Blackie snapped.

Deidre hadn't gotten a chance to say a word. "How can you be so sure?"

"He's all bluff. Hammer's just a big guy who's always on the go. Sure, he drinks too much, but don't we all? I'm just saying, Hammer's not a mean person who picks on people."

The conversation was not going where Deidre wanted it to. "What I came for is concrete information. What you say might be true, but it's your opinion. T.J. needs to build a case that puts doubt in the jurors' minds. He doesn't have to prove Jimmy didn't commit the crime, just foster doubt. That's why I'm here today, to find out about your group, the people he's close to."

Blackie thrummed her fingers on the table for a few seconds. "I know we look tough, but all of us have jobs, pay taxes, work hard. On weekends and days off, we come here to forget our troubles and play like we're bad dudes. The most any of us has ever had against us was a DWI. That's been Hammer's problem."

"Look, I don't even know your name—"

"Blackie," the woman interrupted.

"Right now we need to get away from the nicknames," Deidre said. "What message are you sending if you continue to call Jimmy "Hammer"? And you, what if your name, Blackie, appears in the paper as a friend of his? What does that mean to people? See what I'm saying? From now on, use your given names if anyone approaches you. If you will, I'd like you to answer some questions. What's your name?"

"Caroline Reynolds."

"How long have you known Jimmy O'Brian?"

"I suppose about six years. No, seven. It was the year after I graduated from business school."

Deidre began to think she had made her point. "Where were you last Saturday?" Caroline looked at her through narrowed eyes, and Deidre could see her answer would be guarded. "Look, Caroline, I'm not law enforcement, and you are not a suspect. I just need to be very certain of my timeline. Will you answer my question, please?"

Caroline relaxed a bit. "I was here most of the day. Came up from Duluth around ten in the morning. It was the first nice day we had to ride. I got here first, so I opened up, got the heat going, and made sure the refrigerator was making ice."

Deidre nodded and smiled. She knew Caroline was thawing somewhat. "When did Jimmy arrive?"

Caroline's face screwed up as she tried to remember. "Scy, I mean Eddy, got here next . . . then it was Jimmy. I suppose that was about eleven o'clock."

"So, what did you do for the rest of the day, go riding?"

"No, Jimmy and one of the other guys went into town to get some beer and other shit. The rest of us waited for them. It's only a ten-minute trip."

"They took bikes?"

"No, they fired up the bus you saw back there." Caroline tilted her head in its direction and sort of laughed. "Sometimes we use that when we go out and plan on partying hard. Whoever draws the short straw is the designated driver. Saves us a lot of tickets. Anyway, Jimmy and Eddy were back in an hour with a couple cases of beer. We spent the rest of the day drinking."

"Use anything else?" Deidre asked, smiling while she waited. Caroline squirmed.

"A little weed—but not much, you know?" She looked at her feet.

"What time did Jimmy leave?"

"He was the first one to go. I think it was about four. Anyway, the sun was still up pretty high. He was angry, because he wanted to plan a trip and nobody would listen to him. He cleaned up a little and then said he was heading to town. Rode his bike."

Deidre took her time writing down what had been said. "Did Jimmy have it in for people who were gay?" She waited for an answer.

Caroline measured her words. "You know, we're all straight, and we might say some things that aren't," she made quotation marks in the air with her fingers, "'politically correct.' But we never go looking for them. We sure as heck have never hassled anybody over it, and I know Jimmy wouldn't hurt anybody because they were gay. Oh, that sign out front," she said in explanation. "Eddy picked that up at another bike rally and brought it here as a joke. Nailed it to the wall."

Deidre wanted to ask how she could be so sure about Jimmy but held her thought. "Thanks, Caroline," she said and started to leave, then thought of one last question. "Was Jimmy pretty wasted when he left? Would you say he was drunk?"

"No more than the rest of us," Caroline answered, and Deidre wondered what she meant by that.

*****

It was two thirty when Deidre left the biker's clubhouse and headed back to town. She stopped at the intersection of the Gun Club Road and Highway 2 and pulled out her cell phone.

"Hi," she said when someone at the high school answered the phone. "Is it possible for me to make an appointment to meet with Judith Eliason and her son, Nick, after school today?" The office person asked for information before she could respond.

"My name is Deidre Johnson. I'm helping to investigate the murder of Justin Peters." Again, she didn't divulge whose side she was on, and the receptionist assumed she was with law enforcement. She asked if Deidre could hold while she made a call to one of the classrooms. Deidre had made a quick check on Nick Eliason and knew his mother taught psychology in the school he attended.

The receptionist came back on the line and informed Deidre that school would be out in fifteen minutes. Mrs. Eliason would have a few minutes free at that time. It was less than a ten-minute ride down Five Mile Hill to the school, and Deidre parked in the visitor's lot, checked in at the office, and was waiting outside Eliason's classroom when the bell sounded and students poured out into the hallway. In minutes they had cleared the building, rushing to escape its confines. Deidre waited patiently for Judith to appear.

"Can I help you with something?" the teacher asked as she approached Deidre in the hall. Deidre extended her hand.

"I'm Deidre Johnson, and I was hoping I could speak with your son, Nick. I thought since you work in this building the three of us could meet." She tried to accompany her request with a sincere smile.

A frown crept over Judith Eliason's face. "Who are you, and why do you want to speak to Nick?"

"I'm helping to investigate the death of Justin Peters, which occurred over the weekend, and I'd like to talk to Nick about any contact he may have had with Justin."

"And what makes you think Nick would know anything about that?" Deidre could see she had lit a fuse, and the woman was about to explode. "My Nicky would never hurt anyone! I suppose you've talked to his mother, and she told you those lies about my son being a bully. Well, they're not true." She stepped closer to Deidre and continued her rant.

"I'm tired of everyone saying that Nicky is a bully. He's not. And now you come here accusing him of murder. Back off, lady. You're standing in my personal space." Deidre could tell Mrs. Eliason was trying to intimidate her by backing her against the wall, but she held her ground.

"Mrs. Eliason, I wish you would calm down. No one is accusing your son of murder. I'm only trying to gather information that might give me a clue as to why Justin would have been so badly mistreated."

Judith thrust her jaw out. "From what I hear, you already have his killer in jail. Whatever happened, my guess is that Justin did something to this O'Brian guy to make him commit the crime. You know those people. They have a way of throwing their lifestyle in our faces. Not everybody appreciates that."

"And what do you mean by 'their lifestyle'? Are you trying to tell me something, Mrs. Eliason?" Deidre looked the woman square in her eyes and waited for an answer.

"You know perfectly well what I mean," she shot back.

"I think I do," Deidre replied, her disdain for how the conversation was transpiring evident in her voice. "I presume you are not going to help me speak with Nick."

"I certainly am not!"

"And there is absolutely no truth to the allegations that your son was bullying Justin?" Deidre pressed.

"Absolutely none!"

"Then why, after the school and Nick were threatened with legal action, did the nonexistent bullying stop?" Deidre held her ground, and Judith Eliason went speechless for a moment.

"It's all a lie," she said and retreated to her classroom, slamming the door to make it clear that Deidre was not welcome to follow.

Deidre made a few notes in her book and checked her watch. It was nearly four, time to become a mother and wife again. Heeding T.J.'s advice to not check in with every detail, she didn't drive through town but took the back roads. On the drive home, she began to see the law from the other side of the fence. What had once seemed to be black and white was becoming more gray all the time. By the time she pulled into their driveway, she was nearly convinced the only thing James O'Brian was guilty of was making some very self-destructive decisions.

Chapter
Nine

The ore docks in the harbor stand at least ten stories above the water. Railroad gondola cars lined up on tracks running atop the structure are filled with a partially refined product of the Iron Range made from low iron content taconite, and are emptied into waiting ships bound for eastern steel mills. A secluded bait shop sat near the tracks not far from where they curve onto the docks, and customers had to wend their way through a maze of gravel roads to find it.

It was Monday of the third week of April when its proprietor, Mel, unlocked the door to the shop. He wasn't in a hurry to open, because the lakes were covered with rotten ice, the kind that wasn't safe to walk on. There was still no open water for anglers to float a boat. Business would be nonexistent. He planned to spend the day organizing the shop, unpacking inventory, and preparing for walleye season, which was set to open in May. In the distance Mel heard the sound of an approaching ore train coming down the incline to the docks. He was so accustomed to their passing the sound hardly registered. He had just cut open a carton of lures when everything in the shop began to rattle and shake.

Mel grabbed a shelf to steady himself, but it broke loose from the wall, and he fell backwards onto the floor. He could hear screeching and the sound of metal being crumpled, and it felt like an earthquake, but that made no sense at all in Two Harbors. When it seemed as though the noise and quaking was never going to stop, it did, followed by an eerie silence.

The shopkeeper picked himself up off the floor and looked out the window, but he couldn't see anything. A wall of black dust was rolling toward him, and he knew in a second or two his shop would be enveloped by the cloud. He tried to orient himself, but his mind wasn't cooperating.

As Mel stood in the middle of the chaos inside his bait store, he became aware of sirens wailing. By the sound of them, they were getting closer. In seconds the first fire truck pulled in, followed by two police cars, a state highway trooper, and another fire truck. Just when he thought there would be no more emergency vehicles, two ambulances braked to a stop, sending up mini-clouds of dust that mixed with the particulates already suspended in the air.

By that time, the firemen in the first truck had their hoses hooked up, and Mel saw a stream of water shooting toward the track. In minutes, the water began to pound the dust down, revealing a heap of twisted steel. The wheel assemblies of gondola cars were piled helter-skelter, some buried in the wreckage, some sitting atop a three-story-tall pile. Everywhere he looked, Mel saw wreckage. He knew somewhere under the pile of steel the locomotive was probably buried. He hoped the engineer and brakeman had jumped before the wreck occurred. All he could do was sit on a bench outside his store and watch as he regained his senses.

In his bewilderment, he watched one of the firemen run to a nearby steel fabricating business and gesture wildly to workers who had run out of the building. One of them climbed onto a mobile hoist. Mel saw black smoke escape from its exhaust stack when its diesel engine started. The driver moved the slow-moving machine toward the wreckage, its engines whining because of the RPMs. It seemed to take forever for the driver to reach the spot to where he was being directed.

Workers who had arrived from the docks began to hook chains to something, and Mel watched as the hoist lifted what was left of a gondola car, swung it out of the way, and lowered it to the ground. Time after time the procedure was repeated, first a car, then an axle with a set of wheels attached, another gondola car body, more wheels, until the junk was piled high beside the roadbed. All motion stopped, or seemed to.

The hoist operator inched the powerful machine forward, and Mel realized he had uncovered the engine. Workers on the ground attached chains to the locomotive, and the hoist groaned as its winch was activated. The massive tires of the hoist squatted from the load, and the diesel belched exhaust, but nothing moved. The operator tried again, and Mel saw him shake his head as he eased off on the power.

After a five-minute wait, another hoist, a bigger one, roared up from the railroad shops. The two hoists were parked side by side, and together they were able to roll the engine a few feet up from its side. Mel watched in amazement as a worker risked his life by stooping and crawling under it. He pulled something out and went back under. Just as he dragged another something out from under the deadly trap and got out of the way himself, a chain either slipped or broke, and the engine crashed to the ground.

Mel had regained his senses, or at least he was cognizant of what was happening, and as he watched the EMTs carry two draped stretchers to the waiting ambulances, he knew there hadn't been time for the engineer and brakeman to jump. He locked the door to his shop and left for downtown. In The Pub, he ordered a brandy on the rocks. His hand was shaking as he lifted the glass to his lips and took a gulp. In one motion, he set the glass down and motioned for the bartender to pour another drink. Then he sat and stared at the glass of brandy and ice. Other than him and the bartender, the place was empty. Everyone downtown had heard the crash and had rushed to look at what happened.

*****

DEIDRE WAS UNAWARE of any of the commotion until she and Ben were watching the ten o'clock news on TV. Every channel from Duluth had sent a film crew up the shore, and the two of them sat engrossed by the pictures they were seeing.

First to be interviewed was a safety inspector from the railroad. The reporter asked the obvious question: "Do you have any idea what caused this derailment?"

"Well, let me begin by saying that our condolences go out to the families of those who were on the train. We want to assure them that every precaution was taken to prevent an accident like this, and I'm sure we will find that it was nothing more than an unpreventable happenstance. It's unfortunate, but railroading is a dangerous occupation. Our workers know this and accept the risk. They are paid wages commensurately."

The reporter blinked, scarcely believing what she had just heard. "But, sir, you didn't answer my question. Do you have any idea what caused this derailment?"

He glared at her. "No," he said sharply and turned away to busy himself with another seemingly important duty.

The reporter moved to where a group of workers stood in a circle. She thrust herself into the ring and held the microphone out. "Do any of you have an idea what happened here today?" There was silence until one man spoke up.

"The rail was sabotaged. A whole section before the switch is torn out. The thing is, there are no spikes laying around. None. Listen to me. Somebody pulled the spikes last night and meant for this to happen. When they catch the bugger, I hope they wring his neck, the dirty SOB."

Again, the reporter was at a loss for words, and her confusion was evident as she tried to think of what to ask next. While she was groping for a thought, the railroad inspector burst into the group and told the men to not answer any more questions. They shuffled away in different directions.

Ben and Deidre looked at each other, speechless at the callousness of the official they had witnessed. Ben said out loud what Deidre had been thinking. "All he could think of was covering his own hind end." He turned off the TV in disgust.

Chapter Ten

Ben left for work a little after seven, and the school bus picked up the girls ten minutes later. By seven forty, Deidre was out the door and on her way to Toimi, a wilderness community thirty miles north of Two Harbors. Because of Reverend Isaiah's negative rhetoric about gays, she had decided to pay him a visit this morning, and she suspected he would be found at the small church he ran.

At one time the Toimi area had been inhabited mostly by hard working Finns who tried farming the rocky, yellow-sand soil. They subsisted by raising a few animals, logging in the winter, and poaching a deer now and then. Now, most of its people were older. Their children, not wanting to set down roots in isolation, left the area as soon as they could to find work and live in the modern world. Deidre was curious why anyone would try to keep a church going in such a remote territory. As she drove, she thought of Reverend Isaiah.

Reverend Isaiah—no one knew if he had another name—had come to the area some ten or twelve years ago. He brought several people with him: his wife, Sarah; three sons, Abraham, Jacob, and Joshua; and two teenage girls, Hannah, and Rebecca, who didn't seem to be part of his immediate family. Two other families came with him, but they were seldom seen in town. Altogether, the sect numbered about twenty, including the children, whose ages at the time seemed to span about twelve years, the youngest a toddler.

They were grown now. The oldest boys must have been in their mid-twenties, and the girl who had been a toddler would be about thirteen or fourteen.

The group had used a technicality, what some called underhandedness, to purchase Toimi's tiny rural community church. Its small congregation had failed to register the proper papers with the IRS. They had temporarily lost their non-profit status, during which time they accrued a small property tax bill, a bill they were unaware of until two years later when the property was declared tax forfeit and scheduled to be auctioned off by the county. Reverend Isaiah paid the taxes for the church, then billed the congregation that amount plus exorbitant fees and interest. The few people of the congregation couldn't come up with the money and signed the church over to him. Forty acres of wilderness land was included in the deal.

Every week, the reverend ran an ad in the local paper declaring homosexuality to be a sin and quoting obscure Bible passages from Leviticus declaring that homosexuals should be stoned by the community. Not only that, he offered his services to the gay and lesbian community. Anyone suspecting they were homosexual could come see him, he claimed, and he would perform an exorcism, driving out the demons which caused what he termed "their sinful sexually deviant behavior."

Deidre thought she would not be surprised to find that he or members of his group would be capable of violence toward anyone with alternative lifestyles. She was so deep in thought that she missed the dirt road which led to the church and behind that, the group of buildings housing the reverend's followers. She turned around at the first opportunity and returned to the driveway.

As she parked her car, she saw children and women working in the several gardens maintained by the group, and it reminded her that they were in some sort of survivalist mode. The women all had long hair which hung nearly to their waists in single rope-like braids They wore ankle length dresses and high-collared blouses. Even the little girls were attired the same way, and the boys wore heavy leather workboots that could have used some polish. Long-sleeved shirts covered their arms, and they wore suspenders, which made them look like miniature old men.

Deidre stared at the children. They looked as if they had been made with a cookie cutter, all looking alike to her as though they were closely related. *Too closely,* she thought. None of them raised their heads to look her way when she walked up.

"Hello. I'm looking for Reverend Isaiah." A couple of children looked up but said nothing. The women continued to hoe the rows. "Is the reverend home today? He usually doesn't come into town until Saturday." Finally, one woman spoke, although she didn't look up, nor did she break the cadence of her work.

"Reverend Isaiah is praying in the chapel. Best not to disturb him while he's praying for us. That's what gives us strength to keep working, his prayers."

Deidre could hardly keep from snatching the woman's hoe from her hands and saying, "This is abuse. Don't you know that?" but instead she said "Thank you. Try to have a nice day."

Even though it was only two hundred yards back to the chapel, Deidre drove her car. She wanted it nearby where she could see it, and she felt the hair on her neck begin to prickle, even though she could see no danger. The door to the chapel was closed, but she decided not to knock. This was, after all, a house of God, and she could say she was stopping to meditate if she was chastised. She turned the knob and walked in. As her eyes adjusted to the shadows, she saw a figure rising from the floor behind the altar. The Reverend Isaiah looked confused.

"I've told you never to interrupt my prayer time," he snapped. Deidre noticed he was rubbing his eyes as though he had just been awakened. When he stood, he wobbled on his feet, and Deidre saw that his eyes were bloodshot. She stepped forward, and as she drew near the man she could smell alcohol on him. He reeked of it.

"What do you want?" he demanded. "And who are you that you think you can barge into God's house without being invited?"

Deidre looked at him with disgust. While the women and children sweated as they tended the gardens, the good reverend was in here, soaking up booze and sleeping it off. "I thought everyone was invited to the house of God," she answered, calling on what little church background she had.

"Well," he stammered. "I suppose. But this is a special place for my followers. Why don't you search out another church in town?" He scowled at her.

"Tell you what, Reverend. Answer a few questions for me, and I'll leave. I won't even tell those poor women out there that their spiritual head is a drunk and a hypocrite. Okay?" The reverend didn't move, but he didn't say no. Deidre took out her notepad and a pen. "Where were you last Saturday night?"

"I was here, with the group."

"And they'll attest to that?" Deidre knew it would be no use asking them. They would say whatever they were told to say.

"Of course they'll vouch for me," the eagle-nosed old man said indignantly.

"Well, how about the men in your group? Where were they last Saturday night? Here? Or were they in town?"

The reverend snorted. "They don't leave this place of sanctuary. The world out there is evil, and none of them wants to be tainted by the sin that is everywhere. Our mission here is to remain pure until the great return. The righteous will inherit the earth for a thousand years after Christ's appearance, and we are going to be among the one hundred forty-four thousand, the chosen few." The old man paced the floor as if he were fighting an inward battle. "Look at me. I'm the one who goes to town, who picks up the staples we need, who tries to warn the people of what is to come. Look at me! I'm the one who has allowed myself to be exposed to the demons of the world, and they have grabbed me." As he talked, he became more agitated. "There is no hope for me. I am like Christ, sacrificing myself for the good of many. No, I am the only one who ever leaves this colony of holiness." Reverend Isaiah sat down in a pew and covered his face with his hands. "Please, leave us alone now."

Deidre walked back to her car, which was parked near one of the gardens. She nonchalantly wandered to where one of the young women was hoeing a row of string beans. As she came closer she could see that the gardener was actually a girl, hardly fifteen, Deidre guessed. The girl kept her head down and continued to chop at the earth with the hoe.

"Hi," Deidre said. The girl continued to toil without responding. "Can you stop to talk with me a minute?"

"No," was the one word answer, but as she moved past Deidre, a piece of paper that was folded into a wad dropped from her pocket. The girl moved on, ignoring the paper. It was obvious to Deidre that the girl knew she had dropped it, but made no effort to retrieve whatever it was. Deidre palmed it and walked to her car.

She drove out to the highway from the secluded enclave before she stopped and unfolded the paper. Scribbled in crooked handwriting were two words: HELP US.

Chapter
Eleven

As she drove back to town, Deidre knew in her heart that the reverend fervently believed what he had said. That made her wonder all the more if he might have been capable of killing someone for his beliefs. But then she thought of the severe beating delivered to the dead boy. The reverend was old and frail. No way he could have inflicted that much damage to the victim. But he was filled with an irrational hate for what he believed to be sin.

Now she had a new quandary: what to do about the message. Help who? And help them from what? She shook her head and, deep in thought, drove the two-lane road back to Two Harbors. She decided her only course of action was to take the note to the county sheriff, Jeff DeAngelo.

It was noon when she arrived at the law enforcement center, and she hoped to find Jeff at his desk and that he hadn't left for lunch. As she was climbing the stairs to the second floor, she met him coming down.

"Hey, there's my favorite PI. Do you still go by Deidre, or should I call you Harry?" He was referring to a mystery series he knew Deidre had read, where the PI was named Harry.

"Watch it, Sheriff," she joked, "Or I just might have to punch you out." She playfully jabbed his arm. "Are you heading for lunch, or are you on the clock?"

"You know better than that. Seems like I'm always on the clock, but I am going down to Louise's for a sandwich. Want to join me?" They walked together the two blocks to the coffee shop.

After ordering, they poured themselves cups of coffee and found a table. Deidre looked around to make sure no one was close by, and then she leaned closer to Jeff.

"I might have something that should be looked into. I'm not sure, though." Before she could continue, the waitress brought their sandwiches and asked if they needed anything else. They shook their heads. Deidre continued after the girl left. "I think you're familiar with Reverend Isaiah."

Jeff interrupted. "Now what'd he do? I get at least one complaint a week from somebody he has harassed with his religious badgering. Has he been bothering you?"

Deidre half laughed. "No, nothing like that. This morning, I visited his commune, or sanctuary, whatever you call it. I wanted to talk to him about a case I'm investigating for T.J. Compton."

"That would be the Jimmy O'Brian case?"

Deidre was momentarily stopped by Jeff's question. "Well, yeah. But that's not what I wanted to talk to you about. I didn't feel comfortable at all when I was there. Felt like I was being spied on, and I couldn't get anyone to talk to me, except the rev. I don't know how many people are in his group, but I think there are quite a few more than when he came to Toimi. Anyway, several women and girls were working in the gardens when I got there. I was inside the chapel talking to Reverend Isaiah for about half an hour, and when I came out, I wandered over to one of the gardens and came close to a girl, quite a young girl, maybe fifteen.

"When I asked if she could talk to me, she said, 'No,' and kept hoeing a row of beans, but as she passed me, this dropped from her pocket." Deidre took the folded paper from her own pocket and began to open it. "I think she knew she dropped it, but she made no effort to pick it up, so I did. When I got to my car, I drove out to the main road before I opened it. Look at this." She spread the note out so Jeff could read it.

His brow furrowed as he studied the words, and he didn't speak for several minutes. It would have taken him only seconds to read the message, but he continued to stare at the paper. Finally, he exhaled.

"Something up there isn't right, and this raises the warning flag even higher." Jeff went on to share some information with Deidre.

"You know Johnny Bolene, don't you?" Deidre nodded. "He came to my office about three weeks ago. Said he wanted to talk to me about a hitchhiker he had picked up. Johnny's quite a trout fisherman and said he was heading up to Breda Creek for the evening and stopped to give the guy a ride. When he asked where he was going the guy said, 'Toimi', and Johnny told him to hop in. To make a long story short, the guy said his name was Jeremiah Rude. As soon as he climbed into Johnny's pickup cab he started talking goofy religious stuff, told Johnny that people called him The Prophet. Then he went on to say that he had a prophesy for Two Harbors. Johnny said the guy freaked him out with what he was saying. Rude told him that God looked at Two Harbors as a modern Sodom and Gomorrah, and that God was going to destroy the town because it's a sinful place."

Deidre didn't say anything to interrupt Jeff, and he continued with Johnny's story. "The guy recited a litany of our offenses against God. We drink too much. We don't worship enough. We show no evidence that the Holy Spirit resides in us. I really don't know what he meant by that, but he didn't mince words when he said only God's select would survive to the end. That kind of talk is unnerving to me, but then he began to single out groups who he said were an abomination and had to be cut out like a cancer.

"At the top of his list were homosexuals. He said there was a special place in hell for them. But what troubled me most was his accusation of Lutherans. He told Johnny that they had deeply offended God by welcoming, to use his words, 'the blighted' into their congregations. Rude cited the recent vote taken by the Lutheran

Church accepting gay clergy. Most troubling was his claim that God would use whatever tool he needed to cleanse the earth of those who were born of Satan. By that time, Johnny was at Four Corners and told Rude he'd taken him as far as he could. When Rude got out, he asked how far down the road it was to Reverend Isaiah's Sanctuary. Johnny told me the guy freaked him out."

Deidre had listened quietly to Jeff's monologue, but thoughts had been rummaging around in her head the whole time. "That news freaks me out, too. But what do you make of this note?"

Jeff thrummed the table with his fingers. "I don't want to jump to conclusions, but I don't like it at all. Just last summer, a religious compound was raided near Moose Lake. They found a dozen girls being literally held captive and used as sex slaves by the cult leader. I sure as hell hope this isn't what we have going on here, but this is pretty suspicious. I'll get on it right away. Thanks for bringing it in."

Luckily, they had ordered cold sandwiches, because neither of them had taken a bite. Now they dug into the food, hardly exchanging a word. Deidre broke the silence. "Would you have any objection to my speaking with Johnny about this "Prophet"? I think he has information T.J. can use in his defense of Jimmy."

Jeff took the last bite of his sandwich. "Go for it."

Chapter Twelve

Deidre knew where Johnny Bolene lived, and she hoped the retired ore dock worker wasn't out fishing. She figured the day was too bright and sunny for him to be plying the trout streams, but he was such a fishing fanatic, he might be out scouting a new stretch of water. She rang the doorbell, but no one answered, even though she waited a good three minutes. Following a hunch and a hope, she walked around to the back of the house and spotted movement in his garden. Since the death of his wife, Johnny spent most of his time either fishing or gardening. Today it was gardening.

"Hey, Johnny," Deidre shouted out. "How ya doin'?" Johnny stood up and shielded his eyes against the noon sun.

"Deidre, good to see you. Come on down here. I just finished grubbing out some old cabbage roots I forgot and left in the ground over winter. Too much on my mind, I guess. Either that or I'm getting old." He threw the roots onto a compost heap and laughed as he removed his work gloves. Johnny thrust his hand out to shake Deidre's. "I'm doin' really great. In a week I think I can get the garden tilled up. Might be able to plant lettuce by then."

"How's fishing?" Deidre asked. Johnny's eyes lit up.

"Great. Caught a nice brookie a couple of weeks ago on the Breda." Johnny's face took on the appearance of somebody who had just given away a secret.

"Why, Johnny. I thought season only opened last Saturday." Johnny began to sputter out some kind of an answer, but Deidre came to his rescue. "That's okay," she laughed. "I hope it tasted good. I promise I won't tell anybody. Especially the game warden.

Anyway, it would only be hearsay, because I'm guessing the evidence was eaten a long time ago." She laughed when Johnny let out a relieved sigh.

"I've been worried for a few days," he admitted. "Jeff and I talked, and I had to tell him why I was up in Toimi that day. He said he'd grant me immunity for telling him what I had to say."

Deidre had a hard time not laughing. She was sure Jeff had no intention of turning Johnny in for his crime, but was only making the wayward angler squirm a little.

"That's why I'm here. Jeff said I could talk to you, and I need your help. He said you picked up a hitchhiker that evening, a guy named Jeremiah Rude." Johnny looked like he remembered something he'd rather not.

"Now there is a real crazy. I almost stopped my truck and told him to get out. The guy freaked me out with all his babble about the end of the world coming. Between you and me, I think he's one dangerous dude." He shook his head and spat on the ground.

"Johnny, I've never heard you talk that way about anyone. What makes you think he's dangerous?"

Johnny shrugged. "Just a feeling. That and what he said. I wouldn't trust him any further than I could throw him. He's bad business."

Deidre couldn't quite figure out why Johnny was so emphatic about Jeremiah. "Johnny, can you tell me exactly what he said that riled you up? It must have been pretty frightening to make you so jumpy."

"I can't tell you exactly what he said, you know, word for word. But I can, what do they say, 'paraphrase'? He's one scary guy."

Deidre still wasn't making any progress other than to learn that Johnny had been really rattled. "Let's sit on your deck. I'd like you to tell me as much as you can about what he said." They sat across from each other at the round patio table.

"Like I said," Johnny began, "I stopped to pick up this guy who was thumbing a ride. He was one big man, probably a good six-four and maybe weighed two-fifty, two-sixty. We were about ten miles from town, and I thought maybe his car had broken down. He had only a small backpack, and I wanted to help. Well, he climbed in and thanked me, introduced himself, and told me again how much he appreciated the ride. Said he was heading for Toimi if I was going that way. Then he said, and this is word for word, 'Thank God you came along. God must have a special job for you, because he told you to stop. Halleluiah, and praise God!'"

Johnny paused. "Man, I almost stopped and asked him to get out, but then I thought I could stand his Holy Roller stuff for twenty minutes. For the first few miles, we talked sort of normal, you know what I mean? He wanted to know how far it was, said he'd never been to the North Country. Told me he was from Oklahoma. After a few minutes of chit-chat, he turned to me and asked, 'Are you saved?' Let me tell you, I didn't know what to say, so I said, 'I'm Lutheran.' He looked at me and said, 'So you're not saved. Do you want to be saved right now, Brother?' Well, I just continued driving and didn't say anything, thought we could just ride in silence. But he kept on, getting more worked up.

"'Brother,'—he never asked my name—'Brother, you better repent and be saved because the Lord is going to punish Two Harbors for the way they have rejected his word. That is Sodom and Gomorrah back there, and soon it will feel the wrath of God. It's already started,' he said. Deidre, I have to tell you, I was getting uncomfortable, so I gritted my teeth and drove a little faster. The nut kept talking.

"He told me, 'In some places they call me The Prophet, because what I predict happens. I have prophesied to multitudes, and when they didn't turn from their sin, bad things happened: fires, death, accidents, all sorts of punishment rained down by God's almighty wrath. The same thing's going to happen here. Listen to me because, thus sayeth the Lord.'

"We only had five miles to go to Four Corners, which is where I'd decided to let him out, but that's when he got really scary. He said, 'I heard a young man was recently killed in town. Do you know why? Because he was an abomination before God, he was a homosexual. Leviticus says, "If a man lies with a male, as with a woman, both of them have committed an abomination: they shall surely be put to death; their blood is upon them." Don't you see, Brother, no one murdered him. He killed himself by his sinfulness. Whoever delivered the blow was only a tool of God, not a murderer.'

"By that time we were at Four Corners, and I stopped, but he didn't make a move to get out of my pickup. He kept on with his garbage. 'There will be more, Brother. Believe me, there will be many more: the whores, the drunks, the blasphemers, the idol worshippers. They will all perish under the hand of God. Brother, I don't want you to be one of them.' Strange thing was, he had tears running down his cheeks when he got out. Then, as if he had said nothing unusual, he turned and asked how far it was to The Sanctuary, or whatever Reverend Isaiah named his place. Then he smiled at me and said, 'The Gospel of the Lord.' I couldn't get away fast enough. Kind of ruined my evening of fishing."

*****

DEIDRE CHECKED HER WATCH, 2:20 P.M., still time to see one more person. She hoped her next meeting wouldn't be so unsettling. At two thirty she was parked by the high school's baseball practice field, and as she sat in the warm sun, her car window down and the fresh air blowing in off Lake Superior, she wondered what caused people to be so blinded by their radicalism that they totally missed the beauty of the area, of its people. Her thoughts were interrupted when she saw a group of players approaching with their baseball gear in their hands. Among the players was Nick Eliason, and Deidre could see that he was the alpha male. The other boys seemed to bask in his presence, and although at first glance it might appear that everyone in the group was on equal footing, Nick was clearly the center of their attention. Deidre stepped out of her car and called to him.

"Nick, can I speak with you a moment?" Nick's head snapped up, and he spun around.

"You can't question me without my parents' consent, and unless you've got a court order, I don't have to talk with you." The other boys drifted away, leaving their belligerent leader standing alone in the parking lot.

"You might not know as much as you think about the law, young man," Deidre shot back. "Unless you are subpoenaed to testify, you cannot be forced to answer any questions, even if you are a suspect in a case." Deidre could see a look of surprise on the boy's combative face. "Furthermore, I am not an officer of the law, and I can't keep you from walking into the clubhouse right now." She could see that Nick was confused by this turn of events. "Finally, you are eighteen, considered an adult. No one needs parental consent to ask you some questions. In fact, your parents can't demand that anyone stay away from you. With your adult status, only you can make that demand. So the choice to speak to me or not is yours."

Now Nick really did look confused, and Deidre took advantage of that moment. "All I want is to find out about your classmate, Justin Peters." Nick took a step toward her, and Deidre walked toward him until they were four or five feet apart. She wanted to stay well back from what he might consider his personal space.

"What is there to know?" he demanded as he menacingly tapped the baseball bat near her foot.

"That's what I'm asking. It's as simple as this: Did you know him?"

Nick sneered. "I don't hang around with guys like him. You know what I mean?" Deidre shook her head.

"No. I guess I don't know what you mean. Tell me."

"He was a queer, a faggot, a homo, whatever you want to call him. My guys and I, we don't hang out with his kind." Nick's face was clouded with contempt, but Deidre pressed on.

"But you did know him, right? Knew him well enough to have caused him some trouble a couple of years ago. What was that about?"

Nick started to turn away, and then had second thoughts. He took another step toward Deidre, and now she was feeling like her space was being crowded. "Look," Nick snarled at her, his face turning red. "Just because I didn't like the little creep doesn't mean I killed him. Yeah, we pushed him around a little. Called him some names, but we never put a mark on him. And what did the jerk do? He runs home to Momma, and she gets all bent out of shape, because her precious little boy got his feelings hurt."

Deidre couldn't believe the young man's lack of caring for Justin. His vitriol was just beginning to spill out, and Deidre took advantage of his riled state. "Where were you and your friends the night Justin was murdered?"

He stopped in the middle of his rant. "None of your business, lady."

From the corner of her eye, Deidre saw someone running across the parking lot to them, and she turned her head to get a better look. Nick's mother, Judith Eliason, burst upon them. "I told you to stay away from my son. He had no part in that boy's murder and neither did his friends, so just leave him alone. If you don't, I'll have charges brought against you for defamation of character." The woman was livid, and she thrust her face close to Deidre's. Before Deidre could respond, Nick barked at his mother.

"Ma, get your ass out of my business. I can take care of myself. I've got practice now, and if you two want to go at it, then do it, but I'm out of here." Nick strode away and didn't look back.

Mrs. Eliason turned on Deidre again. "Now, see what you've done? You've turned my boy against me. And for what? Some pervert that we're better off without. I can see why you aren't sheriff anymore. You did our county a favor by not running again, you social misfit. If you'd have done your job back then, maybe good boys like Nick wouldn't have to put up with the riffraff they do." Deidre walked away and got in her car. She left Judith Eliason standing alone, still shouting insults at Deidre's retreating car.

On the way home she made a mental note to revisit Nick another time when she could again catch him off guard. Tomorrow, she planned to visit the pastor of the church she, Ben, and the girls attended.

Chapter
Thirteen

The next morning as Deidre drove to town, her thoughts swung to how her life had taken on a new dimension. The school year would soon be drawing to a close, and the twins would be needing more of her attention. She thought of the plans she and Ben and the girls had made to do some traveling, taking a real vacation together for the first time. Now she was wondering if her job was going to get in the way of their family time, and she began to feel the pressure of being pulled in two directions. She forced the coming dilemma from her mind and parked her car in the church parking lot. Pastor Ike was waiting for her.

"Deidre, I got your message that you wanted to talk to me this morning. Is everything okay? Ben, the girls, you?" He waited for Deidre to respond, expecting that she must have some personal problem she wanted to discuss.

He seemed almost disappointed when she said, "I need some help with an investigation I'm working, and I thought you might know about Reverend Isaiah's group. He's got the church in Toimi."

Pastor Ike looked a little deflated. "I can tell you a little about him and his group. You know everyone sees God a little differently, so we have to be careful not to rush to judgment." Deidre sensed that he wanted to say much more than he had, but was following what he saw as his Christian duty to be kind.

"I know you want to avoid disparaging another group," she offered, "but I'm in the middle of an investigation of a case in which they may play a role. Please, I assure you anything you say to me will remain confidential. I'd like your unvarnished impression of the group."

The pastor looked at the floor for a second or two and then lifted his head. With a sigh, he told Deidre what he really thought.

"I can't say I agree with much of anything Reverend Isaiah preaches. Two of my parishioners started to listen to his interpretation of scripture and came to me so confused that they were on the verge of leaving the church entirely. But that's the least of the problem. Word has gotten around that a man who calls himself The Prophet has joined their enclave, and he is bringing a more militant message to the group. His last name is Rude, but I doubt if that is real. You see, 'rood' is an ancient word for the type of Roman cross upon which Christ was crucified. I think Jeremiah Rude is a misspelling of rood, and I think he believes he's a martyr, willing to sacrifice himself. There's a rumor that members of The Sanctuary are planning to disrupt our Sunday services sometime soon, and they intend to take over pulpits and preach their message of God's wrath. Many of the pastors in town have met, and we've developed a plan for how we will handle such a situation in a non-violent manner."

Deidre listened attentively as her pastor continued.

"I honestly believe, and please don't tell anyone this, I honestly believe that they are a cult capable of twisting the Gospel message to support some very ungodly acts." He shook his head and looked away as though he wished he hadn't added that last statement. Deidre and he sat silently for a moment, neither of them knowing what to say next. Finally, she broke the silence.

"Thank you so much. You've been very kind to share your ideas with me, and don't worry. What you have said will remain between us." She stood and offered her hand, thinking her pastor looked weary this morning.

Her next stop was at T.J. Compton's law office. He had texted her earlier in the morning, asking that she stop in, because he had some important information to share with her. As Deidre opened the door, T.J. stepped around his desk and grabbed her shoulders.

"I think we have it," he exclaimed excitedly. "I think we can put so much doubt in a grand jury's mind they'll never convict Jimmy for Justin Peter's death. There is no way he did it, and I think we can prove it, perhaps not beyond a shadow of a doubt, but logically, I think we can show they have the wrong man."

Deidre was swept up by his exuberance, but she had no idea what he was babbling about. T.J. continued to gush.

"The DNA results of the blood on the shard of glass you found came back. The blood is definitely Jimmy's."

Deidre looked at him as though she were looking at a demented person. *This is good news? It places him at the scene of the murder, no ifs, ands, or buts.*

As if he read her mind, T.J. continued.

"Don't you get it? Jimmy said he vaguely remembered tripping over something and falling down. Remember the slice on the heel of the palm of his hand? It matches perfectly with his story. A man is walking, or in his case staggering, in the dark. He trips and falls. What's his reflex reaction? He throws his hands in front to catch himself and lands hard on the heels of his hands, but there is broken glass on the ground, and he slices his hand. The type of longitudinal cut perfectly matches the gash on Jimmy's hand, and we have the piece of glass to prove it happened."

Deidre stared at him, expecting more. "What?" T.J. asked, looking a little deflated. "You expected more?" Deidre hesitated in answering. "Well, we have more," T.J. continued. "The blood found on Jimmy's boot was on his left boot, none on the right. Jimmy's left-handed. Get it?" He didn't give her an opportunity to say no. "Jimmy had no motive. You told me that the woman in his group—what was her name, Carrie, Carol?"

Deidre corrected him, "Caroline."

"Yeah, that's it. Didn't she tell you that Jimmy had no malice toward gays, no special feeling one way or the other? We can use her as a character witness. And that shell casing you found at the scene. I sent it to a ballistics expert, and his report is very interesting. He said it had been chambered and fired from an assault rifle, and he could identify the type of weapon it had been fired from. Said it was manufactured here in the U.S. by a firearms company, Barrett. He had no doubt it had been chambered in a REC-7, which fires a 5.6 x 45 bullet, a NATO round."

Deidre interrupted T.J.'s river of words. "And you want me to check if any of the bikers have an assault rifle." She smiled at his response.

"Of course," he said, as if anyone would have known that was the next step.

"I'll be back as soon as I have any info." Deidre threw the words over her shoulder as she made a beeline to the door.

Six hours later she was back in the law office.

"I tracked down four of the members of the bike gang. Three live in Duluth and one in a town south of there, Barnum. They all have the same story. Most don't even own a gun, especially an assault rifle. Every one of them volunteered to testify to that in court." T.J.'s smile grew even wider.

"We have enough evidence to verify that Jimmy was just in the wrong place at the wrong time. I'm sure of it."

Chapter
Fourteen

THE DAY AFTER SPEAKING with Deidre and receiving assurances from Jimmy's friends that he didn't own an assault rifle, T.J. paid a visit to the county prosecutor. He was ushered into her office, and the two familiar adversaries shook hands. She invited T.J. to take a seat.

"So, T.J., nice of you to stop by for a chat. How's the law office doing?"

T.J. chuckled. "Come on, Mary. You know this isn't a social visit," he said to the prosecutor, then cleared his throat.

"I know this is highly irregular, but I am requesting that the county drop all charges against one of my clients, James O'Brian."

Mary looked at him a few seconds before answering. "Now why would I do something as ridiculous as that," she scoffed. "Everyone, well, except for you maybe, knows he's guilty."

T.J. jumped on her statement. "That's where you're wrong. I have witnesses who will testify in court that Mr. O'Brian is as much a victim as is Justin Peters. Sure he was drunk, but that doesn't make him guilty."

Mary shot back, "T.J., you know drunkenness can't be used as a defense."

He came right back at her. "You have one piece of evidence linking my client to the crime, the victim's blood on one of his boots. That isn't going to be enough to convict him, and you know it. Drop the case."

"Not on your life," Mary shot back, her neck and face becoming blotched with red spots.

T.J. looked at her for several seconds. "Have it your way, but you're going to be embarrassed when this gets before a jury. I'm requesting that my client be given an expedient trial. His defense team is prepared right now, and I'll be petitioning the court to schedule it as soon as possible." He stood, gathered his briefcase, a few loose papers he had brought to the meeting, and left without saying goodbye.

*****

DEIDRE AND T.J. MET in his office that afternoon to sift through what evidence they had and to determine if they had left any stone unturned. Deidre still couldn't understand how he could be so certain they would win the case. She wondered if he wanted to get it over with so he could concentrate on paying clients.

"Jimmy's trial has been set for June seventeenth," T.J. said. "It's a damn shame he'll have to sit in jail until then, but that's the way the system works. I don't expect the trial to last more than three days. There's no doubt in my mind he'll be exonerated. I believe the community is looking to wrap up this case in a hurry and forget about it. It's not going to be as easy to do that as they think." Deidre wondered from where his optimism stemmed.

The next weeks went by slowly for her. T.J. had no more detective work for her, and about all Deidre had to do was clean house and tend the garden. School let out and the twins had time to loaf around and play their sports. That meant countless trips into town for practice and games. At least once a week she stopped to visit her friend, Sheriff Jeff DeAngelo. For one reason or another, they usually ended up discussing the Reverend Isaiah and his group.

"I went up to The Sanctuary the day after you showed me the note dropped for by that girl," Jeff told Deidre one day. "When I got there, the place seemed as empty as a clothing store in a nudist colony." Deidre thought that was an unusual comparison but said nothing as Jeff continued. "A guard was stationed at the driveway leading to their residences, but he wouldn't let me pass without a search warrant. Nothing had happened that would give a judge reason to provide one, so all I could do was ask him a few questions. He said all the members of the group were observing a day of fasting and prayer. Seems The Prophet had received a vision from God telling him to declare a day of repentance." Jeff shook his head. "I wonder how people can be trapped into blindly following without questioning."

During their conversation, Jeff confided in Deidre that he was sure nothing good was happening at The Sanctuary, and he suspected many of the young people were being held against their will, or at least they were too frightened to leave. He told her he was seeking a court order to allow Social Services to speak with the young girls and women to find out if they were being abused in any way.

"Then, too," he lamented, "there have been other minor crimes going on these last couple of months that we're investigating. Most of the mainline churches in the area have experienced one form of vandalism or another, and signs point to the reverend's group, but nothing's concrete. Even the statue of the Virgin Mary outside the Catholic Church has been defaced. We're going under the assumption that these acts coincide with the threats of church service disruptions rumored to happen sometime this summer. It's difficult to get into The Sanctuary to question anyone, though. Seems every time my deputies or I go there, the group is sequestered for a prayer retreat, or some other excuse that prevents us from speaking to anyone. It's getting pretty frustrating."

It seemed to Deidre the problems in their community were becoming more serious. Investigators were sure that the rails of the track had been sabotaged, causing the fatal derailment the past April. Vandalism was increasing, and people were becoming convinced they were hate crimes. Hostility toward Reverend Isaiah was increasing, and Jeff told her he was worried citizens would form some kind of vigilante group to take care of the problem themselves. On top of that, Jimmy, the biker accused of viciously beating Justin Peters to death, was coming to trial the next week. She still didn't have the confidence that T.J. had in Jimmy walking away, exonerated.

*****

THE BAILIFF CALLED OUT, "All rise," and Judge Einar Jesperson stalked into his courtroom and took his seat. He glared at the gathering seated before him, and there was no doubt in anyone's mind who would be in charge. With his words, "You may be seated," the trial began.

Deidre was not allowed in the courtroom, because she was on the defense's witness list that had been disclosed to the prosecution. T.J. told her to wait in the courthouse, because he didn't think the prosecution would be calling many witnesses. He said that according to the prosecution's list, they intended to call Dan Zemple, the officer who brought Jimmy in on a drunk-driving charge; Sig Swanson, the chief of police; and the ER doctor who had attended to Justin Peters while he was dying. The prosecutor had intended to call a DNA expert to verify that the blood on Jimmy's boot was indeed Justin's, but T.J. had capitulated the point, something that confused both the prosecutor and Deidre.

Other than those few witnesses, the prosecution had few points to make, other than the testimony that Justin was gay and the group James O'Brian belonged to had an anti-gay sign on their premises. She was relying to a great extent on circumstantial evidence, and the damning evidence of Justin's blood on Jimmy's boot. By the mid-morning recess of the second day of testimony, the prosecution rested their case and it was the defense's, T.J.'s, turn. All during the prosecution's presentation and questioning, he had been nearly silent, not raising one objection and hardly asking a question during cross-examination.

Chapter Fifteen

Deidre was the first witness to be called. As she was being sworn in, out of the corner of her eye, she could see T.J. smiling in anticipation.

He casually stepped closer to the witness stand and leaned on his podium with one arm. "So, Ms. Johnson. You are in my employ as an investigator. Is that correct?" Deidre spoke in the affirmative, wishing all the questions would be so easy.

"And on April 18, three days after Justin Peters was beaten to death, did I assign you a job?" Again the question was easy, and Deidre told the jury that T.J. had asked her to do a thorough search of the murder site.

"Did you?" T.J. asked, and Deidre answered that she had. "Please explain to the jury what you did and tell them what you found."

This wasn't the first time that Deidre had testified in court, and she never was comfortable being on the witness stand. She cleared her throat before speaking. "I parked my vehicle on the shoulder of the road near the spot the victim was found. It was easy to identify, because the grass had been trampled down. I walked the entire area, searching for anything I might consider significant, then got on my hands and knees and carefully covered every inch of the scene."

"I see," T.J. interrupted as though he was hearing the story for the first time. "Did you find anything?"

"I did," Deidre said as she nodded. "I spotted a shiny metallic object that had been pushed into the soil by the heel of a boot."

Mary, the prosecutor, sprang from her chair to object that there wasn't proof the print came from a boot. The judge sustained the objection, and T.J. took a different line. "Your Honor, I'd like to offer this plaster cast made by Ms. Johnson of the heel print into evidence, along with photos verifying the time, date, location, and procedure she used."

The prosecution couldn't object, because it was on the agreed list of evidence the defense would produce. T.J. dropped the idea of the boot and switched his questioning to the metallic object. "Did you examine the shiny object you saw?" he asked. Deidre took it from there.

"Yes, I carefully teased the object from the soil and discovered it was an empty shell casing. I used a forceps to place it in an evidence bag, which I turned over to you."

T.J. probed her search efforts. "Did you find anything else while you were on your knees on the ground?"

"Yes, I did." The questioning was going easier than Deidre had anticipated.

T.J. continued, asking, "What did you find?"

Deidre spoke with confidence. "I found a shard of glass which appeared to be part of a broken soda or beer bottle. Using a forceps, I picked it up and placed it in an evidence bag."

T.J. held a bag out for her to see, and asked, "Was there anything of interest on the glass?"

Deidre answered carefully, "There appeared to be something resembling blood covering most of it." She knew if she had said it was covered with blood, the prosecution would have objected and the objection would have been sustained.

T.J. offered the glass shard as evidence and from that time on most of his questions were phrased so they were easily answered, so the prosecutor had little to object to. When she was told she could step down, T.J. smiled at her, but Deidre didn't feel like she had made much of a contribution toward proving Jimmy's innocence.

T.J.'s next witness was a representative of the Red Wing Boot Company. "I believe you have seen a replica of the impression of the heel of a boot or a shoe that was admitted as evidence." T.J. began as he picked up the plaster cast. "In your opinion, was it a replica of this cast?" The shoe man answered yes. T.J. continued. "Can you tell the court anything from this cast?"

Obviously at ease, the shoe representative gave his testimony. "This is the heel print of a Red Wing steel-toed work boot, the Classic 2238 eight-inch model."

T.J. had one more question of the man. "You're positive?"

"I'm positive," he answered.

T.J. had the witness examine Jimmy's boot, which the prosecution had entered as evidence to support her case. "Does the pattern on the heel of this boot match the pattern of the heel print left at the scene of the crime, the one you have testified came from a Red Wing boot?"

The representative answered, "No sir, it does not. Of that I am positive."

"No more questions," and T.J. sat down.

On cross-examination, the prosecutor asked how he could be so sure, and the witness pointed out the many identifying markings. She couldn't refute his testimony.

Next, T.J. called as a witness a ballistics expert and showed him the casing Deidre had found at the site. "Have you ever seen this before?" he questioned.

"Yes. This is the bullet casing you sent to my office for examination."

"And what did you conclude about this particular casing?" T.J. continued his line of questioning.

"This is the casing of a NATO round of ammunition, a 5.6 x 45, to be specific. It was fired from an assault rifle manufactured by Barrett Arms Manufacturers."

"Can you tell when it was fired?" T.J. wanted to know, but the expert said he couldn't. Then T.J. asked how he could be so sure of his conclusion. The witness took out a page from a notebook he carried, and began to explain.

"Objection, Your Honor," Mary calmly interrupted. "The diagram is not large enough for the jury to see."

T.J. smiled at her. "With the court's permission, I do have an enlargement of the diagram. Will it be okay if I set it where all can see?" He looked at Mary, who shrugged at the judge. T.J. had brought an easel into the courtroom and soon had the picture set up. The witness pointed to the various scratches and markings on the enlarged picture of the casing.

"This indentation was left by the firing pin, from which I can reach a logical conclusion." Again, Mary could come up with nothing to discredit the witness.

Judge Jesperson announced that there was time for one more witness before the court recessed for the day. T.J. called Caroline "Blackie" Reynolds, although he didn't use her nickname.

"Thank you for taking time away from your business, Ms. Reynolds," he began, making sure the jury was aware that she was a responsible person in the community. "Do you know the defendant, James OBrian?" Blackie looked at her friend and nodded.

The judge interrupted. "You'll have to speak up for the record."

Blackie enunciated very clearly, "Yes." and the judge almost smiled.

T.J. continued. "How well?"

"Very well. We belong to the same club, have for the last seven years."

Anticipating the prosecution's cross examination, T.J. asked, "That would be the biker group, the Death Riders. Am I right?" Caroline was sure to voice her answer, and T.J. asked, "Tell me, what does your group do?"

Caroline shrugged. "We get together for rides around the state. Sometimes we just hang out and have a few beers. Once in a while we go to a party as a group. Nothing too exciting, I'm afraid."

T.J. smiled at her. "Has anyone in your group ever been arrested for a serious crime, perhaps like armed robbery or assault or," and here he paused for effect, "murder?"

Caroline looked surprised at the question. "Hell no!" she blurted out. "The only one who's even had a DWI is Ham . . . I mean, Jimmy." T.J. had no other questions, and as he took his seat he thought he saw smiles on the faces of a few jurors.

The prosecutor tried to pin Caroline down, wondering if they were such a peaceful organization, why they had such a violent name. The witness laughed. "It makes us sound tough."

The judge asked if T.J. had any redirect questions, and he did. "To your knowledge, did James O'Brian ever own an assault rifle?"

"Absolutely not," she said. On recross-examination, Mary tried to get Caroline to offer some degree of doubt to her answer, but she stood firm on her response to T.J.'s inquiry. At three forty-five, Judge Jesperson called a recess for the day, reminding all parties that court would resume at exactly nine the next morning.

Chapter
Sixteen

The third day of the trial started with little of consequence. T.J. called a series of witnesses to vouch for Jimmy's character: three more bike gang members, each of whom testified that they had never known Jimmy to own a gun, let alone an assault rifle, and the owner of The Pub, which Jimmy frequented. By the time T.J. called Jimmy's employer to vouch for his work ethic, everyone in the court room was getting restless. Even the prosecuting attorney was getting glassy-eyed.

"I call Dr. Marcus Fayler," T.J. said, showing no emotion. The doctor was sworn in and took his seat on the witness stand. "Would you please tell the jury what you do for a living and what is your position?"

Dr. Fayler looked at the jury. "I'm a Ph.D. biochemist, specializing in DNA sequencing. I'm also the owner and president of an independent laboratory, Genetic Measurements Incorporated, which is licensed to conduct genetic testing of all sorts, including DNA analysis."

Deidre realized that T.J. had paraded a number of red-herring witnesses past the jurors and the opposing attorney, lulling them all into a state of near numbness. Now he was preparing to slip in an unexpected thrust.

Mary came out of her doldrums and addressed the judge. "Your Honor, I object to this witness on the grounds that Mr. Compton has done nothing but stall. First we had to sit through hours of testimony from people who told and retold us that the defendant is a nice guy. Now we're going to hear from a DNA expert who will tell us what Mr. Compton has already conceded. The blood on the defendant's boot is that of Justin Peters."

At this point T.J. interrupted. "Your Honor, this has nothing at all to do with the blood on the defendant's boot. Rather, it has to do with a blood sample taken from the shard of glass that has already been accepted as evidence by the court—and by the prosecution, I might add."

Both attorneys approached the bench. Mary's face was crimson. "Your Honor, I demand that this witness not be allowed to testify. At no time during disclosure did the defense make one mention of DNA tests being conducted on what appeared to be blood on the broken glass."

Judge Jesperson glared down from his bench at her. "Counselor, you do not make demands in my courtroom. Do you understand?"

"Yes, Your Honor," Mary answered weakly, and the judge continued.

"Dr. Fayler's name was on the list of witnesses submitted during disclosure by the defense. The broken shard of glass was listed as evidence at the same time. Did you request to be allowed to test it for the presence of blood?"

Mary's shoulders drooped. "No, Your Honor."

"Then I suggest you allow Mr. Compton to get on with his questioning of his witness. We don't want to waste any more of the court's time, do we?" Mary slouched back to her table, plunked down in her chair and held her head in her hands.

T.J. continued with his questioning. "Dr. Fayler, did you test the sample that was taken from the glass shard?" Fayler answered that he had. "Was it human blood?" The doctor answered that it was. "Did you run a DNA test on the sample?"

The members of the jury had perked up and were listening attentively when he said he had. T.J. pressed on. "Was that sample compared to a known sample of DNA?"

By now, Mary feared her case was being skewered, but she wasn't sure how. Dr. Fayler answered T.J.'s question, saying, "Yes, it was compared to a DNA sample submitted by the defendant."

T.J. paused to let that sink into the jurors' minds. "What were the results of your test, doctor?"

With no doubt in his voice, Dr. Fayler said, "The blood on the glass shard was that of James O'Brian." T.J. thanked him and said he had no more questions.

Mary tried to regroup, but all she could do was determine that Dr. Fayler was indeed competent to conduct the tests.

"I call Dr. William Burns." T.J. was on a roll, and he wanted to keep moving.

"You were one of the doctors on duty the night of April 16, were you not?" Dr. Burns said that he was. "And you treated Mr. O'Brian that night. Am I correct?" The answer was yes. "Would you please tell the jury what you observed to be Mr. O'Brian's condition?"

The doctor checked his notes. "He was extremely inebriated."

T.J. turned and looked at his client, and without facing the witness, asked, "In your opinion, do you think Mr. O'Brian was so drunk he could not have administered such a brutal beating?"

No sooner had Dr. Burns said he didn't think Jimmy could have stood up, let alone strike anyone with a forceful blow, Mary interrupted.

"Objection, Your Honor. Defense is asking the witness to form a judgment."

"Sustained," the judge growled and this time glared at T.J., who ignored the glare and quickly moved on.

Facing his witness again, he asked, "Did you treat my client for anything other than alcohol poisoning?"

Dr. Burns paged through his notes. "He had a deep laceration on his right hand requiring seventeen stitches to repair."

"And where on his hand was this cut?" T.J. asked. The doctor held up his right hand and pointed at the heel as he answered.

"When someone trips and falls, what is their reaction?" T.J. inquired.

Doctor Burns looked at his hand as though he were imagining such a fall. "They throw their hand forward to break their fall."

T.J. asked one more question. "If their hand was to land on a piece of broken glass, what would happen?"

The doctor smiled for an instant. "They would sustain a rather severe cut."

T.J. reminded the jury that when questioned, Jimmy had said he vaguely remembered tripping over something when he had gotten out of his truck at the soccer field to relieve himself.

Mary cross-examined the witness, but there was little she could do to refute anything he had said. The judge looked at his watch. "Ladies and gentlemen, it's nearly noon. Court is recessed until one o'clock. Mr. Compton has requested a short meeting with me in my chambers. The prosecution is strongly advised to attend."

The courtroom emptied, and the two attorneys and the judge proceeded to his office.

Chapter
Seventeen

At one o'clock sharp, Judge Jesperson entered the courtroom, his robes flying behind him and a scowl on his face. "The defense has requested permission to put on a demonstration for the jury." He glowered at T.J. "I trust this show is going to lead somewhere."

T.J. picked up a soccer ball he had brought to court, bounced it twice on his table, and placed it on the floor. He pointed at the bailiff. "Sir, will you kick the ball? Not too gently, just a firm kick." The bailiff looked puzzled, but he gave the ball a gentle boot. T.J. asked for a volunteer from the jury pool to do the same. As randomly as he could, T.J. singled out six persons and had them each kick the ball. The jury looked puzzled and an onlooker snickered. T.J. addressed the bailiff. "Sir, are you right- or left-handed?"

The bailiff answered, "Right."

"And with what foot did you kick the ball?"

Deidre could see him thinking about which foot he had used. He answered, "My right."

T.J. asked each kicker the same question, and when he was done, he summed up the findings of his little experiment for the jury. "Do you realize that every person who is right-handed kicked the ball with his or her right foot? Conversely, every left-handed person used his or her left foot to kick the ball. Studies show," and he cited a reference, "Studies show that if a person's dominant hand is their right, their dominant foot is usually their right, and vice-versa." He looked directly at the jurors. "My client is right-handed, yet the victim's blood was found only on his left boot. This little experiment, although perhaps flawed, gives a strong indication that James O'Brian did not kick the victim. If he had, blood should have been found on his right boot, not his left. You are intelligent people, and I know you remember the chief's testimony two days ago." Deidre could see at least two jurors struggling to remember. They wouldn't admit they weren't intelligent enough to remember. "You remember," T.J. went on, "That the chief testified that Justin's blood was found only on one spot, that was Mr. O'Brian's left boot. Why wouldn't he use his right foot? It's his stronger side."

At that point the judge announced that court was recessed until the next morning. Soon the jury would go to work.

*****

AT SUPPER THAT NIGHT, Deidre was in a good mood. She could see what T.J.'s strategy was and thought it had worked. "I'm wondering what we should do to celebrate the Fourth," she asked, hoping somebody would have a good answer.

Megan had the first idea. "Why don't we go into the Boundary Waters, you know, that spot where Dad asked you to marry him?" Deidre recollected the joy she had experienced that night, but Ben brought the idea to a halt.

"Great idea, but we'd need a permit to go there, and I'm afraid they're all taken for the weekend of the Fourth."

Maren suggested they take whatever permit was available, but the others didn't want to go to any lake other than their favorite. Finally, they decided to go on a daytrip into the BWCA, have a picnic, swim and return to Two Harbors in time for the fireworks that night.

Deidre paused to savor the moment. She had two lovely daughters who never once sassed back, who had never once said, "I don't have to listen to you. You're not my real mother." She thought she was one of the most blessed people on earth. For that instant all she wanted to be was a wife and mother, and thought perhaps when

Jimmy's trial was over, she would retire for good. The garden needed weeding and there was always an opportunity to volunteer at the women's shelter in town. *Maybe,* she thought, *being a full-time mom and wife is what I should do.*

*****

Deidre was seated in the gallery of the courtroom at nine the next morning. Mary was shuffling through some notes, preparing to begin the summation of the state's case against Jimmy. She looked neither worried or confident, just business-like.

T.J. sat at the defense table, waiting for his client to be ushered in. He was relaxed, his hands folded in his lap, and a half-smile on his lips. He had his legs crossed and Deidre watched as his foot bobbed, as though in time to some familiar tune running through his head. Jimmy was escorted into the room by a deputy and took his place next to T.J. Unlike his attorney, Jimmy's brow was furrowed and he fidgeted with his fingers while he waited for the jury to enter and the judge to begin the day's proceedings.

The regimen for the day was becoming all too familiar, the "all rise," the judge's order to sit, the clerk's fingers moving over her recorder. The moment of truth was near.

Mary stood and looked at the jury, trying to make eye contact with every person on the panel. Then she began her summary statement.

"Ladies and gentlemen of the jury. You have heard many theories postulated by the defense in this case, but I want to remind you, that is exactly what they are: theories. The one hard fact you have in this entire case is that Justin Peters's blood was found on the toe of James O'Brian's boot. The defense would like to cloud the issue with soccer balls, and broken glass, but the fact still remains that the victim's blood was on the toe of the defendant's boot. Yes, the defendant was very drunk at the time, but that's not an acceptable defense. Dr. Burns testified that when he treated the defendant, he was much too inebriated to have delivered such a brutal beating. But I want you to remember that Mr. O'Brian was brought to the ER and examined by Dr. Burns some time after Justin Peters was beaten. An empty vodka bottle was found in the suspect's truck, evidently consumed a short time before Officer Zemple found him passed out near the breakwater. Mr. O'Brian beat the victim to death and then drank himself into oblivion. His inebriated state, the opportunity to live up to the name of his gang, his physical dominance of the victim, all of these are circumstantial. However, the one fact that cannot be explained away is the blood on the defendant's boot. Ladies and gentleman, there is no doubt in my mind, nor should there be in yours, that Mr. O'Brian knocked Justin Peters down and proceeded to kick him to death. You must find him guilty of this crime, a hate crime at that, because the victim was a gay man."

Mary paused to give her words time to sink in and took her seat, looking exhausted. It was T.J.'s turn. He greeted the jury, put his hands in his pocket in an "ah, shucks" attitude and began.

"My client has an alcohol problem, no doubt about it. He drinks too much, and he drank too much on the night of Justin Peters's death, but that's not an act for which we lock people up for life. Let's run through the chain of events that evening as they pertain to my client. He left the Death Riders' clubhouse at approximately four in the afternoon. He had drunk a few beers. According to his testimony—which, by the way, the prosecution never challenged—he swapped his bike for his truck in Two Harbors. He cleaned up a little. Now it was about four thirty. Witnesses corroborated his testimony that he went to The Pub, where he had a few more beers. He left The Pub at about seven o'clock. He moved on to the Legion Club in town, where he drank with friends for a couple of hours. Now we're getting close to nine o'clock, dusk, and he'd had enough to drink that he should not have been driving. But he did drive, he thinks up near the soccer field. After all the beer, he had to relieve himself. Now according to his testimony, taken by the chief of police, Sig Swanson, he vaguely remembered tripping over something, but he was too drunk to know what. He got back in his truck, stopped at the liquor store, and bought a pint of vodka. The clerk at the liquor store testified that she remembered him and that she saw no blood on him, although he had a rag wrapped around his hand. That is the last James remembers, because he passed out in his pickup." T.J. paused a moment before continuing.

"But let's look at the facts. As testified to by Dr. Fayler, my client's blood was found on a glass shard partially buried in the soil at the soccer field. He sliced his hand when he tripped and fell. Someone else, roughly my client's size, was at the field, because he left his boot print behind, a steel-toed boot according to an expert witness. It did not match the imprint of my client's boot. Justin Peters's blood was found only on the left boot of my client. If Mr. O'Brian had kicked Justin to death, surely he would have used his dominant leg to deliver the blows. Most likely, my client's dominant leg is his right. Certainly, there would have been blood on his right boot had he committed the crime. At best, the evidence against my client is circumstantial. He was in the wrong place at the wrong time, and in an impaired state. No way can you say beyond a shadow of a doubt that James O'Brian committed this terrible crime. Someone else did and should be caught and punished. I trust, and Mr. O'Brian trusts, that you will see through the flimsy case the prosecution has presented in an attempt to close this case in a hurry to appease the public and find him rightfully . . . not guilty." With those words, T.J. sat down.

Judge Jesperson finished his instruction to the jury. He retreated to his office, the jury to the deliberation room. Deidre wasn't as confident as T.J. seemed.

Chapter
Eighteen

The jury was excused to begin their deliberation at exactly 11:39 A.M., and Deidre met T.J. in the hall outside the courtroom. "Let's go grab a bite at Louise's," he suggested. "I don't expect they'll take long to reach a verdict, but we can walk the two blocks down to her restaurant, have a sandwich and some soup, and be back here by one. I'm expecting Jimmy to walk away a free man by four o'clock." Deidre walked beside him, wondering from where his confidence came.

They beat the lunch crowd by a few minutes and were seated with their food before the place filled up. The tiny café was immensely popular with both the locals and tourists who had visited before, and Deidre was grateful they had a table almost hidden in one corner so they could talk about the trial without being eavesdropped upon.

"Do you really believe the verdict will go our way?" Deidre asked, realizing she had become possessive about the case. "I think there are too many people who want an answer to who killed Justin. It'll make them feel safer knowing someone is locked up for the crime, even if it might be the wrong person." She tested her soup to see if it had cooled enough to eat.

T.J. had his mouth full of egg salad sandwich but managed to talk around it. "Did you watch the jurors' eyes? Mary almost put them to sleep, but I felt they were awake when I was giving my summary. I can feel when people are with me, and I felt that today. I honestly think they had their minds made up before the judge gave them the instructions, all except the middle-aged lady, third from the left in the second row." Deidre was amazed at how he could pinpoint one person that way. "She seemed disinterested in what I had to say. She may have had her mind made up, too, but not the way I want. But she's one vote, although I don't want a jury that can't come to a decision. I want a "not guilty" verdict, which I'm certain we'd get if it weren't for her. Hopefully, the others can convince her."

It took them only fifteen minutes to finish their meal. They paid their bill and made way for other customers who were waiting for a table to open up. On the way back to the courthouse, Deidre and T.J. talked about her future as a PI. He said that nothing was on his docket that would require her services, but if anything came up, he'd give her a call. They climbed the timeworn stairs to the second floor, and Deidre wondered how many feet had passed over the limestone steps to have worn the depressions in the rock. She wondered how many people had retreated down those same steps, disappointed or even dejected over decisions that had been handed down. T.J. said he had some business to take care of in the clerk's office, and after that, the recorder's office. She was free to leave if she wanted, but Deidre had too much invested in the case to not be present when the verdict was read.

She read a magazine she found on the waiting bench, visited with a friend she hadn't seen for weeks, and tried to pass the time by thinking about her future. Time dragged, and she almost nodded off a couple of times. Finally, she followed the hallway to the Law Enforcement Center, hoping Jeff wasn't too busy. He greeted her like a long lost friend.

"Come on in and visit a bit. I heard Jimmy O'Brian's trial has gone to the jury. Suppose you're hanging around for the verdict. Any prognostication you'd want to share?" He rocked back in his chair.

"T.J. says Jimmy will be free by tonight. I'm not so certain. The state didn't have much, but I didn't think we did, either. T.J. can talk, though, and he says he could sense the jury being with him. Hope he's right." Deidre switched subjects. "By the way, did anything ever come of the Reverend Isaiah's group? Seems like things have quieted down lately. At least I haven't heard of any more vandalism. The railroad pileup still must bother you, but I don't see the reverend being involved in that. Do you?"

"No. No, I don't see them doing anything that destructive, but something isn't right up there. I still haven't been able to talk to anyone but Reverend Isaiah and that new guy, The Prophet. Every time I go up there, they say a retreat is going on, or it's prayer time, or everyone is down at the river. I'd like to know more, but without a search warrant, we can't force our way in, and no judge is going to issue a warrant because I think something doesn't seem right. We'll just have to wait and see."

She and Jeff talked about their families, a little town gossip, just everything and anything. Deidre felt her phone vibrate in her pocket a split second before it rang, and she instinctively looked at the clock on the wall. It was 4:00 P.M.

It was T.J. "Hi. If you want to hear the verdict, you'd better get to the courtroom as soon as you can. The jury will be coming back in five minutes." He disconnected without saying goodbye, and Deidre imagined him climbing the stairs two at a time in anticipation of what the verdict would be.

When Deidre arrived, T.J. was already seated beside Jimmy, who was pale as a ghost and looked as if he were ready to bolt from the room.

The bailiff called, "All rise!" and the judge entered in his usual flurry. The jury filed in, their faces blank. They were seated, and a couple of them shuffled their feet, several looked at the floor, and one man stared at the upper corner of the room.

"Have you come to a verdict?" the judge intoned. This was the time for the foreperson of the jury to rise and answer, and Deidre groaned inwardly when the stone-faced woman T.J. had singled out in their conversation slowly stood.

"We have, Your Honor," she answered in a strong, measured voice.

"How, then, do you find?"

There was a pause as though she wanted to drag out the suspense, and almost reluctantly she answered, "Not guilty on all counts." She didn't look at anyone or let her face show any sign of emotion, simply sat down and stared straight ahead.

Jimmy slumped in his chair, his face buried in his hands. It was evident to everyone that he was so emotionally drained he was about to collapse. Deidre had had no inkling how much he suffered over being charged with murder, not to mention a hate crime. Finally, he gathered himself and gave T.J. a bear hug that Deidre feared was going to crush the smaller man's ribs. Over and over, he kept repeating something in T.J.'s ear.

Judge Jesperson rapped his gavel to retain order in his courtroom. "James O'Brian, you are free to go on this charge. However, there is still another matter to be dealt with, your DWI."

Before he could say another word, Jimmy, in his exuberance, blurted out, "Guilty, Your Honor. I'm guilty, and will accept whatever you say." The judge almost smiled, but not quite, and T.J. tried to get Jimmy to sit down.

"Your Honor, I think my client may be just a bit overwhelmed by the verdict that has just been rendered and is in no state of mind to make a plea on the DWI charge."

"Oh, no, Your Honor. I know what I'm saying. I'll take responsibility for what I did." T.J. couldn't get him to shut up, no matter how hard he tugged at Jimmy's sleeve. The judge cleared his throat.

"I'm sentencing you to time served in the county jail. I'm also sentencing you to attend a twenty-eight day inpatient treatment program for alcohol and drug abuse, to begin as soon as there is an opening at an approved treatment facility."

Jimmy looked as though he were going to drop to his knees. "Oh, thank you Your Honor," he said and wiped his eyes. As the courtroom cleared, T.J. looked at his client. "Why didn't you let me bargain for you? I might have gotten you off even easier."

"I'm sober now, T.J., maybe for the first time in two years. This was a real scare for me, and I'd have done almost anything the judge asked. He's right, I need some help staying straight. How can I ever thank you for what you've done for me?" He clutched T.J.'s hand, not wanting to let go. Finally, T.J. extricated himself from the larger man's grip and picked up his briefcase.

"Jimmy, I couldn't let an old friend like you go down the tube. Stay in touch, man. Call me anytime you need someone to talk to."

Deidre and T.J. left the courthouse together. "I had my doubts about this one," he confided in her. "I thought the worst when I learned our sour-faced lady was the jury foreman, and I didn't dare breathe until I heard the 'Not guilty' come from her mouth. She looked as though she really didn't want to say the words, but evidently, the other jurors put some pressure on her. It was a good way to end the day." He smiled. "But I'm afraid I haven't any sleuthing for you to do, at least not right now. Any idea what you'll do?"

Deidre stifled a laugh. "I've thought of retiring again, for the fourth time, I guess. I don't know, T.J. Right now I'm sort of at loose ends, not really sure what I want. I suppose things will sift out, and I'll find my direction." They said goodbye, Deidre to go home and T.J. to return to his office. She felt a strange letdown now that the excitement and tension were gone.

*****

DEIDRE, BEN, MAREN, AND MEGAN got going early on the day of the Fourth, leaving home an hour before sunrise while the dew clung in droplets to the grass. Ben had loaded their canoe onto the car the night before, and Deidre had packed food for a shore lunch. One of the rules of the trip was that no electronics would be brought with. No games, no books, and most of all, no cell phones. The girls had grumbled a bit but were over their snit. On the way up Highway 2 they fell asleep in the backseat and Deidre rested her hand on Ben's knee. As the eastern horizon became splashed with pink just before sunrise, she inhaled deeply and considered how lucky she was. She had a wonderful family, a husband who loved her and treated her like a queen, and life was more than good. She closed her eyes for a moment, she thought, but when she opened them, Ben had turned off the highway onto Spruce Road. They were nearly to the landing at Little Gabbro Lake.

As the four adventurers began the portage to the first lake in the Gabbro chain, she remembered the first time she had hiked the trail carrying a forty-five pound pack. That was in early summer, four years ago. Ben had proposed to her on that trip. Today, her pack was light. The girls were carrying most of the noon meal in their packs. Ben was carrying the canoe, and she, more or less, was able to walk unhindered and enjoy the scenery. She saw two brown animals scurry up a tree, and when she got closer, stopped to see what they were. The pine martins' Teddy-bear-like faces peeked around the tree at her from their vantage point some twenty feet off the ground. She laughed out loud as they surveyed her with beady, black eyes. This was going to be a good day.

It took them only an hour to paddle the six miles to a place where Ben was well accustomed, a beach in a secluded bay where other paddlers seldom stopped. For some geological reason, which Deidre didn't know, the sand was coarse and pink. Swimmers could wade out about five yards from shore, but then the bottom dropped off steeply, without any vegetation to tangle around their legs. It was a perfect swimming spot.

The four of them spent the day lolling around, sometimes in the sun, sometimes in the shade. They had cold sandwiches for lunch, along with fresh fruit. Ben had brought a water filter and he siphoned water from the lake, from which they made ready-mix lemonade. Later in the day, they built a small campfire and made s'mores. For supper, Deidre had packed brats and along with chips and lemonade, they had a feast in the wilderness. Their meal was topped off with an instant cherry cheesecake prepared in a Ziplock plastic bag and poured into paper cups, the cracker crust being sprinkled on top rather than on the bottom.

At seven o'clock, Ben announced they'd have to get started, otherwise they wouldn't make it back to the car in daylight. By the time they straggled into the parking lot, even their light packs felt heavy, and they guzzled down cold soft drinks that had been left on ice in a cooler in the car. The trip home was silent, everyone happy but too windburned and tired to talk. Deidre was right; it had been a good day.

Chapter
Nineteen

D<small>EIDRE UNLOCKED THE SIDE</small> door to their house while Ben carted the outdoors gear to the garage. Just as the door swung open she heard her cell phone ring and rushed to pick it up from the kitchen counter. "Hello, Deidre speaking," she answered, a little out of breath. She hadn't taken time to look at the caller ID and wondered who was calling so late at night. It was a little after ten o'clock by her estimation. There was a long pause.

"Deidre, this is Danielle." She repeated her name, "Danielle DeAngelo," as if Deidre wouldn't recognize the name of one of her best friends.

"Danielle, what's wrong?" Deidre answered, worry evident in her voice. Ben stood in the door, somewhat alarmed at the tone he heard.

"Deidre, can you come to the hospital right away? Jeff's been shot. It doesn't look good right now, although the doctors are being pretty tight-lipped. I just need somebody with me." Deidre looked up at Ben and shook her head.

"I'll be there in fifteen minutes. Ben will take care of everything at home. I'm leaving now." She hung up the phone and grabbed the edge of the counter. "Jeff's in the hospital. All Danielle said was that he's been shot, and it's serious. Hold down the fort while I go be with her. Kiss the girls goodnight for me. I don't know when I'll be home. Love you." She kissed Ben on his cheek, raced to the car and sped out of the driveway, leaving a cloud of dust trailing her. Twelve minutes later she ran toward the ER doors of the hospital. She knew the place well.

"Oh, Danielle, I'm so sorry" she blurted out as Jeff's wife rushed to her and threw her arms around Deidre. "Can you tell me what happened?" Danielle was sobbing hysterically, and when she tried to talk, unintelligible sounds came out. Deidre led her down the hall to a waiting room/lounge reserved for families. A man was curled up in a chair, sleeping, but when the women entered, he roused, and seeing Danielle's distress, he left them alone in the room. Deidre guided her friend to a sofa and sat beside her, holding her hand. She waited until Danielle could utter a few words.

"A highway trooper came to my door about an hour ago. He said he didn't have any details, but that Jeff had been shot while he was investigating an incident north of Two Harbors." She sobbed for a few seconds, then took a deep breath before continuing. "The trooper said Jeff was able to make an officer down call before he lost consciousness. One of his deputies was on his way to meet Jeff before he was hit. They were supposed to investigate a call together, but Jeff arrived at the scene first. Because the other officer was on his way, it may have saved Jeff's life. He got there in seconds and was able to apply a compress to the wound."

Danielle broke down again. "Deidre, what will I do if he dies?" she managed to squeak out between sobs. Deidre held her friend tightly as she rocked back and forth, praying a stilted prayer to herself and pleading with a God she really wasn't sure about to spare Jeff's life.

She was still holding Danielle when the ER doctor stepped into the room and sat in a chair next to the sofa. "Mrs. DeAngelo," the doctor began, "we've been able to stop the bleeding and have transfused two units of blood. Your husband is quite stable at this time but isn't out of the woods quite yet. He was shot in the lower back, near his spine. X-rays show that the bullet didn't sever his spinal cord, but it came close enough to cause severe trauma. It did miss his kidney, although it pierced his colon in two places and injured his small intestine as it passed through his body. Fortunately, it missed his abdominal aorta by a couple of centimeters, otherwise he would have died almost instantly from loss of blood. There were other vessels severely damaged, but we've been able to clamp them off.

"We're not equipped to handle such severe trauma at this hospital, and Life Flight from Duluth is on its way. Should be arriving any minute. Do you have someone who can drive you to Duluth?" Danielle turned her tear-swollen face to Deidre, and Deidre nodded without having to say a word. As the doctor stood to leave, they heard the *whomp-whomp-whomp* of the blades as the Life Flight helicopter alit in the parking lot. Deidre and Danielle were on their way to St. Luke's Hospital in Duluth before Jeff was loaded into the flight, and as they left town, they could see the running lights of the helicopter disappear overhead as it headed southwest toward the bigger city.

By the time they arrived at the hospital, Jeff had been prepped and wheeled into a surgery suite. A hospital worker directed Deidre and Danielle to the surgery waiting room, where they sat side by side in silence, Deidre holding her friend's hand. It was three in the morning when an obviously exhausted surgeon came to talk with them. Deidre noticed blood spatters on his surgical booties, and hoped Danielle hadn't looked down.

"Mrs. DeAngelo, this might sound strange, but your husband is an extremely lucky man. Although the bullet did considerable damage, he is in serious but stable condition. We were able to repair his colon and small intestine with little loss of tissue. He's missing about six inches of his bowel, and another four inches of small intestine, but he'll do just fine without that. Both kidneys were spared, as were the blood vessels leading to and from them. Much of the damage was done to what we call the greater omentum, the tissue which holds the intestines in place. In the future, he'll probably suffer adhesions which will have to be repaired, perhaps more than once in his lifetime. That's where much of his blood loss came from, because no other major vessels were damaged. I wish all the news were that good, but there is one injury more serious than the others. The bullet passed very near his spine, and damaged several nerves that emanate from between the vertebrae. It clipped the right transverse process of his fourth lumbar vertebra, chipping off a piece. There was an amount of torque applied to the vertebra, and his spinal cord was badly bruised by the compression of the bullet's passage. He shows no response in his legs, but we're hopeful feeling will return and he will be able to walk again. I wish the news was all good, but there is hope. Unless an infection develops, your husband should make it." The surgeon pushed himself out of the chair and patted Danielle's shoulder as he walked past them.

Deidre wrapped her arms around her friend. "Is there anyone you'd like me to call? I'll stay with you through the night, but I will have to get home some time." Danielle wiped her nose and composed herself.

"I think I'll be okay now. My folks are taking care of the kids, and they called Jeff's parents. They should be here any minute." She had barely gotten the words out when Jeff's mom and dad rushed into the waiting room. They hurried to their daughter-in-law's side, and Jeff's mother took both her hands while his father placed his hand on her shoulder.

"Oh, my dear Danielle. How are you? We met the surgeon in the hall, and he filled us in on Jeff's condition. Thank God he's going to live. Whatever else happens, we still have him with us."

Danielle straightened her back. "You're right. He's still with us." Then turning to Deidre she said, "Thank you, friend. I'm okay now. Go home to Ben. It's going to be okay. I'll call you tomorrow and let you know what's happening. Thank you." She squeezed Deidre tightly, and Deidre could feel her friend shaking, but she had to leave. There was nothing more she could do tonight.

It took forty minutes to drive home, and by the time she crawled into bed with Ben, she had mulled over too many scenarios of her late fiancé's murder and her husband's job with the FBI. She snuggled up to Ben, kissed his cheek, and he mumbled something in his sleep, then rolled over. Deidre fell asleep listening to his measured breathing and feeling his body next to hers.

*****

SHE HAD HARDLY fallen asleep when the alarm went off. Although the twins didn't have anything going on, Ben had to go to work. At the first sound of the buzzer, Deidre's eyes flew open, and for a second or two, she experienced the panic one does when awaking from a horrible nightmare. Then she realized last night had not been a nightmare. It had really happened. Ben was wide awake, too.

"How's Jeff?" were the first words out of his mouth.

"Could be a lot worse," Deidre tried to sound hopeful. "The surgeon was confident that he'll pull through, but Jeff's spine has been injured. They're not sure how badly or how permanently. I thought I'd drive back to Duluth and spend some time with Danielle this morning."

"How's she holding up?" Ben asked, his eyes showing his concern.

"Like you'd expect, I suppose. Ben's mom and dad got there just as I was leaving, so I think she had good support at the hospital. I want to find out what went wrong when Jeff was shot."

They got out of bed at the same time, Deidre going downstairs to make a badly needed pot of coffee and Ben to the bathroom to get ready for work. Over a light breakfast, they discussed what they could do to help Jeff and Danielle over this hurdle.

Deidre set out a bowl of fruit and left a note for the girls. "I've gone to town for a bit. There's cold cereal in the cupboard. Fix yourself toast to go with it, and have a glass of milk. And don't skip a serving of fruit. I'll call later. Love ya, Mom."

Her mind flitted from one thought to another as she drove into town, and by the time she arrived at the Law Enforcement Center she was angry, dismayed, and confused, all at the same time. What was happening to her small town? She climbed the stairs to what had once been her office and now was Jeff's, although it would be a long time before he sat behind his desk again, if ever. She was buzzed in by the dispatcher who sat behind a plate glass window. *I'm glad they remember me*, she thought as she walked into the sheriff's office.

A group of people sat at the conference table, and she recognized three as deputies. Sig Swanson, the chief of police, was seated at one end of the table, and Deidre knew by name two other people, a man and a woman, in civilian clothes. They were members of the county board. No one was smiling. The councilman stood and extended his hand to Deidre, and she took his offer. He held her hand in both of his, and his eyes drooped in a sad way.

"Deidre, so good to see you. I'm sure you're here to learn what you can about Jeff's ambush." Deidre was startled to hear that word, "ambush." She wondered if there was anything a law enforcement officer feared more than to have someone lie in wait and then unexpectedly attack. "Please, sit down and join the conversation." He pulled a chair out for Deidre.

No one said a thing, and finally, Deidre had to speak. "What do you mean, 'ambush'? Can you fill me in, or is it too soon to let out any information?"

Sig cleared his throat. "We wouldn't talk to just anyone, but if we can't trust you, I guess there's no one we can trust." He began to tell what they knew. "For about a week or so, the department had been receiving calls at random times, reporting bogus incidents. They were all made from throwaway cell phones. After each call, the signal went dead, the phone probably having been tossed in the big lake or otherwise destroyed. One call asked that a deputy be dispatched to what was said to be a dog bite incident. When she got to the location, no one was around.

"Another caller reported an accident up Highway 3 by the Stewart River, but there was no accident. There were two or three other calls, but last night, a call came to Jeff's personal phone from a person who claimed to be holding his own family hostage. He rambled on about some grievance or another with the government and said he was going to kill his wife and kids and himself if Jeff didn't come talk to him immediately. He told Jeff where they were, gave him the fire number. Jeff called for backup and left town in a hurry. The fire number was for a driveway, but no buildings were on the site, only a tent pitched back off the road.

"Jeff got out of his car and identified himself but received no answer. He radioed his deputy and said he was going to the tent. Jeff slowly made his way toward it and probably could hear the siren from the other squad coming up the highway. We surmise he returned to his car without going all the way to the tent. Someone was waiting in the brush, and shot him. When the first deputy arrived, Jeff was slumped partway into his car and partially lying across the driver's-side seat. He was shot in the back, and the sniper had vanished into the woods. He must have planned an escape route and evidently knew the terrain well, because the other deputies who arrived could find no trace of him. He just vanished. The deputy called for an ambulance and began to administer first aid. Otherwise, Jeff would be dead." Deidre sat, too stunned to respond. Jeff was one of her oldest friends and a man she deeply respected. For an instant, the image of his wife, Danielle, flashed through her mind, and she remembered back when her John had been slain in a drive-by shooting. She hung her head, not wanting to face the reality of the day.

"Deidre," the councilwoman began as she fidgeted with a pen she was holding. "We were having a discussion before you arrived. I am aware of your history in this town, but I'm also aware of your reputation with most of the town folk. People look up to you, and if Jeff weren't doing such a great job, I think you would have felt some pressure to run for sheriff again. That said, and I know this is terribly presumptuous on our part, we were contemplating asking you if you would allow us to appoint you sheriff during Jeff's absence."

The councilwoman hurriedly added, before Deidre could respond, "Please hear us out before you answer. Something dangerous is happening around the county. First it was the murder of Justin Peters, then vandalism to several churches, not to mention the note you brought in from the girl at The Sanctuary. We've had a train derailment, and now Jeff. All of these incidents have happened within the last four months. It's as though war has been declared on our community. We need a strong leader right now, and we think that leader is you. Please, we ask of you, forget the way you were slighted a few years ago and consider our offer, if for no other reason than that the community needs your services." The woman looked Deidre square in her eyes, silently pleading.

Deidre squirmed uneasily in her chair. She knew she should call Ben and discuss the council's proposal, but she remembered their conversation when she had decided to work for T.J. Compton. He told her she should make her own decision, and he would support her. Yet, she knew she had her family to consider. Then she remembered the look on Danielle's face the night before, the anguish she had displayed. "I'll do it," she heard herself saying, almost as if her voice were that of another person. *There*, she thought, *I did it, and I can't renege on my word now.*

The group exhaled in unison, one of their biggest fears having been set aside. They had lost an excellent leader but had gained another in the same twenty-four hour period. Something had to break their way soon.

Chapter Twenty

THE ENTIRE COUNTY BOARD would have to vote on Deidre's appointment. It was a formality, but one that had to be on the record. They were meeting that afternoon, so Deidre wouldn't be able to begin her investigation until the next day. She intended to waste no time once the board acted. In the meantime, she was exhausted and headed home, where she found a note from her step-daughters saying they were at the neighbors, hanging out with friends from school. Deidre crashed on the couch but did take the precaution of setting the alarm on her cell phone before allowing herself to close her eyes. Within seconds she was asleep.

Three hours later her phone began to play a nerve-wracking tone meant to be so irritating that no one could sleep through it. Groggily, she reached for the silence button and focused her eyes with difficulty. She didn't fully wake until she heard footsteps pounding down the stairs. Megan and Maren leaped from the third step up, hitting the floor with a resounding thud.

"Mom, you're awake. When we came home, you were so sound asleep you didn't hear us. We let you sleep," Megan said. They plunked down on the couch beside her. "How's Jeff doing?"

Maren added, "I'll bet Danielle is really having a hard time."

Deidre put an arm around each girl's shoulder and drew them close to her. "Sometimes I forget how precious you girls are to me. It takes moments like this to remind me." She hugged them tightly. "Jeff won't be able to work for a long time, if ever, and in the meantime, the county is without a sheriff."

Before she could finish what she was going to say, Maren blurted out, "Are you going back to work?" She pulled away from Deidre, just a bit.

"This morning, the county board asked to appoint me to serve as interim sheriff. I didn't have time to talk to you and your father, because they needed a decision as soon as possible. That's what I want to talk about right now." She paused and neither daughter said anything, but Deidre could sense a reluctance on their part. "I know it will put a strain on the family, but there are three reasons I said yes, and I'd like you to know what they are. If, after we talk, you still want me to turn it down, I'll call the chairman of the board and decline their appointment." She looked at the girls and took a deep breath.

"First, I'm good at what I do. The faster I can get on the case of who shot Jeff, the easier it will be to catch the bad guy. I think my primary reason for wanting to catch the culprit is to stand up for my friend. Second, I feel a duty to serve my community again. What drove me out of the sheriff's office happened many years ago, and those who pushed the issue are themselves in jail and will be for a long time. It's rather humbling when people come to you and say they need you. The last reason for my saying yes is that I miss working as an officer. That's what I'm trained to do, and like I said, I'm confident that I'm good at it." The girls still sat silently, thinking.

"Mom, it's dangerous. Jeff proved that," Megan spoke up. "He's good at what he does, too, and he got himself into serious trouble. What if that had been you? We don't want to lose you." There were several seconds of more silence. It was Maren's turn to speak.

"Mom, I'll go along with your wishes. It wouldn't be fair for you to not be able to do what you want because of us. But I'll be afraid for you every day you go to work. Please promise us you'll be careful and not take any chances. We love you so much." She wrapped her arms tighter around her stepmother.

Megan began to pucker up, hardly able to speak. "That goes for me, too, you know. Go for it if you have to, but always come back to us. Promise?" She laid her head on Deidre's shoulder.

Deidre forced the words to come out. "Oh, girls, there are no promises in life, and I can't make promises I might not be able to keep, but you have my word that I'll do everything in my power to come home every day in one piece. I have too much to live for not to be careful." They sat like that for several minutes. Finally, Deidre said she was going to Duluth to see Jeff and Danielle and that she'd like the girls to come with her. "Their kids are going to be there, and I think it will be good for them to talk with you. Maybe you can say things I'd never think to say, seeing as how you're about their ages."

By two o'clock they were on the road, and they arrived at the ICU waiting room forty minutes later. Danielle was there as were her three kids, Angie, Michael, and Trudie. There was a moment of awkward silence when the five kids met. At their age, they wondered if there were special words to be said. Megan broke the ice. "We're sorry this happened to your dad."

Before she could continue, Jeff's children said almost in unison. "Thanks for coming."

Mike said, "We're going nuts sitting around this room all the time." He turned to Danielle. "Mom, could you give us a little money so we can go down to the cafeteria?" Mike asked Megan and Maren, "Want to go down and get a Coke or something? We can see the lake from there, and we can play video games or something."

After the kids left, Danielle shared more openly about Jeff's condition. "Things are so much better today than they were last night." Deidre looked at her friend and thought she hadn't slept a wink. Her hair was disheveled and black bags hung under her eyes. She wore no lipstick, and her clothes were wrinkled. She didn't look like Danielle much at all. "The doctor stopped by a few minutes before you got here and said they'd be moving Jeff to a regular surgical unit tomorrow morning. After two or three days there, he'll be moved up to the fifth floor, rehab. Those were good words to hear." But then she sobbed, momentarily overwhelmed. "Jeff still has no feeling in his legs. The doctor said there is a lot of swelling around his spine and that probably is the cause. We should know within a week if the paralysis is permanent."

Deidre stepped closer to her friend and hugged her. "Jeff's one tough guy, and you know he's going to do everything he can to get back on his feet, literally. I have faith that he'll be back to work as soon as he can." There was a pause.

"That's what worries me," Danielle said so softly Deidre could hardly hear. "That's what worries me."

Deidre led her friend to a lounger chair in a secluded corner of the room and more or less pushed her into it. "I'm getting a blanket for you, and I want you to close your eyes for a few minutes. You might not sleep, but you need to rest." She found a blanket in a nearby cupboard, which she spread over Danielle. Deidre had just sat down by her side with a magazine when she noticed a change in the exhausted woman's breathing. Danielle was sound asleep.

Twenty minutes later she heard the laughter of preteens as a troop of them came gamboling down the hall. Evidently, Megan and Maren had relieved some of the tension, and Deidre could hear them joking and verbally jabbing at each other. They sounded happy. As quietly as she could, she left Danielle's side to intercept the crew before they could wake her. She put her finger to her lips and the chattering stopped. "Your mother is sleeping, and she needs all the rest she can get," she whispered. "Let's go into the other waiting room, where we can talk."

Deidre poured herself a cup of coffee, and the kids sat down in a group. Suddenly, they had become solemn. "I think you know your dad will be moved out of ICU tomorrow, which is really good news. It means he's getting better. And now your mom is sleeping and that's good news, too. She needs her rest so she can be here for your dad. What about you kids? I don't think you want to stay at the hospital the whole time. Do you need a place to spend the night?" She saw her daughters brighten up, because they thought they knew what was coming next. Angie deflated their expected plans.

"Grandma and Grandpa are coming to get us at five o'clock. They're taking us out for supper, and we're staying at their house tonight. They don't live far from here." Deidre thought Jeff's kids looked as if they would rather have spent the time with her daughters, but she wasn't about to get in the way of family plans at such a dreadful time. She thought Jeff's mother and father needed their grandkids more than ever. They sensed someone entering the room and looked back to see Danielle standing. She still looked as if she had been dragged through the proverbial knothole, but she was smiling.

"Thanks," she said as she walked over to Michael and gave him a hug. "Grandma and Grandpa should be here soon to pick you up. Deidre, Jeff gets to have a visitor for ten minutes out of every hour. Do you want to see him?"

Deidre declined the offer, telling Danielle that those precious ten minutes should be hers. Minutes later she excused herself and her daughters. On the way home Megan announced. "That was good. Not fun, but good. We talked a lot about how dangerous police work is, and we told them that you were going to take Jeff's job until he comes back. They thought that was a good idea. We're okay with it." Nothing more was said of Deidre's decision for the remainder of the ride. When they got home, the girls spilled out of the car and rushed to play with their dog. Deidre went in to prepare a quick supper before Ben got home. She hoped he would be as understanding as the girls had been.

Chapter
Twenty-One

On the drive to the Law Enforcement Center the next morning, Deidre had time to reflect on Ben's reaction to her news. As she laid out her plans to take over for Jeff, he momentarily went catatonic, she thought, but he quickly recovered his usual composure and tried to smile. Finally, after several seconds he gave her his blessing, but not without a lecture about being careful and not taking any stupid chances. Then he enveloped her in his arms and told her how much she meant to him. She vowed she would be as cautious as the job permitted, a caveat they both knew was reality. A short time later the phone rang. It was the chairman of the Lake County Board, calling to tell her the appointment had been unanimously approved, and she should begin work in the morning.

She slowly climbed the stairs to her old office, wondering what she had taken on, hoping she wasn't making a mistake. The dispatcher, a new hire, buzzed her in without comment, and she was warmly greeted by Shirley, the sheriff's assistant. Deidre was reminded that time had passed since this had been her office, and nothing felt quite familiar. She entered Jeff's office, picked up the badge and identification pin that were lying on the desk, and wondered where she should begin. She buzzed her assistant.

"Shirley, will you run off a copy of the next two weeks' duty roster, please? Before doing that, though, locate whichever deputy on patrol is nearest the location of Jeff's ambush. Tell him to meet me there in twenty minutes." Shirley responded in a business-like way. Deidre had wished for a little more familiarity on her return to duty, but too much water had gone under the bridge since she had been sheriff. But now she was back at her old desk.

The site of the false hostage incident was ten miles out of town, on the entrance road to an abandoned gravel pit. When Deidre arrived, a deputy was waiting for her. She had vowed to herself—and her family—that she would never go to out-of-the-way places alone.

Deidre parked on the side of the road and walked in to the site. "Hey, Jake. Good to see you," she hollered to the deputy. He was one of the old guard who worked with her when she was sheriff the first time. "How's it going?"

Jake was nearing retirement, and nothing caused him much excitement. "I'm good. A little slow on the draw these days, but good." By this time Deidre was nearly to him. He took a few steps to meet her and grabbed her hand. "Damn good to have you back. Never thought it would happen, but great to have you back. We need someone like you to tackle this mess. I've got a feeling this isn't the last bad thing that's going to happen around this county." Deidre slapped him on the back and offered her thanks.

"Well, Jake, glad to be working with you again. What do we have here?"

Jake led her to where the tent used in the scam was still pitched. It sagged a little, evidently from having been put up in a hurry. The wind had loosened a stake or two, and unless it was taken down soon, it would blow down. Loose fabric flapped in the breeze.

"Fill me in on what's been done at the site so far." Deidre looked at Jake as he removed a notepad from his breast pocket and thumbed through a few pages.

"The interior has been checked for fingerprints, but as you know, lifting them from fabric is almost impossible. The tent floor is made of a synthetic material but had no prints. The exterior frame was dusted, but whoever set it up must have worn gloves. Again, no prints. The tent is a cheapy, the kind you can buy at any discount store, and will be hard to trace. It's new, no stains or any other identifying marks. We think it was bought for this one purpose. No vehicle tracks were found. Seems the shooter, or shooters, must have hiked in through the woods. They knew the area or were good at reading a topo map, because the nearest road, other than the one we came in on, is five miles to the east. North and south the same distance. That's a lot of woods. Somebody went through a whole lot of trouble to plan this. They were out to get Jeff, no doubt about it. Other than that, the first sweep of the area didn't turn up one clue. Whoever did this knew what they were doing. Reminds me of a special forces operation in the military."

Deidre's head jerked around when he said that. "Jake, I've got to make a call from my car. Wait here, I'll be right back." She jogged across the opening to where her vehicle was parked and called in to the office.

"Shirley, I need you to drop everything and get on this right away. Call Johnny Bolene and ask him if it would be okay for a team to come out and take a look at his pickup. Be sure to tell him that he's in no trouble whatsoever, but that his truck might hold an important clue to an assault case. Ask him not to touch anything inside his truck, especially on the passenger side, until the team gets there. Get someone out to his place immediately, and have them dust the inside of the passenger compartment for prints, especially the door handle, the armrest, dash, any of the common places a passenger would place his hands." She listened to Shirley's response. "No, that's okay. They don't have to impound the vehicle, just lift the prints and document from where they came. Thanks, Shirl." She hung up before she realized she had used a nickname for a person she hardly knew. She shrugged, hoping there had been no offense taken. Jake watched her jog back toward him, wondering from where her energy came.

"You gave me a great idea, Jake. If this turns up anything, we might have our first big break. Does anyone have an idea where the shot came from that hit Jeff?"

"We're pretty sure it came from up there." Jake pointed to a spot in the woods some one hundred-fifty yards away. A clump of birch grew in front of a densely branched balsam fir. "As close as we could tell, it came from near that tree. A gunman could sit under those branches, and with the birches breaking up his silhouette, he'd be about invisible. He'd have to be a good shot, though. Probably used a night scope with a laser sight in the dark, although the moon was full."

Deidre suggested that they begin their search at that spot, although she didn't have much hope of finding anything new. As they climbed the sandbank, Jake was wheezing so hard, she hoped he made retirement age. "Too many hours sitting in a car waiting for something to happen," he puffed, his face turning beet red. Luckily, they were near the top of the bank, and he bent over, catching his breath. They walked straight to the spot from where they thought the sniper's shot had come. Deidre got down on her hands and knees and began searching under every blade of grass and every leaflet. It took Jake a little longer to assume a search position but eventually, with a good deal of groaning, he made it. They moved slowly, expanding their search inch by inch.

"Jake, move that leaf again. I think I saw a flash of something shiny." Without moving forward, the deputy gently pushed aside the broad leaves of a bloodroot plant. "There. From your angle, I don't think you can see it," Deidre almost shouted. "See it?" She carefully moved so she could see what was on the ground, and whooped in excitement. "It's a rifle casing. Now we might have him."

With Jake holding the vegetation back, Deidre was able to insert a pencil into the empty's opening and lift it so she could look carefully at it. She gasped, and Jake wondered what she had found that evoked such a startled response. "Look at this and tell me what you read." Deidre wanted verification to confirm she wasn't seeing what she wanted to see. Jake tilted his head so the sun's rays struck the base of the bullet casing at an angle.

"There's a circle with a cross, no wait, that's a plus sign in the center of it. I can make out the letters 'USCCO,' and some numbers." He struggled to read them, eventually guessing the number ten.

"That's what I see, too." Deidre shook her head in disbelief. "I did some PI work for T.J. Compton, and during my investigation of the

Justin Peters murder, I uncovered a casing that matches this one perfectly. I'm betting whoever killed Justin was also involved in Jeff's shooting. Ballistics at the BCA will be able to tell us for sure. One thing puzzles me, though." Deidre stopped to think a moment. "It seems the shooter is a pro of some sort, especially if he used a night scope and laser sight. He made the effort to set up a ruse to lure Jeff out here, planned his escape, and carried out the shooting without being caught, but he left this empty behind. All I can guess is whatever mechanism he rigged to catch the empty as it ejected failed, and in the dark he couldn't locate it. Or else he was in a hurry to get away and took a chance on our not finding it. Doesn't matter, really. We've got it now."

The officers searched for another half-hour on their hands and knees without finding another clue. Finally, Deidre stood up and stretched her back as Jake made a good effort of getting to his feet. She could hear a few snaps and pops as his joints realigned themselves, and Jake limped around for a few minutes, "getting the kinks out," he said.

On the way back to town, Deidre mulled over the one bit of evidence she had in her possession, the spent cartridge casing. It lay in a plastic bag beside her on the car seat, glistening when intermittent sun rays struck it. She was sure it was of the same type she had found at the site of Justin Peters' murder. The head stamp of each empty casing bore markings indicating they were NATO compatible rounds. The letters USCCO meant they both had been manufactured by the same company, United States Cartridge Company, in Lowell, Massachusetts. The number ten on each casing meant they had both been manufactured in 2010. *Too many coincidences,* Deidre thought. *The killer and shooter must have had a spent cartridge in his pocket that fell out when he attacked Jason. Lucky for us, unlucky for him, he lost the brass casing from the bullet he used to shoot Jeff. He might be the same person, or,* she mentally corrected herself, *at least the gun might be the same one.*

By the time she reached her office she was so pumped by the possibilities presented with her find in the woods, she completely forgot that she had requested fingerprints be taken from Johnny Bolene's truck. It was a long shot, she knew, but Johnny was a loner. Chances were that no one had ridden with him since he had given a ride to the hitchhiker named Jeremiah Rude. Deidre wanted to know who that strange character really was.

"There's a report on your desk from the team that took the prints you requested. They ran an ID search on them." Shirley informed Deidre without looking up from her computer screen. Deidre thanked her but received no response. There was a folder on her desk, and she sat down and began to read its contents.

Deidre skipped over the required documentation of time, team members' names, and other extraneous information, allowing her eyes to move to the meat of the report. She read:

> Several coinciding fingerprints and palm prints were found inside the cab of a blue, 2008 Ford F-150 pickup, VIN 23DH2A007J6643THM. The prints were brought back to the lab and were run through the national database with a 99% match to one individual:
>
> David Aaron Schoeneger
> Age: 35
> Height: 6'4"
> Weight: 255
> Military record: Army, special forces
>   2001-2003, Afghanistan,
>   2004-2006, Iraq

Deidre studied the name and stats, and in her mind she was sure she was on the trail of the murderer and ambusher. Everything fit. Tomorrow she would pay a visit to The Sanctuary and have a visit with The Prophet, if she could find him.

Chapter
Twenty-Two

On the ride up to Reverend Isaiah's Sanctuary, Deidre wondered if she should be going alone. That was what got Jeff into trouble, answering a call without backup. But, she thought, it really wouldn't have made any difference if a deputy had been with him. Perhaps the deputy would have been shot, too. Anyway, people knew where she was headed, and if something happened to her on The Sanctuary's property, they would know who to go after. She felt safe, sort of.

When she pulled into the small gravel parking lot of the church, she saw a group of children being hustled away by three women. The doors to the chapel were flung open, and Reverend Isaiah stepped out, his hair disheveled and a scowl on his face.

"Get that police vehicle off our property," he bellowed. "This is sacred ground, and we obey only God's laws here. Your manmade laws hold no sway with us. Thus sayeth the Lord, 'The law of the Lord is perfect.' Your laws are not."

Deidre had nothing to do with religion when she was growing up. As an adult she never attended church until she met Ben, and now she more or less went to be with him and the girls. Suddenly, the words Pastor Ike had read the previous Sunday came back to her.

"But in Romans, Paul wrote, 'Let every person be subject to the governing authorities.'" That stopped the reverend in his tracks, but only for an instant.

He retorted, "Paul was just a man. God says his law is perfect, and it is. That is the law we are following."

Deidre was in no mood to have a theological argument. She had already shot the one scriptural arrow she had in her quiver and knew she could never crack the reverend's shield of self-righteousness. "Listen to me, Isaiah. We can do this one of two ways. You can cooperate with me now, or I can go to a judge and get a search warrant. Then I'll come back with my deputies, and we'll tear your compound apart, board by board. We'll haul every man, woman, and child in for questioning. You choose. Which way do you want it?"

The reverend glared at her, his deep-set eyes piercing her psyche, his eagle-beak nose aimed directly at her face. Finally he snapped, "What do you want from us? We're only here doing God's work, tilling the land, multiplying as we are instructed by Him, and warning the people of your community of God's imminent wrath."

Deidre had a difficult time holding her comments, but she managed to control her voice. "I want to speak with Jeremiah Rude, no one else. It must be a private conversation, either in the chapel or anywhere he chooses." As soon as she uttered those words, she regretted saying them. She had just given him power. *Too late now,* she thought. "I'd prefer the chapel. Tell him he's got fifteen minutes to be here, or I'm going back to town for the warrant."

"Wait here," Reverend Isaiah commanded, and he slouched off toward the compound, his boney shoulders bent against some unseen force. In ten minutes Jeremiah walked toward her, coming from the direction the reverend had taken. Deidre was amazed at the hulk of the figure approaching her.

He surprised her by saying in a quite gentle voice, "Hello, my name is Jeremiah Rude. Some call me The Prophet." He thrust his hand out to shake Deidre's, and she gasped when he wrapped his huge mitt around hers. "Reverend Isaiah said we can sit in the chapel. I'm not sure what you want to talk to me about, but I have nothing to keep from you." He led the way and opened the door for her. The Prophet set up two folding chairs opposite each other and an appropriate distance apart, then motioned for her to sit.

"What do you want to ask me?" he said.

Deidre was a little confused at the man's demeanor. It wasn't what she was what she expecting. "Have you ever heard of a man named David Aaron Schoeneger?" The man's face hardened.

"Yes. Yes, I knew a man by that name." He looked squarely at Deidre.

"Perhaps you can tell me something about him," she said, wondering what he would say.

"When I knew him he was an abomination in God's eyes, drinking, whoring, killing. I knew him too well." Deidre felt as though she were in a time warp. She knew she was talking to David Schoeneger, but he was talking like David was someone else.

"Do you know what happened to him?" she asked. Tears formed in The Prophet's eyes, and he looked at the floor.

"He's dead."

Deidre was at a loss for what to say next, other than, "Can you tell me about his death?" The Prophet looked up at her.

"He died the fall of 2007. He'd been a soldier for the United States, a hard core soldier, special forces. He spent two years in Afghanistan, killing people. He said to me once that he enjoyed what he did, and it was beginning to bother him, the nightmares, the faces he'd see, the sleeplessness. He was sent to Iraq for two years to do the same things. Then, in 2006, he was sent home. Soon after, he died."

Deidre started to realize what was happening. "Jeremiah, is it possible that David Schoeneger is still alive, perhaps using another name?" Jeremiah shook his head, violently.

"No! No, that's not possible. I saw him die." He looked Deidre squarely in the eye, and she sensed that, in his mind, he was telling the truth.

She asked, "Did David ever own any firearms, perhaps a handgun, or even an assault rifle?" He looked at her through sad eyes.

"Yes, he did. He had many guns. Used to hunt a lot, killed a lot of things, including people in Afghanistan and Iraq." Deidre followed with one more question.

"Do you own any guns?"

His answer, strangely, was in the second person. "Jeremiah Rude has never owned a gun."

"Jeremiah, can you tell me where you were last April? I know that's a long time ago, but can you give me an idea?" The man thought for several seconds before answering.

"I was in North Dakota the whole month. Got there the end of March and stayed until sometime in May."

"Can anyone vouch for you?" Deidre wanted to know.

"Several people. I lived in the basement of a small church while I was there. It's called The Church of The Coming Age. It's small, about twenty members, but they all believe like I do, that Christ's return is soon and the world must repent or be destroyed. They liked what I preached, compared me to John the Baptist. One of them had a vision during a service and said I looked just like him. If you want, I can give you the name of their leader. He'll tell you."

When Deidre asked for it, he gave her the man's name and the address of the church. She jotted it down in her notebook. "Where were you Fourth of July night, Jeremiah?"

The big man didn't have to think about that one. "I was right here. We held a special service that night, praying for the people of Two Harbors and that God would turn them from their sinful ways before it is too late. I preached that night." He stopped mid-thought and looked straight at her.

"Sheriff, are you saved?" The question set her back. No one had ever asked her that question, and she didn't know how to respond. The Prophet didn't give her time. "You must repent, Sheriff," he said, becoming more agitated. "Time is running out, and if you don't commit to Jesus, you, too, will burn in hell." By now his voice had risen to a shout, and Deidre became a little alarmed at his fervor. "Please, Sheriff, turn from your sinful ways or you will suffer God's vengeance. For he says, 'I'm a jealous God.' Sheriff, for your own sake, stop whatever sin it is that is weighing you down. I am a prophet. I see you are burdened." Deidre was getting spooked, but she tried to bring the conversation around to her purpose.

"Are you sure David Schoeneger is dead?" Jeremiah's shoulders sagged.

"Yes, like I told you, he died on September 13, 2007, sacrificed on the altar at God's Chosen church in New Orleans. He's dead and will not be coming back."

Deidre sat for a few moments, carefully weighing her words. The interview hadn't gone as she expected. Finally she said, "Jeremiah, I believe you when you say David is dead. But I worry about who has taken his place on this earth. I hope that person never hurts anyone, saint or sinner. I don't think God wants us to take matters into our own hands. Didn't he say, 'Vengeance is mine?' If you know of anything that's not right, here or anywhere, I want you to call me. Okay? Otherwise, Jeremiah, thank you for speaking to me." She stood to leave, and The Prophet only nodded his head. He was still sitting, motionless, as Deidre let herself out.

Chapter
Twenty-Three

By the time Deidre arrived back at her office, there wasn't much of the day left. She looked over a few reports that had been left on her desk, all minor events that didn't require immediate attention. As she walked past Shirley on the way out of the office she announced she was going home for the day and if anything came up to call her on her cell phone. She saw Shirley glance up at the clock on the wall and make a note to herself. "Okay," was all she said.

When she arrived home, both girls were sitting on the swing under a large elm tree. They jumped up to greet her as she stepped out of her car. "How'd it go today, Mom? Catch any bad guys?" one of them blurted out, and they both laughed.

"No, not a one. I had an interesting day, though. Wish I could tell you about it, but this is kind of like your dad's job, I can't say very much." She had an arm around each girl as they walked to the house and couldn't help noticing how tall they were getting.

"What about you? Anything exciting happen today?" Both girls began to talk at once. "You'll never guess what we saw." Maren let Megan tell the story. "After lunch, we followed the river to the spot where we go for picnics sometimes. We thought we'd work on making a campsite for us to use. We pulled some rocks out of the river and made a fire ring." Maren finished telling about their adventure.

"We got tired and waded in the river, but both of us fell in so we were soaking wet. We sat down on that rock shelf that juts out into the stream and were just soaking up the sun. All of a sudden, two fawns jumped out of the woods. They leaped around like two little kids, chasing each other in circles until they saw us. We sat so still, just like you and Dad taught us to do when we're in the woods. They came right up to us, sniffing the air."

"But we didn't touch them," Megan interjected.

Maren continued. "Just then their mother came out of the woods. She snorted, like she was scolding them. One fawn returned to her, but the other ignored her. It reminded me of me and Megan. You know how Megan never listens to you." Megan punched her sister on the arm but laughed.

"Then the mother deer stepped toward the fawn who wasn't listening to her and stomped her foot, real hard," Maren kept her story going. "The stubborn one started to come back, but then the mother deer butted at it with her head. I think she would have scolded it if she could have talked." The girls were delighted to be able to share their adventure.

Megan added, "I wish you could have seen it. They were really cute."

Deidre felt a twinge of guilt for not having been there, but she answered, "That's a memory you two will share forever, and it will be special because it's between the two of you. There'll be a time when we'll have memories together. We do already. Speaking of which, what should we do tonight as a family. Anything?" The three went inside to talk it over and to prepare supper before Ben came home.

Their dinner time was relaxed. Deidre and the girls had fixed chicken on the grill, added fresh beans from the garden, and a lettuce salad. They laughed and teased each other, and Deidre was totally at peace. She had spoken with Danielle earlier and received good news. Jeff had been moved from the ICU to a surgical unit, but the best news of all was that he was experiencing some tingling in a few of his toes. The doctors looked at that with hope he would continue to improve.

The girls cleared the table and loaded the dishwasher while Deidre and Ben talked about their day's work. She was glad they had the freedom to share, although she didn't relate every detail and was sure her husband didn't, either. Megan interrupted them.

"We'd like to hike back to the picnic spot by the river, maybe build a campfire and make s'mores. Want to do that?"

It took only a few minutes to pack up the graham crackers, Hershey bars, and marshmallows, and they set off for their favorite spot. The trail was winding and a little rocky, but they made it to the site in less than twenty minutes, their trek interrupted several times to admire a patch of moss here, a brightly colored lichen there, or a patch of Indian pipes growing near a rotting stump.

The river was flowing at mid-summer level, clear and cool. Along its banks, ferns hung over the water, and where a leaning tree afforded shade, three or four brook trout finned in the current. This was the family's special woodland retreat. Together, they set to improving the site, first pulling up brush by its roots, then stacking it in piles that would be burned next winter. After working for much of the evening, they took off their shoes and waded into the stream.

"Wow! This is cold," Maren exclaimed. She knew it would be cold, but every time they waded in the Knife, one of them would complain about the same thing.

"Sure, it's cold," Ben said with a chuckle. "Up here the river's spring fed. That's why the trout do so well." They washed the dirt off their hands and splashed water on their faces to cool down. By then it was time to climb out of the river, build a fire and let its heat dry them.

The fire was mesmerizing, and no one spoke for many minutes. Deidre dug out the s'mores' makings and they all rushed to skewer marshmallows on toasting sticks. Megan's burst into flame, and she frantically tried to blow it out. Everyone was laughing and chiding her for not having enough patience. "That's the way I like them," she shot back and was the first to sandwich her blackened, melted marshmallow between half of a Hershey bar and two halves of graham cracker. By the time the others were building their first treat, she was on her way to eating her second.

"Hey, leave enough for the rest of us," Maren chided her sister.

By the time it was almost dark, the four washed their sticky fingers in the river, and they all sat on the large rock shelf, watching the stars appear in the sky. "I wish I may, I wish I might, have this wish I wish tonight," the girls recited in unison. Deidre asked about their wish, but they wouldn't tell.

"If we tell, it won't come true," Maren instructed her.

At ten o'clock, Ben announced it was time to go home. "Mom and I have to work tomorrow, and you girls have to catch a ride with the Johnsons to ball practice. Let's go." He turned on the flashlight he brought with, and they began the walk home, sometimes stumbling on roots, at other times getting swatted in the face by branches springing back when the person in front bent them and then let go. By ten forty-five, they were all in bed, and sleeping soundly by ten fifty. All was well in the VanGotten household.

Chapter
Twenty-Four

Deidre intended to hold her first squad meeting that morning, checking on reports from the nightshift and assigning duties to those just coming on. She went through what had been her ritual years before: fix a cup of coffee, pick out a treat from the bakery box on the table, and sort through a few papers on her desk. It comforted her to begin the day in a low key way. She heard the officers trooping in, some tired and needing the lift the coffee would give them, others getting a charge to start the day off on the right foot.

"Anything significant happen?" she asked the night crew. Adamson spoke up. "Nothing in our jurisdiction, but you might want to talk to Sig about the city cops' problem. Somebody broke into the Catholic Church last night and did a heck of a lot of damage. Smashed most of their statues and poured what looks like blood in the baptismal font. They peed in the communion chalice and left it on the altar, then took a crap on the steps leading to it. The place is a mess. Sig was there when I drove by the church on my way here."

Deidre was taken aback. *What's going on in this town?* she wondered. She made a note to visit the police chief that morning. In the back of her mind, she knew she would be taking another trip north to The Sanctuary and Reverend Isaiah. There had been vandalism in town on an increasing regularity, but the act at the Catholic Church was more than vandalism. To her, it had all the makings of a hate crime. The rest of the meeting was inconsequential, and the group stood to leave, some to go home to bed, the others to begin their twelve-hour shift.

As Deidre passed her assistant's desk, Shirley stopped her. "This came in this morning from the BCA. It's the result of the ballistic test on the casing you sent in day before yesterday," she said, and smiled. "You must know somebody down there to get such quick results." Deidre smiled back, took the papers and retreated to her office.

The top page was a note from Melissa, her friend who worked for the BCA.

> I thought you'd need this report as soon as possible. Whenever there is an officer shot, the work is moved to the top if the list. I looked at the report before sending it on to you, and I think you'll be interested in what you'll see. Hope all is well with you and Ben and the girls. Just to let you know, my daughter just graduated from college this spring, majored in criminal justice. Says she wants to be a parole officer. Go figure. Anyway, take care, friend. Hope we can get together soon. Melissa

Deidre contemplated the note for a second or two, a smile barely visible on her lips. then she turned to the report.

> Two empty brass casings sent to our lab from the Lake County Sheriff's Department were examined for identification and comparison. The first was labeled as being found at the scene of the murder of a young man in April of this year, the second identified as having been found at the scene of an officer's shooting.
>
> It is our conclusion that the bullets are NATO compatible, manufactured by the United States Cartridge Company (USCCO) in 2010. It is possible they could be from the same batch. Markings on the casing are indicative that they were fired from the same gun. Scratches produced from the gun's chamber match one hundred percent. The firing pin mark is identical on each, further supporting the theory they were fired from the same weapon.

Markings from the extractor of the gun's automatic loading mechanism, as well as the firing pin indentation, indicate the gun from which they were fired was a REC-7 assault rifle, 5.6 x 45 NATO compatible.

Added to the report was a suggestion, one she had intended to tackle later in the day: "If it is possible to locate the slug fired from either cartridge, we can match them to a specific firearm."

That last line miffed Deidre. What did they think she was, some Keystone Cop stuck up in the woods? Of course it would be great if they could find the slug that had passed through Jeff. Right now, she wanted to talk to Sig, the chief of police, and find out what had happened at the church last night.

His patrol car was still parked in front of the church, along with another squad and two civilian vehicles, when she arrived. She entered the narthex of the sanctuary and was met by a woman, her eyes red-rimmed from tears. She was holding a handkerchief over her mouth, and she sobbed, "Who would want to desecrate God's house like this? We try our best to do what is right. Why this?" She wasn't expecting an answer and rushed past Deidre.

Sig was up front, near the altar, and Father Joseph was at his side. Sig held a notepad and was busy writing in it. As Deidre came closer she could hear their conversation.

"I can't find anything missing," the priest was saying. "Whoever did this was bent on destruction and desecration, simple as that. They knew what is most holy to us, and those were the items they targeted: the baptismal font, the communion chalice, our saints' images. We have, *had*, a copy of the entire St. John's Bible, a considerable gift from one of our parishioners, and they tore the pages out and scattered them around the room, some of which they urinated on. It was pure hate, pure hate." He shook his head.

After Sig was finished speaking to Father Joseph, Deidre approached him. "Not good, is it, Sig?"

His answer was a short, "No." There wasn't much Deidre could do, but she did offer whatever help her department could provide. Sig's old eyes looked sad, almost defeated, and he shook his head.

Back at her office, Deidre looked through the folder containing the evidence that had been gathered relative to Jeff's ambush. The crime looked as though it had been carried out by people who were expert at such things: the calls, the location, the escape route, the probability of the use of a night scope. Why, then, an errant shot that had missed Jeff's vital organs? She attempted to piece together a possible explanation.

The report said that the driver's-side door was fully open and that Jeff was found partially slumped into his vehicle, his torso lying across its front seat, his feet outside and touching the ground. That meant he had probably been standing beside the open door rather than sitting inside. She stared at the photo of his SUV, taken after he was transported to the hospital.

What if, she wondered. *What if Jeff had been leaning into his vehicle and the shooter had targeted his head? And what if, at the split second the shooter began to squeeze the trigger, Jeff abruptly stood up to look around? That would have accounted for him being hit low in the back. Maybe we're looking for a shooter who is an expert marksman but missed because of a fluke.*

Deidre did some mental calculations, considering where Jeff's wound was, the angle from the place the shooter lay in waiting, and the position he must have been in when the shot was fired. It dawned on her as she looked at the photo of his squad that something might have been missed when his SUV had been combed for clues.

The impoundment lot was only a half-block away, and in less than five minutes she let herself through the locked gate. Jeff's squad was sitting next to the fence nearest the back of the lot. She unlocked the driver's-side door, put on a pair of rubber gloves, and ran her fingers along the crease where the backrest met the seat. The seat was intact, no hole. Then it dawned on her. Accounting for the trajectory of the bullet, it would have traveled at an angle across the seat. She checked the passenger side. Concealed in the crevice, she felt what she was looking for: a small hole in the faux leather covering.

"Denny," she spoke into her cell phone. "Could you come across the street for a few minutes to give me a hand?" Denny owned an automotive repair business and was hired by the county to help with any automotive searches. He was trusted and a good friend of Deidre. "I'm going to need help removing the passenger's-side backrest of a 2012 Ford Explorer. Think you could spare a few minutes right away?" Deidre smiled at his response, and in minutes she saw him jog across the street toward the lot, a collection of tools in his hands.

"Hey, Deidre. I heard you'd put on the uniform again. Great news. So, what we got here?" Deidre explained that she needed to have the backrest removed from the passenger-side front seat so she could look at the surface where it met the seat cushion.

"No prob," he said, as he pushed the button that moved the seat as far back as possible. "I think this takes a three-eighths socket," he mumbled to himself, and struggled to get it on the head of a bolt. Deidre heard the *click-click-click* as he worked the ratchet, followed by a grunt as Denny attacked another bolt. He got to his feet and rocked the entire seat assembly forward, used a screwdriver to separate the wiring connection, and lifted the seat assembly out. The entire process took only minutes.

"I've got to take off these side brackets," he explained as he expertly began removing bolts from the braces and with no effort, lifted the backrest away from the seat. Deidre still had on rubber gloves, and quickly stepped in. She wasn't interested in the backrest but the portion of the seat that had been covered.

"There it is, what we're looking for." She stuck the tip of her gloved finger in a hole that was exposed by the removal of the backrest. "I've got to get this over to the lab and have them look at this hole. If I'm right, the slug that went through Jeff is in it." She thanked Denny and made a promise they'd get together for coffee real soon. After locking the vehicle and the gate as she left, Deidre carried the seat over to the Law Enforcement Center, took the hall leading to the lab, and triumphantly walked in, bearing her trophy.

"Hi guys," she exclaimed. "Any chance one of you could help me out? It should take only a minute."

A voice from the back answered, "Help you out? Sure, I'll help you out. The door is right behind you." Jarod came around the corner. He sported a week-old beard, wore a white lab coat over his ragged jeans, and Deidre noticed he had on sandals that were nowhere new. He was laughing. "Good to see you again, Deidre. What are you up to, running a chop shop?" He pointed at the car seat she was holding. Deidre wished she had a smart comeback, but at the moment nothing came to mind.

"That's some kind of welcome. When you gonna shave?" She had at least gotten in a small jab. "Really, I need your help, right now if you can. This seat is from Jeff's Explorer, and I think the slug that hit him is lodged in the padding. Will you try to dig it out so the rifling marks aren't damaged?"

Jarod came closer for a better look. "We sure can." He disappeared for a second and returned with a scalpel and forceps. Deidre noticed the jaws were padded with some sort of rubber. Jarod carefully slit the vinyl cover, and teased apart the fiber padding enough so they could see the shiny object. Then, carefully inserting the forceps, he extracted the slug and dropped it into Deidre's gloved hand. She held it up to the light, contemplating the fact that it had passed through her friend.

"Thanks, Jarod. I'm sending this down to the BCA for analysis, but I'm pretty sure I know what they'll say. Thanks again." She left the seat behind, knowing Jeff would catalogue it as evidence to be used later.

During the short walk back to her office, Deidre questioned what she knew, and the answer was, "Not much." A vicious murder had been committed, a rail line had been sabotaged, a sheriff ambushed, a church desecrated, and numerous smaller acts of vandalism had been perpetrated. She had only one link: two cartridge casings that were fired from the same rifle linked the murder and the ambush. Other than that, everything was circumstantial. The thought crossed her mind that nothing had been done about the note dropped for her by the girl at The Sanctuary. She wanted to have another conversation with Jeremiah Rude. Something told her he had nothing to do with the Catholic Church incident, but on the other hand, something wasn't right with him, either.

The drive to Toimi was quiet, and she stopped in front of the chapel. She decided to walk the road leading to the compound.

As she rounded a bend in the driveway, Deidre saw several women and children working in the many garden patches. Only a couple of them stopped work to stand up and look her way. There were no men around and no one stopped her, so Deidre continued walking until she came to a building set apart from the others. It looked as if it had been a dormitory at one time. From inside she heard a voice being raised.

"You have read the scriptures. From Revelation, the thirteenth chapter, 'And I stood upon the sand of the sea, and saw a beast rise up out of the sea, having ten heads and ten horns, and upon his horns ten crowns, and upon his heads the name of blasphemy.'" Deidre recognized the voice. It was Jeremiah Rude. He continued, his voice rising to almost a shout. "God has shown me the meaning of this, the Apostle John's vision. The ten heads represent ten sins that God abhors and that war against him. They are lust, homosexuality, drunkenness, whoring, murder, incest, greed, cursing the name of God, rejecting Christ, and physical harm to your neighbor." Deidre listened to the responses, expecting a string of amens. Instead, there was a stillness broken by a shuffling of feet. Jeremiah went on to expound on each point, railing against those who wallowed in those sins.

Deidre was amazed at the fervor he managed to maintain right to the end, when he finished with another quote from Revelation.

"And so as it says, 'And to them it was given that they should not kill them, but that they should be tormented for five months: and their torment was as the torment of a scorpion, when he striketh a man.'" Jeremiah added, "'And they shall beg to die, but death will not come.' Brothers, this is why we must remain pure. This is why we must continue to preach to the people of Toimi, of Brimson, of Two Harbors. Even though they are sinners, they are our brothers. Who among us would have his brother suffer the wrath foretold in Revelation? 'I want none of this to befall your brothers,' Thus saith the Lord. Amen." A long period of silence followed, and Deidre heard chairs being moved. A door opened and a string of men began leaving the building, muttering this and that to each other. At last Reverend Isaiah and Jeremiah emerged, walking side by side. They appeared to be arguing over something.

"Good afternoon, Reverend, Jeremiah. I was wondering if I could have a minute with The Prophet, in private?" Reverend Isaiah glared at her but said nothing. Jeremiah half bowed and with his hand, indicated he would follow her, but Deidre had no idea where to go. "Do you have a room we could use? Or would the chapel be better?" Jeremiah said there was a bench on the bank of a small river that flowed behind the compound that would be comfortable, and private. He glanced at the reverend, making his point.

It was a pleasant spot, grassy and shaded by a large maple tree, and looked to Deidre as though it were a place not much used. She and Jeremiah sat on opposite ends of the bench, watching the river slowly eddy its way past. Deidre wasn't quite sure how to begin.

"I was standing outside the meeting hall while you were preaching, Jeremiah. It sounds to me that you believe what you say with all your heart. Am I right?" Jeremiah only nodded, hardly looking up from the river. Deidre continued, "You told me you once knew Aaron Schoeneger. Do you think he would have believed you?" She saw The Prophet flinch.

"It doesn't matter," he responded in a barely audible voice. "Aaron Schoeneger's dead. I watched him die." Deidre sensed that Jeremiah was having a great deal of difficulty speaking, but she asked another question.

"You said you are concerned for every person in the area, that you didn't want them to be, what did you say, 'tormented for years as though they had been stung by scorpions.' I think that's what you said. Do you think Aaron is being tormented like that?"

Jeremiah stole a glance at Deidre, and she was sure saw the glint of moisture gathering in his eyes. "Aaron suffered the sting of those scorpions for most of his life, but Aaron is dead. I keep telling you that. He died, and by God's mercy the scorpion bites have been healed. He is at peace where he's at. He told me that."

Deidre paused to see if he would say more. When he remained silent, she said, "Jeremiah, you told me Aaron is dead. How can he have told you he is at peace, if he is dead?" Jeremiah thought for a second.

"I had a vision, and in my vision he said he was at peace. He also told me to go save as many souls as I could from the life he had lived. Told me his was a wasted life full of pain and suffering, just like the scorpion bites. He doesn't want anyone else to suffer the way he did."

"Aaron," Deidre began, but her companion looked at her.

"You called me Aaron. I told you," and his voice became quite agitated, "Aaron is dead. Please, never call me that again." Deidre sucked in a breath.

"I'm so sorry, Jeremiah. It just slipped out." She knew she'd better not take that tack again.

"Jeremiah," she started over. "Do you know that something really bad happened at the Catholic Church last night?" He shook his head. "Do you agree with that church's theology?" Jeremiah had fire in his eyes when he looked at her.

"No!" he emphatically stated. "How can I when I read about children being molested by priests, when I see the cathedrals they build when people are starving? How can I when they sell indulgences?"

Deidre had virtually no theological training, but she did know that was wrong. "Jeremiah, that hasn't been done for centuries. Could you be wrong in what you say and think?" The question stumped him momentarily.

He said, "I know what I've been taught."

Deidre steered the conversation in the direction of the desecration. "Let me tell you what happened in the church last night. Someone broke in and toppled all of the statues dedicated to the saints. Then they urinated in the communion chalice and placed it back on the altar. They poured blood, we hope it's animal blood, in the baptismal font. They tore up some very valuable Bibles and defecated on the steps leading to the altar. Jeremiah, I have to ask you, do you think that's right, that it's God's will?"

She waited for an answer, and finally, he murmured, "No."

"Jeremiah, this is so important. I don't believe you would do such a thing, but do you think anyone in Reverend Isaiah's group would do that?"

Jeremiah turned to face her, tears trickling down his weather-beaten cheeks. "I don't know," was all he said.

He and Deidre sat for several minutes in silence, studying the river. Eventually she had to leave, and she reached over and placed her hand on his. "Jeremiah, you don't want anyone to suffer, do you?"

He looked her in the eyes. "No, I don't. We're all God's children." Then he surprised her. "Can we talk again, soon?" Deidre assured him they would and said goodbye.

On the way home she tossed around in her mind the conversation that she and Jeremiah had, and she came to the conclusion that he had something he wanted to tell her but hadn't. They would meet again, soon.

When she returned to her office, she found a memo lying on her desk: "Sig would like to meet with you at 7:00 tomorrow morning. Call him if you can't make it."

"Guess I won't sleep in tomorrow", she said out loud.

Chapter
Twenty-Five

Deidre and Sig met in his office, which was located on the north side of town not far from the golf course. As she drove past, Deidre noticed a foursome on the second fairway, the one bisected by a creek. She saw one of the golfers throw his club in the air, his shot evidently finding the water. She smiled and thought, *I hope that's the worst of his problems today.* Sig was waiting behind his desk, and when she entered his office he rocked back in his chair. He looked tired.

"I'm too old for this, Deidre," he said. "I wanted these last few months to go by quietly and then slip out of here to enjoy a long retirement. It isn't going to happen. Did you hear what happened last night?" Deidre looked at him, puzzled, and shook her head. Sig continued. "We have a gunsmith in town, a good guy who does good work. A number of people I know have taken rifles and shotguns to him to have the stock checkered and to have the breeches engraved. He usually has a number of guns, both handguns and sporting guns, in his shop. Last night somebody broke into it and stole everything he had, including his tools. He carried reloading supplies, including powder, casings, and lead of different kinds. They took everything. Most bothersome, they left behind anti-government posters. Do you have any ideas about what's going on around here? I know much of what has happened is my jurisdiction, and you've got some pretty tough issues of your own in the county. But the reason I wanted to meet with you—even before this happened—is that we've got some that overlap your responsibility and mine.

Deidre took a moment to respond. "Let's list everything that has happened and whose jurisdiction they fall under." They began. Justin Peters's murder had happened within the city limits, so it was Sig's case. Jeff's ambush had taken place in the country. That belonged to Deidre. The train derailment was on railroad property and their investigators, along with the National Transportation Safety Board, were working on it. Nevertheless, they knew they were responsible for doing what they could to help. The church was in the city, a police problem, while the note passed to Deidre by the girl at The Sanctuary was definitely something she would have to follow up on. Now the gun theft, that would be Sig's problem, but Deidre was concerned where the guns had gone. They could be anywhere in her county.

When they had the lists in front of them, Deidre said, "I'm having a real hard time seeing a pattern, Sig. Do you suppose we've got several groups that are responsible? Look, Justin's death definitely looks like a hate crime. The Catholic Church, too. The girl who passed me the note, that sure looks like it might be a kidnapping issue, at the least a child molestation issue. The sabotage on the railroad, that might be a terrorism plot. Remember, ten years ago, the ore docks were targeted. I really don't have any good theories about what's going on."

Sig shook his head. "Me either. For now, what do you say we agree to open our files to each other? If you copy what you have to me, I'll do the same for you. That way, maybe we can find some common thread. If we don't catch up to whoever is to blame, I'm afraid something totally disastrous is going to happen."

Deidre left Sig's office no further ahead than she was an hour before. She decided to take a run into Duluth to visit Jeff. He was in rehab, and she wanted to see how he was progressing. On the way, she kept picturing the list she and Sig had formulated, trying to connect one dot to another, but the events didn't seem related.

Jeff's room was on the sixth floor of the hospital, but he wasn't there when Deidre arrived. A nurse directed her to an exercise room, and as she approached its doorway, she heard the physical trainer offering words of encouragement.

"Come on, Jeff, you can do it!" Jeff let out an exasperated gasp and Deidre heard him groan. She wasn't sure she wanted to go in but forced herself. Jeff was standing between parallel bars, his forearms bulging, beads of sweat clinging to his forehead, and a determined look on his face. He was concentrating so hard he didn't see Deidre standing in the doorway. She watched as he struggled to move his left foot forward, the brace on his legs keeping him upright. With what looked like total effort, he managed to shuffle the foot a few inches. The room was filled with cheers. His PT applauded, and from another part of the room, two assistants came running, huge smiles on their faces.

"You did it, Jeff! You actually took a step on your own. Way to go, buddy. I'd give you a high five, but then you'd have to let go of the bars. We're not quite there yet, but it'll come." Jeff tried to smile, but his face was contorted by the exertion. Then he saw Deidre.

"Well, partner, you saw history made today. What'd you think?" Deidre had a difficult time holding back her tears.

"That's really great," she said, trying to make her voice sound upbeat, but inside she was torn up. Her friend's progress was being measured in inches, and she wondered how he was ever going to recover.

The PT assistant brought Jeff his wheelchair, and he settled into it with a sigh. He took Deidre's hand. "I know it doesn't seem like much, but I'm getting better every day. Scans show the swelling around my spine is going down, and I've regained the feeling in my legs down to my knees. I can wiggle my big toes, and put a little pressure on the therapist's hand when I push with the balls of my feet. I'm telling you, I really believe I'll be walking in a month or two. I just feel it, you know?"

Deidre was amazed at his strength, and she thought if attitude made any difference, Jeff's dream of walking again was not far-fetched at all. She helped him wheel back to his room, and they visited until mid-morning, when an occupational therapist carted him away for another work session. On the way back to Two Harbors, Deidre decided to do more checking on a soldier named Aaron Schoeneger.

*****

DEIDRE GENTLY KNOCKED on the door of the county veterans' service officer, even though it was open and she could see the man hunched over the paperwork on his desk. Deidre had never met the man, whose nameplate on the desk read "Jason." He looked up and asked if he could help her.

"I'm looking for the service record of a soldier who has recently moved to Lake County. I doubt if you've been notified, because he's using an alias and I'm sure has severed any ties with the military establishment. Is there any way you can search a database and retrieve his records?"

Deidre was out of uniform at the time, and the service officer looked at her dubiously. "And for what do you need his record?" he asked as he looked at her through squinted eyes. Deidre could tell she should have approached him differently.

"I should have introduced myself," she said as she pulled out her badge. "I'm Sheriff Deidre Johnson of this county. I suspect that this person I'm looking for is in our county and that he is suffering from PTSD. From the conversations we've had, I'm almost certain I'm right."

The officer offered his apologies. "We're careful about giving out information to the public, but in this case, I think we can do a search. What was his name again?" Deidre watched as Aaron's name was typed into the computer, and in seconds the information for which she searched was displayed on the screen. Jason hit the print icon, and she heard the usual clicks and whirs as the printer begin to spew out information. He handed her the sheaf of papers. Deidre thanked him profusely and headed upstairs to her office, where she spread the papers out on her desk and began to read.

Name: Aaron David Schoeneger
Place of Birth: Minneapolis, MN
Years of Service: 2001-2007
Date of Birth: December 12, 1983
Branch of Service: Marine Corps
Duty: Special Ops
Tours of Duty: Afghanistan (1), Iraq (1)
Discharge Date: January 1, 2007
Rank: Corporal
Current residence: Unknown
Awards: Silver Star for Special Ops, Navy and Marine Achievement Medal, Bronze Star (2), Purple heart (2).

Corporal Aaron Schoeneger was assigned to the 2nd Reconnaissance Battalion, stationed at Camp Lejeune, N.C. During his two tours of duty, Corporal Schoeneger was assigned to a six-person recon group, first in Afghanistan, then in Iraq, serving as a targeting specialist for precision-guided munitions. During his time served in combat, Corporal Schoeneger was wounded twice. He was cited for actions exceeding his duty by holding his ground while under heavy fire while laser-guiding missiles to strategic targets. Although wounded in his arm, he refused to leave his post. On another occasion, Corporal Schoeneger was cited for bravery in the face of enemy fire by holding off a squad of the Republic Guard, allowing his recon platoon to escape unharmed to safe positions, then retreated under their covering fire. He was wounded in the operation. On two separate occasions, Corporal Schoeneger placed himself in danger by retrieving wounded comrades and carrying them to safety.

Deidre didn't understand the significance of each award, other than the purple heart, but without a doubt, this Aaron Schoeneger was a military hero, a true warrior in every sense of the word. She wanted to know what, exactly, had been his duties. She called a friend.

"Hey, Leon," she said when he answered the phone by saying "Yo." Leon had been a Marine Corps sergeant until a bomb went off in his barracks in Beirut, Lebanon, destroying his hearing and causing him lasting vertigo. "Leon, I'm checking on a guy who was a Marine, recon specialist. His record shows he was engaged in precision-guided munitions. What the heck does that mean?"

She heard Leon cough, and then there was a moment of silence. "It means he was in the thick of things. You see, some of those smart bombs need to be guided. The way that's done, someone on the ground has to be close enough to the target to light it up with a laser. The missile guiding system locks onto the laser beam and follows it directly to the target. I knew some of those guys. They had balls made out of brass, I think. I'm telling you, they got into some awfully tough situations. Then after the bomb hit, it was recon's job to assess the damage and make a field report back to command. Then came the tough part, getting out. A lot of them didn't make it, and the way things were, they sure as heck didn't want to be taken prisoner. They almost always fought until they either made it or were killed trying. That help you at all?"

Deidre thanked him and promised they'd get together for coffee and a visit soon. After she hung up, she thought she'd make another run at The Prophet to see if she could shake something out of him concerning The Sanctuary and the Reverend Isaiah.

Chapter
Twenty-Six

As she drove north, up Highway 2, she couldn't stop thinking about Jeff. The prognosis was that he'd never walk normally again, the damage had been so severe, but Deidre believed in her gut that his recovery would be complete. *Is my optimism only wishful thinking?* she wondered, then put that thought aside, but she couldn't shut her mind off. A myriad of thoughts streamed through it as the miles sped by. She began to mull over the cases she and Sig had open, the murder of Justin Peters, Jeff's ambush, the church vandalism, even the train sabotage. By the time she reached The Sanctuary, she had come to no conclusions about any of them, didn't even have an inkling how to proceed.

Deidre guided her vehicle to a stop near the chapel, and walked down the dirt road to where the compound buildings sat. As was typical, women and children were working in the gardens, and there were no men to be seen. As she approached two girls who were on their knees, weeding what looked to her like a row of beets, the reverend scuttled from one of the buildings and intercepted Deidre's path before she could reach the girls.

"You seem to be spending a lot of time here," he snapped. "Now what do you want?" Deidre looked into his cold, blue eyes.

"I came to talk with Jeremiah, if you don't mind." She regretted asking if he minded. He should have no say in the matter.

Reverend Isaiah answered, "He isn't here, so it would be best if you leave." He almost spit the words at her.

"But I am here." The reverend spun around at Jeremiah's announcement. "I'm here, and I'd like to talk to you, Sheriff. Maybe we can go down by the river where we sat the last time." He motioned for her to follow, turned and slowly walked away, leaving the reverend standing with a scowl on his face.

When they reached the bench by the river he sat down, releasing an audible sigh that sounded to Deidre more like a sob, but he shed no tears.

"Jeremiah, I'd like to talk to you about Aaron Schoeneger again. I know you say he's dead, but I'm interested in what kind of man he was. He was a hero in the war, wasn't he?"

Jeremiah's shoulders slumped. "I suppose some people think he was, but I think he was a murderer. He killed too many people."

Deidre sat for a moment and then spoke quietly. "Jeremiah, I've been told that an act committed in war is not to be confused with murder. I heard a minister once say that murder is an act committed against innocent people. Killing in war is more an act of self-defense. Would you agree with that?"

Jeremiah didn't answer, and Deidre didn't push. They sat in silence for several minutes before he spoke. "I believe you," he said, and several seconds went by. "But Aaron murdered people during the war. He killed innocents, many of them, children, women."

To that pronouncement Deidre had no response. Eventually she asked, "What was Aaron's job during the war?"

Jeremiah toed the ground and hung his head. "He was in recon. Do you know what that means?" Deidre nodded.

"That means Aaron was in a patrol of about six men who went into enemy territory to gather information. Right?" After she said that, she looked at Jeremiah, who had a far away look in his eyes. Deidre asked another question. "Did Aaron do other things behind enemy lines?"

Jeremiah flinched when she asked that question.

"He was the one that targeted missiles." He heaved a huge sigh.

"Would you use the term 'lit up the target' to describe what he did?" Deidre asked, her voice barely a whisper. Jeremiah's answer was a slight nod of his head. "What would happen then?" Deidre inquired, then sat still.

Jeremiah shook his head. "Aaron told me the missiles would lock onto his laser beam and follow it to the target. It would destroy everything and everybody." The burly man's face remained expressionless. Deidre broke the silence with another question, all the while worrying that Jeremiah would bolt. "Jeremiah, did you have to report to command the extent of the damage done by the bomb?" The instant the words came out of her mouth, she knew she'd made a terrible slip. Jeremiah flared.

"How many times do I have to tell you? I'm not Aaron Schoeneger. He's dead. I saw him die. You asked if I had to report back. I wasn't there. It was Aaron, and he's gone. Please, believe me." Deidre looked in Jeremiah's pleading eyes. She tried to smooth over her slip of tongue.

"I'm sorry. Of course I believe you. Did Aaron have to report the damage done by the bombs to command?" Jeremiah nodded as he tried to control his emotions. His mouth moved as though he was trying to say something, but no words came out.

With great effort, he spoke. "One day he lit up a building he was sure was housing a group of Republic Guard. The missile hit it dead on, and he reported a direct hit, then went to inspect the damage while the other guys of his recon team covered him." Jeremiah stopped and swallowed hard. He began to sob. Deidre could hardly understand him when he said, "The building was filled with women and children. Aaron found them, all dead, all blown to pieces, and he found a little girl, still clutching her doll." Jeremiah broke down and wept openly, his body rocking back and forth. Deidre put an arm around the big man's shoulders and laid her other hand on his arm. They sat that way for many minutes.

"That must have been difficult for Aaron. How did he handle his grief?" Jeremiah looked at her through red-rimmed eyes.

"He drank—more than he ever had. He tried to lose himself in a bottle, but it didn't work." Deidre tried to look him in the eye, but had to look away, disturbed by the pain she was causing.

"But, Jeremiah, I've read Aaron's military record. He saved the lives of his companions. He acted honorably in all ways. Surely, he must have known that in war accidents happen, terrible accidents." She tried to console him.

Jeremiah shook his head. "No, nothing could ever take away the image of that little girl lying in the rubble of the building, bleeding, dead, still holding her dolly to her chest. The only way for him to forget was to die."

Deidre looked at him. "In death, do you think he forgot?"

She hardly got the words out when Jeremiah answered. "No!"

"Jeremiah, is that why you preach the way you do? Is that why you fear for others' salvation, to spare them from what Aaron carried with him to his grave?"

He nodded. "I don't want anybody to burn in hell the way Aaron is burning." Again, they sat for several minutes. Deidre broke the silence.

"You know, Jeremiah, for a time I suspected that you were responsible for some of the bad things that were happening in Two Harbors, but I was wrong. I don't think you would ever intentionally harm anyone. You're a good man, Jeremiah Rude. Thank you for allowing me to ask so many questions about Aaron and for answering them. I won't bother you anymore, but I want you to promise me that if you ever want my help, that you'll call me. Do you still have my card?" Jeremiah nodded.

"Thank you, Sheriff. I've never told anyone about Aaron. Thank you for listening and for not believing he was an evil person. I hope God blesses you."

Deidre stood up, and Jeremiah slowly got to his feet. Side by side, they walked back to where her car was parked. Just before she got in, she saw Reverend Isaiah standing in the doorway of one of the buildings. He had his hands on his hips, and his eyes were filled with hate. On the way back to town, she wondered what could be done for Aaron Schoeneger, or Jeremiah Rude, as he wished to be called.

Chapter
Twenty-Seven

During supper that evening, Megan and Maren were wound up as only twelve-year-old girls can get. Their conversation bubbled, one finishing the other's sentence.

"And today at soccer practice the coach said that if everyone worked as hard as Maren and me—"

Maren butted in, "she said we'd win every game."

"Yeah, and then we had a water break, and—" Again, Megan didn't have the opportunity to finish.

"And Melissa said we were the coach's pets," Maren finished the story.

"That's not fair, Maren. You never let me tell the story, because you always finish it." Megan pouted. Deidre finished the debate.

"You know, Maren, she's right. The next time your sister wants to tell us something, let her finish. Okay? And Megan, it won't help to pout. You'll get your chance. Now, what else did you want to tell"

"Nothing," Megan sulked. She picked up her fork and ate in silence, while Ben and Deidre exchanged glances. Ben asked Maren to pass the potato salad. She did without saying a word. Finally, Ben tried to break the ice.

"What will you girls do tomorrow? There won't be practice."

They both shrugged.

"I've got a suggestion," he tried again. "What if you take a picnic back to our special place on the river? I think it needs some looking after, maybe take the riding mower and trim along the trail and then mow the site. What I'd really like you to do is gather up any loose tree limbs you see lying around and drag them to the wood pile. Just spruce the place up. Mom and I will make a lunch for you. Maybe you can even go wading. I know the water's not deep enough to swim in, but you could lay in the water. Might feel good. What do you say?"

Megan mumbled under her breath, "It'd be okay if *she* didn't have to come with."

By that time the family was done eating and the girls knew it was their job to put away leftovers and wash the dirty dishes. Ben and Deidre decided to take a walk up the road, and while they did they discussed strategy for dealing with their competitive daughters. When they returned and were still in the yard, they could hear shrieks from inside, and both of them made a dash for the door. Before they burst in to break up whatever was going on, they realized they were hearing shrieks of laughter.

They entered the house and saw the sight of Megan with soap suds covering her chin like a beard and trying to imitate Reverend Isaiah. She had Maren in stitches. Deidre had to admit she had the old man's mannerisms down pat, and she knew all the right words to say. They all had a good laugh over it, and the girls wiped up the water they had splashed on the floor.

That night before they went to sleep, Deidre knocked on her daughters' bedroom door. "*Vous pouvez entrer*," Maren called out, and both girls started laughing hysterically. Deidre opened the door and tousled each of them.

"Oh, I can, can I? I suppose I should be grateful." They giggled together for a minute, but Deidre had a serious question for them.

"How do you girls know so much about Reverend Isaiah? Has he ever talked to you?"

Both girls saw she was serious about this and stopped joking. "No, not directly to us," Maren said, "But we see him on the street corner sometimes. Is what he says true, Mom? It just seems that he's always angry about something. Pastor Ike tells us God is a loving God, but Reverend Isaiah is always saying God is mad at us. What do you think?"

"Tell you what, I don't believe what the reverend says, and I like Pastor Ike's God a lot better. I look at you two, and I know God must love me very much to have brought me into this family." She kissed each girl on the top of the head. "Good night, you two. I love you more than you'll ever know."

She and Ben had their usual quiet time after the girls were in bed, and Deidre told him about Jeremiah. "I know that he's Aaron Schoeneger, but he keeps saying that man is dead. I'm afraid he wishes he were, but it's as though he wants to do something to make up for a horrible mistake. I'd give anything to help him. He's really hurting."

The next morning was dreary. A typical Two Harbors fog settled in, covering the sky many miles inland, and a perpetual drizzle saturated the air. *The girls are going to go nuts if they're cooped up in the house all day,* Deidre mused. *I'm not sure I want to come home to that tonight.*

She was at the stove scrambling eggs when the rest of the family trooped into the kitchen and plunked down on their chairs. None of them looked quite awake yet.

"Hey, girls," she said as she dished up the eggs for them, "I know it'd be tough staying home alone all day. How about coming into town with me today? I'm sure we can find something for you to do."

Megan looked up at her, sleep still fogging her eyes. "Oh, sure, Mom. We could shop till we drop, hit all of the stores, both of them." Maren let out a giggle, but Megan found nothing funny in what she had said. "There's nothing going on in this town, nothing exciting, anyway. What can we do there all day?"

Deidre had to admit that the choices were limited. With the fog and the cold, they couldn't enjoy being outside, and she agreed, shopping in a town of three thousand was pretty limited.

"Come on, kids. Let's get going. We'll think of something for you to do while we're in the car." The four of them left together. She gave Ben a kiss at the door and wished him a good day. He mumbled something back about trying. The girls grumbled as they buckled their seat belts. Maren had called dibs on riding shotgun, and Megan was sullen in the back seat. *This is going to be a fun day,* Deidre thought. On the way to town, she threw out several suggestions, all of them meeting rejection. By the time they reached the Law Enforcement Center, nothing had been decided.

"Here's a few bucks. Why don't you kids have a snack at Louise's Café? Call friends and get together with them to play video games. You can always go to the library and read, or what about going to the depot and reading up on the history of Two Harbors?" The girls looked at her as though she were from another universe. "Anyway, let's meet at the Vanilla Bean Café for lunch together. Okay? See you at noon. You've got your cell phones, don't you? Call if you need me." She left the twins standing in the parking lot, hoping they'd find something creative to do, then climbed the stairs to her office.

Deidre had just settled behind her desk and was ready to begin her workday when she heard a man's voice in the outer office. "Is the sheriff in yet? I want to talk to her." She heard her assistant begin to ask if he had an appointment but was cut off. "No, I ain't got no appointment. I just want to talk to her." Shirley started to respond, but Deidre was at her door, hoping to ward off a conflict.

"Sheriff, I want to talk to you," Jimmy O'Brian said as he brushed past Shirley's desk. She began to stand to block his way, although she would have had little success with his bulk.

"That's all right," Deidre calmly stated. "I know Jimmy." Turning to him, she said, "Why don't you come into my office where we can talk." She shut the door behind them, and offered him a chair. As Jimmy lowered his frame onto it, the wood creaked in complaint. "Now, what is it you want to talk to me about?"

Jimmy scuffed at the floor with his boot, and Deidre thought he wasn't going to say anything. Then she saw that his chin was quivering, and his eyes were strangely watery. Finally, he found his voice. "Sheriff Johnson, I never thanked you for all you did for me at the trial. I thought I was a goner for sure, but then you found those things in the grass. If it weren't for you, I'd be serving a life sentence." Deidre began to object, but he raised a meaty paw. "No, let me finish what I came to say. I've been out of treatment for almost three weeks now, and it's bothered me every day that I didn't even say thanks. It's the best thing that ever happened to me. The more I dried out, the more I realized I was killing myself with the booze and the weed. So, thanks."

Deidre could see how uncomfortable Jimmy was, and she tried to steady him. "What's going to happen in your life now?" She looked at the relief in his eyes to think she cared.

"My bosses out at the steel fab shop have been great. Said I was the best welder they had and wanted me back as soon as I finished treatment. I'm lined up with an AA sponsor, a great guy whose been through the mill himself. So, I guess the rest is up to me." Deidre wanted to know about the gang he belonged to. "That's the tough part. They're not going to quit drinking, and they don't want me around to remind them they could probably use treatment, too. I've decided I can't go be around those guys no more. I miss 'em, though. Sure as hell miss 'em."

Deidre could sense the struggle going on in his mind. "Jimmy, I wish you nothing but the best. You'll make new friends. Might take awhile, but it'll happen." She stood, indicating the talk was coming to an end. "I've got a lot to do today, but thank you for stopping in to see me. It means a lot. Take care of yourself." Jimmy got to his feet, a little clumsily, and shook Deidre's hand. It disappeared in Jimmy's grasp. He tried to say something but ended up clearing his throat, let go of her hand and turned his back to leave. Deidre wondered if his shoulders were going to pass through the doorway. As she sat down, she couldn't quite identify what she was feeling, but she had only a moment to contemplate Jimmy's visit before her phone rang.

There was a long silence after she said, "Hello." She could hear someone on the other end of the line breathing heavily, and for a moment, she thought she was the victim of a crank call. The other party cleared his throat as though he were struggling to say the first word.

"Is this Sheriff Johnson?"

"This is she," Deidre replied.

"Sheriff, this is Jeremiah, Jeremiah Rude."

Deidre was rather taken aback. She hadn't really expected he would call her. "Yes, Jeremiah." Her answer was a little too quick, she thought, and she hoped her eagerness wouldn't scare him off. Trying to sound a little more at ease, she asked, "How can I help you?"

He cleared his throat again. "I'm in town. Can we meet someplace to talk?" Deidre suggested he come to her office. Now it was Jeremiah's turn to answer quickly. "No!" He caught himself. "No, I'd like to meet outside, if it's all the same to you. Do you know where the first rock point is from Burlington Bay? There's a park bench on the rock ledge. I'd like to meet there, if you don't mind."

Deidre was quick to tell him that would be fine. They agreed to meet in ten minutes. Deidre looked at her watch and was surprised to see it wasn't even eight o'clock yet. During the short drive to the lake shore, Deidre wondered what he would have to say, and she mulled over more than one scenario in her mind. The thought struck her that the bench Jeremiah had requested to meet at was rather hidden from view, and her thoughts turned to Jeff in the hospital. Could this be another setup? She thought, *No, not in the middle of the morning in broad daylight. Or foggy daylight.* Nevertheless, stranger things had been known to happen, especially when zealots were involved. Then she thought no again.

The path leading to the point wound its way through a dense stand of evergreens, and Deidre began to feel uneasy as she approached the open space where the bench was placed. She decided not to show herself quite yet and stepped a few yards off the trail, where she remained hidden. A few minutes later she heard someone with heavy footsteps coming down the footpath, and she watched as Jeremiah approached the bench, dropped what appeared to be a heavily loaded packsack, and sat down with a sigh. Deidre waited a few seconds, returned to the path, and nonchalantly walked up to him.

"Good morning, Jeremiah. Great view of the lake, isn't it?" She sat down on the end of the bench, turned and looked at the obviously nervous man. "You said you wanted to talk. Anything special on your mind?" Jeremiah shrugged, and Deidre sat quietly as the seconds ticked by.

"Do you remember I told you I felt sorry for Aaron Schoengren, sorry for all the things he did, sorry for the little girl he killed? I want to make up for some of the things he did." Deidre didn't quite know how to respond to him.

"How will you do that?" she asked. Jeremiah stared at the lake.

"I wanted to join The Sanctuary because I thought God had really spoken to Reverend Isaiah, like he's spoken to me. I thought the reverend had the answers to finding peace and to saving souls. I don't want one more person burning in hell, and I'll stand at the gates of Hades, like a warrior, so no one suffers what Aaron is suffering." Deidre waited, wondering where this one-sided conversation was going.

Jeremiah continued. "There are a lot of children at The Sanctuary. At first, I thought they were happy doing the gardening and being taught God's laws. But now I don't think so. There are some bad things happening up there."

Jeremiah had Deidre's full attention. Quietly she asked, "Can you tell me what kind of bad things are happening?"

His shoulders slumped, and he answered. "The men are using the girls, those beautiful little girls."

"You mean they're forcing them to work?" She was certain that wasn't what Jeremiah was hinting at, but she wanted the words to come from his mouth, not hers.

"No," he answered almost unintelligibly. "They're forcing them to have sex with them. Even the older men, even the reverend, I suspect. Night before last they had a wedding. The groom was twenty-five years old and the bride was twelve. Sheriff, she was terrified, cried through the whole ceremony and called for her mother as the groom led her away to their wedding bed, as the reverend called it. The next day I saw her working in the gardens. She had a bruise on her face, and she could hardly walk. If Aaron had been there, he would have found the groom and killed him. There is one girl about that age who is pregnant. She's kept away from the others and out of sight. I only caught a glimpse of her. She was standing in a doorway while the wedding was going on, and I think she was crying."

After he'd made his disclosure, Jeremiah sat still, continuing to stare at the horizon, apparently lost in thought. He added, "I think it's the men of The Sanctuary who are going to burn in hell. If they don't, there's no such place."

Deidre was shocked. She understood the message on the piece of paper dropped by the girl who was hoeing in the garden the day she had visited. With the note as evidence and with what Jeremiah had told her, she knew the next step was to visit a judge and procure a search warrant.

"Jeremiah, what you've told me is very important, but now I need your help, those girls and women need your help. Will you come with me and tell a judge what you saw? He needs to know. And if people are arrested, I'd like you to stand up and tell a jury what you saw. Will you do that?" He nodded. "Do you have a place to stay for a few days?" This time he shook his head. "If I find a place for you, will you use it?"

Jeremiah answered, "S'pose so."

Together, they walked back up the trail to her car, Deidre contemplating what her next move would be and Jeremiah showing little emotion at all. She handed him a twenty-dollar bill and dropped him off at a restaurant called Judy's on the main drag of town before returning to her office. First she called the judge to set up an appointment, then phoned the Salvation Army to make arrangements for Jeremiah. She prayed to God that he would not leave, at least not without talking to her first. Only then did she remember she was supposed to meet her daughters for lunch. It was early yet, but she knew her day would stay busy.

"Hello, Megan? Oh, Maren, are you and Megan at the café?" She heard the answer. "Good. Listen, sweetie, something really important has come up, and I can't make it for lunch. Here's what I want you to do. Walk up to Inga's, Mrs. Olson's, house. I'll call her so she'll be expecting you. I want you to spend the afternoon with her. She'll like the company." Before the call was ended, Deidre heard an audible grumble on the other end of the call, not loud enough that she could understand it, and she smiled as she brought up Inga's number.

By nine thirty, she and Jeremiah were in the judge's chambers, and by ten she had a search warrant for The Sanctuary, to be executed at nine o'clock the following day.

Chapter
Twenty-Eight

Deidre dialed the number for Social Services as soon as she got off the line with Maren. "Hi, Jan," she said when she heard a familiar voice answer the phone. "How's life treating you?"

Deidre remembered the day they'd met, the day she, herself, so desperately needed Jan's help. Deidre was a teenager then and was trapped in a violent home situation with an abusive stepfather. Jan had helped Deidre's family escape the situation. Jan was now past the age when most people retired, but she was still going strong. To Deidre, it seemed the larger-than-life social worker had more energy now than when she was new on the job.

"Hey," Jan answered. "If things were any better, I'd have to pay them for letting me keep this job." She laughed. "What's up, girl? I assume this isn't a social call, because you've got to be up to your eyeballs with work."

Deidre had to admit that it wasn't. "Jan, unless I'm way wrong, you're going to be slammed with I don't know how many psych evaluations in the next few days. We have a probable situation up north involving a number of teens and preteens who have had some rough treatment. And there will be several adult women who are going to need help as well." Deidre went on to explain what Jeremiah had stated in a deposition he had given to her and the judge. When she was finished, there was silence on the phone.

Finally, she heard Jan say, "Is this never going to end? Seems the world just keeps getting crazier and crazier all the time. Okay, we'll be ready. Thanks for the head's up, Deidre. I'll get the staff together before quitting time this afternoon. How soon can we expect our first clients?"

Deidre had already planned her action and could answer without hesitation. "The judge issued a search warrant a few minutes ago, as well as a warrant that will allow us to remove the children from the compound. I suspect the women won't be cooperative, so my deputies will probably be bringing them in against their will. If there are any of the men still at The Sanctuary, they'll be placed under arrest for suspicion of child abuse." She realized she hadn't answered Jan's question. "Be ready by three tomorrow."

The rest of Deidre's day was spent drawing up a plan for how they would approach The Sanctuary the next day. She calculated that about thirty persons would be detained, more if the men were still there. She didn't know why, but she had a premonition that the men would be gone. Perhaps it was because of a similar incident in the central part of Minnesota that had occurred a little over a year before. An enclave had been operating in that area for several years before someone reported to authorities forced marriages between underage girls and older men.

When the authorities made a raid, they found that the leader, a self-proclaimed minister, and most of the men had fled to a similar group living in the mountains of Oregon. To Deidre's knowledge, none of them had been arrested. At any rate, she knew she had to be prepared to haul the men in, just in case her gut feeling was wrong.

She sent out a call to six of her most trusted deputies, most of them remaining from when she had been sheriff. They were getting older, but they were experienced, less likely to respond with force when it wasn't needed. She also called the superintendent of schools and requested the use of one of their busses. The logistics of moving so many people at once was a problem. After assuring him that the district would be reimbursed and that they would use the district's drivers, he relented.

By five o'clock, Deidre was exhausted, but the plan was set. It was time to pick up her daughters at Inga's. She braced herself for gripes and complaints about the boring afternoon.

*****

"Mom, you won't believe what our afternoon was like!" Maren blurted out the moment she hit the back seat of the car. Deidre rolled her eyes, waiting for the bombast. "We had the best time ever." Deidre almost swerved off the road as her head spun around so she could see who was in the backseat.

"Yeah," Megan chimed in the way she usually did, taking the conversation away from Maren, but this time there were no complaints. "We just got to Inga's when she took out this fancy tea set and said, 'Girls, we're going to be grownups today. Choose what kind of tea you'd like.' Then she put two platters of food on the table, one with cheese and crackers, the other with different kinds of dessert."

Maren interjected her comments. "She treated us just like grownups. We sat down, and she had these fancy napkins at our places. We didn't know what to do, so we watched as she poured us tea, and offered us the cheese and crackers."

Megan took her turn. "She asked us questions about ourselves, what we liked, what songs, movies, and all sorts of things. I think she was really interested in what we had to say."

"After dessert and tea, Inga took us out to her garden," Maren continued the story. "She had an interesting history about each flower. Do you know she's lived there since 1965? How old is she, anyway?"

Before Deidre could answer, Megan added, "We spent the rest of the time in her house. She had old pictures of her husband, Eric, and told us stories of what it was like to live in Two Harbors in the olden days and what Eric was like. Then she told us about when you moved in next door. She thought you were too cute to be a sheriff's deputy." The girls became somber for a second. Maren spoke next.

"She told us about the night John was killed. Mom, we're so sorry that happened to you. Inga told us lots of things." Deidre was startled to learn that Inga had picked at some scars she thought were long healed, and the car went silent.

They drove up their driveway. No one had talked for many minutes. The girls got out before Deidre and waited by the driver's-side door. As Deidre placed her feet on the ground, both girls wrapped their arms around her and began to cry. "Mom, we're so glad you're our mother," Megan sobbed, and Maren murmured something Deidre couldn't understand. All three stood there, arms entwined, for several seconds. Deidre laughed and pulled out some tissues to share with them.

"I love you guys. Come on, let's go in the house before your dad gets home and wonders what happened." She gave the girls an extra squeeze and led the way.

*****

AFTER THE SUPPER DISHES were cleaned up and the leftovers put away, the girls asked if they could go to the family picnic site by the river. Ben gave them the go-ahead with an admonition to be home no later than eight thirty. He didn't want them walking on the path in the dark, knowing how difficult traveling in the woods at dusk could be. He and Deidre decided to take a slow walk up the road. The evening was peaceful—no wind, no traffic on the country road, and the birds were beginning to sing their settling-in songs. They held hands as they strolled, and Deidre felt Ben's strength.

"I'm facing a real problem tomorrow morning," she began to unburden herself. "You know that place up north called The Sanctuary?" Ben said he did. "Well, I've got a witness, not a terribly reliable one, I'm afraid, who has signed an affidavit stating that girls as young as twelve are being forced into marriages with older men of the group. The thing that scares me the most, though, is I fear what he's saying is true. We're going up there tomorrow with search warrants and child protection orders. I don't know what to expect as far as resistance. No matter what, it's going to be a pretty traumatic day for the kids who are part of the group."

They walked a few steps in silence before Ben spoke. "Do you think that group is responsible for the crimes that have plagued the area since last spring? I'm wondering if you might find something more dangerous than what you're expecting."

They took a few more steps. "I don't know," Deidre answered pensively. "At first I thought they were our prime suspect group, but lately, I've come to believe they haven't had anything to do with the crimes in town and in the county. Something's going on even more sinister than the reverend and his crew. They're screwed up, but in my gut, I think we're dealing with some force even more dangerous."

By this time they were at the gate that blocked the driveway on the neighboring property, and they stopped to look up the trail. "Looks like they've been doing some hauling in and out of here," Ben observed. "Have you seen any trucks going by our place?" He answered his own question before Deidre could respond. "Of course, none of us have been home during the day lately. It looks like a lot of truck traffic has been moving. Maybe they're logging the back of the property. Somebody, I can't remember who, told me there are some really nice stands of timber in there. Hope they don't clear-cut the whole tract. I think they own almost eight hundred acres. Oh, well, not much we can do if that's what they decide."

The two of them wandered up the dirt road for another half-mile before turning back home. Deidre felt better for having talked with her husband, glad for his unwavering support.

Chapter
Twenty-Nine

Deidre slept fitfully, with nightmares filling her mind, occasionally waking in a sweat. She folded her pillow, changed position, tossed off the blanket on her side of the bed, and then repeated the process. When the clock radio came on, signaling time to get up, she was more tired than when she went to bed. Even a tepid shower did nothing to bring her to a state of readiness for the day. Megan commented on how rough she looked at the breakfast table. On the ride to her office, she tried to play out in her mind how the morning would go.

Six deputies waited for her at the Law Enforcement Center. A large school bus idled by the curb, its diesel fuel exhaust forming an acrid, invisible cloud while the bus driver dozed in the driver's seat. Six department SUVs were lined up, ready to roll. Deidre's vehicle would make seven, enough to transport twenty-one of the reverend's followers, if need be. At eight o'clock, the caravan of law enforcement vehicles started up the road, heading to the church in Toimi and The Sanctuary. At exactly eight fifty they pulled into the church parking lot. There wasn't a soul visible.

Deidre walked up the drive, past two of the gardens, and proceeded to the first building where she had seen children peeking from the windows during her last visit. She knocked on the door, softly at first and then more loudly. She could hear movement inside, but no one came to open the door.

"Whoever's inside, open this door immediately. I have a search warrant signed by Judge Walters, and if you don't open the door, I'll be forced to have my deputies break it down. The choice is yours:

open the door or have it smashed in." She stepped to the side, in case whoever was inside had a gun, and listened for movement. She heard a latch being slid aside, and the door opened a crack. Deidre saw an eye peering out at her through the narrow opening. By its distance from the floor, she assumed it was a child.

"Please let me in. I'm not going to harm you. I just want to talk to you and your mamma." The door opened a little further, and Deidre was greeted by the sight of a six-year-old girl grasping its knob. Her large, blue eyes were opened wide, searching the sheriff's face, seeking an answer to what was going to happen. "Can I come in, please?" Deidre asked. The little girl nodded, then stepped back. Deidre gently pushed the door open and stepped across the threshold. It took a moment for her eyes to adjust to the dimly lit room, but when they did, she was shocked by what she saw.

Three women stood against the wall. In front of them were children, twelve of them, crowded back against the women as though they believed they were about to meet their doom. One girl, who Deidre figured to be about eight or nine, turned and buried her face. She began to cry while the older woman stroked her hair. Every member of the group looked terrified.

"Is one of you in charge?" Deidre spoke quietly. No one made a move. "I need to speak to one of you about your situation. Will someone please come with me?" From where she was nearly hidden behind the group, a young woman stepped forward. Deidre recognized her as the one who had dropped the note on the ground during one of her first visits. Turning to the others, Deidre calmly said, "I want you to stay inside until I get back. There are deputies outside, and I don't want them to have to restrain any of you." She placed her hand on the volunteer's elbow and guided her to the door. When they were outside, she asked, "Is the chapel empty?" The answer was a slight nod and together they walked across the yard and entered the building.

"I know you're the one who dropped the note for me, asking for help. What is your name?"

"Anna," the girl answered. Deidre smiled at her.

"My name is Deidre, and I want to thank you for being so brave. Now, what do you need help with?" Deidre waited for a reply while the young lady fidgeted with her fingers. Finally, she drew in a deep breath and looked Deidre square in the eye.

"I . . . we need help getting out of here. We've been held like slaves long enough, and I want to be free. Anything will be better than this."

Deidre didn't flinch. "Are there any men around?" The girl shook her head.

"They left yesterday. Reverend Isaiah told us that you would be coming any day. I didn't think it would be this soon, though. He said God told him he and the men were to leave immediately to find another place. He said they would send for us when it was safe."

"Do you know where they went?" Deidre asked.

The girl shrugged. "He said they would be looking to the mountains, that God's people had always sought the mountains when they were in danger. He quoted from Psalms. 'I will lift up mine eyes to the hills.' Are we in danger?"

Deidre smiled as warmly as she could and shook her head. "No. You're safe with me, with us. I promise you we're going to get you and your group out of here and to somewhere you can get whatever help you need. First, I want you to help me by answering some questions. How many women and children are in the compound?"

"Thirty-two," Anna said, her voice becoming more confident. Deidre continued.

"Do you think any of the older women will balk at being taken into town?" Anna abruptly stood up.

"Only Sarah. She's Reverend Isaiah's wife, at least that's what she calls herself, although he hardly ever stayed with her."

Deidre stood up to be beside Anna. "What's your biggest concern?" Once again Anna looked Deidre in the eye.

"That the men and the reverend will come back for us."

Deidre scanned Anna and judged her to be about fifteen or sixteen. "Are any of the children yours?" she questioned.

"I have a two year-old son who I left with one of the other women, and I suspect I'm pregnant again."

"Who's the father of your child, and of your expected child if you're pregnant? Do you know and will you name him?"

Anna squared her shoulders. "Reverend Isaiah."

Deidre put her arm around Anna's shoulders and steered her outside. "I need you to show me which buildings house the others and to help me convince them to come with us into town. Can you do that?" Anna's answer was to head for the building from which they had come.

She marched in and announced in a firm voice. "This woman is here to help us. I want you to do what she says. She's promised me that no one is going to hurt you and that she has people who will give us shelter, but we have to go into town. Go with the officers who are waiting outside. I've been out there with them and they did me no harm. They'll treat you with respect, I promise." Deidre thought the others looked at Anna as their leader, and she wondered from where the young lady's authority came. Perhaps it came from nowhere. Perhaps she had just grabbed it.

Tentatively, the group stepped into the sunshine, stopped and squinted at the late-morning glare. Deidre had assigned the three women deputies on the force to be on the team, and two of them ushered the cult members to the waiting bus. The children were in awe of the vehicle and stared wide-eyed out the windows after they had found seats inside.

Anna led Deidre to another building and assertively knocked on its door. "Lydia, it's Anna. You can open the door now. Someone is here to help us." The door was opened a crack, and a baby began to cry. Anna pushed the door open further and stepped in, motioning Deidre to wait. She spoke to whoever was inside but with such a subdued voice that Deidre couldn't make out what was said. A minute later a girl about Anna's age ushered two children out, where they stood blinking in the bright sun. They were followed by a girl Deidre guessed to be about thirteen who carried a baby in her arms. Deidre thought the worst and hoped she was wrong. Anna followed. One of the women deputies met the group and, as she tried to reassure everyone, more or less herded them toward the waiting bus. It helped that some of the group had already boarded.

One building remained that hadn't been approached, and Anna, more emboldened than ever, marched over to it and pounded her small fist on the door. "Open the door. The sheriff is with me and she wants you to come out. She wants to talk to you." As with the other buildings, the door wasn't opened at first. But Deidre could hear a commotion inside, followed by a heated argument.

"Get your hands off me!" someone shouted.

The other person retorted, "Don't you dare open that door! You know Reverend Isaiah said not to allow anyone in, and it is a sin to disobey our husband."

The first person responded, "Husband! Husband! He's no more my husband than he is to the others. He might be your husband, but he's not mine. Now get out of the way."

The door was thrown open, and an obviously pregnant older teen stood in the doorway. "Get me out of here. I can't stand it anymore," she exclaimed as she jumped off the step and ran toward Anna and Deidre. The doorway was filled with the frame of a large, frumpy-looking woman. Deidre figured her to be about forty-five, but she couldn't be sure. She guessed this was Sarah, the woman Anna had said might resist going into town. Sarah's graying hair, which had been pulled back in a bun, was disheveled and coming loose from its pins. She wore a dress that hung to her ankles and over it an equally long apron. She tried to shoo the other women and children back inside, but they were having nothing of it. Eventually, she stood alone, her hands held to the sky.

"God, show these sinners your power. I command you to strike this woman dead. Let your fury rain down on her, Lord. Let fire and brimstone end her evil life right now."

The woman watched expectantly, and Deidre wondered if she really believed the vitriol she was expounding or if she was trying to scare her. Deidre felt a little uncomfortable, nothing she could put her finger on, but that feeling disappeared when a few seconds had passed and nothing had happened. She almost laughed, but caught herself, not wanting to make the situation more tense.

"I want you to come with me," she calmly informed the woman.

"I will not!" came the reply. "You'll have to carry me out of this sacred place. But if you try, God is going to save me." Deidre could tell Sarah was serious.

"Please," she pleaded. "Don't make us have to use force. If you come peaceably with me, everything's going to be okay. Otherwise, I'm going to place handcuffs on you and take you to town in a sheriff's vehicle. Of course, it's your choice. You can decide."

The woman shouted back at her, "The choice has been made for me. My husband said to wait for him, and his word is my law. I will not sin by disobeying him. Do you understand?"

Deidre called for one of the women deputies, and together they approached the doorway in which the woman stood. "Get away from me!" she shrieked and rushed into the confines of the building. Deidre and her deputy followed and discovered her cowering in a corner of what appeared to be a kitchen. She brandished a ten-inch-long butcher knife and waved it in front of her, all the while shouting, "God will give me strength to kill you if you lay a hand on me."

Deidre tried to calm the situation. "I don't think God wants you to be a murderer. Remember what the commandment says, "Thou shalt not kill."

Sarah shouted, "No! It says that we can't commit murder. Reverend Isaiah says its not murder if you kill someone while defending yourself. He said it's not murder if you kill your enemy, and he said all sinners are the enemy of God. If I kill you, I'll be doing God's will, just as whoever killed that boy in town was doing God's will. The reverend said that the boy was a homosexual who refused to seek help for his sin, and it was God's punishment that he died."

Deidre was so taken aback with those words that she could only stand motionless. Finally, she found her voice. "Don't you think that Reverend Isaiah could have been wrong? What if God loves everyone, saint or sinner? Or what if we've heard God wrong and what we call sin, really isn't? That would mean the boy was killed for no reason." Sarah kept shaking her head and continued her rant. Deidre tried to reason with her. "Why don't we sit down and talk about this? Maybe I'll be able to see things your way. Why don't you drop the knife?" Those words only made the incensed woman more unstable, and her words became more and more incomprehensible. Deidre decided it was time to act. With a slight movement of her eyes and head, which she hoped had gone unnoticed by Sarah, Deidre motioned for her deputy to move in from one side, and she began to work her way to the other.

"Stay away from me!" the woman screamed, and thrust the knife at Deidre. With one quick step forward, Deidre was close enough to grab her arm and a struggle for the upper hand turned ugly. With a downward jerk of her arm, the woman wrenched herself free of Deidre's grasp, and she slashed at Deidre. It happened faster than Deidre expected, and with the move, Sarah slit the sleeve of Deidre's uniform and gashed her upper arm. The other officer rushed the scene while the assailant's attention was directed at

Deidre and pinned the knife-wielder's arms to her body. Sarah's strength was amazing, and she was on the verge of breaking free when Deidre brought her nightstick crashing down on the struggling woman's forearm, breaking at least one of her bones and forcing her to drop the knife, which clattered to the floor. The zealot sank, holding her arm and rocking back and forth as she cursed God for having abandoned her.

Deidre kicked the knife to the far corner of the room and, panting from the struggle, tried to help Sarah to her to her feet. The woman wouldn't move, but by that time two other deputies had responded to the sounds of the struggle. Together, the four officers carried the uncooperative resistor from the building and forced her into the screened back seat of one of the SUVs. At eleven thirty, the group was on its way to Two Harbors. Thirty-one women and children rode in the bus and one woman was held in the back of a sheriff's SUV. Sarah kept trying to call down the wrath of God on the officers. The other women and children rode in silence, wondering where they were going and what the future held for them.

Chapter
Thirty

DEIDRE PICKED AT her evening meal, hardly joining in the conversation with her family and spending most of her time deep in thought. She forced herself to supervise the cleanup, and afterward busied herself with mindless tasks. Ben knew to let her continue in her own world and to not try to help. Later, after the girls had retired to their room to read, or text, or do what preteen girls do, he asked if she wanted a glass of wine.

"No, not tonight," she answered with a half smile on her face. "I could sure use a gin and tonic, though, with a twist of lemon. Make it a stiff one." Deidre plunked down in their lounger and tilted it back until she was staring at the ceiling.

"Must have been a tough day," her husband commented when he handed her the highball. You've been pretty much lost all night. Anything you can talk about? If you can't or don't want to, we can just sit quietly together and get a little plastered." Ben smiled at her as he lowered his frame into another easy chair. They sat in silence for a long time, Deidre sipping her drink while she thought and Ben waiting until she wanted to say something.

"We did a raid on that group up north at the place called The Sanctuary. I'm afraid when we find out what went on up there we're going to want to castrate somebody. I can't get the image of that vile preacher out of my mind. It's been there all evening, and I wish I could make it go away." She quit talking and took another sip, a gulp, really, of her gin and tonic. Ben noticed the glass was already half empty. Deidre continued.

"Remember, I told you several weeks ago that a girl had dropped a note for me when I visited the compound. All it said was 'Help us,' and now I know why they needed help."

Ben nodded as he sort of murmured a "mmmmm" to indicate yes, he remembered.

"Today, I found out her name is Anna. She's sixteen, has a two-year-old child, and may be pregnant again. She said the father is Reverend Isaiah. I don't think he's the only child the almighty reverend has fathered."

They were both pensive for awhile, until Ben brought up an incident that had been investigated by the FBI. The person in charge was Gary Rose, a close friend of Ben's. His office was just down the hall, and they frequently ate lunch together. "Is there any connection between The Sanctuary and that enclave that was operating in the east-central part of the state, the one near that small town? What was its name . . . Fiddleson, Askoton, something like that? Anyway, it was all over the papers about a year ago. Remember?"

Deidre finished her drink in two gulps and motioned for Ben to make another. While he was in the kitchen preparing it, she answered him. "That's where Anna came from, a couple of the other girls, too. She said three or four years ago Reverend Isaiah frequently attended the worship services and meetings down there. He and the minister, Joshua Blood, preached together. She said their messages were almost always about hearing God's voice and obeying his command."

Ben interrupted. "That's the guy Gary's been trying to find, Joshua Blood. Those working the case think he headed to the mountains in Idaho, but no one had seen him for over two years. Then, just last week he was spotted coming out of a fast food joint in Salmon, Idaho, with a girl on his arm. A customer thought she recognized him from when his picture was on a local TV channel. She notified the authorities, and with their help, made a positive ID. They're on his trail as we speak and hope to catch up with him soon. He's a slippery one, though, and there's a good chance he'll get away. But we'll eventually get him, just a matter of time. "

"Yeah, well, here's what happened to Anna." Deidre went on to tell Ben what she had learned. "One evening, when Reverend Isaiah was visiting the services run by this guy Blood, the two so-called ministers preached on Matthew 25. I didn't know what that was about and had to ask Anna. She told me it's the parable of the ten virgins. That still didn't mean a thing to me, but she went on to say that the story is about ten virgins waiting in a room for their bridegroom to make an appearance. Something about them being ready for the moment when he arrived."

Ben shook his head in disgust. "I know where this is headed, and I have a feeling it's going to get ugly. But finish what you're saying. I've got to know if I'm right."

Deidre continued. "Anna said the reverend had been sitting in a chair next to the pulpit while Reverend Blood declared that all unmarried women should be ready because at any time God might call on them to become a bride. When that time came, their bridegroom would call their names, and they would be led to a more godly level of living. She said the sermon on that particular scripture lasted for over an hour. Then it was time for meditation, a time to listen for God to speak." Deidre stopped to sip her drink. She had slowed down on the highball. Ben watched her, knowing the catharsis of what she had seen was necessary.

"After fifteen or twenty minutes, Reverend Isaiah shot out of his chair. 'I've just received a word from God,' he declared. 'He has given me the names of three virgins in this room who are to become brides tonight. The names I'm going to recite are girls who will be known as God's Maidens.' Anna said he spoke the names of three girls. She was one of them."

Ben shifted uneasily. "How did Reverend Blood react to this announcement?" Deidre's face showed how revolted she was.

"Joshua Blood lifted his arms and shouted, 'Hallelujah, our God is so faithful! He has selected three from our group to be his wives through Reverend Isaiah. What an honor and a privilege this is for us and for these three chosen virgins. Praise God!' Anna said she tried to talk to her parents, said she was afraid and didn't want to go with the reverend, but they told her it would be a grievous sin to refuse. They told her she would burn in hell if she disobeyed God. And so she was taken away by Reverend Isaiah to his commune, The Sanctuary. That was four years ago, when she was twelve. He raped her the second day she was there. Told her she was serving God. She gave birth to her son when she was fourteen, and now, she thinks she's pregnant again." She drained her glass for a second time. "That bastard. Nothing we can do to him will be punishment enough for what he's done to those girls."

Deidre's story was sobering for Ben, even though he could have just about written the script before Deidre told him. "What about the girls' parents?" he asked.

"That's the part that makes me the sickest. They were overjoyed that God had chosen their daughters for this special purpose. What a sick bunch of ignorant asses. Turns your stomach, doesn't it?"

Ben wanted to spit to get the vile taste out of his mouth. "You know, I'm going to have to tell Gary about this. The parents of the girls found in Blood's group were arrested and charged with parental negligence and a number of other crimes, but I don't think anything was ever discovered about the girls who had been taken to other communes. You understand I have to do this, don't you?"

Deidre nodded and set her empty glass down. She covered her face with her hands and rubbed her eyes. "Social Services got the judge to order DNA tests on the children to determine who their parents are. I have a notion that more than one of them is a product of the reverend's continued rapes of their mothers. We'll get it sorted out, I'm sure, but how do we sort out the feelings and emotions of the children and their mothers? I don't know," she lamented.

Ben got up and helped Deidre from her chair. She discovered she was a little wobbly from her two highballs and leaned heavily on him. They laughed as they made their way upstairs to their bedroom. "Let me run you a warm bath," Ben more asserted than asked. "You okay to get undressed while I do that?" Deidre nodded but said nothing. She had some trouble unbuttoning her blouse, and after taking her bra off she tried to get out of her slacks but stumbled when her foot got hung up in the fabric. Finally, she stood naked in front of the mirror.

"You're drunk," she announced to the image looking back at her.

Before the image could answer, Ben came to help her but stopped dead in his tracks. "Where did that cut come from?" he demanded as he stared at her arm.

"It's nothing," she quickly answered and tried to cover the gash with her other hand. He came over and pried it off her arm and looked closely at the wound.

"Why didn't you tell me about this?" he questioned, the hurt evident in his voice.

Deidre shrugged and looked first at the floor and then into Ben's face. "I didn't want to concern you with a little scratch. It's nothing." Ben would have none of that.

"Nothing? If whoever did this had been an inch closer, you could be dead from a severed artery. How can you say it's nothing?"

Deidre looked at the floor, not knowing how to respond. This was the first time in their married life that Ben had raised his voice to her. She didn't mean to, but she began to sob and fell into his arms, not because of the drinks she had consumed but because the dam holding back her emotions had burst.

"Oh, Ben. I'm sorry to have held this back from you. This has been one hell of a day for me, and I didn't want you to know. When I agreed to fill in for this job, you asked me not to take chances, and I didn't want you to think I'd been reckless." She paused and held him closely. She could feel Ben's arms tighten around her, as if he was protecting her from an unseen enemy. They stood that way for what seemed like minutes.

Calming herself, she said, "Help me to the bathroom. I want to soak, and while I do, I'll tell you every gory detail, although it wasn't as bad as it looks. I wasn't in that much danger, because I had deputies with me." Ben's anger bred by his concern melted, and taking Deidre's elbow, he helped her step into the warm bath. Deidre winced when the warm water contacted the fresh cut. She reclined against the back of the tub with a sigh.

"Okay, here's what happened. Like I told you downstairs, all the men had abandoned The Sanctuary, and we found only women and children. Every one of them cooperated, although most of them were terribly frightened and mixed up in their emotions. Some thought God was going to strike them down for disobeying the reverend. Others believed the men would come back and punish them.

"One girl, the one I told you about, Anna, had the courage to show us around the compound. In the last building, Reverend Isaiah's wife—I think she really is his wife judging by her age—and a few others were holed up. This woman, Sarah, tried to get them to resist, but they all left. She stood her ground. In fact, she retreated into the kitchen, where she grabbed a butcher knife. I tried to talk her down, but the more I talked the more irrational she became. Finally, I had to act. The deputy and I moved so we were on opposite sides of her, and we slowly began to move toward her. She decided to lunge at me with the knife. I used the standard move and grasped her wrist, hoping to be able to force her to drop the knife, but she was a lot stronger than I thought she'd be. She wrenched her arm free and took a swing at me with the knife. Fortunately, she only cut my shirt and gave me this superficial wound. The deputy restrained her but couldn't get her to drop the knife. By that time I had freed my nightstick, and I cracked her across her forearm. I think I broke a bone, because she dropped the knife. It all happened in less than two minutes." Deidre looked at her husband, her eyes pleading for understanding.

Ben was still for a minute, then a half smile formed on his lips. "That's all? Well, I'm certainly glad to hear it wasn't of any consequence. Deidre, what am I going to do to keep you safe? Sit on you?" He came over to the tub, got on his knees, and began to massage her neck. He bent over and kissed the top of her head. "I worry about you every day you're on the job." He took a deep breath. "By the way, who treated you?"

Deidre relaxed, knowing things were all right. "We carry first aid supplies in our squads, and one of the deputies bound my arm. I stopped at the ER on the way home and they put these butterfly strips on. Just told me to watch for infection."

Ben helped her from the tub, even though by now the effect of her two drinks had worn off, and dried her back for her. Together, they went to bed.

Chapter
Thirty-One

THE ALARM WENT OFF far too early the next morning. Ben and Deidre almost had to pry their eyes open, and after two cups of strong coffee they still were suffering the effects of having drunk too much and staying up far too late the night before. They did make it out the door on time, and after kissing goodbye, went their separate ways to work.

Deidre spent most of the morning in her office finishing paperwork from yesterday's raid. The women and girls had been taken to the women's shelter, Superior Escape, and the numbers had swamped their capacity. Some were housed in the facility downtown and others were taken into homes by the women who volunteered at Superior Escape. Deidre didn't think the victims were in imminent danger, and she was quite sure none wanted to flee. They would be well taken care of. Today, Social Services would begin processing their status. In some cases they would try to track down family, in others seek referrals for county assistance.

One arrest had been made, Sarah, the one who claimed to be Reverend Isaiah's wife. She would be charged that afternoon with several counts: resisting arrest, assault with a deadly weapon, assault with intent to do great bodily harm, and contributing to the exploitation of a minor. Actually, that charge was multiple, one for each underage girl who had a child. As she interviewed more of the girls in the days to come, Deidre expected the number who had been molested by the good reverend to grow.

She was wrapping up the paperwork when her phone rang. It was Gary Rose calling.

"Hey, Deidre. How you doin'?" He didn't give her time to answer but jumped into the reason he called. "Ben told me about what you discovered yesterday, and he asked me to call you with this news. Joshua Blood was arrested early this morning in Libby, Montana. That's a small town just across the border from Idaho and not too many miles northeast from where he was spotted last week. I was notified because Blood's name was on the FBI's wanted list, and I was listed as the contact. I asked the authorities to question him about your Reverend Isaiah. Blood said he didn't know anybody like that. Then he asked, 'If I know anything about the northern Minnesota group, can we work some kind of deal?' Right then, we knew he had information you can use with your case."

Deidre breathed a sigh, not of relief but of exasperation. "Listen Gary, would it be possible for me to visit with you this afternoon? I've got some questions about this Blood guy and his group, and I need to pick your brain about a couple of other things related to my case. I guess this could be considered *our* cases, because if the story one of the girls told me yesterday can be corroborated, Joshua Blood will be charged with criminal behavior against her. Let the authorities know. Maybe we can work a deal on one of the charges if he gives up Reverend Isaiah."

Gary told her he had about an hour free at two o'clock, which was fine with Deidre. By one fifteen she was on the road to Duluth. At two, she walked into his office, not even having taken time to stop at Ben's to say hi. Gary was busy at his desk, his head down and concentrating on something that was evidently important. He looked up, startled, when Deidre knocked on the doorframe.

"Hi Gary, sorry to disturb you, but there are a couple of questions I need answers to." Gary chuckled and invited her in.

"No problem. Blood has waived his right to an extradition hearing and is on his way back to Minnesota as we speak. I was just preparing papers for his reception into our custody. By the way, the

Montana authorities are beginning their own investigation of him, and when we're done, he may be headed back to them so they can pursue their own charges. Hopefully, he'll never breathe another breath of free air again."

Deidre took a chair kitty-corner from Gary's desk so she wouldn't be talking across the expanse of its cluttered surface. "Gary, I sure could use some help. I think you know, Two Harbors has been hit with an epidemic of crime, some serious and some more like vandalism. I think at least some, if not most of it, is related to Reverend Isaiah's group. But now that we've discovered a connection between him and Joshua Blood, I wonder if they're responsible for everything that's been happening. Right now, I'm at a loss for what to do except to wait and see if the crime wave stops now that the men have taken off. What's your take on it, Gary?"

He shrugged. "I can't answer that, but I know that just waiting around isn't the thing to do. I'm sure that's not what you came all this way to hear. Specifically, what information are you looking for?"

Deidre knew her time with Gary was ticking away, so she got right to the point. "Was there any indication that Blood and his outfit were involved in any violent crimes?"

Gary cleared his throat and hesitated before speaking. "This was never reported to the papers, and what I'm going to tell you is in the strictest of confidence. If word leaks to the media, you and I will be in deep shit. But I know you, and I know Ben. I trust you completely. When we raided the compound down south, we found a cache of some very serious weapons. Not just a few hunting rifles and handguns. I mean serious arms: fifty-caliber sniper rifles, assault weapons, grenades, fifty-caliber Brownings, weapons an army would need. We're working on the possibility that Joshua Blood was connected to a militia group, but we've got nothing so far except theories."

Deidre let the breath she had been holding escape. "That's what I needed to know. I suspected The Sanctuary was more than a religious colony, but now, it seems to be more than a suspicion. The reverend preached such a violent and hate-filled message, I thought he would be capable of serious crimes. Now I'm more certain of it. I know you work mostly with the interstate pedophile issue, and I wonder if I could talk to the agent in charge of the militia investigation unit. Any chance?"

Gary reached for his desk phone and dialed a number. "Jackie? Gary here. Any chance you can spare a minute or two? The sheriff of Lake County has something she'd like to run past you. Good. We'll be right over."

Jackie's office was at the end of the hall. "Ben seems really happy these days," Gary said as they walked. "I think you two getting together was a lifesaver for him. For awhile there, I didn't know if he was going to make it." Deidre smiled, but before she could comment, they were at Jackie's door. Gary rapped but didn't wait for an invitation. He walked in and plunked his frame down in a chair. Deidre remained standing until Jackie stood, shook her hand, and then sat down.

"Gary tells me you have a possible link between a group north of Two Harbors and our cult led by Joshua Blood. Why do you think that?" Jackie didn't waste time with chitchat.

Deidre felt as though she had been put on the spot, but she responded without a hitch. "A witness told me that Reverend Isaiah, the leader of the Two Harbors group, used to visit Blood's compound, and they preached from the same pulpit, preached the same message."

Jackie cut her off. "How do you know this witness is reliable?"

Deidre's hackles were rising, and the characteristic flush that she hated was beginning to redden her face. Pointedly, she answered. "Because four years ago she was a member of Blood's group. The reverend and Blood singled out her and two other girls who they called God's Maidens. The girls were taken to Toimi and became a part of the group at The Sanctuary. That girl's name is Anna. She has a child fathered by Reverend Isaiah and suspects she's pregnant again. She was twelve when she was taken and she's sixteen now." Deidre paused for a second, then added, "What do you think, Jackie? Do you think she might be a reliable witness? If not, I won't waste any more of your time."

Gary shifted uneasily in his chair, wondering if he was going to have to break up a fight. Jackie blinked, and Deidre continued to stare at her, her jaw set and blue eyes seemingly turned the color of steel.

Finally, Jackie, coughed and settled back in her chair. "I guess I'd say you're right. This Anna would be a reliable witness." In an effort to gain the advantage, she asked, "What did you want to ask me? I have a meeting in ten minutes so we'd better finish our conversation."

Deidre doubted the reality of a meeting, but she swallowed her pride. "I want to know if you have any evidence of a militia group operating in Lake County, my county?" she added to make her point. Jackie squinted at her.

"No, I can unequivocally tell you that we haven't heard of anything happening in *your* county." She emphasized "your" to let Deidre know her thoughts. "If anything comes to my attention, I'll tell Gary, and he can get a hold of you." Jackie looked at her watch and stood up. "Sorry I have to rush off, but I have a meeting to attend." She walked out without so much as a thank you for coming in. Deidre and Gary were left standing in her office, looking at each other.

"What's wrong with her?" Deidre wanted to know. "Does she treat everyone so rudely, or is it just me?"

Gary gave her a crooked, embarrassed smile. "I should have warned you. She can be a real . . . you know. Jackie's interested in one thing, advancement, and evidently, she sees you as a threat. Maybe afraid you're going to siphon off some credit she wants. Anyway, did you get the answer you wanted?"

Deidre was still fuming. "No. I wanted to ask her opinion about what I should do next, if she thought the threat in Lake County is over now that the men of The Sanctuary are gone, and if I can count on the FBI in the case I find out a militia is involved. No, I didn't get my answers." All Gary could do was offer his apologies.

On the way out of the building, Deidre stopped at Ben's office. Fortunately, he was in, and she plopped down in one of his chairs. Before he could even say hi, she unburdened herself. "I just met one of your colleagues, Jackie." Before she could continue, Ben raised his hands to cut her off.

"Say no more. I think everyone in the department has had a run-in with her. I don't think she has a friend in the unit. I'm guessing she's treading on thin ice, because I overheard her superior on the phone the other day asking someone what it would take to get her transferred out of here. Try to avoid her if you can, because whatever is eating at her probably will end up devouring her." They spent a few minutes talking, and soon Deidre began to cool down.

She looked at her watch and stood to leave. "I'd like to go up to The Sanctuary before I go home. Any chance you and the girls could fix supper tonight?" She put her arms around Ben's waist and placed her head on his chest. It was an automatic sort of move, one she made without thinking it might not be appropriate in FBI headquarters. Ben used his free arm to swing his door shut, and it latched.

"Deidre, I love you," he said and kissed the top of her head. "Of course I'll fix something. We can eat a little late so you can sit down with us. But tell me, are you going up there alone, or will a deputy or two be with you? I'll worry if you go alone."

Deidre squeezed him even harder. "I won't go alone, promise." They stood like that for a moment, and then Deidre looked up at him. "I'm so lucky to have you in my life. I love you." She gave him one more squeeze and headed for her car.

Chapter Thirty-Two

THE GRAVEL CRUNCHED under the wheels of her SUV when Deidre turned off the paved road onto the dirt driveway. She was relieved to see a deputy's squad already parked near the chapel of The Sanctuary, and he stepped out of his vehicle when she turned off hers.

"Hi Jake, how's the day been for you?"

"Slow," he answered.

"That's good news. We've had enough excitement for a while. Got anything planned for your four days off?" The two carried on a friendly conversation as they walked to the first building. Deidre was relieved to find the door was still locked, and she tried several of the keys that had been confiscated during their intervention. The fourth key on the ring opened the door. It took several seconds for their eyes to adjust to the dimly lit interior, and when they did, Deidre was struck by the stark bareness of the room.

A homemade trestle table with a bench on either side sat near one wall. Two other six-foot-long benches were pushed up against the empty walls, and a fuel-oil space heater connected to a cement block chimney filled one corner. The unfinished wooden floor didn't even have a throw rug covering it. The only word Deidre could think of to describe it was austere.

The two officers moved from room to room. There were five of them, all small. The last three were bedrooms. Two had double beds, but the third had four sets of bunk beds crowded into the space. All were made up with a single army surplus woolen blanket for a covering.

The kitchen was primitive. One drawer held a couple of butcher knives, and another, forks, spoons, and table knives. Deidre had seen better accommodations at rustic camps. There was no electricity in the building, and a slight shudder went up her back when she thought of what life must have been like for the women and children.

She and Jake moved from building to building, coming to the reverend's last. His was the only one with electric lights, and Deidre turned them on with a flip of the switch. The floor was carpeted with a large, patterned rug. The dining table had chairs set around it, and the kitchen, while not a gourmet kitchen, was well-stocked. She opened a cabinet and discovered an assortment of brandies and wines.

His bedroom had a larger bed than any of the others she had seen, and it had a bureau with several drawers. Most of them were almost empty, but in the bottom-most, she found a case of condoms. She looked at them in disgust, and hoped someday she could get her hands on the hypocrite.

After an hour of searching the property, Deidre gave up. Nothing was evident that would in any way connect the group to a militia. She sighed, disappointed that she couldn't call in the FBI's subversive division.

On the ride home, she pulled out her cell phone. She knew this was distracted driving, but she wanted an answer to a question. She dialed the number of a place run by the Salvation Army , the place where Jeremiah Rude had been given shelter. A person with a cigarette-raspy voice picked up.

"Yeah, what can I do for you?" Deidre was a little unnerved by the gruff greeting, but she recovered quickly.

"I'm looking for Jeremiah Rude. Is he there?"

The person with the gravely voice coughed and then said, "Naw, he took off yesterday."

Deidre was silent from the shock of the message. She rather stammered, "Can I speak to the person in charge of the shelter, please?"

Gravel Voice didn't answer her, but Deidre heard someone shout, "Hey, Marge, some woman wants to talk to you about that Rude guy." Deidre could hear noise in the background and then the sound of the phone being transferred from one person to another.

"Hello, this is Marge speaking. Can I help you?" Deidre thought she sounded as if she were expecting the caller to be asking for shelter.

"Hi, Marge. This is Acting Sheriff Deidre Johnson. I wanted to talk to Jeremiah Rude, but I've been told he left the shelter yesterday. It's important that I know the circumstances of his leaving. Can you help me?"

There was a pause. "We try to be careful about the information we give out concerning our clients." Marge hesitated. "But I think in this case it will be okay. Jeremiah spoke so highly of you, Sheriff. He said you were his personal messenger from God. We provide shelter to those in need, but we also talk to the clients about their future. Our captain is really quite well-educated and competent at holding these discussions. He was able to convince Jeremiah that he was in need of professional help. Captain Williams arranged for Jeremiah to be seen at the Veteran's Administration Hospital in St. Cloud. They have a wonderful psychiatric unit there and have helped several of our previous clients. Captain Williams arranged transportation for him, and Jeremiah should be in their hands by now."

Deidre didn't quite know how to respond. All she could think of to say was, "Thank you for your help. I hope things work out for Jeremiah." She disconnected the call and pulled over to the side of the road. Her next call would be more complicated, she assumed. After finding the number of the VA hospital, she punched in the digits, listened while the phone rang, and was rewarded by being connected to an automated answering system. Deidre listened impatiently while the menu was being read.

"If you know your party's extension, you may dial it now. Otherwise, listen carefully to the following options: for benefits information, dial one; to inquire about services, two; for . . ." and the list went on. Finally, the recording came to the last choice, "For general information, dial zero." She did as instructed and another recording came on. "We're sorry," the automated voice intoned. "All of our operators are currently busy. Your call will be answered in the order it was received. Thank you for your patience." Canned music began to play, and Deidre began to rail at the computer.

"Who says I'm being patient? Come on computer, let me talk to a real—"

She was embarrassed when a voice broke into her rant. "You have reached the general information desk of the Veteran's Administration Hospital in St. Cloud, Minnesota. My name is Lisa. How may I help you?"

Deidre regained her composure, wondering if Lisa had heard what she had been saying to the computer voice. "Lisa, I'm the sheriff of Lake County, Minnesota, and I'm calling about a person who may have checked into your hospital yesterday. Can you help me?"

She received the standard answer. "I'm sorry, Sheriff. What did you say your name is?"

Deidre was becoming agitated. "I didn't, but it's Deidre Johnson."

The person on the other end of the call continued with her standard answer. "I'm sorry, Sheriff Johnson, but you must realize I can't give out information about our patients. I can't verify one way or the other if a person is registered at our facility."

Deidre was growing beyond agitated. "I'm well aware of that. I want you to connect me with the head of the hospital. On second thought, I'd settle for the director of the psych unit, even a head floor nurse would do."

"I'm sorry, without your going through proper channels, I'm not allowed to connect strangers to the people you request."

Deidre had had it. "Listen to me. This is a matter of utmost importance. I'm tired of your 'I'm sorries.' Connect me to someone I can talk to and get an answer, and do it now. If you hold up my investigation for one more second, Lisa," she used the woman's name like a club, "I'm going to call my congressperson and have her staff investigate why I can't speak to whoever is in authority." It was a bluff. She hardly knew the name of her congressperson, let alone how to reach her. The bluff worked.

"I'm connecting you to our director of patient rights and quality control," Lisa barked at Deidre. "She can tell you the same thing I just did, but perhaps she has the authority to back up my words. Thank you for your call."

Deidre felt a little sheepish for having lost her cool, but not much. The phone rang five times and a recording came on. "You have reached Julia Selga, Director of Patient Rights. I'm sorry, but I'm currently away from my desk right now or on another line. Please leave your name, number, and the nature of your call, and I'll get back to you as soon as I can."

Deidre cursed into the phone, but calmed herself enough to leave a message. "This is Sheriff Deidre Johnson of Lake County, Minnesota, calling. It's urgent that I talk to someone of authority at your facility concerning a possible patient with whom I have been in communication. I'm concerned for his mental state, and desperately need to locate him. I believe he may have registered at the hospital yesterday. If so, I feel it necessary to alert the staff to the fact that he may be of danger to them and to himself," she lied, piling on the B.S. She gave her number and added a short closing. "I know the VA has been under congressional scrutiny as of late, and it would be a shame if something happened to this man out of neglect."

Deidre hit the disconnect button but kept talking. "And so, Ms. Selga, I suggest you get your ass out of the coffee room or wherever it is and return my call. Because, Ms. Selga, I'm fed up with being put on hold, talking to the operator who can only say, 'I'm sorry,' hearing that you are away from your desk or on another line—"

Deidre's diatribe was interrupted by her cell phone ringing. She looked at the caller ID and noticed the call was coming from a 320 area code. "Hello," she answered. "Sheriff Johnson here."

"Good afternoon, Sheriff. This is Julia Selga returning your call. It sounded urgent, and I'm sorry that I wasn't able to answer the phone directly. How may I help you?" The director had totally defused Deidre's frustration by sounding as though she really cared.

"I should be the one apologizing for being so abrupt. Too much bad has been happening in Lake County, and I'm afraid I'm becoming overly demanding."

Deidre had no idea why she opened herself up that way, but Julia answered, "That's perfectly understandable with your stressful job. I'd like to help if I can." Deidre realized she was being treated as though she were the patient. Julia's tactical understanding worked.

"Julia," Deidre said, using the director's given name. She, too, could play the psychological game. "Julia, we have a serious situation going on up here. Yesterday, we raided a compound where children were being abused. The leader has fled, and we have only an inkling of where he's gone. We're reasonably sure he's been in contact with a militia group. The person I'm trying to locate, who I believe is a patient at the VA, stayed at the religious compound we raided. I've been told he's seeking treatment at the VA. All I'm looking for is confirmation that he's in your care and hasn't run off to join the felon we're after." She took a deep breath, expecting to hear that Julia was really sorry.

The line was silent for so long, Deidre thought Julia had hung up. "Let me check my computer," the director said. Deidre could hardly believe her ears. "Sheriff, you have to agree that this conversation will go no further than this call. What I'm doing is highly irregular, but I imagine if I don't help you now, I'll be looking at a subpoena in a day or two. Let's save each other the hassle." Deidre didn't tell her it probably wouldn't have gone that far. "Tell me the name of the person."

"Jeremiah Rude," Deidre said, and almost immediately got an answer from Julia. "No one by that name shows on our record."

A thought struck Deidre. "I suspected that name is an alias. Would you try Aaron Schoeneger?" In seconds, Julia came back with her answer. "Yes, Aaron was admitted yesterday, but I'm sorry, you can't speak with him. Perhaps by next week he will be settled in and will be able to receive visitors. That's the best I can do. Sorry."

Deidre heaved a sigh of relief, and for a moment had a feeling of joy that Aaron was going to be getting help. "Thank you so much for your assistance. You have no idea how relieved I am that Aaron will be treated. Please tell him that I wish him well and that I would like to visit with him soon. Thanks again." Julia said goodbye and hung up.

As she finished her ride home, Deidre thought, *At least something good might come out of this mess.* It was after six when she pulled into her driveway. She was almost too tired to think of eating.

Chapter
Thirty-Three

Deidre felt as though she had been run over by a truck and left for roadkill. She and Ben had sat up until eleven thirty, discussing what Deidre's next move would be. The women and children from The Sanctuary were being taken care of by Social Services, and Reverend Isaiah and the other men of the commune had made good their escape. Jeremiah Rude seemed to be coming to grips with reality. That left the unsolved crimes: the railroad sabotage, and of course, the murder of Justin Peters. Deidre voiced her concern to Ben that she didn't believe things were going to calm down until she could find a link to those crimes and make an arrest.

Now she was on her way into town, intending to spend the day in her office catching up on paperwork. Things didn't work out that way. When she entered the sheriff's office, two deputies were sitting at a desk with an elderly man who was obviously flustered. His hair was disheveled, and his eyes darted around the room. Before she could make out the conversation, she could hear that he spoke with a heavy German accent, and Deidre thought the man was near tears. One of the deputies looked up.

"Sheriff, you'd better come listen to what Joseph has to say." Deidre didn't take time to even grab a cup of coffee and approached the group. "This is Joseph Feldmann. We were called to his residence at five o'clock this morning to investigate vandalism." Deidre looked at the old man and wondered why anyone would want to single out someone like him.

"What are we talking about?" she wanted to know. The deputy glanced at his notebook before speaking. Deidre thought he was stalling.

Finally the deputy spoke. "We're dealing with another hate crime. Spraypainted on his house were the words 'Die Jew,' and someone had drawn a swastika on his sidewalk. But that's not the worst. A figure was hanged from a tree limb in his yard with a placard on it. In red paint was printed 'Joseph Feldmann.'" Deidre was shocked, and felt a stab of pity for the old man sitting in the chair.

"Joseph, will you step into my office for a minute? It's private there, and we can talk." she turned to the deputies. "Will you draw up your report on this? Go back to Joseph's home and scour the area for any clues that may have been missed. After you're reasonably sure you've got everything, call in a cleaning crew and have them take care of the mess on his house and in his yard. Be sure to wear gloves, cut down the effigy, and bring it into the lab so they can get a look at it." Deidre led the way for Joseph and held the door to her office open for him. Inside, she offered him a chair, and Joseph eased his decrepit body into it. Deidre estimated him to be in his late seventies or early eighties.

"So, Mr. Feldmann, do you have any idea who might have done this?"

The old man shook his head, and then, speaking in his thickly accented voice, said, "I thought all this was over. Not here in America. Not here." He continued to shake his head. Suddenly, Deidre knew what he meant.

"Did you live in Germany?" she asked.

The old man's shoulders slumped. "Yes," he answered. "Many, many years ago—with my parents."

"During the war?" Deidre asked. He looked at her through watery eyes. "Ya," he answered, "During the var." Without prompting, Joseph began to tell his story.

"It was the summer of 1942, August, when German," he pronounced it as 'Churman,' "soldiers broke into my parents' home during the night. We were forced to leave in our nightclothes and go down to the street where we were herded into the back of a truck. I still remember the smell of the canvas-covered sides and top, the smell of exhaust, the smell of fear." Deidre was engrossed in what Joseph was saying.

"My two sisters, my father and mother, and me, all crowded into the back of this truck with twenty or so other Jews. I recognized them from our building. The road was rough and we were headed out of town. As we neared the city limits, a motorcycle pulled up alongside the truck and waved it down. The rider, dressed in an officer's uniform, came to the back of the truck where I was leaning against the latched tailgate. He looked at me and said, 'Get out!' I looked at my parents and they nodded. My mother wept into her handkerchief, and Father stared straight ahead. I climbed out of the truck." Joseph paused as though to catch his breath or to let his voice strengthen. He continued without prodding.

"The officer drove away on his motorcycle, and I never saw him again. I have relived that moment over and over in my mind for seventy years. My only answer is he was an angel of God." Joseph stopped talking and sat, wheezing while he stared at the floor. Finally Deidre broke the silence.

"What happened to you?" she quietly asked.

Joseph's head jolted up. He had been so deep in thought, it was as if he had forgotten Deidre was in the room. "What happened to me?" he asked, echoing her words. "What happened to me? I walked back to my community and went to a Gentile neighbor's apartment, a middle-aged couple with three children of their own. When Mrs. Bachman answered the door she said, *'Mein Gott, es ist Joseph.'* My God, it's Joseph. She took me in, and I became a part of their family, a fourth child. I know now what a risk it was for them. I don't know how they kept the other children from giving away our secret. I was ten years old and small for my age. I looked very young and stayed home all of the time. I didn't go outside for more than a year, and then for only a few minutes at a time.

"After the war, I was sent to a displaced person's camp, and was labeled a DP. I didn't get out until 1948, when I was fourteen years old. I had no job, no skills, other than I could read and write well. I never heard from my mother, father, or sisters again. In the camp, I learned English, and made a few pennies translating letters from America for those who didn't or couldn't learn a new language. I began to write answering letters. In time, I became a very good writer.

"When I was able to leave the camp, I had corresponded with a newspaperman in Superior, Wisconsin. You know, just across the bridge from Duluth. He operated a Jewish paper, printed in both Hebrew and English. He sponsored me and I came to America, thinking I was leaving all of the hatred behind.

"But now this. I am an old man, too old to raise a finger, too old to care anymore." Deidre looked at his sad face and knew that wasn't true. All those memories Joseph had locked away for decades had been let out, and he was hurting. She groped for words.

"Joseph, I'm so sorry. There are evil people in this world, always have been, probably always will be. But there are countless wonderful people, too. Remember the family that took you in? Remember the newspaperman who gave you your job? Remember all of your friends here in Two Harbors? Is there anything I can do for you?"

He looked at her, his eyes blank and his voice thin. "Will you give me a ride home?" They rode in silence to his house, which was located just outside the city limits. It seemed like part of the city, but was in the jurisdiction of the county.

"*Mein Gott, was dast ist!*" Joseph slipped back into his native tongue. The street was lined with parked cars. Two people were scrubbing the sidewalk, and three or four with power sanders were tackling the hate painted on Joseph's house. Three tent awnings had been set up on his lawn, which looked as though it had been recently mowed. Under the canopies, tables had been set up, on each a bouquet of flowers. A gruff-looking man, a neighbor who Joseph had spoken to only a handful of times, came to the sheriff's car and opened the passenger-side door.

"Come on, Joseph. We're having a party." He helped Joseph from the car and steadied him as they walked to the yard. Joseph was confused by all the fuss, but Deidre had tears in her eyes as she drove away. In her rearview mirror, she saw a knot of neighbors gather around the tottering old man. He held his cap in his gnarled fingers and she could see a light breeze riffle his thin, gray hair.

Chapter
Thirty-Four

Deidre tried not to be held in her own world of thought, but it didn't work. During supper, her smiles had been forced, her conversation stilted, and her food tasteless. She couldn't get out of her mind the vision of Joseph's house so sadly defaced by painted ethnic slurs or the idea of him being hung in effigy in his own yard. On the other hand, the image of his neighbors cleaning up the mess and gathering around him made her throat constrict so she had difficulty swallowing. After dinner, Ben asked if there was anything he could do to help. Did she want to talk? Deidre shook her head, then made a decision.

"I think I want to walk down by the river to our picnic spot. I need time to sit and think, to try to fit the pieces together. I've thought for quite some time that all of these crimes have been linked, although Reverend Isaiah's group is not involved in them. That case is separate. Now I'm certain we are dealing with one group, a hate group. If you don't mind, I need some time alone to sit in the peace and quiet of the woods and see if some kind of inspiration comes to me. Ben, dear, I'm just plain weary."

Ben held his wife close, rocking her from side to side, comforting her. "I'll make sure the girls tidy up the house before you get back. You go relax, but please, come back before dark. I don't want you tripping over a rock or a root and spraining your ankle or doing a face plant." He grinned. "Go unwind."

Deidre started down the path that led to their favorite spot by the river. She had a small tablet of paper in her hand and her cell phone, although she had contemplated leaving that at home. The electronic device had become too much a part of her to do that, and she tucked it into her pants pocket. The early evening air was still, and she spotted the leaves of a red maple beginning to change color. It was mid-August, but in the evening, the smell of autumn was beginning to creep in. The thought crossed her mind that the girls would be starting school with all of its activities in two weeks, and she wondered how the family would juggle the hectic schedule now that she was back at work. Maybe she shouldn't have been so eager to get out of the house and rejoin the work force. *Well, too late for that*, she thought.

She reached the picnic spot, found her favorite resting place under a sloping cedar tree, and sat down. The river was only feet away and she listened to its gurgling and splashing over the many exposed rocks. She closed her eyes and let nature calm her spirit. Eventually, Deidre came back to earth, and she opened her eyes to her surroundings, took out the notebook and a pencil and began to doodle. First, she listed the crimes and incidents in chronological order:

1. Jason Peters's murder.
2. Jimmy O'Brian arrested for murder and drunken driving
3. Reverend Isaiah preaches hate
4. Jeremiah Rude comes to the area
5. Train derailment
6. Catholic Church defaced
7. Jeff checks out The Sanctuary
8. Jeff ambushed
9. Men at The Sanctuary fly the coop
10. Joseph Feldmann vandalized

Deidre doodled under her list, "Find a common thread." After Jimmy O'Brian's name she wrote, "No." She was certain he had nothing to do with the acts that were being committed. After Jeremiah Rude she wrote, "No," and drew lines through the two men's names. She drew a line through Reverend Isaiah and the men at The Sanctuary. They were going to pay for their crimes against the women and children they had virtually held captive and sexually assaulted, but they were gone before Joseph's house had been splattered with hate. In her gut, Deidre knew that the crimes, other than The Sanctuary, were connected. Her list was whittled down to five. Now she needed a common thread. It came to her mind that the remaining five could be lumped under one heading—terrorism.

At the bottom of the page Deidre scribbled athletic teams and the name "Nick Eliason." She looked at the words and crossed them out. She thought Nick was a spoiled jerk and thought even less of his mother, but she was positive they would not have been involved in such malicious acts. That left only the option that the crimes were being committed by someone or some group she didn't know about.

The more she pondered that thought, she realized that in the case of the train derailment, it would take more than one very strong person to have pulled the spikes holding the rails in place, and even if one person had done it, time would have been a factor. She estimated a piece of track to be about thirty feet long. That would span almost ten cross-ties, she figured on her pad. Cross-ties required two spikes to hold the rail in place. Whoever had sabotaged the track needed to pull at least twenty spikes, each requiring a straight up pull of about two tons per square inch. Then they would have had to unbolt the connecting pieces of steel at each end. She knew the bolts were close to an inch in diameter.

No, Deidre concluded. A group of school boys couldn't have done that, and neither could the scarecrow-like men of The Sanctuary. Whoever did it needed a lot of brawn. Some of the biker group had that, but there weren't enough of them. She had to be looking for a group whose members were very strong. That left out women, possibly. There had to be several of them, and they had to be filled with a rancorous hate. The thought scared her, because she had no idea who she was looking for. She printed "Militia?" on the paper.

Deidre moved away from the tree she was using for a backrest, stood, and stretched. Suddenly, from behind, her arms were pinned to her sides. A dark, cloth bag was thrown over her head and tied around her neck, and she felt her wrists being drawn together behind her back. She felt the pain of plastic ties being cinched tight. Another pair of hands grabbed her legs and she toppled over to the ground, striking her head so hard on a rock that she saw stars. It was like a display of fireworks being shot off in her brain. Dazed, she felt herself being hoisted over somebody's shoulder, and whoever it was began walking. Deidre heard the sound of splashing water and felt her bearer stumble. He had waded the river.

Chapter
Thirty-Five

IN MID-AUGUST the sun sets at eight o'clock in Two Harbors, and by seven thirty, Ben was getting a little worried. He hoped his wife hadn't gotten so involved with her thoughts that she lost track of time. By eight, he was truly concerned, and when he looked at his watch for the tenth time, it read eight thirty. Ben knew something was wrong.

"Girls, hold down the fort," he called out. "I'm going back to the picnic area to find out what happened to Mom. I hope she didn't fall and break a bone." He rushed out the door, then had to come back to retrieve a flashlight with batteries that worked.

The trail wasn't smooth, difficult to maneuver in daylight, treacherous at night. Ben fought the urge to run. In ten minutes he was at the picnic area, and his heart sank. He hadn't met her on the trail, and she was nowhere to be seen. He panicked.

"Deidre!" he hollered over and over, cupping his hands to form a megaphone and aiming in every direction. He stood silently for several minutes, listening for any sound—her voice, a breaking branch, a moan. Nothing. Ben shined his light around, and its beam reflected off something white under a cedar tree near the water. It was Deidre's notebook. He stooped and picked it up and in his state of confusion, got his fingerprints on the pad without thinking he might have damaged a clue. It was hers, all right. He recognized her unique style of penmanship.

Ben turned to home. This time he ran as fast as he could, picking his way over the rough trail. He rushed to the phone and dialed the sheriff's office while the girls looked on, confusion clouding their faces.

*****

FOR DEIDRE, EVERYTHING became a journey defying her senses. She knew they crossed the river, because she could hear the splashing, but after that the only sound she heard was the swishing of brush as they plowed through the tangled thickets. She could feel the muscles of whoever was carrying her like a sack of potatoes thrown over his shoulder, and she was able to guess he was a very large person. He continued to push on as though the weight of her body was negligible. Deidre was having difficulty breathing through whatever was pulled over her head, and she felt beads of sweat form on her forehead, trickle down her face, and drip off her nose. She lost track of time.

In the distance she heard voices but couldn't make out what was being said, and the trail seemed to become smoother and wider. She no longer felt the brush swat at her, and her assailant picked up his pace.

"Good work, Lieutenant," a voice called out. "Take her inside." Deidre heard a door open, swinging on hinges that could have used some oil, and the tread of heavy boots pounded the wooden floor. Her body was lowered and she felt the jolt as she was dropped unceremoniously. Deidre could tell she had been placed in a corner, because she could feel the adjoining walls press against her back. She was totally confused but still tried to make out what was being said around her.

"Private, go tell Captain Blake that we have her. She's ready for our interrogation and photographing."

Deidre heard a voice answer, "Yes, sir!" and heard the sound of his heels clacking together. She pictured him giving some sort of salute at the same time. From what she could gather from her limited senses, Deidre thought she heard the one who had been addressed as "Lieutenant" move a chair and sit down. She smelled cigarette smoke that made her cough. Someone laughed. Deidre shifted her weight, trying to find an elusive comfortable position, and she heard the door swing on its complaining hinges. Someone walked heavily toward her.

"Get her up on that chair," she heard him command.

"Yes, sir!" came the answer.

She was roughly jerked to her feet by unseen hands, steered in a direction, spun around, and pushed backward. For a moment she felt as though she were falling but then felt herself caught by the seat of a hard-surfaced chair. Her feet were bound to the chair legs, and she felt a pull on her wrist bindings, then a snap as they were cut. Deidre put her hands in her lap and massaged the bruises on her wrists. She thought they were unusually damp and wondered if it was blood. Trapped in her darkened world she felt hands groping her body, at first thinking she was being sexually assaulted, then realizing she was being frisked. She felt the hands remove her cell phone from the front pocket of her tight-fitting jeans.

At that instant, Deidre became acutely aware of how vulnerable she was. Not that she hadn't known it before, but now, reality hit her like a club. Whoever had her could do anything they wanted—and probably would. Her mind raced as fast as her heart was beating, and for one of the few times in her life, she was on the verge of panic. Suddenly, the hood that had been pulled over her head was jerked off. She found herself sitting in front of a bright light. Deidre was totally blinded by the glare until her eyes could adjust. Even after that happened, she could see little. By squinting and turning her head slightly to the side, she could just make out the forms of three people standing behind the floodlight. She could feel its heat on her face. The forms looked like men, large men, but one of them was even bigger than the others. She thought he must have been the one who carried her through the woods.

"You are Sheriff Johnson." It was a statement, not a question. "You have two daughters, step-daughters, actually, and your husband is Ben VanGotten. He works for the FBI and is stationed in the Duluth office." The voice continued with her biography. "Eight years ago, you thwarted a terrorist attack on the docks in Two Harbors. Seven years ago, you broke a meth ring being run out of Superior National Forest. Five years ago, you collaborated with the FBI to rescue Native girls from being sold as sex slaves. Most recently, you have worked as a private investigator for an attorney in town, and after the elected sheriff was careless enough to let himself be ambushed, you accepted an appointment to fill his position. Is there anything else you'd like to know about yourself? We have more."

At first, Deidre was shocked and also puzzled at what they knew and wondered why they were telling her. Then it dawned on her: they were trying to break her, psychologically. If they knew so much about her, what must they know about her family and their movements? The thought hit her that they were trying to make certain she knew they were completely in charge. Rather than intimidating her, Deidre became furious. She resolved she would say nothing, show as little emotion as she could, give them nothing to work with. Minutes of silence passed, and the floodlight's heat was almost unbearable.

The same voice calmly intoned. "You must be thirsty, sitting under the glare of that hot lamp. Private, get the sheriff a bottle of cold water." Deidre heard the lid of a cooler being opened and in seconds a uniformed man stepped in front of the light with a dripping water bottle in his hand. Deidre reached for it.

"Uh-uh-uh-UH-uh," the voice behind the lights warned. "I didn't give you permission to hold it. Private, remove the cap from the bottle." Deidre expected she would be given a drink. "Private, you look thirsty. Why don't you drink some of the water?" She watched as he guzzled the bottle's contents, allowing a stream of water to spill from the corners of his mouth and down the front of his uniform. When he had drained the bottle, he burped and tipped the bottle upside down so the remaining drops fells on the floor. "Okay, now you can give the sheriff the bottle to hold," the voice said. The private handed her the empty bottle, and Deidre realized she was being manipulated in a very cruel and reasoned way. She threw the empty bottle at the light.

"Now, now," the voice cajoled. "Losing your temper will do you no good." For the first time since her capture, Deidre spoke.

"Who are you, and what do you want from me?"

"Oh, so you do have a voice. For a while, I thought you were mute." He chuckled. "Who are we? That's an excellent question. One whose answer is neither here nor there. What do we want? Another excellent question. We want to use you for bait. That's all."

The implication failed to sink in. Deidre's head was swimming, and she felt as if she was caught in the middle of a nightmare that wasn't going to end. She was getting thirsty to the point of real discomfort, and incongruently, she had the pressing urge to relieve her bladder. *Bait? Bait for what,* she wondered. She was exhausted to the point of wanting to lie down but couldn't.

Chapter
Thirty-Six

By eleven o'clock, Ben was frantic. Two deputies had arrived and Jackie, from the FBI, was on her way. At first, she had been reluctant to come, but by telling her of Deidre's notation, "Militia," Ben had convinced her that it might be beneficial for her career if she were to uncover a subversive group. Jackie arrived at Ben and Deidre's house shortly before midnight. By that time, Megan and Maren had grasped the severity of the moment, and they sat curled up on the couch with their eyes wide open to what was happening and shivering with apprehension.

*****

It had been over three hours since the cloth bag was pulled over Deidre's head, and she felt bruised and battered. She could endure the minor pain she felt, but it was the constant heat from the lamp that was wearing her down—that and the lack of water. The light was so bright that she wasn't able to keep her eyes open without them watering, and when she closed them, she saw spots. What caused the most discomfort was that her bladder felt as though it was going burst.

"Can I go to the bathroom?" she asked through parched lips.

"Sure, go ahead," came the answer, but no one moved to assist her. When she tried to stand, she lost her balance and forcefully sat back down. She heard somebody snicker. What confused her was that her captors had stopped asking questions. Their only interaction was when she seemed to drift off in a half-sleep, half-daze. They would prod her, forcing her to open her eyes, not allowing her even a moment's retreat into herself. She knew her spirit was slowly being eroded away, and sometime during the ordeal, she lost control and felt urine flow down her legs. For the next hour and a half she was forced to sit in a puddle of her own water, and she could feel the burn of ammonia on her behind. By that time, Deidre was too weak to be humiliated, and she sat in a stupor. One of her guards prodded her to lift her head, and she thought she heard a click like the shutter of a camera closing. She didn't care.

A wave of relief flooded over her when the light was finally turned off, and she felt the bindings on her legs being cut. Deidre tried to stand, but she couldn't get her muscles to lift her, and she fell into her own puddle of urine on the floor. Strong hands grabbed her arms, hands so large they completed encircled her biceps and cut off her circulation. For an instant, she thought the hands were blood pressure cuffs being pumped too tight. Then she felt herself being dragged across the floor, her legs trying to support her, but in the end becoming useless. Whoever had hold of her shoved her into a corner and let go. She collapsed in a heap, and the stench of her hour-old urine was acrid in her nose. She closed her eyes and drifted off, not to sleep, but to a state of semi-consciousness.

*****

At midnight, Ben's phone rang. He looked at its caller ID and was startled to see that the call was coming from Deidre's phone. He fumbled as he tried to slide the unlock icon. "Deidre! Are you all right?" The voice that answered wasn't hers.

"Hello, Ben," the caller said. "As you have probably already guessed, this isn't your wife on the phone, although she is sitting right beside me. You might say she is our guest."

"What do you want?" Ben demanded.

"First, I want you to calm down and realize that I'm in control. Then, I want you to listen carefully. After I hang up, I'll be sending you a series of photos of your wife. They will have been taken by her phone and sent to you from the same. That way you'll know that we do have her in our custody. Stand by to receive them." The line went dead.

"What was that about?" Jackie asked, for the first time seeming to take an interest in what was transpiring. The deputies moved closer in anticipation of what Ben had to say.

"Somebody's holding Deidre. They didn't identify themselves but said to expect some pictures that are being sent to us right now." He had hardly spoken the words when his phone chimed, indicating he had a message coming in. Ben hit the message button and a series of pictures opened up on the screen.

In the first, Deidre was seated on a chair. Everyone could see that her legs were bound to it, but her hands were free, resting in her lap. To Ben, she seemed to have a defiant look on her face. Although her hair was mussed and her clothing looked disheveled, she had no visible signs of injury. He took heart in that fact, and scrolled to the next picture. The time signature on it showed it had been taken thirty minutes later, at eight forty-five. Tears came to Ben's eyes when he saw the change in his wife's appearance. In this frame she looked exhausted, as though she had spent the past half hour slogging through loose sand. Her eyes sagged and she sat slumped. He scrolled to the next photo, taken at ten thirty.

In that photo, Deidre had an empty water bottle in her hand. By the bedraggled look on her face, Ben guessed that she had not drunk its contents, but that look was contrasted by the fire in her eyes, anger, and she sat more upright than she had in the previous picture.

"Look at that," one of the deputies remarked. "At least they gave her something to drink. Maybe they aren't being too tough on her."

Ben knew his wife's expressions. "No, she was given an empty bottle. They taunted her with it, but look at her eyes. Instead of breaking her, they pissed her off. I know that look too well." He half smiled to himself. "If I know her, she was getting wound up to throw the damn thing at them." He went to the next photo.

Jackie involuntarily sucked in a breath when she saw it. Deidre was definitely stressed. Her eyes had lost their fire, and she was more slumped than she had been in the first picture. Her lips looked cracked, and her facial expression was lifeless. It was obvious she had experienced a long three hours since the first picture was taken.

The last picture had been taken at midnight, only seconds before the call, and it was the most disturbing. Deidre looked so totally beaten that Ben could hardly recognize the woman he loved. She sat in a pool of what he assumed to be urine, and her pants were soaked, the light blue denim having turned a darker blue on the inside of her legs. She hung her head so Ben couldn't see her eyes, and one arm was by her side while the other was still bent so her hand rested in her lap. Deidre looked as if she had given up, and the image broke his heart. Tears spilled from his eyes and he wept silently. Before anyone could say a word, the phone rang.

"Agent VanGotten, I assume you've seen the pictures of your wife by now. She looks tired, doesn't she? We'll allow her to get some sleep soon, but I wanted you to see her and how quickly we can break people. Physically, she's still fine, although I can't guarantee that will remain the case. From your training, you must know how carried away some interrogators can become." Ben heard him laugh, but before he could say a word, the voice continued. "I'll get back to you with more pictures after she has rested, and we can talk then."

"Wait! Don't hang up!" Ben shouted into the phone, but it was too late.

He turned to the others. "Some wacko has my wife and is using torture tactics on her for some reason. Why? There's nothing she knows that's secret. She's the sheriff of a county with ten thousand residents, for crying out loud. What can they possibly want from her?" Ben's questions went unanswered, but Jackie broke his lament.

"First, we have to get a triangulation to locate from where these calls are originating. In the elapsed time from when we think she was picked up until the first picture was taken, she could have been transported miles from here, even to a Range town." She was referring to Iron Range towns like Hibbing, Virginia, or Eveleth. "Obviously, you'll be getting another call. We'll be working on triangulation until then."

*****

DEIDRE HAD LAIN in the corner for what seemed like only minutes when the rough hands grabbed her and pulled her to her feet. This time she could stand, but when she attempted to walk, her legs didn't cooperate. She felt pressure on her back, pushing her forward, and she moved with shuffling steps in the direction she was being guided. Through swollen eyes, the chair came into focus, and she made out the silhouette of the powerful lamp. Her body was pushed so she was seated in the all-too-familiar chair, and the ties were placed around her legs again.

When the light was turned on, the heat was intense, and in her delirium, Deidre remembered a biology class she had taken in college. They had gone to a plant-growing lab that had high intensity lights to mimic the strength of the sun on the equator at noon. The heat had been unbearable, and now, she felt as though she was a specimen under one of those lights. In seconds, she was in agony.

"Well," the familiar voice said, "Here we are again. Are you warm enough?" Deidre didn't raise her head, and the speaker hadn't really expected an answer. Her mouth was so dry it felt as though it was filled with sand, and her tongue stuck to the roof of her mouth. She hadn't had a drop to drink since supper, and she had no idea how long ago that had been. Deidre sat in silence for an eternity—in actuality, fifteen minutes. "Would you like to see a bottle of water?" the voice asked. From behind the glare, she saw an arm reach out and watched through her blurred vision as a bottle was set on the floor in front of her. The moisture in the air condensed on the outside of the cold plastic and collected in a ring at the bottom. Deidre would have given anything to have been able to lick it off the container. Another eternity of silence ensued before the voice spoke.

"I'm going to place a call to your husband and then hand your phone to you. Here is what you will say to him: 'I'm doing okay, but there is no chance for me to escape. I haven't had anything to drink since I got here, and I'm so thirsty. Can you come save me?' Can you remember that?"

Deidre's mind was as blurred as her vision, but she nodded, trying to remember the words she had been instructed to recite.

Chapter
Thirty-Seven

At four in the morning, Ben's phone's message alert signal went off, and his heart missed a beat when he saw the caller ID—Deidre. He opened the message app and immediately a series of pictures materialized. In the first, Deidre was in a fetal position crammed into a corner. She had no blanket, and Ben could see the urine stains on her pants. She appeared to be sleeping. In the next frame she was attempting to stand, and it was obvious she wasn't succeeding very well. He scrolled to the next. Again, his wife was strapped to a chair. The time on the picture was 2:45 A.M. Another picture, taken only a few minutes later, showed Deidre staring at a water bottle sitting on the floor in front of her. The condensation on the bottle could clearly be seen. Finally, the in the last photo, Deidre was slumped in her chair, her eyes glazed, the bottle still on the floor, but now, the condensation had evaporated as its contents warmed to room temperature. Ben squinted at the time signature, 4:00 A.M. The photo had been taken only minutes before.

He hit the recall button on his phone and stared at the home screen. While he was still holding the phone, it rang—Deidre. "Deidre. Where are you?" he blurted out.

A long moment of silence ensued, during which he thought he could hear the phone being passed from one person to the next. "Listen to me, darling." It was Deidre, but Ben could hardly recognize her cracked, hoarse whisper. "I'm doing okay, but there is no chance for escape. I haven't had anything to drink since I got here, and I'm so thirsty." The next words Ben heard were almost shouted, spit out in rapid fire. "Don't come here! It's a trap! Stay away!" Ben could hear a scuffle, and then the phone went dead.

*****

ALMOST BEFORE DEIDRE got the warning out, a larger-than-life figure emerged from behind the light, and with one quick step, he stood in front of Deidre. Because of the intense backlighting, he appeared as a silhouette; Deidre had yet been able to see her assailants. With one swipe he grabbed the phone from her, and with the other hand, he slapped her across her face, splitting her lip. The figure moved behind the light, and the room was silent for another eternity. Finally, the voice spoke. "That was a stupid thing to do. Now, you are both thirsty and bleeding. What do you think your husband will say when he sees this picture?" For the first time it dawned on her that they had been sending pictures of her to Ben.

"What do you want from me?" Deidre croaked from her dry throat and swollen lips. "Either way, you're going to kill me. I know that. Why should I ever cooperate with you?"

The voice responded. "Cooperate? Why, you *are* cooperating. At least, we are helping you to cooperate. You aren't aware that this is the beginning of a war. Within weeks, this scenario will be carried out in thousands of communities across the nation. We are in the process of restoring this nation to what the founding fathers had in mind. Jews will be taken care of. Blacks will be harnessed as they were meant to be, and society will be cleansed of perverts. Churches that do not preach the true word of the Bible will be eliminated, and our nation will once again be the ruler of the world. By *allowing* us to use you, you are doing your part to restore our country to its roots." He chuckled. "Everyone will have to make some sacrifices, some more than others."

A shiver went up Deidre's spine as she realized she was being held by an ultra-rightwing militia, and that she was viewed as an expendable pawn. She decided she would do nothing from that time on that could be used for their purpose. She vowed to not say another word, no matter what. Considering her situation, she knew she had no options. She heard the ring tone of her cell phone. Whether intentionally or not, her captors had made it possible for Ben to call them. Deidre heard a one-sided conversation.

"No, we will not let her go . . . Yes, we are mistreating her . . . We want you to come and rescue her. That's what the FBI is good at, isn't it? Rescuing people? Or do you spend all of your time spying on decent, law-abiding citizens? If you want your wife, come and get her. And while you're at it, why don't you come confiscate our guns at the same time? . . . Where am I? Come on, Ben. I know you have been triangulating our calls. Do you want me to stay on the line a little longer so you can find the exact location? It shouldn't be difficult for you with your connections."

Deidre heard a whispered conversation, but she couldn't make out the words. Then she heard, "Turn off the light and give her some water. We don't want her dying before they decide to come." To her relief, the light went almost black—she could see a lingering glow at its center—and a trim man in fatigues handed her a bottle of water. She gulped it down, some running down the front of her shirt, some spilling on the floor, most going down her throat. In seconds her stomach revolted and she threw up.

"Here's another. Sip it this time!" he commanded, and she did as she was told. He cut the ties on her legs and for a second time that night, Deidre was led to the corner and shoved into it.

*****

BEN COULDN'T BELIEVE his ears as he heard Deidre's warning, and he stared at the phone as though it were a bomb. His urge was to throw it against the wall, but he gained control of his emotions and resisted the impulse. Instead he dialed back Deidre's number. He was almost startled when a man's voice answered. The deputies and Jackie stood silently by, listening to the one-sided conversation.

"Let my wife go . . . You're mistreating her. Let her go! . . . Where are you? Tell me so I can find you! . . . Damn it! Don't hang up!" Ben went back to staring at the phone.

Jackie had spread a map out on the dining table, and she was busy with a straight edge, drawing lines. She hunched her left shoulder, holding her cell phone to her ear to free both hands. As the person on the other end of the call spoke, she changed the position of the straight edge and continued marking the maps. Ben heard her say, "Uh-huh, uh-huh. Okay, got it. Thanks," and she hung up.

Jackie looked at her work. "That was a Verizon rep. I had cleared with them the possibility that we would need to trace a call, and they were very cooperative. Those three initials, FBI, open a lot of doors. Ben, you're not going to believe this. The calls you received were sent from a mile and a quarter from here." She spun the map so it faced him and pointed at a spot. "She's being held here."

Ben was dumbfounded. Jackie was pointing to a site on the property adjacent to theirs, the large tract of land that had once been owned by a paper company. He sat down, shaking his head. "I don't understand. That's just wild land. Nobody lives on it. In fact, it didn't even have a road into it until two years ago, and the road has seldom been used. We've never seen anyone drive in or out. Once in a while there would be tire tracks, but I never gave it a second thought." He paused for a moment. "My God, who's living back there?" He stared at the floor, still holding the dead phone in both hands.

"That's what we need to know," Jackie said, stating the obvious. "I'm calling for a helicopter flyover. Maybe they can take some pictures, and we can decide what to do next."

Before he could respond, the phone signaled another incoming message. Ben opened it to another photo. It was Deidre, still bound to the chair, but now, he could plainly see a trickle of blood running down her chin. She appeared to have lost consciousness. His heart beat wildly, and he clenched his fist in desperation.

Chapter
Thirty-Eight

Ben sat down and looked at the map spread before him on the table. "I think it would be a mistake to come in with copters for a fly-over of wherever they have Deidre. It would be showing them that we're biting the bait they've set before us, and I'm afraid it would only exacerbate her situation. There's a reason they're showing so many of their cards to us. He told me to come confiscate their weapons, and I think they want us to show up so they can demonstrate their firepower. Jackie, I'll follow your lead if you have a better idea, but I think I should go to that location," he pointed at the map, "on foot to see what we're up against. If I can pull it off, we'll gain the advantage of knowing their position without them being aware that we have them in our sights." He looked at her with a plea on his face.

Jackie looked at the map. From where they stood to where the calls originated was a half-hour walk if the surface was level. She knew it wasn't. It would take Ben a good hour to traverse the distance. Considering that his steps would be cautious and his approach watchful, she guessed more like two hours.

"Do you know that country?" she wanted to know. Ben stood up and paced the room.

"Jackie, I was raised only two miles from here. No, I've never been on this particular tract of land, but I grew up exploring the Knife River. I grew up hunting in these woods. I trapped along the river and camped out too many nights to count. If I'm anything, I'm a guy who knows the woods. If anyone is going to reconnoiter these people, I think I'm the best bet. Say the word, and I'm gone."

"Go for it," was all she said.

Ben made a quick trip to the shed where his camping gear was stored. He grabbed a compass from one drawer, pulled on a pair of well-worn boots, and donned his lightweight camo jacket. The last thing Ben put in his jacket pocket was a compact pair of binoculars. He stopped back at the house and tromped upstairs into their bedroom. His service handgun was in the top drawer of the bureau. Ben inserted the ammunition clip into the gun's magazine. He'd wait to chamber a round until he was outside.

Heading back downstairs, Ben suddenly became aware that he had totally neglected the needs of his daughters who were curled together on the couch in the living room, holding each other. They were asleep in that uncomfortable position, and Ben's heart broke when he saw them. Gently shaking their shoulders, he woke the girls, and when their eyes opened, he could tell they had fallen asleep while they were crying. Ben cradled his daughters in his arms and rocked them back and forth.

"Oh girls, girls. I'm so sorry. I've been so wrapped up in myself that I totally forgot you." He squeezed them tighter. "It's going to be okay. I'm leaving for a short time. We know where Mom is and that she's still okay. When I get back, we'll have some answers, I think. I'll be gone about three hours, maybe a little longer. Right now, I want you to get on your cell phone and call Pastor Ike. Explain to him that I asked you to call, and that I'd like him to come to the house to be with you. Can you do that?" They nodded as Ben stood to leave. He walked through the kitchen toward the back door.

"Take it slow," Jackie warned, and clapped him on the shoulder as he walked past her. "You got your cell phone with my number set on your speed dial?" Ben nodded once and started down the path on a trot. The sky in the east was turning pink. It would be totally light in a half-hour.

When he reached the picnic spot, he slowed to a walk and took a deep breath to get his emotions under control, found a place where he could step from rock to rock, and crossed the river without getting wet. On the other side he followed the bank for a few steps to the place where he thought the captors might have crossed with Deidre. Without having to really look, he spotted a branch that hung loose, broken off from the main stem of a shrub. Under it, he saw the imprint of the heel of a boot pressed into the moist soil. It was a large boot.

Ben stopped for a second to get his bearings. He looked at his compass and turned to face the direction he calculated would intersect with the origin of the phone calls. Then he remembered he had his cell phone in his pocket, took it out, and set it on airplane mode. He didn't want it even vibrating and giving away his position. He moved a few feet and found another broken branch. He knew he was going in the right direction. For the next half-hour he worked his way through the brush in this manner, finding a scuff mark on the ground here, a crushed fern there, and then another broken branch. Between his compass and the signs left by whoever had grabbed his wife, he could follow the trail, but the going was slow.

Two hundred yards in from the river, the alder brush and high bush cranberry bushes thinned, and the terrain became higher. Ben found himself on a ridge forested by paper birch interspersed with an occasional balsam fir. An almost invisible trail ran along the crest. He was accustomed to seeing these trails, most of them routes animals such as white-tailed deer followed, especially during the autumn and early winter. He hoped Deidre's abductors had taken this easy route. According to his compass, he was headed in the direction pinpointed by Jackie's triangulation. Ben had walked only a few hundred feet when he spotted a stem of hazelnut brush broken off about three feet above the ground.

For a second he stopped, looked closely at the jagged end of the break, and decided it was fresh. The inner bark was still green, and the loose end of the shrub was still supple. Ben was sure he was on the right path and that the trail would lead him to Deidre.

Now he had to fight the impulse to hurry, and the thought crossed his mind that the trail might be booby trapped. He kept a constant pace for another twenty minutes, and once, when the early morning breeze picked up for an instant, he thought he heard voices in the distance. Then the breeze died and so did the voices.

He hadn't seen a sign of anyone having used the trail since the broken hazelnut bush, and doubts began to rise in Ben's mind. Ahead, beside the trail, he spotted a crushed bracken fern frond, and he stopped to look more closely. Then, further off the trail he saw another. It wasn't obvious among the standing fronds, but as he studied it, he was sure whoever had taken his wife had made a detour.

Ben dropped his hat on the trail at that spot so he could return to it and slowly moved ahead on the path, his eyes scanning the ground and forest ahead of him. He had gone only a few yards when he spotted what looked like a place where the ground had been disturbed. It looked as though the dried leaves and duff of the forest floor had been scraped aside and then replaced to hide something. He got on his hands and knees and carefully lifted a leaf off the top, then another. One leaf, one twig at a time he carefully worked his way down until eventually he saw a piece of metal protruding upward. He had dug far enough. It was a landmine, armed, he was sure. Cautiously, he backed away, returned to where he had left his hat, and took the same detour Deidre's captor had taken. Ben located and noted a landmark so if he returned in a hurry, he wouldn't stumble on the mine.

It wasn't difficult to follow the route they had used, because it was impossible for them to walk off the trail without leaving signs: a piece of dislodged moss, a crushed fern, a broken twig. The signs led him around the spot where the mine had been set and back to the trail. He deliberately slowed his pace to a crawl and unconsciously walked slouched over. He plainly heard a voice, couldn't make out what was said, but knew it was human. He stopped in his tracks and knelt on the ground, his ear turned toward where he thought the sound originated. The voice spoke again, and again it was unintelligible. Ben thought he could make out three separate voices but he wasn't sure.

He was almost positive the trail would lead straight into their camp, and wondered if it didn't appear to be a little more used. Then again, he wondered if it was his imagination.

If this is a way to their camp, I would think they'd have someone guarding it, Ben thought, *and if they do, I'd be walking right into their trap. That's what Deidre said, 'It's a trap.' But from what direction should I approach them?* He had an idea.

The ridges in Lake County were left by glaciers thousands of years ago, and they tended to run parallel to each other. Between the ridges of glacial till lay lowlands with a rill running their length. It's wet land, most often covered with the rotting trunks of fallen trees, and everything is moss-covered. The areas between the ridges are brush-choked and difficult to navigate. *I doubt if they expect anyone to blunder onto them by coming through the lowland. I'd be surprised if that possibility is even on their radar,* he thought as he mulled over the situation.

Ever so slowly Ben moved laterally from the trail, being careful not to leave a trail of disrupted vegetation behind. It took him several minutes to reach the stream running parallel to the ridge he had left. Ben followed it and knew he was getting close. He managed to snake his way under a dead cedar that had tipped so that it almost touched the ground, skirt around a huge erratic boulder left by a glacier, and climb over the bare trunk of a fallen ash tree. He was feeling confident and became careless. A dead limb of a towering white spruce snagged his coat sleeve, and the tinder-dry wood splintered with a sound as loud as a gunshot. Ben froze in his tracks, then sank to a crouch behind a pine stump left by loggers a century ago. He stayed in that position for ten minutes, sure he would hear someone coming to investigate. No one came.

He slowly crept forward, acutely aware that one mistake might be fatal and forced himself to slow his progress, continually checking to be sure no dead wood was in his way. The distant voices became clearer, and he could make out individual words: army, caliber, surprise, war. Ben slowed his rate of advance even more. In fifteen minutes he knew he was in the low area below and behind where Deidre was being held. He crawled to higher ground, then got down on his belly and snaked to the edge of a clearing. Before he could stop himself, he gasped.

In front of him were five buildings, one long and narrow with windows spaced every ten feet near the eaves. It reminded Ben of pictures of army barracks he had seen. The buildings were grouped around what looked like a parade ground, in the center of which was a flag pole with a banner fluttering in the breeze. Ben didn't recognize the insignia. Another building appeared to be an office cluster. He couldn't put a finger on why he thought that, but it was his first impression. The third building had a number of vents protruding through the roof, and he could see steam emanating from two of them. He thought he detected the smell of fried food and assumed that structure was a kitchen and mess hall. The fourth structure was smaller, seemingly out of place with the others. It had no windows and only one door. *My God,* Ben thought, *Deidre's in there.* He wanted to run to her but knew it would be suicide. He shifted his attention to the fifth building and decided it was a bunker, probably where they kept explosives and ammunition.

He struggled to get his binoculars out of his jacket pocket, and put them to his eyes. After adjusting the lenses into focus, he began to scan the camp. Where the road entered—he assumed it was the same road he and Deidre had wondered about on their walks—two guards were stationed, and he focused on them. Ben recognized the arms they carried, Barrett REC7 assault rifles. Sweat formed on his forehead as the picture became clearer. Without a doubt, he was on a recon mission for what was to come.

Ben kicked himself for rushing off from home. In his haste he had forgotten to bring a notebook, something that would have been more than valuable, because now he was forced to memorize everything. He counted four more groups of guards on station, and on the backside of the compound a guard tower stood about twenty-five feet above the ground. He identified two guards up there, possibly three, but he couldn't be sure. Lounging on the parade ground were another dozen men, all dressed in uniforms with insignia on their sleeves. That made twenty-four soldiers—he didn't know what else to call them—who were visible.

He assumed there were more, probably another group of twelve who had stood guard through the night. It appeared that no one in particular was in charge, and Ben thought there must have been at least another half-dozen men who were acting officers, but where were they? Then, too, others must have been in the mess hall, maybe as many as a half-dozen more.

As he continued his surveillance, two man exited the building he had decided to call the prison. Their uniforms were different, and they had the bearing of superiority. Ben watched the men who were lounging jump to their feet and stand at attention when they passed. He knew he was right in his assumptions. He guessed the number in the group to be about fifty, give or take a few. At any rate, a formidable number.

He took one more look through his binoculars at what he knew in his heart to be Deidre's prison and slowly backed down to the low ground. Tears welled in his eyes, and he said a silent prayer for her as he made his way back from where he had come. He'd be back. And he prayed, *Please God, don't let us be too late.*

Ben's journey back to his house went much faster. Once he cleared the area of the land mine, he broke into a dogtrot, concentrating on his footing and not much feeling the brush that swatted him in the face as he pushed through it or the bite of deer flies that burrowed into the fringe of hair that escaped from under his cap. It was eleven o'clock when he slammed his way into his kitchen, gasping for breath as he rested his hands on his knees.

Chapter
Thirty-Nine

"I FOUND THE PLACE," Ben managed to get out while he sucked air. "They have a military outpost set up about a mile or so from here. "Get me a paper and pen so I can sketch things out. Then we have to decide what we're going to do."

Megan and Maren were standing in the doorway between the kitchen and the dining room, their eyes wide open and filled with concern. "I'll get the paper," Megan volunteered and spun on her heels. Maren could only stand and gape at her father. Ben remembered that he had put his cell phone on airplane mode and that he wouldn't have received any messages since then. He entered his code, touched the settings icon, and removed the lock symbol. Immediately, a number of messages were downloaded. In the first, Deidre was again bound to the chair, and she looked worse than before. She had dried blood on her lip and chin. Her head hung so her chin rested on her chest, and Ben could see that she was so weak she could barely sit up. In the next frame, a rope had been tied around her neck and pulled taut overhead, forcing her to sit up straight in the chair to avoid being strangled by the noose. Ben felt a sense of panic and rage, but there was nothing he could do. The last picture showed her drinking from a water bottle. Her eyes were closed and her head was tilted back. A rope burn was visible around her neck, and it was obvious her torture was escalating.

A voice message had been left, and when Ben opened it, he discovered it was the same man's voice from before. "Hello, Agent VanGotten. Your wife is quite photogenic, don't you think? Well, the next move is yours. If you don't make a move soon, her condition is sure to worsen. I guess we could say, only you can save her." The message ended.

Before anyone could stop him, Ben hit redial on his cell, and the call was picked up after the third ring. "Hello, Ben. Glad you called back. I thought for a while that you had abandoned your darling little wife. She is a looker, isn't she?" Ben lost it.

"You SOB, if your lay another finger on her, I'm going to tear your arms off when I get to you. We know where you are and how many of you there are. Damn it! We'll be there, so be ready!" Jackie grabbed the phone from his hand and turned it off. Ben realized he had given the enemy information he shouldn't have. Now they knew they had been observed and would increase their border security. "Sorry," he said and hung his head, then he began to sob. "We can't just leave her there." He looked into the faces of the officers gathered around him. One of the deputies put his hand on Ben's shoulder but had no words.

Jackie was the first to respond. "Ben, here's the paper you asked for. Begin by showing us what you saw." He began to make a rough sketch of the compound, along with his estimates of size and distance.

"I'm guessing she's being kept here," he said, pointing at the square on the paper representing the windowless building. Ben continued. "I counted about thirty people I could see, but estimate there might be around fifty. The guards I saw were all equipped with Barrett REC7s, but that's not the worst of it. On either side of the compound were redoubts housing what looked like Browning fifty-caliber machine guns. They're set for war." He shook his head in resignation.

Jackie took him by the shoulders and gave him a jerk. "Don't you give up. We haven't started to fight back, and we will. Keep your head up, and trust us. You and Deidre aren't alone by a damn sight. Just sit tight for a couple of minutes. I've got two calls to make." She stomped out the door, and Ben saw her pacing in the yard, her cell phone to her ear. In a few minutes she returned.

"I just called our boss," she said, looking Ben square in his eyes. "He's organizing a SWAT team as we speak, should be here in two hours. He said to notify the state troopers and have them bring their armored vehicle as soon as they can. Right now it's at headquarters in St. Cloud. I called and they're on their way. Should take them under three hours to make the trip, because I doubt if they'll follow the speed limit. While I was making that call, he was on the phone to the governor and will be calling back with good news, I'm expecting." Jackie had just uttered those words when her phone beeped. She put it to her ear.

"Yes, sir!" they heard her say. "Yes, sir. . . . We'll be ready . . . Yes, we can use his house for a command post . . . Yes, sir." Jackie took the phone down from her ear. "The governor has activated a unit of the National Guard out of Duluth. He talked to the commander, who's in the process of mobilizing his men. The governor will be here in four hours so he will be available to make instant decisions." She looked at Ben. "Keep the faith. We'll do all we can. Why don't you go talk to your daughters? Your pastor visited them until a few minutes ago, but he had a funeral to attend and had to leave. The girls just went back to their room. Go be with them. There's not much we can do until the big guns get here and we make a plan, but be ready if the group sends another message to you about Deidre. We don't want to miss it if they do."

Ben forced himself to climb the stairs and as he walked down the hall past his and Deidre's bedroom, he was blindsided by a whiff of her perfume. All of his emotions erupted to the surface, and he turned to the source of the smell, sat down on the bed, and buried his face in his wife's pillow. Silently, he wept until he couldn't weep any more. Then he made his way to the girls' room.

Megan was sitting in the window bay, staring off across the neighbor's hayfield. Maren was lying on her bed, earphones on, listening to some song. Her eyes were closed, but Ben knew she wasn't sleeping. He touched her foot. "Girls. Can we talk?" Without a word, Maren removed her headset, and Megan came to sit beside him on the bed. "Mom's in big trouble," he began. "I won't lie to you. She's being psychologically tortured, but not brutalized, at least we don't think so. I'll be honest with you, her treatment could escalate to something more brutal. As of right now, the National Guard has been called to help us. The FBI is sending a SWAT team, and the state troopers will be here. Mom's deputies are here in full force, and we have reinforcements on the way. Even the governor is coming." He forced a smile. "Get cleaned up. The TV cameras won't be far behind."

"Oh, Dad. How can you try to make a joke right now? We're so worried. Nothing matters but getting Mom home safely." Megan scolded.

Ben looked at his daughters, and he couldn't help but notice how grown up they were becoming. "Right now, all I can do is believe this is going to turn out okay." He closed his arms tighter around them and held on. "It's going to work out. It has to. I bet neither of you have eaten anything today. Come on down and we'll grab something from the fridge. Reinforcements will be here by evening, and we don't know what we'll be doing then."

Maren laid her head on her dad's shoulder. "Do you think . . . do you think, you know. Do you think they're . . ." She was groping for words, and Ben thought he knew what she was thinking. He finished her sentence. ". . . sexually abusing her? There's nothing in the photos that make me believe that." He thought, *At least I hope to God they're not.* "Come on, girls, let's all go downstairs. It will be better to keep busy, and we can use a couple of gofers."

Three abreast, they squeezed their way down the stairway without falling, and were greeted by everyone in the kitchen. His phone signaled an incoming text message.

Ben's fingers almost froze as he fumbled with the buttons, but eventually he pressed the right ones and the message opened. It was a video sent via text, and he hurriedly clicked on it. It was a recording of Deidre. She was having a difficult time holding her head up, but Ben noted that the blood had been washed off her face. Through her chapped lips she began to speak, and Ben saw thick spittle begin to form in the corners of her mouth.

"Ben. As you can see, they're keeping me alive. The heat lamp is brutal, but I'm making it. When are you going to rescue me? I can't hold out much longer." Ben saw a flicker of fire in her eyes and her head came up. She shouted as best she could through her dry lips. "Don't come! It's a trap!" From out of nowhere a hand swept into the picture, and Ben heard a resounding slap as Deidre's head jerked to one side, and Ben saw her topple from the chair.

Chapter
Forty

Half-dazed from what she had endured, Deidre calculated she'd been held for at least sixteen hours, and her estimate was not far off. Of those sixteen hours, twelve had been spent strapped to a chair under the blaze of the heat lamp, and her face felt as though it were on fire. She knew she had suffered burns as serious as if she'd fallen asleep on a beach while sunbathing. Her lips were dry and cracked, and when she ran her tongue over them, she could detect the salty, metallic taste of blood. She gently touched one side of her face and winced as pain shot up her cheek, and she could feel its puffiness with her finger tips. They had shoved her into her corner again, and she brought her knees up to her chest so she could rest her forehead on them. She wrapped her arms around her legs, curling into a defensive position, trying to block out all that was around her, and drifted off into a confused half-sleep, half-stupor.

It seemed as though she had momentarily closed her eyes when one of the uniformed men kicked her shoe. She instantly jolted awake, confused, wondering where she was. Then reality set in. She was dragged to the chair which she had begun to hate, fear, and accept, all at the same time. There was no wondering what would come next. The pattern was set, and true to form, seconds after she was bound, the light came on. She closed her eyes and dropped her chin to her chest in an attempt to shield herself from the intense rays.

This time, somebody stepped forward but off to the side, and she could see that whoever it was, they were taking a picture of her. It registered in her fuzzy mind that they were using her cell phone. He came a step closer. "We're going to make a video using your phone, and this time I want you stick to what I tell you to say. Tell him, 'As you can see, they're keeping me alive. The heat lamp is brutal, but I'm making it. When are you going to rescue me? I can't hold out much longer. Please come soon. The captain says he wants to talk with you to negotiate a deal with the FBI. All they want is to be heard. Then we can go home together.' Can you remember that?" Deidre nodded. "Good, let's try a rehearsal." She nodded again and tried to recite his message word for word but only got most of it right. "That's okay. You got most of it."

She saw him fiddle with the phone and signal her to begin. Deidre heard herself talking as though she were eavesdropping on a conversation. "Ben, as you can see, they're keeping me alive. The heat lamp is brutal, but I'm making it. When are you going to rescue me? I can't hold out much longer." Captain Blake stood a little off to the side, a smirk of victory on his face. Suddenly, Deidre went off-script. "Don't come! It's a trap!"

The captain thought they had broken her, but he was wrong. He drew his hand back and swung with all his might, hitting her square in the face, and Deidre was knocked off the chair. She lay in a heap on the floor, unable to gather enough strength to get up.

"Stupid!" the captain screamed. "When are you going to learn that you have no way out unless we decide to let you go? That's the last time you'll get to hear Ben's voice. From now on, he'll see your pictures, but I'll do the talking. Do you have any idea what you look like? No, of course not. You don't have a mirror. You're a mess, and with every hour that goes by, you look worse." He ordered the light shut off and sat down on the chair that was Deidre's torment. She lay in a crumpled pile at his feet.

"I'm sure your husband has gathered some officials who will try to decide what to do. They're probably wondering what they're up against, and I've expected a surveillance copter or plane to fly over. If not that, I've expected someone to reconnoiter our position on foot. The lieutenant who carried you to our outpost left a faint trail that could be followed. He even planted a fake landmine to make it look as though we didn't want anyone observing our position. You see, we *want* them to know what we have. You're right, this is a trap, but not for Ben. We fully expect that when word gets out about the land mine, about our armament, about our defense, the National Guard will be called in, and when that happens, the war for the salvation of the United States will have begun."

Deidre was hardly cognizant of the captain's words. Her head throbbed with each beat of her heart, her face felt like a balloon that was ready to burst, and her thirst was becoming unbearable. The captain reached behind him, and she heard the lid of the cooler open. She expected him to taunt her with cold water, but instead, he unscrewed the cap and handed the bottle to her. She controlled the urge to chug it down and sipped a mouthful at a time. The captain continued his monologue.

"There are countless groups like ours scattered across the United States. Most of them are stationed in remote area, like this, but a few are set up in cities, right under the officials' noses. Of course, as of yet, the groups are loosely connected, but some of us have a vision of strengthening those connections, forming a web of fighters from coast to coast. We have plans." The captain looked at Deidre and realized she had drifted off to her own world. He thought it interesting how the human brain could shut down to avoid unpleasant events.

She didn't know how much later it was, but Deidre woke to find herself in the corner. Someone had thrown a blanket over her, and when she tried to move, she ached all over. Rough hands grabbed her underarms and she was hauled to the chair, and she wondered if she could stand another round of the heat. She waited with terror wracking her mind for the inevitable, but it didn't happen. She saw she was being photographed, and then was pulled back to her corner, where she was dropped. Deidre pulled the blanket over herself, covering her head, and lay on the bare floorboards, shivering, although the room was warm.

Chapter
Forty-One

Ben was wracked with waves of alternating anger and total despair, and he paced the floor. Once, he stopped by the window that looked out over the garden that Deidre loved. Late summer flowers bloomed, dahlias and cone flowers, behind them a crop of hollyhocks flanked by sunflowers. He choked back a sob and turned away from the scene. His throat constricted so he could barely swallow, and he stumbled on the way back to the table. A topo map was spread out on top of the county map on which they had first located the coordinates of the camp. Now he knew where it was, knew where his wife was suffering, knew what they were up against, and his heart sank. To him, the situation looked hopeless, especially because they had no idea what motivated the group holding her.

If they were out to simply kill a sheriff, she would be dead by now. On the other hand, if they were seeking information, she had none to give them. To Ben, her abduction made no sense, and he wondered with what kind of radical bunch they were dealing. He made a trip upstairs and looked in on his daughters. They were on their beds, sleeping, and he smiled. Ben remembered back to when his father had suffered a heart attack and he had curled up on the hospital waiting room couch and fallen asleep. To him, sleep was the great escape. Like father, like daughters.

Quietly, he closed the door and slipped back downstairs. On the way down, the thought struck him that when the Guard arrived, along with the FBI SWAT team, he would want to go with them. But there was no way he could leave the girls alone. Ben was at a total loss for who to call. Jeff's wife, Danielle, had trouble enough of her own to be bothered. He couldn't ask her to come and relive the night Jeff was shot. Without warning, Inga popped into his head. It took him one try to reach her.

"Inga, this is Ben, Deidre's husband. Inga, we've got some big trouble here, and I need your help. Is it possible that you could take time to be with our daughters, and would it be asking too much to have you drive out and spend the night with them?" For an instant his gut relaxed when Deidre's dear friend said she'd be there in twenty minutes, and he was thankful she didn't ask for an explanation. Ben didn't know how urgent his voice had sounded.

While the other officers were busying themselves as they waited, Ben sat at the table, reworking in his mind what he had seen of the camp. He had no idea how they would ever be able to storm the place and rescue Deidre. His contemplation was jarred by his phone's tone, another text message coming in, and he opened it. It was another picture, along with a text. Ben's hands trembled and he lost the battle as he tried to fight back tears. Deidre was sitting in the usual chair, but this time the bright light was turned off. It didn't matter; she looked totally defeated. The result of the blow he had seen delivered on the video was clearly evident. Her lip was swollen, but now to match that injury, her left eye was swollen shut and beginning to turn purple. Across the side of her face, he could make out the raised imprint where the four fingers of someone's hand had struck. She could barely keep her head up, and the life spark had totally left her one visible eye. He groaned so loudly, two of the deputies and Jackie rushed in to see what had happened.

"Look at the picture and then look at the text. When are we going to do something?" The three officers crowded together, jockeying for position so they could see the screen of the phone.

One of them read the text out loud. "'Time is running out,'" the officer intoned. "'Come get your wife before it's too late. Realize, we are in a state of war, and I can't guarantee her safety forever.'"

"We've got to get moving, quick." Jackie said, and then, by the expression on her face, the others could see she had an idea. "They've been telling us to come and get her. It's a challenge, a taunt, and I think things are going to continue to escalate until they get a message that we've accepted the challenge. The longer we wait to respond, the more they are going to up the ante with Deidre. I think Ben should send a text back simply stating that we're coming. Perhaps they'll lay off her if they know they've accomplished what they want." A rigorous argument ensued, some agreeing with Jackie, others being hesitant. Finally, Ben spoke.

"I'm not sending that message. If they think they have us on the way, what's to stop them from killing her? We have to maintain what little leverage we have." Jackie gave up the argument and Ben stepped outside.

He checked the time on his phone. Almost four o'clock. Ben chafed at how slowly time was passing. He wished all the units that had been called out were on hand, working on a plan, getting prepared to move. While he was standing on the porch, Inga pulled into the driveway and hurried out of her car. Ben was surprised how nimble she was and how quickly she walked across the yard.

"Ben, what's happened? Are the girls okay? Deidre?" She looked at Ben's lined face and knew whatever it was, it wasn't good.

"It's Deidre," he said, putting his arm around Inga's shoulders and guiding her into the living room. "She's been kidnapped by a militia, and they're holding her in a camp back in the woods. We don't really know what they want yet, other than they keep taunting us to come and get her." He choked up, and Inga held his hand. When he could speak again, he asked, "Will you stay with us, take care of the girls, while this mess plays out? They need somebody with them, and I can't be right now. You're the best person I know for the job."

Inga patted his hand. "Are they upstairs in their room?" she asked, and started to move to the stairs before he responded. Ben nodded, but it was to her back. She was halfway to the top of the stairs. As he was returning to the kitchen, a column of FBI vehicles pulled into his yard, including an armored vehicle. The sight of them brought hope. He recognized the director of the Duluth division, who stepped out of the last car to pull in and park, and Ben strode toward his boss.

"How you doin', Ben?" the director asked. "When the others get here, I've got some news that everyone will be interested in hearing. Until then, is there anything I can do to help? God, this must be a nightmare for you."

Ben toed the ground, then looked up. "Just knowing that things are beginning to materialize means a lot to me, sir. Come in and meet the others. You know Jackie, but there are a half-dozen deputies from Deidre's force who want to help. Don't cut them out is all I ask."

Together, they walked up the steps, but before they reached the door, the sound of a veritable convoy stopped them. They turned to see a line of drab-painted vehicles swing into the yard. Parking space was getting to be a problem, and Ben motioned them to drive into his neighbor's hayfield. A sergeant clamored out of the lead truck and began barking orders, and an organized chaos erupted. The leader of the group came to join Ben and the director, and Ben was dumbstruck to see he was wearing battle gear. Once inside, introductions were made, and the major, whose nametag read "Jensen," laid out a new set of maps that were far more detailed than those they had been using. He had just placed a red-headed pin on the locus of the camp when another ruckus sounded outside.

The governor's entourage drove in directly after the Guard, followed by a horde of media people. The place was becoming a circus, and something had to be done. At the present, no one was in charge, and Ben gave an order. "Deputies, would you guys go out and move those reporters back? Set up a perimeter, and tell them they'll be shot if they cross it, or something." Major Jensen agreed, and told them to forget the line about being shot but to tell them they'd suffer the consequences if they bucked the orders. *I'll figure out the consequences after the fact,* he thought.

Ben expected the governor to make a grand entrance, but instead the man calmly walked into the room and asked if it would be okay if he stayed to listen to what was being planned. Ben looked at him through new eyes, and the politician moved to a position out of the way but where he could see everything. Major Jensen offered a customary welcome and got back to looking at the map.

"One of you has been in there. Who was that?" he asked. Ben raised his hand and stepped forward, wondering what his role would be. Again, any communication was interrupted by a disturbance in the yard, and through the window, they saw another armored vehicle arrive, accompanied by three state trooper vehicles. All hands were on deck for what Ben visualized to be an all out assault, and he wondered what would happen to Deidre if that occurred.

The National Guard soldiers unpacked and began setting up large tent shelters. Ben could see the uniformed state troopers helping to carry gear into the first one erected, and he thought at that rate everything would be ready in an hour.

Chapter
Forty-Two

Deidre was awakened by a kick to the bottom of her shoe, and her good eye sprung open. The other remained swollen shut. She tried to move, but a stiffness like she had never experienced locked her muscles and joints. Rough hands grabbed her arms and lifted her to her feet. She tried to walk, but could only manage small, shuffling steps. The man with the rough hands steadied her as she was directed to the spot across the room where the chair sat. She slowly lowered herself to a sitting position.

"You look rested," Captain Blake said with a mock grin wrinkling his lips. "Not very presentable, but rested." He stepped toward Deidre and in one motion grabbed the front of her blouse with both hands. She heard the buttons pop off the front and felt the fabric tear. Instinctively, she brought her arms up to cover her near nakedness. Captain Blake motioned with his head, and two of his underlings stepped forward. Each grabbed one hand and stretched her arms out from her sides. She was held in that pilloried position while a revealing picture was taken. When they let loose of her hands, she pulled her blouse shut in front and covered herself, sure that worse was to come. The same soldier helped her back to the corner, and no one touched her again. She slithered down the wall until her butt contacted the floor, and she doubted if she would ever see her family again.

*****

The major had just started quizzing Ben about the recon he had done in the morning when Ben's phone came alive. He knew who it was and dreaded opening the text message. As soon as a new picture filled the screen, he sank onto a chair. "Damn them, no!" He repeated over and over again, "No, no, no! Not my wife!" Jackie pried the phone from his hands and gasped when she saw the picture.

Deidre looked as though she had been run through a gauntlet. One eye was completely swollen shut. Her hair was an absolute tangle, and it appeared that she had wet herself again. One side of her mouth was black and blue, her lips on that side swollen to twice their normal size. And now this. She was held in an exposed position while her picture had been taken, causing her humiliation. Jackie could see there had been physical harm done. She made a positive note: there was fire in Deidre's good eye.

"Ben, this looks bad, I know, but I don't think their sexual assault has gone any further than this. Did you look at Deidre's eye? She hasn't given up yet, and damn it, don't you either!" She grabbed Ben's shoulder and shook it. "We're going to begin formulating our plan. Now you can sit there in a heap, or you can join us. The choice is yours. No one would fault you if you backed off and let us take care of it."

Enraged, Ben stood to his full height and moved to the table without saying a word. Jackie saw the same look in his eyes that she had observed in Deidre's. Inwardly, she breathed a sigh of relief. The governor stepped forward at that point.

"FBI Director Benton has an announcement to make before we get down to the nuts and bolts of this operation. Director Benton."

The director stood up. "Since yesterday, there have been five reports from across the nation of incidents such as what we have going here today. In five different states, a law enforcement officer has been taken and tortured. The strange thing is that in each case, assailants made no attempt to disguise their actions. As a matter of fact, they taunted law enforcement to come after them. We think this is a pattern that will repeat itself in days to come. In two of the five cases, an assault was launched on the militia's compounds. Right now, they are in standoffs. The hostage in each is still alive, but the Guard has no way to rush the captors without putting him or her at risk. Here, Major Jensen will be in charge, but we will function as a team to try to end this episode with as little violence as possible, and we're going to try to end it quickly."

Director Benton stepped away and motioned for the major to take over, and Jensen stepped to the table where the map lay open. "This is the location of the camp." He pointed to the red pin protruding from the map. "Look at the contour lines that ring that spot. All of you know how to interpret a topo map, but I want to draw your attention to what we have here. The isolines form circles around the pin and because this region is relatively flat, each line represents a five-foot interval. In this case they're spaced relatively far apart, indicating it's a flat area approximately two hundred yards long by a hundred-fifty yards wide. Does that jive with what you observed, Agent VanGotten?"

"Pretty much, sir," Ben agreed. "With the exception that there were three hummocks that should show on this map, because I would estimate their height at about eight feet. If the contours show every five-foot change in elevation, but the mounds aren't on this map, that leads me to believe they're not natural but were pushed up after the map was made. As best as I can remember, they were located here, here, and here." Ben pointed out the three locations, and he mentally kicked himself again for having forgotten to take a notebook with on his recon mission.

Major Jensen thought about what Ben said. "Chances are what you saw are disguised bunkers. I think we might be walking into a well-designed field of enfilade fire. The three mounds roughly form a triangle, and I can easily visualize a squad being trapped in a crossfire. Because of the site selection, the layout of the buildings, and the probable redoubts, it looks as though we're facing an opponent who has been trained in setting up firebases, probably ex-military. I'd stake my rank on that. We're up against professionally trained people." He pondered his own words.

Director Benton broke the silence. "Well, Major, I'll follow your lead on the plan, but in my opinion we should think of taking full advantage of the lay of the land. My guess is, they're hoping we make an all-out attack from the road. Do you think we can follow these ridges and come in from the north and south, catch them in a pincer move?"

Ben watched to see what the major's response would be, and it gave him hope when he saw the man considering what Benton had proposed. "No." Jensen shook his head. "I think they would like us to consider what you said, come up the ridges. That's where they'll be lying in wait."

Ben thought this was shaping up to be like a page from a magazine he read when he was a kid. It was called "Spy vs. Spy," a good guy in white and a bad guy in black. Otherwise the spies were identical. They were always trying to figure out each other's moves. *If I do this, he'll do that, but he wants me to do that, so I'll do this, but he'll anticipate that I know he wants me to that, so I'll do what he thinks I was going to do in the first place.* He found himself caught in a maze of thoughts that circumscribed a circle. He was brought back to reality by the sound of his name.

"Ben, I asked you a question, You okay? You with us?" It was Jackie speaking. Ben looked up, embarrassed.

"I'm sorry. I haven't slept for almost thirty-six hours, except for a couple of catnaps before everyone got here. What did you ask?"

Jackie restated her question. "How wet are these low areas between the ridges?"

Ben was with her. "Pretty dry this time of the year. In the spring, after the thaw, they would be almost impossible to walk through, but we haven't had any significant rain for two weeks and they're dry, at least the one I went up. It was easy going, except for the brush. It gets pretty thick in those low areas."

Benton jumped into the conversation. "According to the map, every low area has a stream running the length of it. Any idea where they empty into?"

Ben had that answer. "They all drain into the Knife. This whole area is a watershed that eventually ends up in Lake Superior. Like the ridges, they run parallel to each other." It dawned on him that Jensen hadn't said much but was allowing everyone to contribute ideas. It was turning into a brainstorming session, and the major wasn't pulling rank, instead letting ideas flow. Without saying a word, he pulled another map out of his case and laid it next to the one they had been working off. He lined up the edges so the lines and stream markings matched. Together the two maps showed a complete picture of the land, that which Ben owned and the portion of the neighboring tract where the militia's compound was located.

Jensen took out a third map, this one showing the county road that ran past Ben's home. "I don't see any road or trail leading to the compound. Is it that recent?" he asked, looking at Ben. This time Ben was tracking what was going on.

"It is. I think it was put in two, maybe three years ago. We thought it was the beginning of a logging operation, but they never hauled anything out, and we more or less forgot about it. It starts here." He placed his finger on the new map. "That's all I know. The property is posted, and I never had a reason to trespass."

Chapter
Forty-Three

Major Jensen studied the map before them. "Get Chief Warrant Officer Eggart in here. I want him to take a look at this map." In a matter of seconds, the enlisted officer came running across the lawn and into the kitchen, which was now serving as headquarters.

"Yes, sir," he barked, and stood at attention. His commander put him at ease and asked a question.

"Look at this map. If you were laying out a road, beginning here," he jabbed his finger at the spot where Ben had said there was a gate, "where would it go?"

Eggart studied the contours for a minute. "Sir, may I draw on this?" The major nodded. Picking up a pencil, the warrant officer began to draw a fine line. "I'd follow this ridge to where it almost joins the one above it. That way I'd only have to fill in this short distance. If I took a sharp left on the next ridge, sort of hairpin back, I could connect with the third ridge at this narrow piece of lowland." He continued drawing a line, explaining his rationale as he drew on the map. When he finished, the trail he had delineated resembled a piece of ribbon candy that continually looped back on itself. There could be three miles of road to advance the mile to the back of the property and end at the red pin, the location of the militia's base.

Eggart looked at Major Jensen, oblivious to the others in the room. "That's my opinion, sir." He assumed his attention pose.

"That's all, Warrant Officer. Thank you. Resume what you were doing before I called you.

"Yes sir!" Eggart responded, turned on his heel and left the room. Major Jensen studied the map.

"It would be easy enough to do a flyover and get an aerial view of the road, but I don't want to do that for two reasons. One, I don't want them to know what we might be considering. Let them wonder what's going on. Two, we don't know what kind of armament they have. The black market is filled with everything from high caliber machine guns capable of bringing down light aircraft to shoulder-launched missiles that can track even jets. We're not ready for that kind of escalation—yet. We have to consider they have a hostage."

Inside, Ben froze. They weren't holding a hostage, they had his wife, the woman he loved, his children's mother, at least the only mother they really remembered. He caught the major's eye and saw a sudden recognition.

"I'm sorry, Agent VanGotten. I had forgotten your relationship to her. I got caught up in the logistics of this. Try to have faith that we're going to rescue her as quickly as we can. Here's what I want you to do. Every hour, on the hour, until we are ready to move, call and demand to speak with her. Not only will that keep her hope alive, it will also let her captors know that as long as she's alive, we won't bomb the hell out of them. I think they want to draw us into a firefight, so they can kill as many U.S. soldiers as they can before they go down. They intend for this to be a suicide mission for themselves, why I don't know, but they want to take as many of us with them in the battle."

Ben was torn by his emotions. On one hand he wanted to jump at the chance to talk to Deidre. But on the other hand, he feared what he would find out. He had no choice but to call, and with his heart beating wildly and hands shaking he hit the call icon next to her name on his phone's contact list. The phone rang so many times he expected it to go to voicemail. At the last minute it was answered by a man, the same voice he recognized from previous conversations.

"So, Ben, you're still there. How can I help you?" the captain asked as though this were a simple business call.

"I want to talk to my wife."

Captain Blake snickered. "She's sleeping right now. Do you want me to wake her?"

Ben lost his cool. "Listen, you miserable SOB, I want to talk to her now. Do you understand? Right now, and if I ever get my hands on you, I'm going to tear your head off and shove it where the sun don't shine."

He knew he had made a mistake and had shown his desperation. "Now, now, Ben. We both know that's physically impossible," the captain chided him. "There's no use getting testy about this. The answer to your problem is simple. We have your wife. You come and get her. That's all we want."

There was no more conversation, but Ben could tell Blake hadn't hung up. He could hear footsteps and other sounds in the background.

"Ben?" It was Deidre's voice, but he could hardly recognize it. She sounded unbelievably tired, and her voice cracked as she tried to speak. He couldn't get past the way she slurred her words.

"Deidre!" he shouted into the phone. "Deidre, don't give up. We're coming to get you. Do you hear me? We're going to get you out of this. I promise." The phone went dead in his hand, and Ben slumped into a chair, his jaw set and his eyes steely. Jackie came over and laid her hand on his bent back.

"We'll get her back. I promise." She walked away without saying another word. It took Ben more than a few seconds to pull himself together, and when he did, he returned to the kitchen.

"She sounds about in the same condition as the last photo we saw. What are the plans?"

*****

AFTER BEN'S CALL, Deidre was offered a half-cup of water, and her lips burned as it penetrated the cracked skin. She sipped it slowly, remembering what had happened the last time she gulped down her ration. She reeked of stale urine, but so far had resisted the urge to defecate. In her condition, it really wouldn't have mattered much, though. She was defeated, and the call had hardly registered. In her mind, there was no hope.

"They'll be coming for you soon. In a way, I hope your knight in shining armor gets his princess out. It will make for a nice story in the news. But," Captain Blake paused. "If not, I suppose that will get reported, too." He turned from her and walked away. Deidre pulled the blanket over herself and collapsed into a fitful sort of sleep. It had been almost twenty-four hours since her capture, but it seemed like an eternity.

*****

BEN COULDN'T REMEMBER his last real meal, and it dawned on him he hadn't eaten much in the past twenty-four hours. And the girls, what must they be doing? He had totally forgotten about them, and he rushed upstairs and opened their bedroom door without knocking. He was momentarily shocked to see Inga sitting on the edge of the bed, and then remembered he had called her to be with them. He took in the sight, and for a moment thought he would break down.

Inga had one of the girl's Bibles open on her lap, and she was reading to them. He recognized the Twenty-Third Psalm. Her calm voice had an almost mesmerizing effect, and he stood in his tracks, listening to the words. When she finished, Inga patted the bed beside her, indicating she wanted him to sit down. She took his hand and began to pray. When she finished, she closed the Bible and stood.

"The girls and I have done a lot of talking today, and we think it would be good if I took them to my place. They know you have too much on your mind right now to be able to worry about them. Can I take them with me for the night?"

Both girls came and sat with him, one on either side. They buried their faces on his shoulders, and Ben could feel their tears soak through his shirt. Megan looked up and then buried her face again, but Maren spoke.

"Dad, this must be killing you. We know how much you love Mom, and we don't want to get in the way of your doing what you have to do. Just promise us you'll be careful. How would we get along if we lost both of you? Inga will take good care of us, you know that. So, please, just take care of Mom." She buried her face, and Ben looked helplessly at Inga.

"You're a special person, Inga. I'll try to get word to you as soon as I can about our situation. I'm not sure right now what the plan will be." The girls packed their bags quickly, drying their tears, and together the four of them went downstairs. Ben watched Inga drive away with his precious daughters.

A field kitchen had been set up by the Guard, and Ben, realizing he was famished, ate for the first time since Deidre had been abducted.

Chapter
Forty-Four

Ben's spirits revived a little with food in his belly, and he paced back and forth on the porch while Major Jensen and the others in charge finished their meal. He knew they had to take care of their own physical needs or they'd be good for no one, but still, the minutes dragged and he became more restless with every sweep of the second hand on his watch. Finally, the group trooped back to HQ, his kitchen, and began planning in earnest. Ben discovered, to his relief, that Jensen was one of those people who processed while doing innate tasks, like eating.

"Okay, here's the way we're going to play this," the major announced. "My men are divided into fire teams of four, and each squad is going to follow a stream toward the compound. There are five ridges that, if followed, will come within a quarter-mile of our target. The men will follow the low ground between the ridges and approach from the southeast. Five ridges, six fire teams of four men each, that makes twenty-four men."

"Excuse me, Major," Director Benton broke in. "Wouldn't there be only four low area between the ridges?" The major looked at Benton as though he resented the interruption.

"There are five ridges, four low areas in between, and a low area on the flank of each outer ridge. That makes six low areas, twenty-four men." Benton nodded, feeling as though he had just been chastised. Ben felt uncomfortable for his boss and wondered if that would be the end of the FBI's input. Major Jensen continued.

"I'm going to send another six fire teams up the road and past the entrance, where they'll cut through the woods and locate the same five streams. They'll follow them down, making their approach from the northwest. That makes forty-eight of us, about equaling Agent VanGotten's estimate of the militia's strength. Any comments so far?" He cast a quick glance at Director Benton, and Ben wondered how many others had noticed. No one said a word.

"I have no intention of going in on equal terms, though. Three more fire teams, another twelve of our personnel, are going to come in from the direction of the entrance road, hitting the ridges perpendicular to the direction in which they lie. They will be the first to engage the enemy in a frontal attack. This will be mostly a diversionary move."

Ben was getting more uneasy by the minute, because the major was talking as though Deidre didn't exist, and he was about ready to break his silence. He had opened his mouth to say, *What about my wife? She's in there, you know.* But before the words came out, Jensen continued.

"Our initial concern is to rescue Sheriff Johnson, which is why I don't want this to be an all-out assault. Agent VanGotten?" Ben's mouth snapped shut before he could say something he'd later regret. "You said you were quite sure you knew which building your wife was being held in. Tell us about what you saw that makes you so sure."

Ben cleared his throat and pointed to a building in the sketch he had made earlier. "This one. I observed two individuals who carried themselves like officers go in and out of it twice in the few minutes I was there. Also, it has only one door—here." He made a mark on the side of the building facing the central grounds. "It has no windows, and looked to be made of concrete blocks. If I were to hold someone, it would be in there." Jensen took a second to digest Ben's information and supposition.

"What if that's their armory, and your wife is being held elsewhere? We're not sure she's even being held at that exact location."

"Yes we are." It was Director Benton speaking. He hadn't been cowed after all. "We ran a triangulation on the phone calls and texts we've received via Deidre's cell phone. That's the origin of the transmission. And if you're thinking they've moved her, the last call made by Ben was received by them in the same place." He stood his ground, looking at the major, not confronting him, but letting the officer know that he expected to be considered part of the team. "And another thing. I doubt at this stage of the game they're going to be moving her. You told Ben to call her on the hour to make sure she's still alive. I know what you're trying to avoid, risking your people to rescue a dead captive. But, and I ask this not to undermine your authority, because you are in charge and your men are your responsibility, but think of what Sheriff Johnson has been through. To wake her every hour and expect her to respond will only sap what little strength she has remaining. If we do that, she'll be of no help aiding in her own escape."

Major Jensen looked at the map, then looked up. "You're right. I wasn't thinking when I made that order. Point taken. Agent VanGotten, do you have any idea how to breach the walls of this building?"

Ben was taken by surprise and had to think. "I know she's in there, but I don't know where. If we blow a hole in a wall, it might be one she's leaning on. It would be impossible for anyone to sneak around to the front and break down the door, even if it weren't reinforced. I don't know." He shook his head in frustration.

"Is there a way for Deidre to provide us with the information?" Jackie thought out loud. "What if a couple of hours before our operation begins, Ben calls her to check on her wellbeing? Could we frame some questions for him to ask that would provide us with a clue by her answers? For instance, he could ask if she is being kept in a separate room, or if that is too obvious, ask her if she is comfortable where she's being held. I think it's worth a try, anyway. Then we can plan to set a charge where we think she isn't."

The thought bolted through Ben's mind. *Where we think? We're getting set to roll the dice with my wife's life at stake!* He was about to object when Benton spoke up again.

"Major, what do you think of that idea?" Benton asked. "I know it's taking a chance, but it's better than going in blind. Any information we can gain will increase our odds of succeeding." He turned to Ben, and expressed what Ben had been thinking. "I know the idea isn't foolproof, but we have to do something." He turned his attention back to the major.

Jensen nodded with his lips puckered and his brow furrowed. "You're right. There are no certainties, but we have to do something. We'll follow the agent's suggestion." He glanced at his wristwatch and Ben looked at the clock on the wall. It was eight thirty and getting dark outside, twenty-four hours since Deidre had been carried away, and he wondered if any plan would work. Major Jensen's voice pulled him back to the room.

"We want to be at the compound by daybreak. All units will be ready to move out at 0400 hours, which should give us time to reach our positions. The three units coming in from the northeast will fire a round of shots at 0630 hours to get their attention and create a diversion. A hole will be blown in the wall of the building that seems to be a bunker, and a designated team will storm the interior and bring Deidre out. Once she's been safely extracted, a full assault will begin. I want the state troopers to have their armored vehicles ready to crash the gate of the entrance road and move in to our perimeter. County deputies are in charge of maintaining order here. The FBI SWAT team will join the state troopers and act as reinforcement. Unfortunately, I doubt if we will come out of this unscathed. I've been in contact with the Guard units at the other sites, and those who have engaged the enemy report strong resistance from well-trained militiamen. They report their adversaries are well-equipped for battle." He concluded by asking if anyone had questions.

Ben spoke up. "Sir, where do I fit into the picture?" The major looked at him. "Where do you want to fit in?"

Ben's impulse was to say he wanted to be among those who entered the building. Then he remembered Megan and Maren. "I'd like to join one of the units, but I'll let them do their job. I just want to be close and observe. Does that sound ridiculous?" Jensen looked at Ben and shook his head, and Ben thought he was rejecting his request. Then it dawned on him that the major meant no, it wasn't ridiculous.

"You will arm yourself, though, and you will be ready to defend any of my personnel as needed. Agreed?" Ben nodded.

The major dismissed them and joined his warrant officers to finalize the plans, but not before admonishing everyone to get a couple hours sleep if they could. Ben went into the living room, sat on the couch, and stared at the floor. The room was too quiet. Jackie tiptoed in and took a seat in an easy chair next to where he sat.

"I'm sorry, Ben. You must be at your wit's end," she said in a quiet voice. "You really love her, don't you?" He looked up, surprised at her directness, and nodded. "You know, after your wife, Jenny, died, I thought of you often." She paused, and Ben started to say he appreciated her thoughts, but Jackie continued. "No, I didn't think of your sorrow. I thought if I waited a year, maybe two, that we could get together. Then, only a few months after Jenny died, Deidre came along. I saw you change almost immediately, and I was sure you were making a big mistake. It was too soon, I believed." Ben was beginning to feel uncomfortable, but he didn't know what to say.

Jackie fiddled with a hangnail on her thumb and didn't look at Ben. "I really expected you to come to your senses and ditch her when you were thinking more clearly. Then I'd planned to move in." She chuckled a little. "But it didn't happen. I saw her demanding nothing from you, saw her meeting your needs with no strings attached, and I knew I had lost." Ben looked at her and saw a tear roll down her cheek. "She got what I wanted." Jackie squared her shoulders and smiled at Ben. "I don't know why I'm telling you this. I guess I wanted you to know how I felt, but I'm going to tell you straight out, I'm happy for you, that you got what you needed. I hope with every bone of my body that you get Deidre back. She's been wonderful for you and your daughters, but I want you to remember, I'll be here to help you pick up the pieces if you should need me."

Ben looked at her and was saddened by the confession she had just made. "Thanks, Jackie. It was difficult for you to tell me this, I know. I'll remember your offer. I will." Jackie almost ran from the room, and Ben was left sitting, alone.

Chapter
Forty-Five

It seemed Ben had slept only minutes, propped up by a couple of throw pillows on the corner of the sofa. Someone was shaking his shoulder, and confused, he almost called out Deidre's name. It took a few seconds to clear the cobwebs from his sleep-deprived mind and focus on reality. The hand belonged to Director Benton.

"Wake up, Ben. It's three thirty, and Major Jensen is moving out at four sharp. You don't want to be left behind." Ben rubbed his eyes and shook his head to come fully awake and regained his bearings enough to stand up. He groped his way to the kitchen and poured himself a large mug of black coffee that scalded his mouth with the first slurp. He was wide awake now. He went to his study, opened his gun cabinet, and removed his service sidearm, a nine-millimeter Glock.

The heft of the weapon felt good in his hand, comfortable, and he removed its clip, worked the action to make sure there wasn't a bullet in its chamber, and slid the clip back in, hearing the click when it seated. He put two additional loaded clips in his pocket, and the thought crossed his mind, *If thirty shots aren't enough, it'll be too late anyway.* He gulped the rest of the black coffee, laced on his field boots, and stepped outside. The coolness of the early-morning calm contrasted with what he was feeling in his guts. The major and his warrant officers were conversing in a group, and Ben moved near them, not pushing his way into the knot but hovering on its perimeter.

"Ben," Major Jensen greeted him. "This is Warrant Officer Jameson. You'll be attached to his group, the one in the center lane of low grounds we'll be using as our routes. It's time for you to make the last call to your wife to try and get her exact location. Let's step over here." He placed his hand on Ben's elbow and steered him to the porch. Ben brought up the favorites list on his phone, tapped Deidre's name, and heard the phone ringing. By the fifth ring he was getting agitated, and he fully expected to be connected to her answering machine by the seventh. On the sixth, a groggy voice answered. "Why, Ben, I thought you had given up on seeing your wife again. I suppose you want to talk to her, make sure she's still alive."

Ben couldn't disguise the anger in his voice. "What do you think? Let me hear her voice." In the background he heard shuffling sounds and muddled voices, then what he wanted to hear.

"Ben," Deidre croaked. "Ben, I'm still here. Are the girls okay?" He couldn't believe she was thinking of them.

"Yeah, yeah they are. Now listen to me and answer with only yes or no. Do you understand?"

Deidre answered, "Yes."

"Are you next to a wall?"

"Yes."

"Are you in a corner?"

"Yes."

"Can you tell me which one?"

"No."

"Is it opposite the door?"

"Yes."

Ben heard the sound of a tussle on the other phone, and Captain Blake's voice came on. "Passing information, were you? That's okay with us, to a point. Come and get her, now that you know she's alive. We're waiting." The line went dead.

Ben glanced at Major Jensen. "She's alive but sounded like she's been through the wringer, sounded really weak. She was able to let me know she's in one of two corners of the room—on the back side from the door. If they hold her at the present position, we can blow a hole in either side or the back, if the charges aren't too big and if they're placed in the center of the wall." The major nodded and went back to his planning group, leaving Ben standing alone. He thought, *It might work if they don't move her.*

"Ben, we're set here," Jameson called to him. "You lead us to the river. From there, our fire teams will fan out, each moving up their assigned route."

The trail was familiar, and Ben felt more at ease now that they were moving. An unusual calm descended on him as he realized that in two hours Deidre's ordeal might come to an end. He refused to let the alternative outcome enter his mind. By the time they reached his family's picnic area, everyone was warmed up from the pace and ready to do their job. Using hand signals, Jameson motioned for the fire team leaders to go to their particular areas. At exactly 0420 they began moving on the militia's compound. Ben followed the four-member group to which he had been assigned.

Ben had warned them in the pre-operation briefing that the first many yards along the river bank would be particularly tough going. The rivers in northeastern Minnesota are bordered by dense thickets of tag alder, a tree-like shrub that tends to grow in tangled clumps. Mixed in are high bush cranberry bushes that reach a height of ten to fifteen feet, but the worst impediment to passage are the scattered stands of hawthorn with stout one-inch thorns protruding from their branches, thorns sharp enough that they can be pushed completely through the fleshy part of a hand. The Knife River was no exception, and travel through the thick hedge of vegetation was difficult in daylight, let alone the blackness of night. Fortunately, the moon was still high in the sky, affording a bit of light. In front of him, one member of the fire team cursed under his breath as a bramble snagged his skin and rasped away a layer.

After ten minutes of arduous travel through the tangle, the team broke into the open ground of the ridge. The plan called for them to use its more open terrain until they were closer to the compound, then drop down to the low ground to their left and follow the creek that ran behind the building they were sure held Deidre. From that time on, Ben would stay behind in the cover of the trees while Fire Team B, his group, executed the rescue.

The team was good, he thought. All he heard was the swish of ferns brushing past their legs and an occasional light snap as a twig was crushed underfoot. Had he not known they were there, Ben might have thought he was alone. In the distance he heard the peaceful hoot of an owl, and once, he heard a small animal scurry off to the side, a fox perhaps. The air wasn't warm, wasn't cold. It was late August, the time of year when the early morning hours held a hint of autumn but not the threat of frost that would come later in September. Under normal circumstances, Ben would have been in his glory, but this night, he was on a mission.

Jameson stopped the group with an almost inaudible signal, and everyone, including Ben, gathered around him. He whispered, "We are almost to the spot where Ben said a landmine was located. We'll go around it and come up on the ridge on the other side. If I'm not mistaken, we're still over four hundred yards from our objective. Am I right?" He looked at Ben, and Ben nodded. "Okay, single file and pick up your feet. We're getting close enough that I don't want any more noise than necessary." The group followed the team leader, Ben taking up the rear.

After coming back up onto the ridge, Fire Team B paused, and Ben checked his watch: 6:10 A.M., 0610 hours. Twenty minutes until the action would begin. He felt the grip of apprehension take hold of him, and he knew the decision for him to not be directly involved in the action was right. He was much too closely involved to make the necessary split-second decisions and was almost frozen with fear, not for himself, but for Deidre. A hundred yards closer to their objective, they crept down to the stream below the ridge.

Because of the trees and dense foliage, none of the team could see what was happening in the east, but the sky was beginning to lighten. In ten minutes it would be turning a faint pink, followed by the rose-colored edge of the sun breaking the horizon. Animals were already sensing the change, and to his right, Ben heard the erratic shuffle of dry leaves as a squirrel took a few hops, stopped to listen for danger, and then continued making its way to a stand of hazelnut brush laden with a husk-covered bounty.

Somewhere above him, he heard the hammering of a downy woodpecker. It beat out a rhythm, followed by the flutter of its wings as it flew to another tree. Not far from his head, he heard the scratch of a small creature moving down the tree, and in the dim light, Ben made out the inverted shape of a nuthatch moving down a tree trunk as it searched for a meal hidden in the bark's cracks and crevices. In the distance, a blue jay croaked its raucous call. For an instant, the forest went silent only to erupt in more sounds a second later. He checked his watch again, 6:24.

Ben had a fleeting moment of panic, wondering if the other groups had gotten lost. He hadn't heard a sound except for the light footsteps of his own team since they split up at the river. For an instant, he panicked, and then became acutely aware of what the word faith meant: faith in the other teams' abilities, faith in his own team's training, faith that he would be holding Deidre in just minutes. Then his faith faltered, and panic set in worse than before. She had to be okay, he told himself.

*****

HUDDLED IN HER CORNER, the blanket pulled up around her face and her knees curled to her chest, Deidre had no sense of time. She dozed fitfully, her mind wracked with dreams that seemed all too real. Every time she dozed off, another series of terrifying scenarios would build until she jolted awake. With a spasm, she kicked her legs at a nonexistent adversary and readied herself for a fight until she realized there was no adversary to be fought.

The building in which she was being held had no windows and only one door. She had been left alone, but as she looked across the room at that one exit, she knew there had to be at least one guard posted outside. The thought never crossed her mind to sneak across the room and try the doorknob. Even if she had thought of doing it, she wouldn't have, fearing reprisal. She shifted her position and felt a sharp jab of pain in her neck. It was enough to cause her to call out, and she remembered the last time Ben called.

She had heard a sound at the door, before it swung inward. Captain Blake had strode over to her, and Deidre pulled the blanket higher around her chin, waiting to be dragged back to the chair. Her cell phone was in Blake's hand, and he had thrust it at her, a sneer of victory on his face. "For you."

Deidre had tried to speak, but all that came out through her dried lips and parched vocal chords was a croak. She swallowed hard, trying to force some lubricating spit to form and tried again. "Ben. I'm still here. Are the girls okay?" Considering her condition and situation, she had realized that was a totally inane question, but that was the first thing to come to her mind. Then she had heard Ben say to answer his questions with only "yes" or "no."

Yes, she understood him. Yes, she was still against a wall. Yes, she was still in a corner. No, she couldn't say which one. Yes, it was across the room from the door. At that instant Blake had grabbed the phone from her and shut it down.

"What was that about, some kind of code?" Deidre had looked at him defiantly through her open eye and said nothing. He took a kick at her out of frustration and she felt his boot crash into her ribs. Then he stalked out of the room, slamming the door as he left and leaving her more bruised than before. At that moment, Deidre doubted she was going to make it out alive.

For the moment she tried to move to be more comfortable, this time favoring her left side where Blake's boot had struck her, and she dozed off again. She had no idea how long she dreamed, but when she woke, she winced when she tried to move. Her side ached, her legs were so stiff she had to force them straight, and her face throbbed. The building was as silent as a tomb, and Deidre thought maybe that was appropriate. She heard some faint sounds and strained her ears to make out if she was imagining or if they really existed. At first she heard a faint tapping like a Morse Code, *dot-dit-dit-dot-dot* and for a second imagined someone was trying to communicate with her, then realized it was probably the sound of a woodpecker, possibly beating on the eaves of the building.

As she was listening to the bird beating his brains out, she heard something scurrying across the roof. It stopped, and Deidre heard the chatter of a red squirrel. She visualized the little rodent sitting on its hind legs and scolding the guard outside the door. Ever so faintly, she thought she heard the warning cry of a blue jay, "Thief!" and she remembered the Native American tale of how Mother Nature had cursed him with that call, because he stole from other birds.

Wishing she could be outside, watching the animals, Deidre realized she knew what time of day it was—daybreak, those few moments when the woods came alive after the silence of night. She smiled and her face felt sore, stiff, and not her own, but she could take a pretty close guess at the time, six o'clock in the morning. It would be daylight soon, and she wondered if she would live to see another sunrise.

Chapter
Forty-Six

BEN LOOKED AT HIS WATCH for the fifth time in five minutes. 6:29 A.M. Before he could think, *One more minute*, the morning tranquility of the forest was shattered. His watch had been a minute slow, or else a fire team coming in from the road had gotten ahead of the game. A volley of shots rang out, and he was aware of the members of Fire Team B crabbing their way up the steep rise to the side of the blockhouse where Deidre was. He watched as they disappeared into the grayness of the early morning light, and then he was alone.

*****

JUST AS DEIDRE BELIEVED she had discovered a shred of reality with the bird sounds outside and the movement of an animal, the peace was shattered by a volley of gunfire answered by the rattle of a machine gun, as well as the retort of assault rifles. Captain Blake and another man, who by his uniform she believed to be an officer as well, rushed into the room. As the second man stooped and fumbled for something on the floor, Blake roughly grabbed Deidre's arm and jerked her to her feet. The second officer lifted a steel ring in the floor, opening a trapdoor that Deidre hadn't noticed. She was shoved toward it, and Blake whispered in a sinister voice, "There's a ladder. I'm going down first, you follow," he jabbed his finger at her. "And you come last," he said to his subordinate.

In seconds, Blake had disappeared into the blackness of the hole, and as instructed, Deidre followed. She felt particles of something shower down on her head when the last man came after them, and for a second, all light vanished when she heard the trapdoor slam shut. There was a metallic scraping sound, and it registered in Deidre's consciousness that the door was being bolted from below. Before the blackness of the dank-smelling tunnel closed in on her, Blake turned on a flashlight and shined it in her eyes. At the bottom of the ladder was just enough room for the three of them to stand and maneuver, and Deidre felt herself pulled forward and then pushed from behind. She was leading the parade to somewhere.

Before she took two steps, the ground and surrounding walls of the tunnel shook and more dust and dirt filtered into her hair. Almost simultaneously, Deidre heard the sound of a blast and then silence. Whoever was behind her gave a shove and she moved forward.

After stumbling along for more steps than she could count, Deidre saw that the tunnel ended in what looked like a solid wall, and as they approached it, she could see that it was a heavy, bolted door. Blake reached around her and slid the lock back. He pushed on the door with one hand, and it wiggled, but didn't open. He pushed again and made a little progress. The second man, who hadn't spoken or been addressed by name, stepped in front of them and leaned into it with his shoulder. Deidre heard something like branches breaking and a tree falling. Blake shoved her through the opening so forcefully she stumbled and almost fell. She sensed him right behind her, and then he grunted, and his sensed presence disappeared.

Deidre stumbled forward and heard someone say, "Don't move an inch, you bastard."

*****

THE GUNFIRE CONTINUED, and Ben could discern that it was coming from two locations. He could also make out those shots that were being returned from the militia. They were less sharp, because they were outgoing. Then the louder and more rhythmic pounding of a large-caliber automatic weapon cut loose. Ben experienced a momentary sense of hopelessness when he heard the sounds of war.

Fire Team B and Ben had stopped near a rock outcrop before moving in on their rescue mission, hunkering down to await the distracting fire of one of the decoy fire teams. During those minutes they waited, Ben had surveyed the spot and noticed that next to the rock outcrop a dead fir tree lay at an unusual angle. Something about it didn't look natural. After the fire team headed toward the camp, Ben stayed crouched down next to the outcrop partially hidden by the dead tree. He flinched and then hunkered lower when an explosion ripped through the bedlam, and for an instant, there was silence, as though everyone and everything had been stunned. During that brief lull, he heard a sound like metal on metal coming from beside the rock he sheltered behind. The tree moved ever so slightly. He stepped closer to the rock shelf protruding from the ground and held his breath.

The dried branches of the tree wiggled, and this time Ben heard the scrape of something being pushed open. He realized he was standing next to an escape route from the militia's compound. He grabbed for his service revolver and pressed against the rocks to the side of the tree. Someone gave one more push from the inside, and what had looked like a natural windfall fell away as a slanted door, like those for root cellars on old farmsteads, opened. But this was no root cellar.

As Ben watched, a figure was pushed out of the opening into the morning air, and it took him a moment to recognize Deidre. She was hunched over, holding her ribs, and she staggered as she tried to walk on stiffened legs. From behind, he could see that her hair was in tangles and matted to her head. Then she turned her head, and Ben almost gave away his position by uttering a gasp. Deidre's face was beaten. Blood crusted around her nostrils and her lips, and one eye was swollen completely shut. Almost no part of her face was without a bruise of some degree, and she looked as though she was going to collapse. A hand had her by the back of her neck, and that hand was attached to an arm that looked to be clothed in a uniform.

As the uniformed man followed Deidre through the opening, Ben stepped forward and raised his pistol. He slammed the butt of the Glock against his head, and the man fell unconscious. Ben grabbed him by the collar and with one heave pulled him to the side, leaving the opening to the escape route unobstructed. Completely confused, Deidre stood in the growing daylight, unsure of where to turn. Before she could move, Ben heard another sound coming from the escape door, and he stepped to the side. Another uniformed man took one step from the entrance and when he saw Deidre standing alone, paused.

"Don't move an inch, you bastard!" Ben blurted out, but the militiaman turned anyway, only to see the barrel of a nine-millimeter handgun pointed directly at his face. From the distance of three feet, its bore looked like a cannon, and he threw his hands in the air.

"Don't shoot!" he shouted. "You got me. It's over!"

But it wasn't. Ben could still hear the rattle of the machine gun. It sounded like there may have been more than one, and he remembered the three large hummocks he had noted on his recon mission. As he stood there, covering the second man to have emerged from the hatch and waiting for Blake to come to, the members of Fire Team B spilled down the bank toward him. Jameson began to bellow above the din, "She wasn't—" He stopped. "Deidre, is that you?" Then he gathered in the sight. "Who the hell is that?" he demanded when he saw Blake sprawled on the ground, blood flowing from a wound on the back of his head.

The plan had been for Fire Team B to blow a hole in the wall of the building, rush in, grab Deidre, and pull her to freedom. When the rescue was complete, they would retreat to the lowland and fire a flare, signaling to the other teams the rescue had been completed. Then all would withdraw a short distance, sealing off the perimeter of the camp so no one could enter or leave. That part of the mission complete, an FBI negotiating team would move in and try to get everyone in the compound to surrender. The plan was intact, but now Fire Team B had two prisoners to contend with. Jameson had a problem on his hands. What to do with Deidre and Ben and the two militiamen in his custody? He made the only logical choice.

Turning to his rifleman, Jameson said, "You return to HQ with the prisoners. Ben, Deidre is in no condition to walk out of here. Can you carry her?" Ben nodded and moved toward his wife, but she was so dazed she perceived him to be a threat and tried to beat him off. Luckily, her strength was so sapped, she could barely swing her fists.

Blake let out a groan and rolled over onto his back. He reached for the back of his head and gently fingered his scalp, and the team leader pounced on him, relieved him of the sidearm he carried, grabbed the front of his uniform, and jerked him to a sitting position.

"You're going back with Rifleman Petroff. If you try to escape, he has orders to shoot you. Understand?" Jameson commanded. Blake tried to focus his eyes, but they wouldn't cooperate. Finally, he was able to nod. Jameson pulled his captive to his feet and shoved him in the direction he wanted him to go. "Rifleman, you heard my order. I meant what I said. Shoot either one of them if they try to make a run for it." The trio, two militiamen and a national Guard soldier, started off on the trail leading back to the Knife River.

Ben swept Deidre off her feet in one move, and draped her over his shoulder. He heard her moan as his shoulder made contact with her ribs, but he knew they had to move away from their current position. It would be too dangerous to stay that close to the compound. The sound of gunfire had ceased, and an eerie quiet draped the woods, as even the animals had gone silent. Deidre was light to carry as they started out, but an eighth of a mile later, her dead weight became too much for Ben. He set her down, and for an instant he feared she had died. As he held her head in his lap, the lid to her unbruised eye fluttered, and then it opened. He felt her bury her face on his chest, and he gently enveloped her in his arms. The rifleman had ordered his prisoners to stop, and he stared at the couple on the ground.

"That's okay, Petroff," Ben said. He didn't know the man's first name. "You go on ahead with those two. We'll be okay. We just need a minute or two to rest, and we'll be right behind you. I don't think anybody will be chasing us. They're bottled up back at the compound by your unit. We'll be okay." He held Deidre closer to his body while Petroff herded the prisoners up the trail.

It was full daylight by that time, and the day was sunny. Through the forest canopy, Ben could see swatches of blue sky, and the small animals had begun to resume their activity. There was no gunfire in the distance, and had it not been for the sight of Deidre's bruised face, they might have been enjoying a tryst in the woods. She tried to smile but winced in pain.

"Can you walk?" Ben wanted to know. Deidre tried to shrug her answer, but the pain caused by the movement of her shoulders made her inhale sharply. Ben stood up and tried to help her to her feet, and after struggling, she was upright. With him holding her under her arm, Deidre shuffled down the trail as best she could, but Ben was broken by how weak she was.

Chapter Forty-Seven

An occasional shot could be heard in the distance, although from where Ben and Deidre were standing, they could have been mistaken for hammer blows or other construction noises. At seven forty-five, they reached the river, and Ben gently picked up Deidre in his arms. She had just enough strength to assist him by clutching his neck and shoulders as he waded the few yards to cross the stream. He slipped on an algae-covered boulder when they were midway to the other bank and went down on one knee, soaking his pants and bruising himself, but they made it. As he pulled them onto the bank, Ben silently gave thanks that they were on home turf. The compound seemed a continent away in that instant.

He didn't put Deidre down, but decided to get back to the house as quickly as he could, and stumbled several times on the rough trail but didn't fall. The closer to home they got, the lighter his wife seemed to feel, and Ben nearly ran the last few yards to the porch of their home. They were met by Director Benton, Jackie, and two of Deidre's deputies. As they took her from him, he pleaded, "Get an ambulance as quick as you can."

Benton said nothing but pointed toward the driveway, where Ben saw the lineup. Two county ambulances were idling, along with a number of military ambulances. Medics were running across the lawn from the county vehicles. They helped lay Deidre on the couch in the living room and began an examination. One was on his phone, but Ben couldn't make out his conversation. The other turned to Ben. "We're going to transport your wife to the hospital in Two

Harbors. I can't find any critical wounds, but until we get some scans taken we won't be sure. You can follow us in your own car."

Ben looked at his boss who said one word: "Go!" It took minutes to load Deidre into the ambulance and it pulled out, sirens blaring and lights flashing. Ben followed as closely as he could, but they soon outdistanced him. He knew the law about being an ambulance chaser, and he didn't need to be stopped by a zealous patrolman and given a ticket.

By the time he pulled into the hospital parking lot, he could see that the ambulance had been unloaded and a flood of relief swept over him. As he rushed through the ER doors, he was met by a security guard, who reached for his sidearm and aimed it at Ben. Shocked and confused, he raised his hands in a sign of surrender, then realized he still had his Glock in its holster on his hip. "Wait!" he shouted. "I'm FBI and that's my wife they just brought in." The guard didn't lower his gun, and Ben was somewhat relieved to see that his finger wasn't on the weapon's trigger and that the safety was still in the "on" position. His heart was pounding in his chest and time stood still.

"Where's your badge?" the guard demanded.

"In my wallet," Ben answered as calmly as he could. "Left back pocket," he continued. The guard still eyed him warily.

Noting that Ben's holster was on his right hip, he instructed, "Lower your left hand, slowly, and with your thumb and forefinger, take your badge out and lay it on the table." He nodded at a stainless steel surface placed in front of the metal detector that entrants were supposed to pass through. Ben did as he was instructed and finally realized the guard was doing exactly what he was trained to do. ERs had become like battlegrounds in too many instances. The guard asked Ben to step back from the table, and he picked up the wallet, fumbled it, because he was watching Ben closely in case he made an errant move. He knew to remain calm and not lower his hands.

After scrutinizing the ID in the wallet, he told Ben to turn around and face the wall without lowering his hands. Ben felt the retaining strap on his holster unsnap and felt the weight of his pistol lift. He heard the guard step back.

"Move away from the wall and turn around slowly," he commanded, and Ben obeyed. "You can lower your hands and step through the metal detector." Ben did has he was told, and heard the beep of the detector go off. The guard eyed him worriedly. "What do you have in your pockets?" he asked, none too casually. Ben saw him slip his finger inside the trigger guard.

Oh, God, he thought as he remembered he had stuffed a ten-shot clip into his other rear pocket. "I'm so sorry," he began to explain. "In all the confusion of wanting to be with my wife, I forgot I've got an extra clip of ammunition in my other pocket. How do you want to work this? Do you want me to dig it out, or do you want me to get up against the wall again, and you do it? If it were me, I'd put me up against the wall." The question caused the guard to pause. Never before had a suspect given him the choice of how he wanted to proceed. It began to dawn on him how ridiculous the situation was becoming. He almost laughed.

"Tell you what, Agent VanGotten. You move really slow, and empty all of your pockets. Rules are rules, and you can't take this crap in with you." Ben did as he was told, removed his watch and laid the ammo clip beside it. As he dug deeper he found the compass and another clip he had forgotten in the pocket of his vest. He looked at the guard and shrugged. This time the detector allowed him through, and he rushed to the nursing station.

"I'm Ben VanGotten, Deidre Johnson's husband. She was just brought in, and I want to be with her." The receptionist didn't have to check her records.

"Follow me," she said as she led the way past several curtained compartments. She held the one marked "ER9" back, and Ben really looked at his wife for the first time since she had been taken.

*****

MAJOR JENSEN and Director Benton huddled together with the rifleman who had brought in the prisoners. They had been turned over to the state troopers to hold. After a short briefing, the major consulted with the governor, filling him in on what had transpired so far.

"Governor, it's our opinion that we should negotiate with the remaining militia. We have their lead officers, and we think we can get most of them to surrender, especially if we play the card that their commander was caught skipping out. If that fails, we need your approval to stage a full-scale assault."

The governor held his head in his hands for a long ten seconds. He remembered a group called the Branch Davidians and the negative press that incident had evoked. At least there were no reports of women and children in Blake's stronghold. On the other hand, a report had recently crossed his desk outlining the possible fallout of giving in, and his thoughts went to a rancher from a western state who two years earlier had forced an armed standoff with the government. The report went on to say the stalemate gave a false sense of victory to the rancher's supporters. Since the authorities backed down, there had been seventeen incidents of anti-government extremists firing on law enforcement. Politically, it wouldn't look good to appear weak. Finally, he lifted his face from his hands.

"You have my orders to attack this group, if necessary. But first, try to negotiate a surrender. That way, everyone wins, to some extent, anyway." Major Jenson made plans to move the command post nearer to the action and was soon on his way to what had become a siege.

Chapter
Forty-Eight

An IV bag hung from a stand near Deidre's bed, and the tube leading from it disappeared under the sheet that covered her body. Her good eye focused on him, and he could see tears in it. Ben brushed back the hair from her forehead, stooped, and kissed it.

"Oh, my Deidre, what did they do to you?" She tried to smile at him, but only one side of her mouth moved. Her lips on the other side were too swollen to respond. "You never realize how much you love someone until you almost lose them. I'm so sorry I didn't go with you when you went to the river."

Deidre attempted to sit up and grimaced as she tried to speak. "Don't talk crazy," she croaked. "You know how stubborn I am, and I'd have said I wanted to go alone. None of this was your fault." She shifted in her bed. "What's happening with the Guard and the rest of the folks? Are they taking care of those guys?" Ben said he didn't know what was happening. "Then get back there. I need a full report as soon as possible. Those are the people who killed Justin Peters, who shot Jeff, and who vandalized Joseph's place, not to mention all the other crap that's been going on around here. I'd bet next month's paycheck they sabotaged the rail line, too." She sank back down on her pillow. "Well, get going. I'm going to be out of here soon. I'm okay. Go!" She smiled as best she could, but Ben didn't move.

The curtain parted, and the ER doc had to duck a little to get under it. He carried a clipboard. "Well, the good news is, I've seen worse." He smiled. "Nothing is broken and the scans showed no signs of internal injuries. The way you feel, you probably won't believe this, but your biggest problem is that you're extremely dehydrated, which we're fixing right now." He pointed to the IV. "Lactated Ringer's, salt and glucose solution. Otherwise, all of the injuries are to your soft tissue, except for three badly bruised ribs. I'd say you're either very lucky, or your abuse was planned to make things look bad without killing you. Either way, we'll be holding you for about the next four hours to see how your body responds to being hydrated. If all goes well, you'll be released by six this evening. You won't be doing any skydiving for a while, though. Any questions?"

Ben looked at Deidre as he asked the doctor, "It's okay for me to leave her while I take care of some other business?" The doctor chuckled.

"We'll take good care of her."

Ben kissed his wife one more time on about the only part of her face that wasn't turning black-and-blue. "I'll be back!" he said, impersonating a movie star from one of his favorite adventure movies, took one more look at Deidre, blew her a kiss, and left.

*****

ONLY THE DEPUTIES and a highway patrol trooper remained at his house. They told him that Major Jensen and Director Benton had moved HQ to the haul road leading to the militia's compound. The two prisoners had been moved to the Lake County jail by state troopers. The deputies expressed their surprise that Ben was back. He had retrieved his sidearm when he left the hospital, and he checked it again, making sure it was loaded, checking the safety last. He decided to walk the few hundred yards up the road to the new HQ, and as he did, Ben remembered all the conversations he and Deidre had had while they strolled the county road. He was jerked back to the present when a short volley of gunshots erupted somewhere back in the woods. Feeling some apprehension, he wended his way up the haul road, thinking his fear was unfounded but half expecting a militiaman to step out of the woods onto the trail. A half-mile in, he spotted a shelter ahead where several Guardsmen were posted. Ben's unease lifted, and he approached the spot where Jensen and Benton were discussing the situation.

"Ben!" Director Benton said, taken by surprise. "What are you doing here?"

Ben grinned a slight smile. "Deidre sent me. She wants a report on what's happening."

Jensen shrugged. "She's one tough lady. Who wins the arguments in your house?"

Now Ben actually smiled. "She does."

Benton got down to business. "Here's where were at. Jackie and another negotiator are in there right now, trying to set up some kind of communication system with the resisters. We'll try talking them out first, but the governor has given his go-ahead to use force if necessary. We suspect we can get some to surrender, but there will be a hardcore group who will fight. We need to figure out how to separate them so we can act."

*****

AN FBI NEGOTIATOR, Andy Cooper, had been flown into the Two Harbors airport earlier that morning. A guardsman had been there to pick him up, and it was only a fifteen-minute drive to the HQ, where he met Jackie. Being the agent in charge of the Militia Division out of the Duluth FBI office, she was the one to brief him on the situation. Together, they had made their way to the front, and now hunkered down with Fire Team C. They both knew the silence of the place was deceiving.

At the present, there was no way to establish communication with the militia, except by bullhorn, and Andy checked to make sure it was turned on and the volume was cranked up. "My name is Andrew Cooper. I'm a representative of the FBI, and I'd like to discuss the situation with whoever is in charge." He clicked the bullhorn off and listened for some sort of response. "Can you hear me? If you can, just holler." More silence. "We've got to talk. If we don't, the governor has given the word to destroy your compound. People will get killed if we do that. If you can hear me, and if you have a cell phone, call this number." He slowly recited the number of the phone he held in the hand not grasping the bullhorn, then he repeated the number two more times, slowly.

Andy and Jackie settled down behind a hummock of dirt and timber that had been pushed aside when the road had been dozed, and they waited. Jackie wished she had looked at her watch when the message was broadcast. Time dragged, and it was impossible for her to estimate how many minutes had elapsed. Andy's phone rang, and its tone jolted both of the negotiators. "Hello," he answered. "This is Agent Cooper speaking. Who am I talking to?" Jackie could tell by his expression that he was getting an answer. "Listen, Lieutenant, I have another agent with me, and I'm going to put my phone on speaker so she can be a part of our conversation. Okay?" There was a pause. "Okay, you're on speaker phone. What are your demands?"

The person Andy had referred to as the lieutenant hesitated for several seconds. The negotiators could almost hear the wheels grinding, and they wondered what was going through his mind. They had expected some sort of manifesto to be read, but it was as though this guy was unprepared, as though he really wasn't sure what to demand.

"We want to have a TV crew come into our compound and interview us." Andy looked at Jackie and shrugged.

"Do you want to be interviewed or somebody else?" Again there was hesitation.

"I don't know. We'll decide that later."

"Okay," Andy seemed to agree. "Okay, we can arrange that, but listen. Why not come out of your bunkers, and we can meet the reporters at a neutral site. That way they'll have time to set up, you'll have time to figure out exactly what you want to say, and we can all ease off a little. No use having a lot of people dying over this."

The lieutenant answered immediately. "You government fascists, I know what you're doing. How stupid do you think we are? You'll get us out there and gun us down. We'll be buried, and nobody will ever know about us. We'll just become another government cover-up."

Andy shook his head in disgust. "Listen to me. We all want to end this peacefully. What exactly are you trying to accomplish?"

"We can't allow things to go on as they are. Our government is nothing but a bunch of liberals who want to disarm this nation, take away our guns, and when they do, we'll be subjugated to their dictatorial wishes. We won't be able to defend ourselves."

Andy listened to the lieutenant's message and then responded. "We understand your fear that your guns will be taken from you, but surely, you must have other grievances. I'd like to know what they are."

A few seconds went by, and the lieutenant came back on. "What kind of government do we have that is intent on cramming perversion down our throats? Homosexuals, all they do is weaken our fighting ability. And blacks, in their arrogant demands they intend to take over. They're as bad as the Jews, who have all the power in this country. Our government is a mess and is failing to protect true Americans, people like us who bleed red, white, and blue."

Andy took a deep breath. "All right, Lieutenant. What do you want us to do?" There was silence for too long, and Jackie thought the lieutenant had hung up on them. Then he came with his demand.

"I want you to get a TV crew on the scene. Then I want you, Agent Cooper, to come out in the open. I'll do the same. You bring six of the Guard with you, and I'll bring six of my men with me. We'll meet in the parade ground, but I want evidence that the meeting is being recorded by the TV crew. I want to see them on the periphery with their cameras. I'll give you two hours to set this up, and then all hell is going to break loose if you're not back to me." The phone went dead.

Agent Cooper and Jackie withdrew to HQ, which was only a short distance behind them. Both Director Benton and Major Jensen were waiting to hear the report, and the two negotiators filled the leaders in on what was demanded. Ben listened intently, wishing that Deidre could be there hearing all of what the militia representative had said. Jensen called the camp set up at Ben and Deidre's home and asked to be connected to one of the TV crews that were waiting. Not only one, but three crews from different networks wanted to be involved in the action, and Jensen marveled at their dedication, even though it might have been preempted by their desire to get a scoop.

In an hour, the camera crews were ready and waiting to move with the negotiating crew. Agent Cooper strapped on a bulletproof vest, as did the six Guardsmen who would be accompanying him. The camera crew had been outfitted by the Guard and wore the same protection as the negotiators. They were set to meet the enemy and begin face-to-face talks.

Agent Cooper, Andy, hit the redial button on his phone. "Lieutenant, we're ready to come out. When we see you and your entourage advance to the parade ground, we'll do the same. The camera crews are ready, as you asked, but they have been instructed to stay well on the perimeter. They are my responsibility, and you'll suffer severe repercussion if they are assaulted in any way."

Four fire teams under direction of Major Jensen had been set up so they could train their weapons on the militia who would be at the meeting. They were sure the other side had their weapons at the ready, also, but everyone felt confident nothing would happen as long as the TV crews were taping. When the militia stepped onto the parade ground, Andy rose from behind his cover, and escorted by the guardsmen, began to approach the clearing. They were almost to the midway point when they were cut down by a barrage of heavy machine gun fire that raked back and forth across their group. Jackie saw them fall, watched as Andy tried to stand up but was mowed down by another volley, and the group lay motionless.

The fire teams answered with their own firepower, and in seconds, the militiamen were on the ground, too. Fourteen people lay dead on the parade ground.

At first, the TV crews had been so engrossed in their filming, it didn't register what was actually happening, but when it did, they dove for cover. But before that happened, they had on tape the National Guard soldiers being slaughtered and an FBI agent being mutilated by the machine gun slugs. Several hundred yards to the rear, everyone at HQ heard the gunfire and knew something had gone terribly wrong.

It took only a few minutes for Warrant Officer James Riley to reach headquarters with the news of what had happened, and Ben saw the jaw muscles of Major Jensen bulge. Director Benton picked up a stone and hurled it at nothing in the woods. Then he turned to Jensen.

"What in the hell are we going to do now? This has turned into what we feared most, a public relations disaster."

Major Jensen was beyond furious. "Our only option now is to complete the operation, and public relations be damned. I'm calling up two armored vehicles that are waiting. The older models that have been sold to public law enforcement agencies won't do the trick against their weaponry. We have the latest, M114 Humvees. They aren't perfect, but they're battle tested. I'll have them here, armed and ready to go, in twenty minutes."

*****

DEIDRE FELT AS THOUGH she was a captive in the ER. She had been given three IV bags of Ringers, and had gone to the bathroom more times than she cared to remember. Her headache had subsided, and she felt her strength returning by the minute. True, her left eye remained swollen shut, and her ribs ached with each breath, but nothing was so bad that she couldn't stand it. The thought of what was happening without her knowledge was eating at her, and she wanted out of the hospital. Fortunately, she was overruled by the medical staff and was forced to stay put. They did mollify her somewhat by reminding her they would evaluate her case by early evening.

*****

As Major Jensen had promised, the two Humvees arrived at 1400 hours military time, 2:00 p.m. civilian time. Ben was left out of the decision-making loop, but Benton allowed him to be privy to the operation. He looked at the two armored vehicles and was overwhelmed by the sight of a guardsmen perched atop each, manning Browning .50-caliber machine guns. There was no doubt about their mission.

Ben saw the crews huddling with Major Jensen—one soldier turned and shot a stream of tobacco juice at the base of a tree—and Ben marveled at how calm they seemed. They were, he realized, preparing to go into battle. The group broke up, and each soldier returned to his respective armored vehicle. In minutes, they were on their way to the compound, only a five-minute ride from where he stood.

Jackie had returned to her cover behind a mound of earth and tangled logs. She held the bullhorn that Andy Cooper used earlier in the conflict, and she cradled it as she heard the rumble of the Humvees coming up the road. They stopped a short distance behind her, and she knew it was time to make one more plea. She tried to get her voice under control so she wouldn't sound like a screeching, hysterical woman.

"Listen to me. We are giving you one chance to drop your arms and come out with your hands on your heads. Whatever you are trying to do, you have reached the end of your time. You have one minute to surrender. If you do not comply with my request, the National Guard has orders to attack, and that won't do you any good. You will not survive. Do you understand me?" She put the bullhorn down, looked at her watch, and waited, observing the second hand sweep its way past the numbers on the dial.

After the minute was up, a voice rang out. "If you want our guns, come and get them. This is being recorded by the TV crews, and when they play it on the news, the public will see just how much of a Fascist regime we live in. We're ready for you and will die as patriots." Another two minutes passed, and the forest shook as the V8 turbo-charged diesels of the armored carriers revved up, propelling them forward. Ben could hear the roar of the engines, and seconds later a steady burst of gunfire. Then silence.

Jackie felt the ground shake as the three-ton vehicles made their charge, and her ears rang as the Brownings spewed their bullets at the bunkers sheltering the militiamen. The plan had been to enter the triangle formed by the three redoubts but not to run directly at the apex of the triangle. Each Humvee would make a run at the bunkers at the base angles of the triangle, take them out with bursts from their machine guns and then converge at the apex. Fire teams would advance from the periphery and mop up whatever needed to be done.

The Humvees were on the militants before they could react, and with the speed that the armored vehicles reached them, they had little chance. The guardsmen swept in and destroyed the bunkers, leaving a trail of destruction behind. Soldiers on foot followed so closely, the survivors of the attack had no time to gather their senses and react.

Jackie heard one warrant officer yell, "Over there, in the corner. Drag him out." She heard scuffling but no shots. As quickly as it had begun, the action was over, and she dared to look over the berm behind which she lay. At least twenty National Guard troops were actively patting down a number of militiamen. In one bunker, two were administering first aid, and she could hear sirens not far away. The National Guard ambulances were on their way, as was the county's ambulance crew and Search and Rescue. She realized she still held the bullhorn, tried to put it down, and couldn't. Her fingers were frozen around its handle, and they were white from clenching it so hard. When she stood up, she realized she was shaking all over. Only then did she notice a member of the TV crew approaching her, his camera held on his shoulder, its red light aimed directly at her. She was being recorded. Jackie stumbled onto the parade ground and passed near one of the bunkers. Four dead militiamen lay sprawled in various distorted positions. *They look too young to be here,* she thought.

She went over to where Andy, her partner only two hours ago, lay, and she folded his dead arms across his chest, then stood looking at his face, wishing he'd wake up.

After ten minutes of wandering around in a daze, Jackie felt someone come up behind her and place a hand on her shoulder, and she turned to face the person. It was Ben, and he wrapped his arms around her as she slumped so her head rested on his chest. He held her for a long time, repeating over and over, "It's done. You're okay. You're safe." Finally, he let go of her and stepped back. "I'm sorry," was all he said, and she saw tears in his eyes.

Chapter
Forty-Nine

A sweep of the compound went far more uneventfully than Ben would have thought. Major Jensen ordered a few of his men to detain the TV people until he could speak with them. The rest went through each building, searching for, and finding, a few militia stragglers who thought they might escape by sitting the search out in hiding places. In the final count, twelve militiamen had been killed and fourteen wounded. Ten had been captured, not counting Captain Blake and his guard. Three guardsmen had been wounded, none severely, and the medics were attending to their wounds. Their count didn't include the initial casualties of the fracas. Ben wondered if all battlefields looked this calm after the storm.

The Guard ambulances arrived almost as soon as the firing was over, and now they were wrapping the bodies of the dead in blankets and loading them into the vehicles. Agent Andy Cooper's body was taken away by the Two Harbors Rescue Squad. Director Benton, Major Jensen, and two warrant officers returned to Ben's place to meet with the TV crews. Ben decided to walk home, hoping he could sort through the myriad of feelings he was experiencing.

*****

It was four thirty when Ben walked into his kitchen. The major had rolled up his maps, and the table was cleared. The Guard still had their tents up in his field, but everyone was moving at a slower pace. The major entered the room with Benton, and their faces lacked many of the worry lines that had creased them before.

"Can we sit in your living room, Ben? I'd like you to know what's happening so you can relay the information to Deidre." Ben accepted, and the trio made their way to the other room and settled into the couch and chairs. "First, we have Captain Blake and his guard being held in the Lake County Jail." Ben signaled for him to wait a second and retrieved a pen and notepad. Jensen continued. "There are three others we think might be useful to us when we begin our interrogation. They're being held in the jail, too. Seven have been transported to the St. Louis County Jail. All are in isolated cells so they can't rehearse their stories."

"What about Jackie?" Ben wanted to know, and Director Benton filled him in.

"Jackie is pretty shook up. She's been taken to St. Luke's Hospital in Duluth for evaluation. That was pretty traumatic, seeing Andy cut down the way he was. She'll be seeing an agency-provided psychiatrist tomorrow and for however long she needs. And what about Deidre? Are there provisions for her recovery?" Ben hadn't even thought about that, and as he was pondering the question, he heard the kitchen door open. He wondered who would be letting him- or herself into his home, and he rose to investigate.

"Deidre!" he shouted. "What are you doing here?"

She looked at him, smiled a crooked smile and tried to wink her one eye that wasn't swollen shut. "I live here. Remember?" She limped to him and threw her arms around his waist. "I couldn't stand being in that hospital another minute. I don't have any holes in me, other than from all the needles they jammed in my arms, and the ER doc said there wasn't much they could do for me that couldn't be done at home. So I called a deputy to give me a lift, and here I am. Aren't you glad to see me?"

Ben rocked her back and forth and started to squeeze. He felt her wince and tense up. "Easy big fella," she said. "That rough play is going to have to wait for a while, I'm afraid," and she laughed the laugh Ben had come to love. His wife was home. "Have you called the girls?" she asked, and Ben realized he'd been so involved with everything, he hadn't let them know a thing.

"Just a second." He let go of Deidre and phoned Maren. She must have been waiting with her phone in her hand, because she answered immediately. "Maren, I've got someone who wants to talk to you." He handed the phone to Deidre.

"Hi, my daughter. How you doin'?"

Even Ben heard the scream on the other end of the call, followed by, "Megan, it's Mom! Come quick!" Deidre heard a crash as Megan overturned a chair in her haste, but in seconds she was telling them she was safe, and she made no effort to stop the tears that rolled down her face, wetting the front of her shirt. After reassuring her daughters she was okay and promising that she would tell them all about it, Deidre hung up. Ben and the other two officers were waiting for her in her living room. It had never felt better to sit on her couch next to her husband and lay her head on his shoulder. Suddenly, she was exhausted, but she wanted to hear what Benton and Jensen had to say.

"Deidre, you're one tough person." She was glad Jensen hadn't said "woman." She didn't want to be singled out as though being a woman and being tough didn't go together. She smiled as best she could. "I had just begun to give Ben a message for you, but now you can get it straight from the horse's mouth, although some people say my words come from a different part of my anatomy." Jensen laughed like Ben had never heard him laugh. He definitely was beginning to relax.

"We're going to start interrogating Blake tomorrow morning at the jail." Director Benton informed her. "We've called in a couple of experts from the agency. They should be getting into town sometime tonight. Not many flights come into Duluth."

"Anyway," Major Jensen added. "We singled out three of the militiamen who showed signs of being intimidated, and we think we can break them and use them against Captain Blake. Maybe then we can get down to what this was all about. It looks to me that it was a setup to create martyrs or to jumpstart a recruitment scheme. I don't know, just guessing."

Benton picked up the conversation. "We would like to have you join us to observe the interrogation. You are the sheriff, after all, and this is your county. Do you think you'll feel up to it?"

Deidre shifted her position next to Ben and winced from a jab of pain in her ribs. "I'm going to feel like hell in the morning. I know that, but I want to see those bastards squirm. What time?"

"The interrogator is scheduled to begin with one of the lesser figures at nine thirty."

"I'll be there." Deidre felt herself stiffen in anticipation of facing her abductor.

*****

THE OFFICERS DIDN'T HANG around long after that. Ben phoned Inga as soon as they left to ask her if she minded bringing the girls home. He asked her to stop at their favorite pizza place, Do North Pizza, and bring them a family size deluxe and a liter of root beer. It was time to celebrate.

He ran a bath for Deidre, helped her get undressed and into the water. As he sat on the edge of the tub, he couldn't help but get a lump in his throat. She had a huge bruise on her side where she had been kicked, and there were scratch marks on her chest from her blouse being roughly torn open. Ben was relieved she had not been sexually molested. He knew he would have been able to look past it, but he wasn't sure if Deidre could have ever bounced back. She was always so strong and self-reliant that he wondered if she could have coped with having her womanhood violated. It hadn't happened, and he put it from his mind.

But her face, her beautiful face, that was so marred. The bruises would heal, and he hoped so, too, would her psyche. As he gazed at her naked body, Deidre opened her eye that wasn't swollen shut. "What?" she asked.

"You're beautiful. Even when you look like hell, you're beautiful."

Deidre laughed. "Well, I'm certainly glad you think so. Really, even though I look like hell? I love you, Ben. More than I can tell you." She lounged for another five minutes and asked for his help getting out of the tub. He had to practically lift her out.

Ben wrapped a towel around her, and she felt so tiny beneath his hands. He automatically wrapped his arms around her, and held her close. "I was so scared I couldn't think straight. Nothing else mattered but getting you back." He bent and nuzzled the soft skin on the back of her neck, and kissed her ear. Just then, they heard the door open and two voices call out in unison, "Mom!"

Ben helped Deidre finish drying her back and said, "Hold that thought. I think I'd better get downstairs and ward off the charge." He kissed Deidre's bare shoulder and raced downstairs.

They ate together that night, five of them including Inga. The party lasted until seven forty-five, when Deidre announced to everyone that she needed to get some sleep. The twins volunteered to clean up, Inga left for home, and Ben escorted Deidre up to bed. This time the girls knocked on their parent's door and asked if they could tuck them in. After much ado about sleeping tight and not letting the bedbugs bite, they turned out the light and quietly shut the door. Ben and Deidre heard them giggling, a sound that was worth more than winning the lottery. Deidre lay on her side, and Ben curled up behind her, and they fell asleep in an instant.

Twice during the night Deidre thrashed around and called out in her sleep. Ben held her closer.

Chapter
Fifty

In the morning, when the alarm clock went off, Deidre moaned when she tried to move. Every muscle of her body was stiff, and she hurt as if she were one giant toothache. She tried to open her eyes, but only one responded, and her entire face felt swollen and beaten. Ben touched her and she flinched.

"How you doin', dear?" he asked, wondering if she would be able to speak, because her lips were so puffy and dry.

"Like one big cow pie," she answered with a croaky voice. Ben wondered what a cow pie felt like but, wisely, said nothing.

Instead he answered. "Pretty rough, huh? Why don't I call in for you and tell them you can't make it to work today? The agency gave me a week off to get my head on straight. You certainly deserve some time to recover. What say we just ease back into life?"

"No!" was Deidre's definite answer. She couldn't see Ben shake his head, because he was lying to her bad side, but she heard him sigh, then say, "Okay, tough girl, let's get you out of bed and into the shower. I've got a fresh icepack in the freezer, but the one you used last night didn't do much good. Up you go, girl."

Deidre felt Ben's hand behind her back and felt the pressure as he helped her get into a sitting position. He helped her swing her legs over the side of the bed, and then guided her to the shower. Her steps were so short and halting, she felt as though she should be in a nursing home, and she thought she'd skip looking in the mirror until after her shower. Ben turned on the water and tested it with his hand to make sure it was a safe temperature and helped his wife step under the cascade. Deidre let out a sigh of relief as water began to wash away some of the stiffness and pain. After ten minutes she almost felt human again.

"Know what I want?" Deidre continued before he could answer. "I want a nice cup of black coffee. Not just a cup of coffee—a *nice* cup of coffee. And toast slathered with butter. And two eggs over easy, not too hard, not too runny. What do you say, Chef Ben? Can you handle that order?"

Ben laughed. His wife was coming back. He escorted Deidre downstairs and filled the first part of her order, then went back upstairs to wake the girls.

"Hey, hey, hey!" he called out as he knocked on their door. The response was several grumbles and groans. "Go away. We talked too much last night and didn't get much sleep."

"Okay," Ben seemed to give in. "But I'm taking Mom into town at nine o'clock, and you're not going to get a chance to see her until later. And, too, you'll be spending the day alone." His message was greeted with another round of grumbles, and finally, one of the girls, he couldn't tell which one, answered.

"Can we go into town with you guys and spend the day with Inga?" Ben smiled. Deidre's old friend had won his daughters over.

"Sure," he answered. "At least, if she doesn't mind. I'll give her a call. Breakfast is served in twenty minutes." He heard their feet hit the floor, and he retreated down the stairs. Mission accomplished.

After breakfast, the girls cleaned up while Ben tried to help Deidre loosen up with some range of motion exercises. She held an icepack over her eye and groaned as he manipulated her joints, especially her legs and ankles. The girls helped her to the car, even though Deidre tried to shoo them away. They were an intact family, and Ben took a deep breath. Life would be good again, he was sure.

Megan and Maren were dropped off at Inga's—she had agreed to let them hang out with her for the day—and arrived at the Law Enforcement Center with time to spare. Both Jensen and Director

Benton were waiting, and Deidre was introduced to two new faces, the FBI interrogators. Where Major Jensen had been in charge of the National Guard troops who had led the charge yesterday, Benton was clearly the man today.

"Deidre, Ben, these are Agents Jonathan Morst and Shelly DeLand. They'll be working the suspects today and for as long as it takes to get what we want. We've got chairs set up on the other side of two-way mirrors of the interrogation rooms. We'll try to work only one room at a time, but two rooms will come in handy. You'll see why. Well, let's get at it."

Deidre and Ben walked to the windows and looked into the rooms. In the first, Captain Blake sat bolt upright in his chair, a scowl on his face. In the other, a rather timid-looking man who probably wasn't yet twenty years old sat hunched over the table where he sat. He picked at his finger, then shifted in his chair. Finally, he put his forehead on the table's surface, not that he was resting. To Deidre, it looked as though he was nursing a headache. He jolted upright when the two FBI agents entered the room and took a seat across the table from him.

"So," Agent DeLand started. "I'd like you to give us your name."

The young man sat at attention. He couldn't stand because he was handcuffed to a restraining ring in the table. "My name is Jesper Landman. I am a citizen of the United States of America. I am a corporal in the Populus Reipublicae Militia."

"Okay, good." DeLand praised him. "And what is the objective of your organization, Corporal?"

Jesper looked straight at her. "My name is Jesper Landman. I am a citizen of the United States of American. I am a corporal in the Populus Reipublicae Militia."

Agent Morst exploded from his chair. "Enough of this crap. We really don't care who you are or what you belong to. Tell me what you assholes are up to."

Jesper looked at the agent, who was now pacing around the room like a caged lion. "My name is Jesper Landman. I am a citizen of the United States of America. I am a corporal in the Populus Reipublicae Militia.

Outside the glass, Deidre, Ben, Jensen, and Benton were watching. Jensen let loose an expletive. "Whoever these people are, they've got their recruits trained like military. We'll never break them down at this rate."

Benton smiled. "Don't get impatient, Major. This is just beginning. Give us an hour or two."

Inside the room, Shelly DeLand took over. "Take it easy, Jon. Can't you see that Jesper is trained to deal with us? Let's go to work on the easier guy. What's his name?"

"Blake, Captain Blake." Jonathan replied, disgust hanging from his words.

"You'll never get to Captain Blake. He's like a rock!" Jesper shouted at them.

Shelly came back with, "Well, last night he called to one of the jailers, wondering about cutting a deal."

"Never! He'll never give us up!" But Jesper's words were spoken to a closed door. Shelly and Jon joined the group outside, and the five of them watched Jesper fidget for five minutes. He didn't look so brave when he was alone. They went down the hall to the room where Blake was manacled to a similar table.

"Good morning, Captain Blake." Jonathan began. "We're being observed from behind that glass." He nodded at the two-way mirror. "Of course with your training you knew that, I'm sure. What you don't know is that Sheriff Johnson is out there, and she has identified you as the one who gave the orders while she was captive. I guess that makes you responsible for what she went through. Am I right?" Before Blake could begin his litany, Morst continued. "Oh, don't give us your spiel. You are Steven Blake. You are a United

States citizen. You are a captain in the Populus Reipublicae Militia. Say, you must have a university professor in your group, to come up with that kind of Latin. Of course, any idiot can go to the Internet and find out how to say anything in any language."

Shelly cut in, "Populus Republicae Militia. What kind of boy scout group is that? What do you do, go out on field trips on your vacations and play war? Well, yesterday wasn't play, was it?"

Blake looked at her. "My name is Stev—" Shelly cut him off.

"Yeah, yeah. We know the lingo, so stop boring us. Corporal Landman has been very cooperative this morning, especially after we told him we were indicting him for murder."

"I knew he'd crack at the first sign of pressure. Every organization has a weak link, and he's ours." Blake's words had no effect on the empty room. The agents were outside before he finished the first sentence.

DeLand and Morst didn't stop to talk, but went right to Landman. "How you doin', Jesper? Comfortable? Want us to get you anything? Water, a soda? Heck, we'll even let you have a cigarette, if you ask for it." This time Jesper didn't go into his prepared statement, but he licked his lips in anticipation of at least some water. "You know, Jesper, we can't give you anything if you don't ask for it. Need anything?"

Jesper licked his lips again, but sat still. "Water."

Jonathan tilted his head. "Water? What about it? There's a lot of it outside in the lake. We've got drinking fountains full of it. You know, Jesper, we could even get some for you, if you ask for it. But, 'water,' that doesn't tell me much."

Shelly gave her pitch. "Did you mean you wanted a drink of water? Because if that's what you want, you'll have to be more clear. 'Water?' Why that could mean just about anything. She sat back and waited. Jesper waited, too.

"Can I have a drink of water?" he finally asked.

"Why, sure. Agent Morst will be happy to get it for you." Morst left the room and stood outside while Shelly kept working.

"We talked to Captain Blake after we left you. He said we'd never break you, because you're too strong. Said that you'd be willing to take the fall for the group's actions if it came to that. In fact, he said that you were the one who beat to death that poor boy, Justin Peters, and that you were the one who painted all the hate slogans on Joseph Feldmann's place."

Just as Jesper was about to say something, Morst came in with a cold bottle of water. He tossed it to the prisoner, who fumbled it and lost control of it. Shelly picked it up off the floor, wiped it off, and opened it before handing it to Jesper. She noticed that his hands were shaking, and he used both of them to lift the bottle to his lips. Just as he was about to take his first swallow, Morst batted it away, and it hit the wall, fell to the floor, and spilled its contents.

"Enough!" He bellowed. "I can't get it out of my mind that you were the one who killed my friend, Andy. You were the one who gunned down the National Guard troops. As far as I'm concerned, you can stay in this room and dry up like a prune." Jonathan stormed out of the room and slammed the door behind him. Then he watched Shelly do her thing. She retrieved the half-empty bottle, wiped it off again, and handed it to Jesper, who was visibly shaken.

"Take a sip," she said, and Jesper looked as though he expected her to pull the bottle away at the last instant. He took a drink.

"I didn't kill that homo," he finally said. "I saw it, but I didn't do it. And I didn't fire a shot yesterday. You've got to believe me. I did some of the painting at the old Jew's place, and I was there when they pulled the spikes from the rails, but I never hurt nobody."

Shelly nodded to him. "I think I believe you," she said, and left the room. Jesper put his head down on the table and didn't move.

"Well, back to the captain," Morst said in a matter-of-fact tone. He looked at his watch. "Pretty good progress in only two hours."

Chapter
Fifty-One

For the rest of the morning and into early afternoon, the two FBI interrogators played their game of good cop/bad cop, alternating between the two prisoners. They believed they had the strongest of the militia in Captain Blake and the weakest in Corporal Landman. Everyone, including Deidre and Ben, could see that the corporal was tiring, weary from the barrages of messages about what Blake was saying. Twice he had asked for more water and twice he had asked to go to the bathroom. Each time he asked, his wish was granted.

Blake, on the other hand, was a tougher nut to crack, and he belligerently refused to speak. In between sessions, however, his discomfort and anxiety began to show by the way his shoulders slumped, and he held his head in his hands.

Sometime around one o'clock, the interrogators split up, Shelly going to Jesper's room and Jonathan to Blake's.

"Jesper," Agent DeLand began, her voice sounding sympathetic. "I've asked Agent Morst to not be here. He can be . . . a little heavy-handed. I think you and I can get more done one-on-one without him blowing a gasket every time you say something. Is there anything you want, anything you need?" She looked at him with a reassuring smile.

"My wrists are getting rubbed raw from these cuffs. Is there any way I can have them taken off?" It was the most Jesper had said at one time since his claim of being innocent of murder.

"Boy, that's a tough one, Jesper. I suppose we could give it a try, but first, I need your word that you'll stay put in your chair and won't try anything funny. Remember where you are, and who I am. You do realize I have a call button, and if I press it, this room will be filled with more cops than you've ever seen in one room? Understand?" Jesper nodded. "No, I need to hear it from your mouth. Do you understand?"

Jesper nodded again, but this time said, "I understand."

"You understand what, Jesper?"

"I understand that if I try to attack you, I will be swarmed by police officers."

"Okay. Good. Here goes." The agent leaned across the table and opened the locks on the cuffs around the suspect's wrists. He rubbed the skin and flexed his fingers but made no move to leave his chair.

"Would you like to stretch your legs, walk around a bit?" Shelly asked.

"Yes, I'd like that," he answered.

"You'd like what?" she asked.

"I'd like to walk around the room."

"If I say you can, you'll move to the far wall and stay in front of me?"

"I'll stay in front of you near the wall. You have my word."

"One last thing. You do realize I have a call button and can have help in here in less than three seconds?"

"Yes. I know you have a call button and can have help here in seconds if I don't follow your orders. Now can I get up?"

Shelly nodded. "You can stand up and walk around a bit. Your legs must be awfully cramped."

Outside the room, Deidre and Ben watched as Jesper tried to loosen up his legs. He looked like a pet dog who wore a shock collar and would do anything to avoid being zapped. They were amazed at the change in his demeanor.

*****

DOWN THE HALL, Agent Morst was approaching his subject differently. "Captain Blake. My superiors have decided that we'll get nowhere if we continue to allow Agent DeLand to badger you. I'll be dealing with you alone." Blake looked a little puzzled but said nothing. He was still defiant. "Tell me, Captain, is there anything you need?"

For the first time, Blake broke his silence. "I want a lawyer," he demanded.

Jonathan Morst smirked. "Sir, you don't have that option."

"I know my rights," Blake shot back. "And I demand to have a lawyer present."

"Look, Captain," Morst said matter-of-factly. "You are being held in a county jail for expediency's sake. It was the nearest place with interrogation rooms." Blake looked at him, not grasping what was being said. "You're in a military uniform, not a United States military uniform, I might add. You set up a military outpost on U.S. soil, and seem to have put together your own army—small, that's true, but an army nevertheless. Then, too, you sent this message to Agent VanGotten. Here is a transcript of what it said." He slid a piece of paper across the table to Blake.

"Time is running out," the message read. "Come get your wife. Realize we are in a state of war, and I can't guarantee your wife's safety forever." Blake read the message and shrugged, still not picking up on its implication. "What's that got to do with my having a lawyer present?"

"By your own words, you have declared war on the United States of America. That means you will be tried by a military tribunal, and the laws governing the Miranda Act and the right to an attorney do not pertain. You are being held by the U.S Army and the FBI as a combatant prisoner of war, a war you declared."

Major Jensen and Director Benton had discussed in detail what tact should be taken and had decided on a strategy. They concluded that the need for immediate information precluded legal correctness. There were too many witnesses to what had happened to allow Blake and the others to plead "not guilty" in a civil court of law and get by with their crimes. Even if anything they said during this interrogation period was thrown out, there still remained enough bullets in a prosecutor's gun to get a conviction. They had decided to use the wartime ploy to get the information they needed in the most efficient manner, and that was to create doubt in the prisoners' minds.

"So, you see, Captain Blake," Jonathan emphasized the word Captain for effect, "You will not be seeing a lawyer. Right now, Agent DeLand—you do remember her, don't you, the nice-looking redheaded woman agent?—she's having coffee with Corporal Landman, and they are having a most interesting conversation. Want to know what they were talking about?" Morst didn't wait for an answer. "They're talking about a young man beaten to death last spring. They're talking about a railroad being sabotaged, about an old man's home being defaced, about a church being desecrated. They're talking about a whole lot of things and who was responsible. The last I heard, Jesper was naming names. Funny how often yours came up."

Blake flew into a rage and tried to stand up but his wrist shackles prevented him from rising. He pounded his fists on the table, becoming more infuriated as Jonathan calmly sat inches out of his reach, smiling. It might have been the smile that broke the dam.

"You smug SOB!" Blake shouted, a vein in the center of his forehead standing out like a purple cord. "In a year, or two years, or however long it takes, you're going to regret being a puppet for this thing we call a government. Do you have any idea how many militias are in existence in our country? In 2007 there were forty-three; 2010, three hundred, and today, more than twelve hundred. We're in every state of the union. One group has active chapters in thirty-nine states. We are over three-hundred thousand strong, three-hundred-thousand voices ready to give our lives to preserve our

Constitution. It's time we take a stand against those goddamned liberal tree huggers who want to take away our guns, the very right given to us in the Constitution. But you government puppets don't get it, do you? Once the government has all our guns, we will become nothing but slaves to the regime. We won't be able to fight back. Conservative, liberal, it's all just a conspiratorial conglomerate. One side pretends to fight the other, but inside, they're both the same, power-hungry animals of prey."

Flecks of saliva gathered at the corners of Blake's mouth, and sweat beaded on his forehead, but still, he continued his rant. Agent Morst was enjoying every moment, knowing the best was yet to come, and he sat with a sardonic smile on his face, egging the captain on.

"You can sit there and smile, you smug governmental puppet, but listen to me. The only thing preventing our side from taking back the Constitution is that we are not yet united. Last week you got a small taste of what can come if we do. I and five other militia leaders networked and decided to start disturbances in six different states. All we need to do is show the others that unity is possible. We decided to invite disaster so the government's actions would be recorded by the TV networks. Do you think we don't know the power of the media? Several of our people had iPhones recording, and by this time, images of our troops being attacked and mowed down by soldiers in Humvees has gone nationwide. Thanks to you, our increased recruitment power will double our forces."

Blake's throat was getting so dry he could barely speak, but he continued his rampage with no prodding. "The plan was for each of the leaders of the six groups to escape and set up new militias, and then use the leverage from the raids as a starting point in unification. Last year the Michigan militia planned to kill law enforcement officers and then bomb their funeral processions, hoping the violence would incite a larger conflict with authorities. Unfortunately, their plan was disrupted by the FBI. But more of the same will come. Look at the Internet, and read the signs. Last July, online celebrations broke out after news of two L.A. police officers being ambushed and killed was released. The site, Police Log, has 800,000 fans by now. It will be a war, Agent Morst. It'll be a war. And the militias of the nation will band together in such numbers we will not be crushed."

Blake slumped in his chair, his vitriol completely spent. Agent Morst stood up. "Okay, Blake. Thank you. Why don't you call your lawyer? I'm done with you." Blake looked at him with disdain as the reality of what had happened sunk in.

*****

JESPER LOOKED TOTALLY DEFEATED, even before Shelly made her next appearance. "Jesper, I want to inform you that you have the right to remain silent. Anything you say can and will be used against you in a court of law. You have the right to an attorney. If you cannot afford an attorney, one will be provided for you." Shelly looked at Jesper sympathetically and continued as though she were repeating the words only for him. "Do you understand the rights I have just read to you? With these rights in mind, do you wish to speak to me?"

For a second she thought Jesper was about to talk, but then he said in a voice barely above a whisper, "I think I need a lawyer."

"Jesper," Shelly said in a way that appeared to show real concern. "I fully understand your wish and anticipated your decision. There is a public defender waiting outside to represent you if you will accept him as your counsel. Shall I ask him to come in?" Jesper nodded, and this time Shelly didn't demand that he speak his request. She went to the door, motioned to someone, and a man in a dark suit and carrying a leather briefcase entered.

He walked straight to Jesper and held out his hand. "Hi, I'm Bill Svor, a public defender. You must be Jesper Landman. Let's sit down and see what we have here." He brought Shelly's chair around to Jesper's side of the table and joined the young man. They were short a chair, and Shelly disappeared out the door. When she returned she carried two chairs and was accompanied by another woman. The two of them sat at the other side of the table. Jesper was totally cowed by this time.

"Jesper, this is one of the prosecuting attorneys for Lake County, Ivy Mack," Shelly said. "She's here to talk to you and your attorney, that is, if you both agree." Jesper looked at Svor, who nodded his approval. Jesper said it would be okay.

Svor started the conversation. "So, Ms. Mack, what do we have on the agenda?"

Ivy pulled a stack of papers from her briefcase. "Mr. Landman, we are prepared to file a number of charges against you: conspiracy to commit murder, conspiracy to commit kidnap, weapons charges, six counts of murder," she paused. "The list goes on, but those will do for starters. Alone, what I've read to you is enough to put you in prison for the rest of your life." Jesper's eyes widened, and he began to sweat profusely. His attorney shifted nervously in his chair before speaking.

"That's quite a list, Ivy. What else do you have?"

"Bill, this is the most complicated case I've ever run up against, and I think your client could make my job a whole lot easier if he will cooperate with me."

Bill cleared his throat before speaking. "And will you please define 'cooperate' for us?"

Ivy picked up a note of hope in Attorney Svor's question. "We need the names of those who committed the criminal acts. Who beat Jason Peters to death? Who was involved in the train derailment? Who was involved in the desecration of the church? Who was involved in the hate crime at Joseph Feldmann's's home? Lastly, who was the sniper who ambushed Sheriff Jeff DeAngelo?" She spread her hands on the table palms down and waited for an answer.

"And what does Jesper get in return for this kind of cooperation?" Bill asked.

"The state is prepared to reduce the charges to aiding and abetting, which, as you know, carries with it a maximum penalty of two years in jail and/or a $10,000 fine. That's quite a deal, Counselor, and I think you should advise your client to accept it. Otherwise, we're going for the max on this one. Believe me when I tell you that Captain Blake has shown he is more than willing to throw you under the bus, Jesper. Think about it."

Bill Svor drummed his fingers on the table while he thought, and Jesper looked at his attorney's face, trying to pick up on his reaction. Bill's expression was noncommittal, and when he responded, it wasn't to Jesper but to Ivy.

"I'd like to confer with my client in private. That means all cameras and recording devices are turned off, and I'm invoking client-counselor privilege." Ivy nodded. She and Shelly left the room, reasonably certain they would get their way.

After several minutes of waiting in the hall, they heard a rap on the door, and Ivy let herself into the interrogation room.

"Jesper and I have conferred, and he agrees his position is tenuous at best. However, he has one overriding concern, and that is for his own safety. What guarantees can you give him that he will be provided with protection?"

Ivy had anticipated this scenario and had discussed the issue with the FBI to great length. They agreed that Jesper would be placing himself in danger, but on the other hand, they didn't believe that the case warranted a full witness protection plan.

"We're prepared to provide protection for you as long as the trial continues. We're not prepared to provide a new identity or secret location." Ivy saw Jesper begin to squirm, and Bill reached over and patted his shoulder as a sign to hear her out. Ivy continued, "We're willing to provide you with transportation to anywhere of your choosing in the U.S., after you've served your sentence, of course. We're also willing to provide you with funds to complete a two-year program at a technical college. After that, you'll be on your own, free to move anywhere you'd like, whenever you'd like. As I said, it sure beats sitting in prison for the next fifty years or more."

The attorney and his client put their heads together and whispered several words back and forth. Bill looked up. "My client accepts your proposal. If you draw up the papers, he'll sign them today."

Without smiling, Ivy reached into her briefcase and withdrew a sheaf of papers. "I have them ready. I'll step out of the room for a cup of coffee while you go over them with Jesper. By the way, would either of you like coffee?" They declined. "Okay, I'll be back in a half-hour to witness the signing." Her shoulders felt incredibly light as she left the room.

When she returned, the papers were on her side of the table, signed. "I have one question I'd like to ask," Ivy said. "I think your attorney will allow you to speak to it now that the agreement has been made. How did your people know Deidre would be at that spot on the river so they could grab her?"

Jesper looked at his attorney, and his legal counsel give him a nod. "I liked to follow the river when I had time. It's peaceful there. One day, I saw Deidre sitting by those cedar trees. She looked like she was meditating or something. I mentioned it to Captain Blake, and he decided to set up surveillance of the spot. He had men posted there on a rotating basis for more than two weeks. When she came there again, they nabbed her. Captain Blake is a patient man."

Deidre was chilled by the realization. *What if they had gotten Maren and Megan?* She shivered a little, and Ben held her close. She and Ben had watched the entire proceedings, and now they felt a letdown as the anticipation of what would happen wore off. It was almost as though Deidre didn't want the process to slow down. She wanted to move to the next step immediately.

Chapter
Fifty-Two

On the way home, Deidre and Ben stopped at Inga's, picked up their daughters, and swung into their favorite takeout restaurant, where they picked up a preordered special. None of them spoke the whole way home, only sat and inhaled the aroma of their evening meal.

At the supper table, the girls asked what had happened and what the future held. Deidre was as honest with them as she could be. Her eye was beginning to open as the swelling diminished, and Maren wanted to know if she could see anything out of it. She had to say that her vision was still very impaired but that her face seemed less sore. She attempted a smile to prove it. After supper, as they retreated to the living room, Maren hugged her mother. Deidre winced, causing the girl to step back with a pained look on her face.

"Mom, did I hurt you?" she asked with concern.

"Honey, don't ever stop hugging me." She put her arms around her daughter and gently squeezed. "Just be a little gentle for a while." The two held each other for several seconds and Megan joined them. Ben called to them and patted the couch. All four of them squeezed together, and they sat touching each other without saying a thing. After several minutes the girls got up and kissed Deidre on the cheek.

"We'll be in our room if you need us. We love you, Mom," Megan said. Maren echoed her sentiments.

Deidre rested her head on Ben's shoulder, and they didn't move for a long time. "Fix me a bath, will you, dear?" she asked.

He smiled. "Want bubbles, too?"

*****

IT TOOK TWO WEEKS, but by then Deidre's face had pretty much returned to its normal configuration. A large blood clot obscured the white of her injured eye, but she could see clearly through it. She had a lingering scab on her lip, and her ribs still made her wince if she turned too quickly in the wrong direction. Yet, she knew her body was healing. About her mind, she wasn't too sure. Almost every night she had nightmares and woke with sweat soaking the sheets. Ben was patient, never complaining about his loss of sleep and holding her until her trembling ceased. She had taken personal leave from her job as acting sheriff, and the under-sheriff was helping clean up the mess of paperwork. It wasn't as bad as would have been expected, because the FBI had taken over much of the case.

*****

TWO MONTHS PASSED. Deidre had been back on the job for three weeks, and as she drove to work, she mulled over what her future might hold. She slowly climbed the stairs to the sheriff's office and took note of the banners hanging across the conference tables. A sheet cake, still in its box, sat on the end of the table, and the smell of freshly brewed coffee hung in the air. The place was empty, and she hoped no one would be late. She was early, although morning report would be later than usual today. Deidre retired to the sheriff's personal office and sat behind the desk. She shuffled a few papers, straightening their corners, and put the two loose pens in the mug near the edge of the large desk calendar. It was October 17, and she placed an X over the square representing yesterday. It was gone, and she thought it appropriate that today's square was fresh and clean, no impending disasters.

Deidre didn't feel well, hadn't for a week, and she had scheduled an appointment with her doctor in the afternoon. First, she had a few duties to attend to. Shirley, the sheriff's assistant, came in shortly after she had closed the door to her office, and now Deidre sat behind the desk, holding her head and trying to quell her nausea. Morning report was delayed until eight o'clock, and she dearly hoped she wouldn't be sick before then. At five to eight she left the shelter of her office. Nearly every deputy was either sitting or standing in the room. She had just joined them when they heard the security lock on the outer door buzz, followed by the buzz of the inner lock.

Jeff DeAngelo entered the room, carrying a cane in his right hand and his briefcase in his other. Everyone in the room stood and began to applaud, followed by the under-sheriff extending his hand to Jeff.

"Welcome back, Sheriff," he exclaimed as he pulled Jeff toward him and administered a crushing bear hug. The welcome was followed by a chorus of voices, all agreeing with the under-sheriff's words. Deidre stepped up, holding the key to the sheriff's office.

"Jeff, this is one the happiest days of my life. Here are your keys, here is my badge, here is your department back, and don't ever do this to us again." She laughed joyously, even while her eyes glistened. "Welcome back, friend."

The crew was able to celebrate for nearly a half-hour, and finally Jeff had to settle them down for their morning meeting. He pulled his chair up to the table and calmly started the day as though nothing unusual had happened while he was gone. Deidre slipped away so quietly, no one paid any attention to the fact she was no longer present.

*****

BEN HAD TOLD DEIDRE that when the FBI's preliminary report was drawn up, she would have the option of reading it, and one day in early December, they rode to Duluth together. He and Deidre would spend an hour with Director Benton, and Ben would spend the remainder of the day working in his capacity as an FBI agent. She was going to do some Christmas shopping, then pick Ben up after work. She was relieved that her bout of not feeling well earlier in the fall had subsided, and her old energy had returned.

"Deidre, come in," Benton invited her. "It's really good to see you after these several weeks. You look as though you're pretty well healed. How you doing with the nightmares?"

She appreciated his concern. "Getting better. I'm down to seeing the shrink every other week, and soon only once a month. She's happy with my progress. Thanks for asking."

Benton got right to the point. "I thought you might like to read this." He shoved a paper across the desk toward her and Ben. They picked it up and looked at it together.

Monday, December 18
Re: Militia Incident August 13, Two Harbors, MN

On the above date of incident, a militia known as the Populus Reipublicae Militia created a situation (see Addendum A) to draw the Minnesota National Guard into a firefight. The intent was to force an armed conflict and martyr some of their own troops. The plan included kidnapping the acting sheriff of Lake County, Deidre Johnson, and use her as bait for their trap (see Addendum B). The outcome of the operation can be found in Addendum C.

Upon interrogation of those militia who were captured unharmed, a plot was uncovered to strengthen militias, known and unknown, across the United States to the point where, if united under one command, they would be capable of mounting an all-out war against the government of the United States. Plots of this nature were carried out nearly simultaneously in six states (see Addendum D). There has been an increased number of incidents of police officers being ambushed to foment a feeling of empowerment by various militias (see Addendum E).

Deidre flipped to that page and skimmed through a few of the incidents that were listed.

March, 2011: Members of an extremist group were charged in Wisconsin with seditious conspiracy and attempted use of weapons of mass destruction in connection with an alleged plot to attack law enforcement and spark an uprising against the government of the United States of America.

April 27, 2012: The leader of a Christian militia planned an elaborate, two-part training session for this month and told members it was okay to "kill anyone who might stumble upon the operation."

September 13, 2014: A late night ambush outside a state police barracks in Pennsylvania's northeastern corner left one officer dead and another critically wounded.

As Ben and Deidre scanned the addendum, it became painfully clear that, nationally, violence against government officials was increasing exponentially, and much of it was for the purpose of fueling what they hoped would be a massive armed revolt. With what happened to Jeff and Deidre, the addendum's contents hit too close to home. They turned back to the body of the report.

> The members of the Populus Reipublicae Militia remain in custody and the legal process continues to work its way through the courts. The FBI is doing everything it can to engage the U.S. attorney general's office.

Deidre looked at Director Benton. "Scary stuff."

He nodded. "Their tactic will be hit and run fighting. For instance, they want to destroy bridges, railroads, communication towers, and human targets. Right now a disease I call anti-government fever is gripping our nation. I truly believe that the rhetoric of some of our congresspeople is akin to throwing gasoline on the fire, raising the temperature. Only time will tell how hot it will get."

Chapter
Fifty-Three

Deidre's day of shopping was a joy. Outside, the thermometer registered twenty-five degrees, about average for December in Duluth. The stores were filled with shoppers, and she couldn't help but smile at the sight of families, the little children staring wide-eyed at Christmas scenes in the store windows. She felt a twinge in her abdomen, reminding her she had a doctor's appointment the next day, and she prayed everything would be all right.

As she walked past the newsstand in a book store, the headlines of the *Duluth Herald* caught her eye, CHILD ABUSER NABBED IN OREGON. Deidre dug in her purse and paid the dollar for the copy, went to the store's coffee bar and ordered a tall decaf with cream and three packets of sweetener. As she sipped the steaming brew, she concentrated on the article. It said that a man named Jerome Burk, alias Reverend Isaiah, had been arrested the day before as he tried to purchase flour and other staples in a grocery store in Enterprise, a small village in the eastern part of Oregon near the Idaho border. It went on to say that he would be extradited to Minnesota to face charges of statutory rape of several girls and false imprisonment of women. Authorities were searching for other men who had belonged to a group in northern Minnesota called The Sanctuary.

With a degree of satisfaction, Deidre finished her coffee and left to pick up Ben. On the way down the hill to the Federal Building, she wondered what would become of the women who had been coerced into living Reverend Isaiah's version of God's will. More so, she feared for the emotional wellbeing of the children spawned there.

She put those thoughts out of her mind when Ben got into the car. "How you feeling?" was his first question.

"Oh, pretty good," Deidre answered. "I do get a little tired by this time of the day, though."

"What time is your doctor's appointment tomorrow?" He continued to fret over his wife's health.

"In the afternoon," she answered, and then changed the subject.

"I sure hope the girls like what I found for them today. I couldn't resist buying them matching jeans and sweatshirts just one more time. Lately, they've made it pretty clear that they want to establish their individuality. When we get home, take a look, and you can tell me what you think of the outfits."

For the remainder of the trip, they talked about banal topics—the weather forecast, what color lights they should have on the tree, whether they should try the lutefisk at the restaurant downtown or not. Ben was a little concerned that Deidre was avoiding the subject of her health, but he knew not to press the issue.

That night Deidre seemed particularly moody, and Ben chocked it up to her being tired from shopping all day. She fell asleep in his arms the way she did most nights, but tonight he had a difficult time getting to sleep. He could feel his wife's chest rising and falling with each breath and could hear the soft whisper of her breathing. With his free hand, Ben gently stroked her hair, brushing it back from her face, and was overcome with the love he felt for her at that moment. He pictured her face, and even though it was dark in the room, he could visualize every line and contour. At that moment, he loved her more than life itself.

*****

THE NEXT NIGHT, the four of them sat down for supper, Ben and Deidre on one side of the table, Megan and Maren on the other. Deidre had made a special meal that included fresh pie made with apples picked from their own tree the last fall and stored in a cool room in the basement. She also made Aloha Burgers: a hamburger patty with a slice of pineapple on it and a tangy sauce, all on a toasted English muffin. She put out wine glasses, and filled them with a sparkling grape juice.

"A toast to our family," Deidre said as she raised her glass. The others followed suit, and they clinked them together in a mutual salute. "I have an announcement to make." The twin girls looked at her face and immediately assumed something must be wrong.

"You went to the doctor today, didn't you?" Maren more stated than asked. "What did he say?"

Deidre took her time answering, looking first at her plate and then up. "Well, he says I'm pregnant."

Megan was just about to take a bite of food, and her fork clattered to her plate. Maren blurted out, "How did that happen?" The words had barely left her mouth when Megan jabbed her in the ribs, and Maren's face turned the proverbial three shades of red. "Oh," was all she said. Now that their secret was out, Ben sat there, grinning.

"And the doctor said something else," Deidre added. Ben looked up, a question mark written on his face. "He says I'm having twins!"